ISLE OF WAITING

GW PROUSE

PROUSE BOOKS

Isle of Waiting

GW Prouse

Author: GW Prouse

Editor: Megan Amato

Cover Artist: Faera Lane

Title Page Art: @Maeowl

Chapter Headers: Jess Robling

Map: Fantasy Realm Artists

Copyright © 2025 by GW Prouse

All rights reserved.

No part of this book may be reproduced in any form or by any electronic or mechanical means, including artificial intelligence (AI), information storage and retrieval systems, without written permission from the author, except for the use of brief quotations in a book review.

ALSO BY GW PROUSE

The Realms Curse Duology:

A Nameless Curse
A Nameless Oath

Standalone Within an Interconnected Series:

Isle of Waiting

CONTENT WARNINGS

The following is a New Adult retelling of fairytale and mythology with topics such as death, death of a family member, assault, stages of grief, famine, manipulation, sexual content (described as smoldering by readers/not overly explicit), illness, stabbing, fatal wounds, discussions of death in childbirth (of mother not child), and of homelessness. Please take care of yourself first before reading further if any of these topics may be heavy for you.

With that being said, this is **NOT** a dark romance. While Isles does contain dark fantasy elements, at the core it's a story about death, grief, hope, and love.

For those who know grief stems from love and loss, but love anyway.

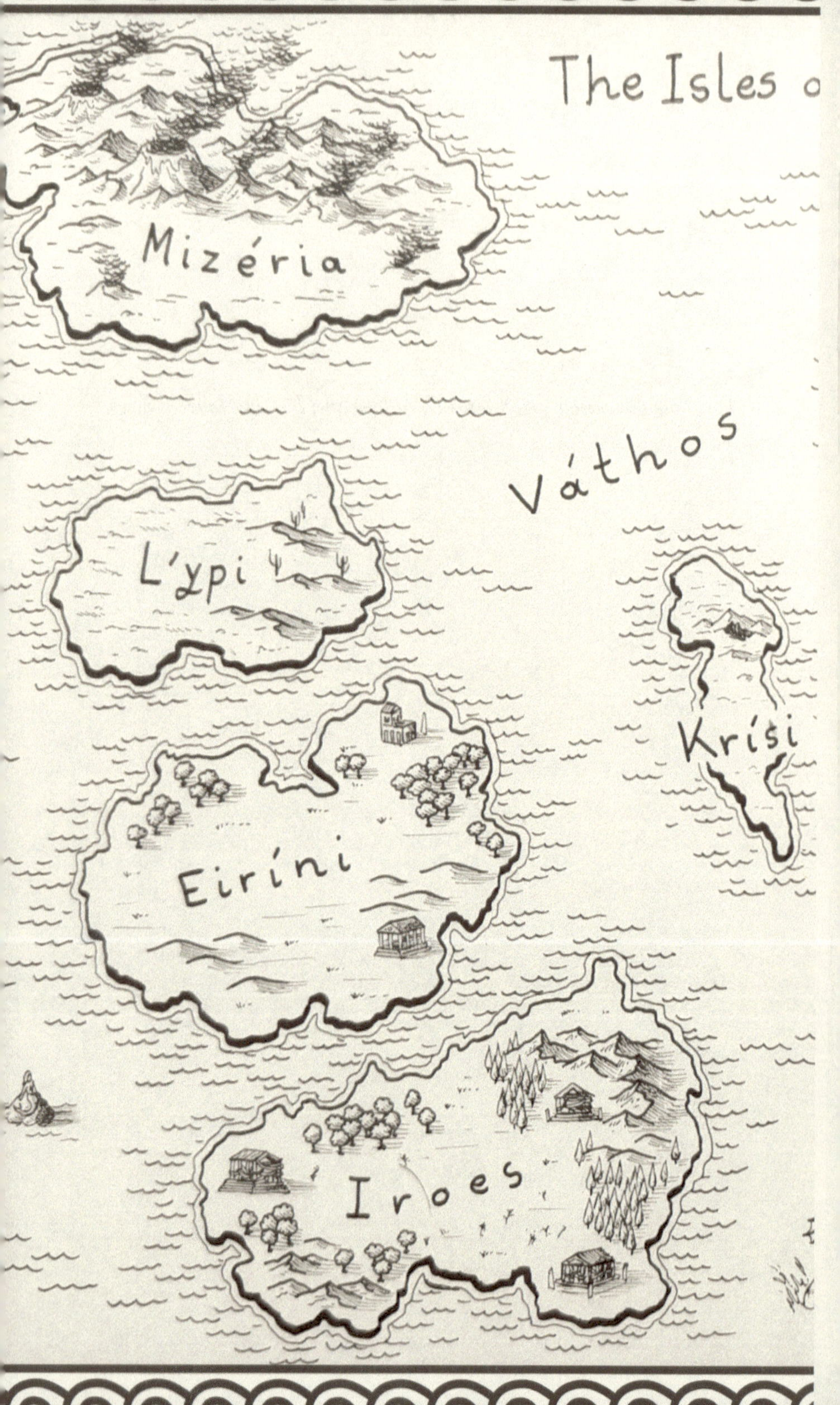

The Isles o
Mizéria
Váthos
L'ypi
Krísi
Eiríni
Iroes

f Nékros
N
W
E
S
The Dock
Pixie Meadow
Anamoní
The Camp
Nereid Lagoon
Shade's Tree

Chapter 1

Kora

*T**he Immortals Have Not Abandoned Us.*

THE HEADING WAS typeset in bold black letters on the pamphlet under Kora's shoe, forgotten by the receiver of the handbill as soon as it reached their fingertips. She bent over and removed the parchment from under her boot, stuck to her sole by the grime on the cobblestone path. She stuffed it in her pouch, unable to litter. One small thing she could do for the world slowly dying around her.

A pedestrian pushed past, and her friend Ariana grabbed Kora's arm for balance to stop herself from falling into a puddle of questionable substance. Straightening, she kept hold of Kora as she peered down the dingy alley. "What are we doing here again?"

Kora considered ignoring every instinct telling her to walk down the darkened space, follow her twin brother and finally uncover his secret. But something stopped her. "You saw him. William went this way."

The two-story stucco buildings framing the alley had dead

bougainvillea vines arcing between the space. There were no windows, and the only alcove was a side door to one of the vacant shops. Behind them, the crowd bustled and moved through the street with the few near-empty carts pulled by forlorn donkeys.

The sun was already stifling, baking in the late morning. It was busy for a Tetárti, the middle of the week and one of the only two days the market was open. Most did their shopping on Kiriaki to start off their week. If there were more people present, that meant the limited produce would be even harder to come by.

"Of course I saw him." Ariana let out a fawning sigh, fanning her hand to cool her pink cheeks. Her light brown hair was tied in a bun at the nape of her neck, and a wicker basket hung from her other arm. "Not that he notices me."

Kora resisted rolling her eyes as she debated following him. A groan from the alley diverted her attention towards a figure covered in a dark tattered blanket who was slumped against the wall.

Ariana took a step back. "If you think I'm going down there, you're wrong. We must do our shopping." She held up the list her mother had given her. Kora's was in the pouch that hung from her shoulder. They had started to go together, *chaperoned* by her brother William every Tetárti for the past eight months after the errand boy had passed from pneumonia. Another death caused by the lack of medicine and proper nutrition. Now that Ariana was sequestered in Greece, their parents decided it was best they went together to the market.

She wouldn't abandon Ariana but that didn't mean she wasn't tempted to go if it meant finding out what her brother was up to. "Where is your sense of adventure?"

Ariana scoffed. "On a ship with no crowds." She peered down the alley again, her nose wrinkling. "And besides, there is adventure and then there is being smart. We are *not* walking down there."

William did, Kora thought to herself. Although, that particular thought might inspire her friend to reconsider her stance. Ariana loved the chance to try something new—as long as it didn't involve crowds. Or land, in particular. On board her father's trade ship was where Ariana stored her confidence as they traveled to different ports around Greece and Europe.

Kora would be lying to herself if she said she wasn't jealous of her friend's relationship with her merchant father. He allowed her to travel with him, and had given her more responsibility with bookkeeping and navigation on their ship. Until the famine spread beyond Greece to surrounding countries and even continents, disrupting textile trade and putting him out of business. Now he worked with the British Consulate alongside Kora's father to broker agreements for the trade market.

Kora gave one final sigh, then turned away from the alley and the slumped figure. Ariana was right. *They* were not looking for trouble, but William might be.

"Let's go." Kora grumbled a few choice words to herself about her brother's recent shift in character. Playful, charismatic, and loyal to a fault—the old William wouldn't have left them in the square. For five months now, he'd become more distant—quiet. Secretive. He disappeared without an explanation. Stopped drawing. Was caught more than once in deep conversations with people Kora didn't recognize or ever see again. Whenever she'd ask, he would wave her off and tell her she was imagining things. They used to tell each other everything. *'Two peas in a pod,'* their father would say. Now William was aloof and silent.

Ariana didn't ask her to speak louder, used to her mumblings. "We should find someone to check on that person, though. I don't know if they are well."

They headed towards the grocer that sat caddy cornered at the intersection of three cobbled streets. Pigeons landed on the road, looking for scraps. A man kicked at the birds to scare them away from an overflowing trash can before rummaging within it himself.

A sign with the echo of *Seamstress* marked by dust where the letters had fallen, hung by the remaining metal loop as it dangled above the dark entrance. Empty counters and bare mannequins within told of what it used to be. A woman leaned against the exterior wall of the shop. Two small children clutched the hem of her tattered skirts. Anxious dark eyes peered through bedraggled hair. The skin on her arms were red and blistered from the sweltering never-ending heat.

"Please?" Her voice croaked as she jangled a tin can, the hollow sound hinting at only two or three drachmas. Like everyone else, Kora diverted her eyes to the dusty cobbled stone. A breeze picked up litter that was strewn along the road and spread the stench of overfilled trash cans and piss-ridden corners. The stories her Nanny told her often spoke of the beauty of the Athens she had been raised in before the famine. It was slow at first—until it wasn't.

According to Nanny, it had begun with the fountains. They had to be turned off to save water. Flower gardens went ignored in favor of food production and keeping livestock alive. By the time Kora's mother was her age, the humid never-ending heat dried out trees and grass. At the time of her parents' wedding, import was their biggest asset. Her mother told stories of walking amongst the vineyards, of shops filled with fabrics of every color and type, and gardens that were pockets within the city when she was a child.

Kora had been a toddler when the animals began to die—only the resilient surviving. When her youngest brother Michael had been born, famine had spread to the rest of Europe and beyond. Three years ago, medicine had become more difficult to make and therefore find. Businesses closed. The apothecary had officially closed two months prior, and doctors were now the only ones authorized to dispense prescriptions and medicinal herbs since there wasn't enough stock.

One of the city security guards walked towards them in a

pressed blue uniform slightly stained with sweat marks and grime. By the patchy beard he was attempting to grow on a youthful face, he looked only a few years older than Kora's twenty.

"Excuse me." Kora stepped in his path. "Someone in the alley looks like they may need help."

He glanced in the direction Ariana pointed. "Everyone needs help these days." With a heavy sigh, he headed towards the alley and reached for the baton at his hip. With an abrupt stop, he whirled around with a scowl on his face that only made him look younger. "You two shouldn't be out here alone."

"My brother is meeting us at the grocer." A lie. William wouldn't be there until noon when they were meant to head home with their purchases.

The guard's brow furrowed. "Be careful."

Ariana gripped tighter to Kora's arm. "We always are."

Her friend's eyes darted around the crowded street. Kora patted her hand, then adjusted the basket she carried further up her arm. The closer they got to the center of town, the slower people moved. Ariana's antsy glances and fidgeting increased with the crowd.

They stood in line for the grocer, Ariana still gripping onto her arm.

Ariana glanced over the list again, a frown line forming between her brows. "Mama is dreaming. There hasn't been silk in the grocer for months. Why does she keep asking for what we can't have? It won't change."

Kora resisted saying the word—hope. At least, that was what Kora clung to. But for both her family and Ariana's, it was more likely naivety. Neither set of parents could accept to what extent famine had hit Athens. Wouldn't accept that life had to change, and that their wealth and food could keep others from begging on the streets. What they thought their money could buy didn't exist anymore.

When the doors opened, the crowd perked up, moving closer

in. The market's proprietor, Kyrie Zervas, stood at the entrance with a greasy blue striped apron tied around his waist and grim expression marked by a grizzled gray beard. "Five at a time." He glared at the first few people—a warning to step back. "Don't need another fight like last week."

Kora let out a groan as he remained at the door with his arms crossed, letting in the first group of shoppers. "Great. Now we have even less of a chance of getting anything good."

Ariana leaned out of line slightly, and started to count in a whisper, her finger bouncing with each number. "We will be in the fourth group. Not too bad."

"Not bad if we want to eat potatoes all week again." She shouldn't complain. Not when others weren't lucky enough to get anything at all. Like that small family begging for scraps. Kora felt something like guilt in her gut, but when scraps were all that was left, it was harder to give them away.

"If the gods don't return soon, I don't think we have much chance of surviving," Ariana said somberly.

Snickers broke out from behind them, and Kora peered over her shoulder to find a group of young men with toothy grins leering at them. "Can we help you?" She plastered on a saccharine smile as she held the gaze of the nearest man.

"Definitely not." The brown-haired man chuckled under his breath. "Not if you believe in the gods. Waste of breath."

Kora's shoulders tensed as she turned away. It was a *waste of breath* to try to make them see reason.

"You know...we could take the place of your gods." A blond-haired man moved in closer, glaring down on them. To some, he'd be considered a handsome gentleman. A chiseled jaw, broad shoulders, sparkling blue eyes, and full lips. Then he sneered and all those thoughts disappeared. "We are much more worthy of your worship." His friends laughed again.

Kora's hand tightened into a fist. Ariana squared her shoulders before turning a sharp glare towards him. "Stay away from us."

Their answering snickers and leering attention held a warning. Kora straightened, drawing back her shoulders alongside her friend.

"You aren't inside yet?"

The *boys*, because they certainly weren't men, stepped back at William's words. Kora met gray eyes that mirrored their father's. A serious expression marred his usual boyish smile, arms crossed as his attention drifted to the group of boys before returning to them. He was slightly taller than the group, and the presence of a man must have been enough for the others to reconsider their attention. "Anything I should know about?"

"They were just leaving us alone." Kora lifted her chin. "And look at you arriving before your usual time. Actually going to help us today?"

William ignored her pointed tone and glanced towards the door. "Why are you in a line with Kyrie Zervas standing outside looking ready to tear us apart?"

While Ariana explained the groupings, William shifted his stance, putting himself between them and the group of boys behind them.

Kora held the wicker basket out towards William who took it without complaint. "You get to carry this now. After the past few weeks of abandoning me, you deserve the responsibility."

At his growing smirk, she thought of his retreating back in the alley earlier and asked, "Where did you go off to this time?"

The grin fell as William's jaw flexed, and he looked away from her sharp gaze. "Met up with a friend. Nothing to worry about."

"Which friend?"

William shrugged, dodging her question with one of his own. "Did mother tell you who was coming to dinner tonight?"

Kora's shoulders slumped. "No, because mother doesn't tell me anything." Not when it had to do with Kora's future. Which likely meant that another suitor would be their guest. Wonderful. "But don't think I'm going to ignore the fact you didn't answer my question."

"It's no one you know, Kora. Don't worry about it." He gave her a grin, which faded at the sound of a chant from the direction Kora and Ariana had come.

The three of them shared a look just as the group behind them joined in the chant and their words became discernible.

"The gods are dead! The gods are dead!"

The words repeated over and over. Others joined in chanting the phrase, and the rhythmic sound of marching had Kora turning just as abruptly as William to watch a procession heading their way. She hissed as a sharp elbow met her left rib as the men shouldered past and pushed her into the wall. After a few disorienting seconds, she ignored the pain to push herself from the wall. An unidentifiable sludge coated her bare forearms. Her gaze fell to her hem and she dreaded the stains at the back of her blue cotton skirt. She wouldn't think about what the rancid sludge was. William stepped forward with fists tight at his sides, but Kora grabbed his arm. "Don't. There are too many of them."

William looked from her to the growing crowd. What had started out as ten had grown to forty or fifty people chanting the same words. Parchment sailed through the air as the protestors tossed them in the breeze. Feet trampled as others passed their line, tearing the parchment and the headline landed at the toe of her boots.

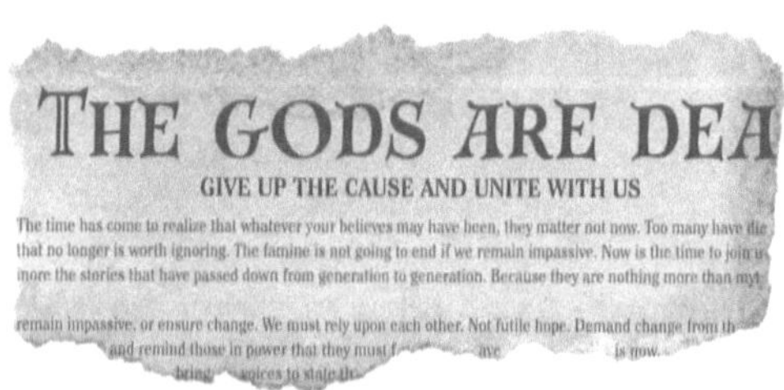

The opposite to the handbill filled with hope that she'd put in her pouch earlier. Her fingertips ached to reach down and tear this blasphemous paper into pieces. To catch them all and throw them back into the face of the faithless.

But instead, she remained in her spot with Ariana gripping her arm tightly. William glanced at the group that continued moving down the road towards the palace before turning back to them. He shoved the basket into Kora's arms. "Stay together. Get the shopping done. I'll be back soon."

Kora made to grab for him but only grasped the basket's handle. "William, come back."

He waved her off. "I'll be back before the shopping is done."

Kora started to follow him as he twisted through the shoppers, but Ariana pulled her back. "Don't."

She met Ariana's worried gaze and nodded, moving back beside her. Even so, she scanned the crowd for her brother's brown bowler hat and coat, but with so many people, her view of him was lost.

The chant echoed in her ears as the protestors continued their call.

The gods are dead.

The gods are dead.

Ariana tugged her towards the door where gruff Kyrie Zervas pouted down at them. "You're next."

Kora opened her mouth, but he raised a hand to stop her. "I already know what you're going to ask." He stuffed his hands into his pocket and removed two linen packets, one smaller than the other. "Potatoes and pomegranate seeds. That's all I got left."

She stifled a smile. "The usual price?"

He considered her, frown lines deepening. From the twitch at the corner of his mouth, Kora knew if no one else was around, his expression would have softened. But Kyrie Zervas had to keep up his fierce reputation. "For you. Yes. Hope they work."

Kora nodded, although she wanted to hug him. Potato seeds were common, but pomegranate were much harder to come by.

Ariana swung her basket to her other arm as they entered the shop, the boxes of produce scattered on tabletops in the center of the shop, the clink of jars as people added dried goods to their bags, and the musty scent of lemon spray. "Well, at least one of us will have some luck." She nodded towards the seeds. "I'm surprised you still ask. He hasn't had anything for you in weeks."

Hope.

Kora glanced towards the quieter streets, everything back as it had been. The chanting a thrum in the distance. Someone still needed to have hope.

Chapter 2
Kora

William met them at noon as usual to walk them back home. Kora had found a spool of cream thread—not the requested green—a loaf of bread, half of the mutton chops her mother had requested, dried currants and raisins, and green beans and corn from the list. None of which covered the smell that lingered on Kora from her impact with the wall. She had caught her friend stepping away more than once, but Ariana had politely remained quiet about the stench. It had caused a few concerned glances and more than one of the shoppers to waft away the foul air in front of their nose.

Ariana turned to the second-story house next door, waving as she made her way up the pebbled path. William had offered to take the basket, but Kora needed something to hold onto. Otherwise, she might throttle her brother. With Ariana present, she hadn't wanted to barrage him with questions, but things had gone on long enough. They walked up the steps to the two-story white stucco house with blue trim, and she was ready to pounce and make her twin answer for his actions when the front door opened.

"Pros Theoú." Mother stood in the front entryway with wide

amber eyes that Kora shared, and her gray streaked hair fashioned in a pouf on the top of her head.

Now wouldn't be the time to talk with him.

Kora adjusted her arms to better accommodate the basket and respond, only to be interrupted by her mother's gasp.

"What is that smell?"

This is where William was meant to support her, but he remained silent with a side glance and a small grin. Kora glared back. "It's me," she answered reluctantly. "There was a big crowd at the market today and someone bumped me into a rather disgusting wall." She stuck close to the truth. Even if she wanted the answers to her brother's whereabouts, she didn't want Mother to berate him for not protecting them. Then they may no longer be allowed to go into town.

William winked at her. "We got everything we could. Fresh fruit is nearly non-existent. Silk is gone, Mother."

Kora rolled her eyes. He acted as though he had procured their findings. "Cucumbers are no longer available. I think we should remove them from the list."

Their attempts to change the subject did nothing. Mother pursed her lips and then called over her shoulder. "Aster, your help please."

Kora's arms began to ache from the basket digging into her skin. She stood on the mosaic entryway with black and white stones creating an owl amidst a border of pomegranate flowers and concentrated on the pattern—anything to avoid meeting her mother's gaze.

The cook, only a few years older than Kora, appeared in the doorway, wiping her hands on a cream apron. "Yes, Mistress?"

"Take those things to the kitchen and ask Nanny to prepare a bath for Kora."

Aster rushed forward to take everything, but Kora held onto the basket. "I can help."

"No, you cannot. We have guests tonight, and I can't have you smelling like *that*." Mother tutted and pointed to the wooden bench beside the door. "The floors have been cleaned. Remove your shoes before you come in, then head straight up to the bathing room." She cast a reproachful glance in William's direction. "You're next."

"We just dined with father's associates a week ago. Isn't it too expensive to have these dinners during a famine?" Kora tried to keep the whine from her voice, but by her mother's sharp gaze, she had failed.

Mother's chin rose. "This famine has been happening for years, and it does us no good to stop our lives. Besides, we are sharing our food with others."

As if they needed to share with the wealthy when the less fortunate were suffering. Her mother continued, interrupting her unspoken thoughts. "You'll be on your best behavior. At your age, I shouldn't have to have these conversations with you." She turned to head inside, before pausing and peering over her shoulder. "Mr. Waltman is an important member of the British Consulate, and your father's friend. His son Eric is showing much promise for one at such a young age. You'd do well with him."

Kora hid her tight fists in the folds of her dress. Another son of an influential family. Of course.

William nudged her arm. "At least he's young?"

Kora's jaw clenched. She knew there was nothing more to say on the matter. Her mother had repeatedly lectured her not to assume the worst of these suitors. As Mother often reminded her, she could be entertaining a middle-aged man and was about to if Kora chased all the eligible bachelors around her age away. It wasn't her fault that their idea of stimulating conversation was if she made the baklava, wanted more than two children, or had mastered cross-stitching. Mending and minding was as far as their interests went. They didn't like it when she asked their views on the famine or their thoughts on the recent article in the *Gazette*.

Unacceptable discussion when you were meant to court one another.

Mother smiled at William. "Take the spool to Nanny please.

She has plans for a lovely dress." Then she turned her attention to Kora, a feline grin appearing. "I also need you to talk your sister up at dinner tonight. Lay on the flattery but steer clear of the truth. It scares them away."

William did his best to hide his chuckle, forcing Kora to elbow him in the side. "You're just as bad as she is," she hissed as they followed their mother inside.

He didn't try to stifle his laughter anymore.

KORA'S HAIR was set in curlers. A thin cotton robe was tied snug around her as she settled the book against bent knees. She had found the perfect position on her window seat long ago. On a warm Athens day like today, she would open the large window to allow in the occasional breeze. Three pillows from her bed were positioned cascading vertically against the wall with a small throw pillow wedged in the corner to prevent them from sinking upon impact. The quilt Nanny had sewn was folded on her lap. It was lightweight compared to many of the others she owned. Fabric in shades of blue with gold and ivory stitching glistened when the sun hit it just right. Perfect to drape over her during those random autumn storms, but now it was used to prop up her arms while she read.

She took out the torn piece of parchment that she'd found stuffed in her pouch earlier. The pamphlet reminded the public that they shouldn't give up on the gods.

Even with a book in her lap, she found her mind wandering. She peered out the window towards the barren garden in their yard. She'd rather be there now, working with her hands in the soil and making another attempt to grow fruit and vegetables with the seeds she'd received today. Except for sweet and red potatoes, nothing else had successfully grown. Every other experiment and attempt were in a pile of dead vines and roots in the corner of the yard to be used as compost for her next try. A hint of hope followed by death and desperation. She hadn't given up yet. One day the plants would flower and produce.

When her door swung open, she fumbled the pamphlet into the book on her lap and stuffed it between the folds of the quilt. Michael bounded inside and jumped upon Kora with a giggle. "Don't let him find me."

He flung the quilt up, the book smacking Kora in the nose, and covered himself in its clutches. Kora rubbed the spot where the book had accosted her. As she searched for it in the mess of limbs and blanket, William strode in with his hands in pocket, eyes downcast and a corner of his mouth lifted. A quick glance in her direction and wink told her he was pretending not to know Michael's location.

William bent over and picked up the book at his feet. "*Botany and the Gods,*" he read the title. "I thought Mother gifted you a book on hosting tea parties?"

Kora pinched her eyes shut, annoyed with them all even as Michael peeked out from the blanket. William stilled, like a cat observing its prey. Snoops. Sometimes it was hard being the only girl in a household of boys. "I had some downtime, and I can read what I want."

Her twin's brow rose as he scanned the stack of leather-bound books on her side table. "But now the gods? Botany wasn't enough?"

He was one of few who knew about her little experiments. Attempts to plant seeds within different parameters and elements in hopes for them to sprout and produce. Some were a success— they had plenty of potatoes. Others had proven more difficult. She couldn't wait to see what would come from the pomegranates and had resisted opening her notes to dive into different ideas.

She followed William's gaze to the horticulture texts. "I wasn't in the mood to try something new today."

He opened the book—the one thing she hoped he wouldn't do—right to the page holding the pamphlet. "What's this?" His brow rose.

She glanced down at her little brother. If it was just her and William, she would have talked openly, but with Michael present... "Nothing. I meant to throw it away."

William opened his mouth to respond, but Michael shifted in her lap. "Can you tell me a story tonight?"

On instinct, Kora looked towards the window in search of the shadowed figure that she swore she'd seen floating there once or twice. More than likely a figment of her imagination, *he* —or so she assumed by the pompous shape of the shadow— had appeared a few times in the past eight months, and she hypothesized that he was one of the immortals thought long gone.

"Please, please, please," Michael begged.

She considered knocking him off, but he began petting her arm lovingly. Being seven and the youngest, he was the most coddled but that wasn't something to fix as far as Kora was concerned. She pulled him closer, and he curled right into the crook of her arm, sticking his tongue out at William in the process.

William closed the book with the handbill within and glanced over the cover. With a heavy sigh, he handed the book to her. "Always the researcher. You should leave thoughts of the gods alone. You saw how things are in the market today."

"What happened today?" Michael perked up, ready for a good story, be it truth or fiction.

Kora sighed and reached down to cover Michael's ears. "You know he can't keep a secret," she whispered. "So hush or mother will have questions for you." She left the threat dangling between them before removing her hands from her brother's ears and snuggled him closer. "The gods must exist somewhere out there. Maybe they just need a little help."

"And you think you'll find your answer in that?" William pointed at the book, his nose crinkling. "Just don't let Mother see you reading it."

As if that was enough to summon the woman, Mother

appeared at the doorway, pushing the door open. "What is going on in here?"

Kora fumbled to hide the book behind Michael, pinning a glare at William. "Just chatting, Mother."

Mother adjusted the silver flower brooch at her throat—even though it was already in place as it always was—smoothing the skirt of her creaseless lavender dress. Her attention shifted to Michael's prone form. "Your father phoned. He'll be home by six. I expect you all to be on your best behavior." She pinned a motherly glare on William. "Understood?"

William took that moment to pounce at Michael who had shifted off her lap, and the two went barreling out the door in a fit of laughter. They almost ran into Mother who darted aside, arms high in surrender as she backed up against the wall.

Kora stood, about to follow them, when her mother shifted in front of the open door. A subtle reminder. *Proper ladies do not run.*

Mother pursed her lips, resting her hands on her hips and glanced over her shoulder at the boys. "They get that from their grandfather. Your father didn't make it into his position without learning to be responsible. I'll have him talk to them tonight."

Kora almost told her to let them play a little longer but kept her mouth shut. Even if William was her twin, someone needed to play with Michael. He deserved to be a child for as long as possible. The world didn't allow such sentiment for long.

Prior to meeting father, Mother had grown up as a middle-class girl expected to stay within her station and didn't dare dream of anything more. It was in the third year of Father's appointment as a British Ambassador in Athens when he met Mother. They fell in love and eloped shortly after—the reason Kora was certain they'd never met their paternal grandparents—and a year later they had William and Kora.

It had been a whirlwind romance. One Kora wouldn't have if her mother had her way. She was to think about the future laid out *for* her. Think of the titles she didn't want—wife. Mother.

Not when others sounded a lot more adventurous and exciting. Student. Professor. Traveler. She dreamed of writing stories. Studying horticulture. Growing gardens full of not only vibrant flowers but fresh fruit and nutritious vegetables. Of being more than what was expected of most young women. While some had begun to attend university—it was 1904 after all—Kora's mother had more traditional and old-fashioned ideas.

Mother gave an exasperated sigh. "Nanny will be in soon to help you finish getting ready." Then she turned on her heels and strutted away.

Kora stared at the hiding spot of the book and bit back the prayer on her lips. It had been a while since the gods had listened to her pleas.

Chapter 3
Captain

Mortals believe the gods have abandoned them.

Captain had often heard the souls' whispers as they crossed the Depth—the dark, placid ocean of the dead. Had seen the shock and disbelief at the gods' existence when in the mortal world they were turning into myth.

It angered him.

A cry echoed across the deck and into his chambers. A reminder of where he was. Where he shouldn't be.

He hated it here. All of it. He longed for the cloud-expanding horizon of his home on Synnefo—Cloud Mount—which floated, hidden from view, above the mortal world. The smell of the changing seasons instead of the stagnant mustiness of death called to him. He yearned to oversee the mortals who lived instead of ferrying souls of the *dearly* departed.

A panorama view of the Isles of Nekrós could be seen from the window of his quarters on the *Charon*. The separate quadrants visible with the slow rising sun. A sand bar divided the other isles of the realm from Ananomí, the Isle of Waiting. A dark cave that jutted out from the midst of the sand bar was their destination—Krísi—the Isle of Judgment.

A knock at the door interrupted Captain's brooding. Staring over the Isles of Nekrós had become a residual habit. A never-ending monotony of fulfilling the task someone else was meant to do. Pitiful.

"Enter."

Captain cringed at the sound of the door creaking open. Another annoyance. Everything about this place sent tension coursing along his spine. His first mate took two steps in, the clop of his boots reverberating on the wooden planks.

"How many came aboard, First Mate?"

"Six, sir." There was a twinge of fear in the soul's voice, forcing the corner of Captain's mouth to twist up in response. He liked it when the soul, Smith, was nervous. Hesitant.

Captain met his apprehensive gaze. The soul stood at attention with two fingers pressed against his wrinkled forehead in salute and brown eyes staring blankly ahead. "Are any of them from Shade's collection?"

Smith nodded. "Yes, two of them, sir."

Two? It wasn't enough. Not compared to the number of souls the immortal had on Anamoní. Where the newly arrived souls were brought. The Isle of Waiting wasn't visible from Captain's window as it was located on the opposite side of the Váthos Sea.

Captain's jaw ticked, but he waved the first mate away. "Prepare to set sail."

Smith nodded and limped from the room.

Captain picked up his hat and placed it atop his trimmed, dark brown hair. Adjusting its position, the ostrich feather fluttered in the breeze as he headed out the door. The scent of sea, sand, and ash brushed past him as the sun beat against his face. In front of him stood a line of new souls—freshly acquired from Anamoní and the mortal world. Shade didn't collect all the dead. Télos and Herald delivered them straight to the dock. It was only his brother's chosen few who remained behind and haunted Captain's thoughts.

Captain stopped in front of the new arrivals and regarded each in turn. One couple, two girls, held hands. They both stunk of Anamoní—the scent of damp forest and sandy beaches. The souls from Shade's Camp.

Two others, a young boy and an elderly woman—unrelated—held onto each other. Captain could sense it was just as much comfort for the frightened child as it was for the grandmotherly soul. "Welcome aboard the *Charon,* your ferry to the Isles of Nekrós. Payment is due to pass."

Captain's eyes narrowed on a teenage boy at the end of the line. His gaze remained downcast, hidden under a tangle of blond hair. He fumbled within his pocket and held out a drachma. Smith passed, taking each offering from outstretched palms. He handed them to Captain who examined the six coins. The corner of his mouth curved at one of the coins as he fisted them. The crunch of metal caused one of the girls to flinch with a small yelp.

He opened his hand, revealing dust within his palm. He blew the dust from his hands and the shimmering shards lifted into the air with the wind and the sails expanded. "Get comfortable. We'll arrive before nightfall where you will meet the Judges and take your rightful place. May they find mercy on you."

The Charon's sails caught the wind and the ship started towards its destination. The ship didn't need anything more than drachma—no crew beside Captain and Smith. His first mate's job was simple. Meet the souls at the dock, load them in the rowboat, and bring them to the ship. Captain ensured this happened and that someone took the coins.

Which was why Captain was *still* here. When word had first reached him that Shade had abandoned his post, he thought nothing of it. The King of the Dead had always run the isles well and deserved the opportunity to visit the living world. Their power needed balance. Responsibility was still required to wield it fully. But when a few days turned into months and then a decade,

Captain had arrived to find Nekrós in disarray and Anamoní busting at the seam with souls. So, he had stepped in. Now, after six decades, Captain was done placating his brother's whims. No amount of coaxing, tricks, or conniving had worked. Shade had been a step ahead of him in a way Captain had been unable to comprehend.

Captain glanced towards the horizon at the Isles of Nekrós expanding before him and took his place at the helm. An unnecessary habit—the ship knew its course—but the spokes of the wheel grounded him to his temporary duty. The new souls remained huddled together in the middle of the main deck, only a few whispers to be heard.

A long slithering spine of spikes broke the surface of the otherwise calm ocean. Captain's half smile lengthened as the serpent's body curved, disappearing beneath the murky water. The ship rocked, and the first mate rushed to the rail. He steered clear of the starboard side, knowing what was to come. When the boat bobbed on the water, a quiet fell over the souls as they stilled. The air was stagnant and with it a thrill pulsed through Captain. Fear was palpable as the new arrivals huddled closer together.

A few green iridescent spikes broke the surface again, much closer to the *Charon*. Shimmery scales in shades of silver and blue were visible as the serpent curved up higher this time. A nose rose a few inches above the surface and with a snort, water sprayed over the railing. A few of the souls screamed as they were pelted with giant drops.

"Hold tight," Smith hollered and gripped the banister.

Before the souls could do as commanded, the creature rose with its long body arching in the air and splashed down to complete its leap. Wide-eyed faces paled with the souls' gasping pleas. Waves rose, jostling the boat from side to side, up and down. Souls, unable to hold on, slid across the deck and their wails escalated as they tumbled in a heap.

Captain's laugh broke through the hysteria and frightened eyes turned towards him. Unlike them, he stood erect and dry.

"One of you" —he pointed at the souls— "are not meant to pass. The serpent has been sent to collect you."

The souls looked at each other and broke apart, darting furtive, accusatory glances. Even the couple had separated. Only the youngest was still gripped tight around the elderly woman.

Before anyone could object or point fingers, the serpent broke the surface again. Its great maw came up alongside the boat with its mouth opened wide showing jagged yellow teeth. The *Charon* nearly heeled onto its side by the impact as his brother Halieus's beast came into full view.

Captain pointed a finger towards the mass of souls. "You. Stand and face your judgment."

The serpent belly flopped, splashing water over the *Charon,* which nearly tilted over again.

The screams of the souls mingled with the creaks and groans of the ship. The serpent breached again before floating above the surface, its long tail keeping it in place. Its webbed fins had appendages with five pointed talons that added to its width and ferocity.

The boat rocked as each step Captain took down to the main deck echoed with precision. "You." He pointed again to the frightened mass of souls.

When Captain stood over them, he stopped, giving each a pointed look before pausing on the lone boy who had kept his face diverted. The boy's eyes widened as they met Captain's gaze. The soul shuddered. The water from the serpent's towering maw plunked on the deck around Captain. "You thought you could trick a god? You don't have the proper payment to pass."

The horrific moan of the sea serpent forced every mortal to cover their ears. Power permeated around him. It felt good to cause fear—when it was well deserved. It had been more enjoyable in the living world when it involved begging and an embarrassing puddle between their legs. Here, there was little left to beg for.

Captain held out his hand and a scythe appeared within his

grasp. Its obsidian handle connected to the hooked blade that shined like silver storm clouds against a dark sky. "Smith."

The first mate limped forward and grabbed the boy out of the crowd. He dragged him around Captain—the soul giving little fight in his shock—and dropped him unceremoniously in the center of the deck. The boy whimpered as Captain turned, flinging the tails of his red coat behind him.

He knew he looked formidable, powerful, and the thought only made him tighten his grasp on the scythe handle. The Judges had given it to him—the one symbol of Shade's power they were willing to share in the interim.

"You will face punishment for your lies." Maybe there were some perks to this job after all.

The boy curled himself over his knees but peered up beneath his hair. "Punishment?" He shuddered under Captain's glare, his eyes darting to search for an escape. One that didn't exist.

"For not having payment, you will spend eternity within the Depth."

"Where was I meant to get payment?" The soul climbed to his knees, hands clasped together in front of him as a wash of anger temporarily replaced fear. "There were none to bury me. No family to say goodbye. They all died because you left us. You left us to starve and suffer. What are we supposed to do?"

Frustration clenched Captain's chest, stiffening his back and shoulders. He must remain on task. "Your attempt called the serpent. Face your end."

The serpent's scream rocked the boat again. The souls screamed. Captain grabbed the unrepentant soul by the scruff of his coat. He kicked and screamed, fighting for his freedom, but Captain flung him towards the creature. A streak of lightning sprung from the scythe, mixing his and his brother's power, and it encased the soul who froze in midair. The boy's mouth hung open wide in a silent scream as lightning flung him right into the sea serpent's open mouth. With a chomp, the creature lowered back into the water, an inky orb of black slid from between those jagged yellow teeth and fell into the water like sludge. The pointed tail was the last to disappear.

Captain gestured to Smith. "Let's continue."

The scythe disappeared, and Captain folded his hands behind his back. "The rest of you just stay out of our way."

The others only stared, too frightened to move. Captain ignored them as he ascended the steps to take his place back at the helm.

Chapter 4

Kora

Mother held out Kora's arms from her perch in the foyer and took a quick glance over. "You look lovely. Nanny outdid herself. Now, stand on the steps and be ready to greet our guests."

Over her mother's shoulder, William stifled a laugh as Michael fidgeted with his bow tie. Kora bit back a scathing comment for her twin as her mother pointed to the stairs. "Actually, go to the landing. That way as the door opens, you can descend the steps and make an entrance."

"Is this necessary?" Kora grumbled as she stomped up the steps.

"Ladies don't stomp."

Kora's tongue stung as she clutched it between her teeth, her grip tightening on the banister.

Voices sounded from the outside steps. Before anyone knew what was happening, Mrs. Darling bustled her brothers towards the drawing room, giving Kora a final harried wave as she disappeared with them.

She pinched her eyes closed, imagining herself anywhere else but stuffed in the silk navy bodice with the waist cinched tight by a cream bow and neckline lower than her personal comfort. Lace trimmed the collar and skirt. It had been the last of the silk purchased earlier in the year. A waste of money as far as Kora was concerned. She'd rather be in her garden under the bare branches of the only remaining tree.

When the door began to open, she knew that this was her cue.

With her chin held high, footsteps silent on padded leather soles, Kora took each step one at a time. Her father's cheerful voice greeted her as he opened the door and two other men entered behind him laughing at whatever he'd said.

Then she met the younger man's eyes. Dark brown. A gentle wave in his dirty blond hair. His olive complexion tinted red from the sun. As his attention grazed over her, Kora felt something twist down her spine. She'd seen him before. But where?

"Ah, Kora. You're here to greet us. Splendid." Her father removed his bowler hat and hung it by the door, his laugh lines and graying blond head illuminated by the remaining sunlight. He held out a hand that she willingly took and gave a small curtsy to their guests.

"Gentlemen, this is my daughter, Kora. My dear, this is Mr. Waltman and his son Eric."

Polite and respectable. Her mother's lectures as of late settled in her mind. "It's lovely to meet you both. If you would like to follow me, I can take you to the dining room. I believe dinner is about to be served."

"Then brandy after?" Mr. Waltman grinned. "I have heard you have an eclectic collection."

Mr. Darling laughed and gestured for them to follow Kora.

"Careful, Gene. I'll think you only came here for my liquor."

Kora didn't dare comment. She had wondered how many of these bachelors and their families came for the promise of free alcohol that was hard to come by rather than marriage prospects. Most who still had the hard drinks had been part of a long line of collectors. If her family wanted to parade her around while pouring another glass, that was their prerogative. She wished only that she didn't have to be a part of that equation.

Eric, Mr. Waltman's son, moved in alongside her. "I have looked forward to getting to know you, Kora."

At the sound of his voice, she recognized him—one of the boys who had stood behind her at the market today. Her stomach twisted further. "Oh, and why is that?"

"I've heard a lot about you. Your beauty is the gossip among our peers."

Gossiping bachelors? Lovely. In other words, who could seduce her first. A game for them.

"Really? You didn't seem so keen to meet me earlier." She kept the venom from her tone. Well, she tried to.

His grin spread, twisting into that sneer she remembered vividly. Before she could respond, her father made introductions to the rest of her family who met the Waltmans at the entrance of the dining room.

Before she knew it, they were seated at the table—Eric beside her, and William across from her. Her brother had also recognized the miscreant from the market, judging by the pinched brow and darting gazes William kept pinning on their guests.

"So, what are your interests?" Eric took a sip from his glass, and Kora turned away from the drop of wine that pearled on the rim—like blood.

"Gardening," Kora said absentmindedly. "And when my mother requires it, cross-stitching and piano."

"Must be difficult right now. Any luck?"

Kora considered him for a moment. These weren't the questions she was expecting. Usually as soon as she announced her interest in botany, the other person would dismiss her lack of knowledge because *nothing can grow right now.*

"Some. Potatoes of course." Kora stabbed said vegetable with her fork and took a bite. "And what is it you do? Besides harass young women at grocers?" she whispered the last part with a touch of vindictiveness.

He gave a boastful smile. "I spend most of my time assisting my father. He plans to retire soon, and I'm in line to step into his place. Learning the ropes, per se."

If his attitude was any indication of how he would be within the consulate, she hoped someone more qualified would take his place. "Must be interesting work. Are you working alongside the government to come up with alternatives for the people of Athens?"

Eric's brow furrowed. "I mean, what we can. It's hard when they're under the impression that our predicament is caused by missing gods. Not much we can do."

"There is plenty you could do if you learn to work together instead of fighting all the time," William interjected, casting a glance down the table at their parents deep in their own conversation. Michael's eyes fluttered closed, oblivious to the tension as his head nodded as he fought sleep, a boiled potato on his fork halfway to his mouth. "Maybe the gods would be inclined to return if they knew we wouldn't ravage our own lands and treated it with the respect it deserves."

Eric snorted. "Were you born here or in England?"

"Why does that matter?" Kora's brow furrowed.

William's grip tightened on his knife. "Because he believes we should side with the English belief." He glared at Eric, his voice low. "Just because our father is English and works for the consulate, doesn't mean we don't accept the ways of our ancestors and those who have cultivated and worked this land for generations. Britain is here for trade and treaties, something you seem to blame Greece for lacking when you're no longer able to keep up your agreements. The famine is affecting us all. And until the gods return, which they won't have reason to if there is resistance, then we all continue to suffer."

Kora blinked in surprise. She had never heard William speak so passionately about anything. Except for his paintings when he was younger. But that had been something that had fallen to the wayside two years prior. "Will—"

Eric interrupted, leaning towards her twin with a dark expression. "The gods no longer exist. And it's not our fault. You'll see that soon enough."

William nearly was to his feet when Father cleared his throat. "If we are finished, we can move to the drawing room. How does dried fruit and wine sound?"

Aster and Nanny entered to clear plates as everyone stood. Kora held back, not wanting to be forced to stay in Eric's company for another minute. She waited for William who was glaring daggers at their guest's back. "He's not good enough for you. I'll let mother and father know he should never step foot into this house again."

"William, what is going on?"

His gaze shifted, softening slightly on her. "I'm all right. I let him rile me up. Go on ahead. I'll be there soon. Need to make a stop at the washroom." He left without a word, but her gaze followed him down the hall and dropped to his tightening fists.

Nanny had scooped up Michael and was carrying him out when Kora stopped her. "I'll take him to bed."

The matronly woman smiled, happy to relieve the young boy to someone else who could climb up the stairs. Her back had taken enough strain from carrying children to bed for the last twenty years. "Not the one, my dear?"

"No, Nanny. He's not."

She patted Kora's cheek before brushing a wisp of hair from Michael's eyes. "The right gentleman is out there. Don't lose hope." She shuffled off to assist Aster with the rest of the table.

Once Kora had fought a reluctant Michael into his night-clothes and tucked him into bed, she trudged towards the drawing room, and anxiously attempted to come up with a realistic excuse to escape. At the bottom step, she paused at the sound of a door clicking shut down the hall.

William hastened down the hallway—in the opposite direction of the drawing room. She followed, only to find him tiptoeing towards the front door. He didn't look her way, but his movements hinted that he was up to something. She followed out the door, pausing at the pomegranate and owl mosaic.

Her mother would curse her when she found out she wore her best dress shoes outside, but the leather souls were silent against the cobbled pathway. A breeze brushed through her hair. Rare in this heat. It urged her forward, beckoning her out. She glanced over her shoulder at the laughter in the drawing room. Considered for a moment if she should turn back and grab a shawl before she closed the door.

William turned away from the town center, heading towards the Temple of the Immortals and the Royal Garden. This time she wasn't going to lose him. She was determined to uncover what he was up to.

Chapter 5
Kora

illiam turned away from the Royal Garden and headed towards the Temple of Theileus—the King of the Immortals. But it was quiet. Too quiet for an evening where a soft breeze fought off the usual heat. Few walked the streets, some sitting on benches. Birds fluttered overhead but didn't sound their usual squawk or crow.

She reached the outskirts of the temple, using the shadows from the minimal remaining sunlight to hide. Beggars were out, a few curled up under trees while others were wrapped in blankets to protect themselves from the elements. Opposite to the usual bustle of parishioners who came to offer sacrifices and gifts in hope for the gods' return. A crackle in the air held the promise of action. Adventure. Fear...

Kora did what she could to remain out of view. The trees that speckled the field protected her until she reached the steps of the temple and crouched low. Voices rose on the other side. All she needed was a last run to hide against one of the tall Grecian pillars, and she was certain she'd be able to see what was going on.

She took a deep breath, and made a run for it, thankful for the quiet soles of her shoes. Kora pressed her back against the pillar, catching her breath while she listened to see if anyone noticed her. Nothing.

Carefully she turned and peered around the edge of the pillar with her hands pressed against the stone and on the grass below the steps found a group of twenty to thirty gathered. There were gentlemen in bowler hats, a few covering gray hair. The grocer, Kyrie Zervas, spoke to a man wearing a toga and a crown of bare olive branches around his head. Young men spoke louder and over one another. Only a handful of women could be picked out amongst the crowd. Kora might be able to slip in among them but was worried someone might recognize her as she had also spotted two of her brother's friends.

A voice sounded from the center of the congregation, calling for their attention. The stone was cold as she pressed her body against it. It was a strain to listen over the mumble of the crowd, but as her breathing evened out and her heartbeat no longer pounded in her ears, she could hear the speaker's words.

The man with the toga spoke, his voice rising in a crescendo. "...and no longer will we suffer at the loss. We will collect an offering to the immortals to beseech our pleas. Our people, the few remaining livestock, land—none of us can take this famine any longer."

A cheer rose.

Kora scanned the crowd for her twin. *This* is what he had gotten himself into—a group searching for the immortals? He knew her stance on the gods. Why wouldn't he tell her about this? William's actions after the day's protest suddenly made sense. His words at dinner. Even his frustration at seeing the pamphlet from the protest that morning.

The speaker continued, "Some have decided that our ways are inferior to their own. That the gods are gone forever, and we are calling upon deaf ears. We need to come together and stand united against their hate and heresy."

She was barely listening as she searched for her brother. Her gaze narrowed on a deep gray dinner coat, now flung over the shoulder of a familiar figure, his confident posture at the forefront of the crowd. William faced her direction, but his attention was on the speaker with a fist in the air, a cry of agreement on his lips. She pursed her own, debating what she should do next. Continue to listen, confront him, or return home and face her mother in her rumpled dress and sweat-rimmed hair?

William was the safer choice.

As she stepped out of her hiding place, a young gentleman snapped his suspenders and puffed up his chest as he stepped into the center of the crowd with a pointed finger brandishing the speaker. "Blasphemy," he screamed. "What you claim is untrue. We're being punished by the immortals because of those like *you*. Those who blame them for our circumstances. Those who cry at their feet as though we are due their attention. They don't care about us. We must fend for ourselves. Tear down the temples and move on."

Kora's breath caught in her throat as a few others muscled their way to the inner edge of the circle.

The speaker straightened, standing a few good inches above the other. "Be gone! Your kind aren't welcome here."

The man chuckled. "Your kind are the scum bringing us down."

Kora's attention shifted when the last of the sunlight reflected off metal. Eyes widening, she pushed through the crowd and screamed, "He's got a knife."

They turned in her direction, William's eyes widened as they met hers before chaos spread. The man with the knife rushed straight towards the speaker, the blade gripped at his side. Screams wracked the air as the crowd fled, her pulse rising and ears ringing. Without thinking, she rushed towards the last place she saw William. She elbowed through the panicked crowd towards her brother. A shoulder shoved her aside, and she nearly fell while others dodged her. Fights broke out among the infiltrated group. William came in and out of view as he fought through the crowd, searching for her too as her name on his lips guided her direction.

"William!" Someone pushed her from behind, and she cried out as she caught herself on a tree trunk, the brittle bark cutting into her hand. She whirled around and gasped as golden teeth flashed, a jagged scar under his right eye. But more alarming was the dagger in his hand pointed in her direction. "You little—" He lunged towards her, and Kora froze against the tree, unable to move her limbs when suddenly she was pushed aside, the ground knocking the air from her lungs.

She wiggled, gripping hold of a dried root to drag herself out from under something heavy, her hands shaking, and the scarred man running away in her periphery. Kora stared at her scraped palms, willing them to stop shaking before she searched her surroundings to find William beside her, hunched in on himself. Kora blinked, rushing to stand as she grabbed hold of his shoulder, ignoring the sting of the scratches on her hands. "Will, we need to go. Now."

With her assistance, he stumbled to his feet, hissing as he tried to straighten.

"What's wrong?" Kora wrapped his arm over her shoulder, practically dragging him away as he limped along beside her.

"We must...get out of here," he spoke through choked grunts.

The sound of guards' whistles in the distance had the few remaining scattering as others ran towards the injured. Tears streamed down fearful faces that rushed past.

Kora, distracted by the chaos, nearly tripped on an outstretched leg. The toga wearing speaker was on the ground, his gaze towards the heavens. His breathing gargled and blood pooled at his side. "We should help him."

"I've got him." One of William's friends stopped and swooped down to press a bundled jacket to the speaker's side to stop the bleeding. "You two go. Hurry, before the guards arrive."

Kora picked up their pace, and William did what he could to match it. Fear and adrenaline kept her going even as her legs wobbled from her twin's weight. The field and temple behind them, the sound of the guards' whistles quieted as they entered a neighborhood with houses close together and barely familiar in the limited moonlight. The sun had set at some point. Kora didn't remember when.

William's breathing became labored after they passed bare olive trees that led to their neighborhood. They just needed to cut over the knoll and they would be home. She had no idea how they would account for their current appearances, or if her mother would ever forgive them for disappearing from dinner.

"What were you thinking?" Kora shook her head as dead grass crunched under their feet. The neighborhood lights acted as a beacon, the street lamps aglow. Over the knoll, down to the corner and they would be home. "I thought you knew better then to get involved in one of those groups."

They reached the bottom of the knoll. "Kora..." William stumbled, falling to his knees. "Not—" He hunched over. "Not now."

"What?" Kora dropped beside her twin. "Will, what's wrong?" She frowned as light caught on her red-coated hand. A stickiness she hadn't noticed lingered as she opened and closed her hand, and she stared. Blood. It wasn't hers. William's.

The scream stuck in her throat, her eyes wide.

His eyes fluttered and he coughed, crimson-tinged saliva speckling his cheek. "Kor—" He coughed again and fell onto his side as his body curled in upon itself.

He'd been stabbed.

No!

"William." Kora looked at William's stomach. His coat had been lost at some point, and his once white shirt was stained with dirt and blood, visible by the lantern above them. Her insides plummeted as fear wrestled against pure panic for purchase. He coughed and more blood seeped from the wound, bringing her back to the present. Action—he needed help and needed it now. She looked down at her dress. Why hadn't she grabbed her shawl? She could have used it. The lace trim was torn at the bottom of her skirt. With shaking hands, she tore it at the seam and pressed it against his wound to try to staunch the bleeding. When did this happen? How—

The image of the scarred golden-toothed man flashed through her mind. This was all her fault.

"Why didn't you tell me you were hurt?" The blade had been meant for her—he had pushed her aside and taken the hit.

"I...I thought we could make it," he sobbed, eyes brimmed with tears.

Blood coated her hands, the lace no longer white. She increased the pressure to his injury as she fought her own tears. "Never mind. Don't speak, William." Kora pressed harder, willing the wound to stop seeping. She looked up, searching her surroundings for anyone walking by. For one of the doors from the houses across the street to open. Someone had to be around—anyone would do. "Help," she bellowed the word at the top of her lungs. "Help!"

Frustration gnawed at her insides at the answering silence, but Kora bit it back. She needed to keep William calm. Keep herself under control.

She turned to her twin, praying to the immortals for help whether they had abandoned humanity or not. Some guidance. Anything to halt the inevitable. To anyone who would listen to her pleas as she desperately tried to stop the flow. Frantic thoughts crowded her mind. Panic grew as she considered if she should run. Slam on doors. Keep screaming for help. But the bleeding...there was so much blood. What could she do? "Please, someone help us!"

"What's goin' on here?" She twisted to look over her shoulder, careful not to loosen her hold. A figure stood on top of the knoll, looking down at her with apprehension.

Relief and something like hope rose with the words in her throat. "Help, please. We need a doctor. Someone."

The man drew closer, coming into view and his attention lingered on her for a moment, before it settled on William. His eyes widened. "What happened?"

"I'll explain later. Please!" Kora begged. William coughed again, the lace not doing enough. "Do you have something to stop the bleeding?"

The man snapped to attention at her voice. He tore off his vest, and she took it from him, replacing the lace with it. He staggered a bit as he bent over and took William's body into his arms. William groaned at the shift. The man smelled of alcohol and sweat, but even though he wasn't exactly steadied, he straightened and began to jog down the street with the vest pressed tight to William's wound. Kora suddenly wanted to be strong enough on her own. She'd be faster. Get her brother to safety sooner.

As if sensing her urgency, the young man quickened his pace. William hung limp in his arms and didn't object as they rushed towards the first home.

Kora banged on the door until someone answered. "Call a doctor. Hurry."

The gray-haired woman looked past her and towards William and gasped. With a quick turn on her heels, she was out of sight.

Kora thanked the immortals, hope filling her. But there was so much blood—there was so much. "Hold on, Will. Please."

A few seconds later, a man was at the door, and Kora was barely cognizant as they ushered them inside. William was placed on a table. Bandages. Bins of water. The woman on the telephone in the hall speaking words Kora couldn't understand. Things happened quickly as strangers snapped orders and bustled around her brother. Through it all, she held William's hand, ignoring the cool touch of his skin against hers.

Chapter 6
Kora

It had been two days. Two days since the incident. Two days since the doctor had done everything he could, and William had been transported home to the comfort of his own bed by the very strangers who had helped them that night.

Now, Kora glanced over William's body as his breathing became ragged. She considered running for her father. Or the doctor who was right outside the door. But she could hear their conversation. Tears stung her eyes.

"There is no medicine," the doctor whispered the words, but not quietly enough. "The pharmacies are out until the next ship-ment arrives."

Her father sounded exhausted. "When is that?"

It felt like forever until the doctor answered. "We don't know. It was meant to arrive today—but didn't."

"And surgery? You said he needed it."

"If I attempted it without the proper anesthesia..." He lowered his voice, but not enough. "That was also supposed to come today."

Infection had spread. His kidney had been damaged. They had closed the wound, but the procedure to fix the organ would be traumatic and impossible with William conscious.

Kora's hope waned. She'd considered more than once running

to the temple. Beseech the gods to hear her pleas. But she couldn't, wouldn't, leave William's side.

There was nothing else she could do. Nothing but wait. *But for what?* William couldn't die. Her body shuddered, but she willed her hand to still. To be strong for him. Her grip tightened as she breathed alongside him, throat bobbing as she bit back tears. "Everything will be fine." The words felt false on her lips. Where were the immortals now? William's skin became paler. "I love you. But please—hold on. They will figure out something. They must." The doctor hadn't really given up, had he? Her parents hadn't, could they?

A chill ran down her spine as William fought for each breath. Death hung around them. Cold. Empty. She wouldn't allow it to take him.

Not now. There had to be medicine and supplies arriving soon. Kora soaked the rag again then reached for her brother's hand, holding it tight as she dabbed away the sweat clinging to his skin. "Do you want me to tell you a story?"

Tears stung her eyes as he gently nodded his head.

Kora cleared the fear from her voice and lowered her head to his ear, pressing his cold hands between both of hers. She hadn't told him a story in years, not since they were much younger. When one of them would have a nightmare and climb into the other's bed. A story was what he'd always asked for when he'd woken with fear and had helped him sleep easier with happier dreams.

"There was once a boy who dreamed of silhouettes. They were shadows of people of all different shapes and sizes. He would dance, play and run about with them until they became whole— more than just a figment of a thing but a solid corporeal being."

William closed his eyes, his breathing slow, but a sense of peace flitted across his face. It frightened her further, but she continued with his hand gripped in hers.

"And as these new individuals took shape, new friends emerged. Some were recognizable, others not. The boy had surrounded himself in times of darkness with those who were closest to him, and they warmed his heart as they continued to celebrate." A sob choked her words, forcing her to pause. Her heart quickened as William's hand grew colder in her own.

She cleared her throat, his skin clammy to the touch. The playful brother, the obstinate sibling—the twin she recognized was slowly disappearing. Yet, somehow, her words kept on. "As they continued to play, he knew he'd never be alone. Would always be safe. That even the unknown held opportunities and adventures."

William took a long, gasping breath. It seemed like the world went silent as his chest stilled. For a moment, it felt as though nothing moved. As if life had paused. William's face had leeched of color, removing any trace of who he had once been. With a deep inhale that clawed at her throat and stuck in her lungs, her entire body shuddered. If she moved, she worried life would resume around her and that wasn't possible.

Not without him.

Another breath? Movement? He had to still be here and at any moment now he'd prove it. She kept her hand resting against his face as it began to cool beneath her palm.

An owl hooted. The flower-patterned drapes fluttered from the open window as a breeze curled around her. Life around Kora resumed. Even if she couldn't bring herself to accept it.

Numb. Incoherent. Everything was stinted of color and sounded like those moving pictures they'd seen in town once before the theater closed. Silence...shock. Nothing registered, and her body shook from a chill that moved through her limbs. Kora watched her brother's prone body with her hand rested on his chest, searching for a heartbeat that no longer existed.

The world continued around her, but Kora couldn't look away. As if he would disappear the moment she broke her stare. Be forgotten—

It was sudden.

Unexpected.

Above William, a shadow appeared, slowly forming in the shape of a human. She gasped, her entire body stiffening.

At first, she thought it must be someone's shadow. She turned around and searched the room. But the door remained closed. She turned back to find the shadow had straightened with its legs spread and fists settled on its hips. Then the shadow materialized —just as the silhouettes had done in her story. As the figure became whole, *he* looked utterly human. A being who wore a tattered cream shirt and dark brown pants torn at his calves.

And he was floating.

Her eyes widened, but when her mouth hung open in awe, no sound came. She recognized him. The young man at her window.

The new arrival reached out his hand towards William. Kora almost held out hers, to see if he was real, but stopped when a shadow rose from her brother's arm to grasp hold. Kora's eyes darted around her to see if anyone else could see what she saw. But no one was there. She turned back just in time to see the shadow fully emerge from her brother's body. The strange man met her gaze. His blue eyes sparkled with mischief under a messy layer of auburn hair that added to his intrigue. She'd only ever seen his eyes hidden amidst a shadowed face.

He tilted his head, brow furrowing at her attention.

"Who are you?" she whispered.

Those eyes widened—a mirror to her own—shock etched in his sharp jaw. And just as quickly as he'd materialized, he was gone. As was the second shadow. As though they had never existed.

The sounds around her suddenly amplified—rushing feet coming in her direction as the door flew open—all came back in a high-pitched cacophony, jarring Kora from her near-catatonic state. Had she cried out? She couldn't remember.

What had just happened? Maybe it was nothing—her imagination and grief playing tricks on her? Or was that one of *them*? One of the gods everyone thought gone.

She nodded to herself. An attempt to try to calm the shock coursing through her body. The grief tried to take hold.

Noise filled the room. Her mother's wails. Her father's agony. The doctor's attempt to push her away to get to William. Too late. A strange sense of calm came over her as she stepped aside without letting go of William's hand.

The doctor stumbled to a stop beside her brother's body. He pressed his stethoscope to her brother's chest. Tried to open his eyes.

"It's too late." Kora's voice didn't sound familiar. Instead, it was distant, disconnected. "He's gone."

She wiped her face. Her cheeks chilled with tears. Father tried to pull her away, but she was frozen in place.

Kora watched as the doctor checked William over. Why? She didn't know since there was nothing he could do now. Not when her brother's soul was flying off with someone or something else.

Chapter 7
Shade

Shade's jaw tensed as he flew over Athens streets, the newly acquired soul soaring along beside him. Mist thickened the deepening darkness as night settled, hiding the inhabitants of the city from view. Nothing to sidetrack him from imposing thoughts.

He had messed up things this time. Somehow, she'd seen him when he'd promised himself that it wouldn't happen again. He'd first seen her eight months prior when he'd overheard her comforting her little brother after the death of their family's messenger. He'd been curious about the young woman with beautiful amber eyes telling stories about the gods. At first, he'd been distracted because the story had been about him. His isles. And for once the stories weren't filled with damnation but of wonder. The way he always wished mortals would view death.

But even he couldn't use that excuse as one visit turned into six. Once he swore she had met his gaze as he sat at the window ledge. That was at least two months ago. And he still continued to stop by—undeterred. Curious.

Until now. When he felt the tug of death and traveled into the mortal world to retrieve the soul.

This wasn't the first time Shade had heard the words uttered by mortals to loved ones on their death beds. He usually tried not to listen in. To give them privacy, but today he couldn't resist. Not as her brown curly hair fell loose from a messy chignon, framing a tear-streaked face with those amber eyes that shone like firelight.

How had she seen him? Then and now? Shade hadn't allowed it, had he? With all his experience collecting souls, not once had another seen him.

Except her.

And maybe it had just been his imagination. He shook his head. No, she had made direct eye contact when she spoke to him. Her surprised expression was proof enough that she knew he was there. Would she tell anyone? Would they believe her? Mortals were never meant to see him unless he wanted them to. At least not the living, breathing, heart still beating mortals. The dead were another story altogether.

Shade pinched his eyes closed, pushing thoughts of her from his mind. With a warm smile, he turned to face the soul beside him. "What's your name?" A safe start, even if he knew already.

The soul scanned Shade with an arched brow and pursed lips. "William."

"I'm Shade." The soul studied him with an analytical gaze. "Just a few more souls to collect and then we're on our way to the Isle of Waiting."

"The waiting place?" The boy's jaw twitched. "It's real?"

"You question the existence of the waiting place but not the fact you're currently flying with an immortal?" Shade asked, a playfulness in his tone he didn't feel. "Where did you expect me to take you? You're dead. We don't just leave souls hanging around the mortal world. It wouldn't bode well for you, or for the living."

"Couldn't be sure. Not with the current state of the world because of your absences. At this point, we question if the immortals cared anymore," William snarled.

"It's for the best we don't intercede as much as we used to. You're too young to know the troubles our presence caused in the past." Empty words Shade had repeated many times.

"Those are damn excuses," William snapped. There was some fire in this soul. "I wouldn't be surprised if the dead still scoured the earth because half the people are looking close enough to it lately. Do you even notice the famine happening? Or know why I'm here now with you?"

"Yes." Shade needed to change the subject. Not just because of the accusations, but because of the truth in his words. The mortal world had changed. There was no denying it. Fewer clouds glistened the dark horizon on his visits. Rain rarely covered the land. The once fertile hills were bare. Even the vineyards along the coastlines of nearby islands had diminished. But Shade wasn't the only one to blame for the mortal world's current trouble. "I know this is hard for you, but change will happen. When it's time, mortals will flourish again. You're a hearty people. Besides, you're dead. There is little you can do to change the path of the world below."

William took a deep breath.

"Like that." Shade nodded. "You don't need air anymore."

The soul shuddered, turning away from him. "Didn't even think how final *death* sounded until now."

Good, he was getting the soul on track. This was a time for a bit of selfishness and self-reflection. There was no way to change William's fate—his life had been cut short, and it wasn't Shade's choice to do so. Time of death was beyond his ability. It was not too dissimilar from Shade's own fate—he hadn't liked being chained to the Isles of Nekrós. His brother was the one who forced him there. It was long overdue for Captain to see, first-hand, what he had sequestered Shade too. The dead—always and forever.

The immortals wanted Shade to reclaim his title and allow Captain to step back in his role as King of the Gods, but Shade wasn't as willing to do as they wished.

Besides, Shade enjoyed the games they played.

The sun had long set as they flew closer to the beaches along the Saronic Gulf, giving a clear view of the nightlife. People walked along sand strewn streets. Some stopped to watch the ocean—moonlit waves crashed against the pebbled shore. A few laughed as they chatted with family or friends. Others rushed past, shoulders hunched to their ears, hands stuffed in pockets as they went on their way without caring about the world around them. They all had one thing in common—life. But even Shade couldn't deny William's words at the sight of the man huddled against a lamp post with his jacket tight around him and a hacking cough deep in his lungs. Or the family in the alleyway with no shoes on their feet and children with gaunt faces and sunken eyes.

Mortals tried to hide so much from each other, which only made Shade more curious about their secrets.

Things had started to change once Captain arrived at the Isles of Nekrós. There had been little nuances at first. The temptation of change like the spread of a great oak's roots. The seed turned into a sapling, and then as the trunk expands and grows, the roots stretch out of control and in any direction they chose, disrupting everything around it. Chaos reigned. Wars broke out.

But it was Captain who had called the immortals back. Not Shade.

Beside him, William cleared his throat. "Why do I have a body?"

Shade turned onto his back and slowed until he was flying a few feet under William, looking up at him with his hands rested behind his head. "It's not a body per se. Not like the one you left behind. It's a vessel currently housing your soul and will continue to do so until you face judgment."

"Judgment? You mean at the gates of the Isles of Nekrós?"

Shade nodded. "Correct. Unless you don't have payment, then the sea serpent has rights to you."

"Wait." William's eyes widened, and Shade could see fear in his expression for the first time. "I don't remember a sea serpent in the stories."

Shade knew he shouldn't but laughed all the same. "I don't think you need to worry about being claimed by the sea serpent."

William blinked a few times. "What will happen to me?"

"You'll meet the Dikastés who will place you within a realm of the Isles of Nekrós."

"The Judges?"

"Yes."

"But you said we are headed to the Isle of Waiting?"

Shade sped up a bit, the tug for the next soul pulling him forward. "Yes, but only a few souls have the option of remaining on the Isle of Waiting until they are ready to pass on."

"Select few? Who gets to make that choice?" William swallowed, glancing around at the mortals below.

Shade twisted around until he was flying on his stomach again. "Me."

"I always knew the immortals hadn't completely abandoned us." There was a smile in his tone.

Shade cocked his head at the soul and considered his words. *Not my fault,* he reminded himself. He glanced down at the passing landscape as he banked left towards Britain.

William sighed. "We need your presence and guidance to steer us right. That's what I was fighting for. To find a way to bring you back. But you're here—just obviously don't care."

Didn't care? This soul hadn't lived long enough to know what had come before. When the gods had meddled, trouble ensued from their own internal wars with mortals caught in the crossfires. It wasn't something any should want to return to.

"We're doing exactly what we should—separating our troubles from yours. Most of us spent too much time involved within our own disputes to do anything for mortals anyway." Even as he said it, warm amber eyes filled his thoughts. Her fear had been evident. As had the hope and awe that flashed across her face as she'd held onto the young man beside him.

The soul's mouth set. "We need you." He looked down at the

mortal world as it shrunk from sight the higher they flew. "They need you."

"And that's why I'm here. To take you where you belong," Shade added a bit of gravitas to draw the soul out of his nagging.

Silence settled between them for some time as they flew over France. They were nearing their next destination when Shade broke it, unable to resist. "Who was the young lady with you?"

"My twin." William sniffled. Even if the soul felt sadness and loss, there were no more tears to be shed now. "Kora."

Kora. It fit her.

William quieted, likely stuck in his own head. It wasn't unexpected—it was a strange experience to no longer be tied to mortality. At least, that was how many of the Lost Souls had explained it to Shade. He didn't know from personal experience. It was both the blessing and curse of being immortal.

Sometimes Shade envied the living—mortals didn't just exist to inhabit the world, but to create things. To leave a mark. Affect change, hopefully in a positive way. Death, for the immortal who oversaw the dead, had never been an option. Never ending torturous pain—yes. But not the bliss and release of taking his last breath or the chance to be uncertain about tomorrow. He would be lying to himself to say he didn't crave just a moment of utter chaos where he could lose it all. He'd never understand since there was nothing for him to lose. Not truly. He'd lost his heart long ago when he lost his best friend. But it hadn't been the end of him. Shade still breathed, continued on. Death for an immortal was eternal damnation or resting in Iroes—the Isle of Heroes. He'd been there plenty and didn't find it relaxing.

Immortal was such a funny word. It came with the gift of life without the possibility of rest. And it certainly came with expectations.

That was why Shade wouldn't return to his supposed 'place'. Although the Isle of Waiting had become his home, it wasn't a reprieve from the orbs—the figments of what the mortals had once been—that remained within the Isles of Nekrós.

"Will the immortals ever return?" William swallowed deep.

Shade laughed. "Someday. They can't be held back forever." The mortals would wish them gone again when that happened. They wouldn't like the gods sticking their noses into their business, stealing loved ones from others, or creating more drama than necessary all for glory or recognition.

But he was growing tired of this line of questioning. "Let's get these last souls. Then it's time for some real fun."

"Will...will I see anyone I know at the Isle of Waiting? Someone who has passed before me? Like my grandparents?" William fidgeted, his bottom lip caught between his teeth. He glanced over his shoulder with longing weighing on his expression.

"Doubtful." Shade did a back flip. "Most of the souls move on after a period of time."

It was often like this. A wish to return. To say proper farewells, but more so a yearning to stay near the ones they know. This was why Shade was here—not only to escort them to the Isle of Waiting, but to see these moments. To grasp some type of understanding of how they lived, mourned, forgave...loved. Something to help him understand his own loss. The friendship and companion stolen from him so long ago. His mother's choice to leave. His brother's abandoning him. "They will learn to live with the memory of you."

"What's it like on the Isle of Waiting? Do I get to stay?"

"I still haven't decided." A lie. His smile widened. "As for what it's like...you'll see."

"Making friends again, Shade?"

He inwardly groaned at the sound of Télos' voice. "What are you doing here?"

The immortal appeared in front of him, cutting him off as they had been ascending into the dark sky. When he had thought only the stars accompanied them. The God of the Dead was wearing his usual black trousers and tunic, dark unruly hair always ruffled by the wind. Shade grinned. "Hello, Télos."

His friend crossed his arms, all but ignoring the deceased souls that he too had collected hovering at his back. "You're not supposed to be here."

At one time, his friend wouldn't have been able to sneak up on him, but since he'd broken from the Isles of Nekrós, his power had dwindled. Something he'd never admit aloud. "I'm helping. The dying called me to come retrieve their souls."

"That's because your brother won't let the gods return home." Télos' bushy brow rose. "Fix that and then the dead wouldn't be coming in droves, and I could handle my job alone."

"You try telling Captain to do anything. He won't listen to me."

Télos' gaze hardened. "Seems stubbornness runs in the family."

Shade peered over the immortal's shoulder at the three collected souls. "Want me to take them with me? We are going to the same place."

His friend sighed. "Theileus only lets me do my job because it is connected to yours—and since he happens to be lording over your domain. Going to consider taking back your mantle? Things would run properly again."

"Old debate. Same answer." Shade shrugged. "And don't let Captain hear you calling him by his true name. It really angers him." With time, they had learned that power came with the knowledge of their true names. Some, just like Shade, protected that information.

Télos shook his head. "I really don't want to get into the middle of this, but I hope the two of you figure it out soon." He gestured towards the souls behind him. "Take them straight to the docks, Shade." He held out a hand.

Shade considered not taking it. He didn't like to make deals with just anyone. But when a notch appeared between the god's brows, he grasped his hand and shook it. "I'll take your collection straight there."

Télos opened his mouth, about to call him on the obvious

word but instead sighed dramatically. "If you need to talk, you know how to reach me."

And then he flew off, back towards the mortal world. That tug pulled at Shade's navel. Not back to the earth below, but to Nekrós. He'd been gone long enough. Soon it would hurt to be away. It was time to go home. "Follow me."

Not that the souls who filed in behind him had a choice.

Chapter 8
Captain

Captain rested his hands on the spokes of the helm of the *Charon*. The towering volcanic ash, pungent scent of sulfur, and spurting lava of the Isle of Torment were visible as they sailed along the strip of land that made the Isle of Judgment. The souls had been delivered—Captain's job complete. Night encapsulated the Isles of Nekrós. Anamoní spread wide ahead, its rigid peaks a silhouette in the sky. Much more welcoming than the peaceful meadows and torturous land-scape they left behind. No wonder the island had beckoned to Shade. It was temptation compared to the stagnant isles of Nekrós.

The ship creaked as the water moved beneath it, floating still as Captain waited. Soon it would be his turn to meet with the judges—the Dikastés—to *talk*.

It had been another day of considering what to do about his brother and obsessing over what he couldn't control. Sometimes free will really was a pain in the ass. Manipulation was considered one of Captain's greatest strengths. But none had worked on the God of the Dead. Not the temptation of power, a need for redemption, a want for more riches, or promises to send Shade whoever he wished to warm his bed.

Shade had denied all the bargaining chips Captain had dangled in front of him. Attempts to trick him to return had done nothing but proven how smart his brother truly was. It only strengthened Captain's reasoning to why he'd placed Shade in such a position. Not only to get him out of his hair—the last thing he needed was a smart conniving god who may want his throne—but also to ensure he stuck his nose out of Captain's business.

A gale howled, heeling the ship portside. The summons he had waited for. Captain called for the scythe and as the cool handle appeared within his grip, the power of the Dikastés encapsulated him. He closed his eyes as it covered him, and when he opened them again, he stood before the three thrones upon a large pedestal in the center of a dark cavern. A flame warmed Captain's back. It was used by the Judges to foresee where the souls were meant to be placed. It was unneeded now, so it burned low.

"You wanted to see us," the figures hissed in sequence. All three sat upon their thrones with gnarled wrinkled fingers gripping armrests. Dark cloaks covered each being except for crooked noses that extended from beneath their hoods. Captain had a feeling he didn't want to see what was waiting underneath.

"I come to beseech your assistance. We all know Shade needs to carry the mantle of God of the Dead again. This charade has gone on long enough. There must be something you can do." Captain lifted his chin, his eyes darting between the three figures.

Silence. For one breath. Two. Then the figure on the left spoke in a booming rasp. "There is nothing we can do."

"We may choose the fate of the souls, but not the fate of an immortal," the middle added.

The third chuckled. "You are his ruler. If you cannot make him do something, what makes you think we can?"

Captain's jaw clenched, his eyes narrowing to slits. They shouldn't question his authority—and yet he had no retort. No false claims to their words. With a tight mouth, he glanced over each of the Dikastés before him. They may not rule this realm, but they had more knowledge of it than Captain. There must be something that could force his brother's choice. The shale rock surrounding them glistened from the braziers scattered around the cave. Captain's power wasn't in the flames but was within the skies. He called upon it and a bolt of lightning ricocheted off the stone at the entrance. The figures shuddered in their seats.

"Do not come here to threaten us. Just because we speak the truth you don't want to hear—it does not mean we can fix what is done," the three voices spoke as one, the sound grating against Captain's ears.

"It was not a threat, but a reminder," he ground out. "There are secrets the isles possess. You must know many of them. Share with me a way, a chance even, to lure Shade back to his position. From there, I will do the work."

The cloaks shifted to look at each other. If they were talking or communicating, Captain couldn't hear a single word.

The middle figure rose as the others settled back in their chairs. They steepled their fingers while the center judge stepped to the edge of the pedestal. "There may be one way, but it will take a conniving mind, and you know how *our* king is always a step ahead."

Captain growled. "Noted. But I think we all want him to be back where he belongs."

"That we do. He has a certain finesse others are less capable of."

At this point, he wouldn't be surprised if the judge was smiling. It only infuriated him more. "Get out with it. Or I can leave and you three can figure out this mess all on your own. The souls will remain in limbo and Nekrós can crumble. Is that what you prefer?"

"No, we do not." The judge straightened. "The Fruit of Death. If mortals eat it, they die. If immortals eat it, they are forever connected to the Isles of Nekrós."

"I've never seen this fruit. And he wouldn't eat it no matter my attempt to trick him to do so."

"That is not what we advise anyway. He's already eaten the fruit—has long been tied to the Isles. He's only extended his reach. Only the King of the Dead can find the pomegranate tree, and he's lost that right by thwarting his duties. Make him need it. Make him want to find the tree, and he'll have to resume his title."

Captain blinked. It was something, yet... "How in the hells do you expect me to make him want the Fruit of Death?"

All three Judges shrugged in unison "You are smart. He has a weakness, everyone does. Make him *want* the fruit."

The Dikastés chuckled, and the middle one pointed a gnarled finger at Captain. "There is one truth Shade may not know. A secret dangerous if ever uncovered. It has happened once, but myth has changed the story. You must swear upon your power that you will only use this knowledge to return your brother to his proper title and in no other way."

Captain tilted his head. "I'm listening."

"It can cure any affliction for a mortal *near* death. Even one that resides within the Waiting Place and has not yet faced judgment."

"Shade won't give the souls a chance at life. They are companions, nothing more," Captain grumbled. They were grasping at straws. Either that or the Dikastés believe mortals to be self-sacrificing fools.

"Opportunities will appear. The Fates have advised. You just need to look and listen." The Dikastés turned and took their place back on their thrones. "Kalí týchi, Captain." Then with a sudden snap of darkness, Captain was back in his chambers upon the ship.

He leaned over his desk, ready to throw everything off it in frustration. They thought luck would be enough to draw his brother back to his throne. Captain sat down in an armchair, tapping his index finger on the wooden corner in succession. It might be time to include Halieus in his schemes. Of course, that would also mean he'd have to hear an abundant amount of 'I told you sos', but it's not like Halieus had a way to force Shade back to the Nekrós. The Dikastés gave him something, but was it enough? Or maybe Captain was too close, and Halieus's insight would be helpful. It would also mean all three kings of the realms would be in the Isles. Not his smartest idea, but if it yielded results…

Halieus would want something in return. Nothing ever was given without a cost. Even if it would be for the good of all.

The putrid smell of death wafted from under the door and tightened his resolve. He needed to go home. Away from the rot and decay. It was time to oversee the mortals, and he knew the other gods were impatient to return to the mortal world. They wanted, almost needed, to cause some chaos. And Captain needed to be there to make sure it wasn't too much. *Some* was a little fun, after all.

Captain stood and opened the door, making his way towards the deck. He peered over the expanding blue ocean. The dock jutted out in the distance. Empty. Then a speck formed in the distance as it broke through clouds, forcing him to pause. It wasn't alone, four other dots trailed behind. Captain stood at the helm and waited. But it didn't come. No crow—no announcement of Shade's return.

It had been his brother's tell-tale call. A playful sound—or so Shade believed—that had been adored by their mother who had coddled the youngest sibling. Captain had once believed that their mother had known her youngest son's future, and that was why she showered him with extra attention. Played with him. Doted on him hand and foot. But now, Captain was tired of his brother's games. It was just another excuse for attention.

"Smith."

Smith rushed to his side. Captain held out his hand and for a moment it hung there until the soul seemed to realize what he requested. Smith rested the spyglass onto his waiting palm. Captain peered through the glass and searched for the specks within the sky—it was Shade with four new souls on his tail.

Something wasn't right. He never had returned without announcing it for everyone within hearing distance. As annoying as it was, the crow had become an expectation. Captain lowered the spyglass, but his attention remained on his brother as he spoke to Smith. "Before we anchor, signal Taea."

Chapter 9
Shade

S hade itched to fly but walked alongside William as they crossed the sandy white shore towards the forest. They'd dropped off the other souls straight to the dock to await passage and made their way towards Camp. William took in his surroundings with the awe the isle was afforded.

Most of the sand dislodged from his feet as the beach turned into thick foliage of shrubs, dirt, and grass. Shade dodged leaves and pushed back low hanging branches from his path, keeping them out of William's way. They reached the clearing in record time. When Shade came to a stop, William almost ran into him.

"What is this place?" William's eyes widened as he turned in a half circle, taking in the clearing. Lean-tos, hammocks, and dilapidated structures were scattered along the edges within the trees. Souls exited them, most with curiosity dancing in their eyes. Rope ladders fell from hammocks or tree houses and a few souls climbed down from their resting places. They wore the clothes they arrived in—well, most of them. All had discarded their shoes at one point or time, deeming them unnecessary. Dirty, stained faces tilted in their direction. Only a few bathed but it wasn't like they stunk anymore. No living body, no odor.

"Welcome to Camp—the home of the Lost Souls." Shade waved his hand and gave a mock bow. As he straightened, a sense of pride forced his shoulders back and his chin to rise as the others surrounded them. "A refuge where you will be able to choose when you want to cross to the Isles of Nekrós. Until then, enjoy some fun and games, and a bit of adventure."

"But you said—" William's eyes widened. "I thought that—"

Shade waved off the soul's incredulity. "Not everyone is meant to cross at their leisure."

A girl stopped beside the others as they circled around the immortal and the new soul. She brushed thick hair behind her shoulder. "You say that to all the souls who come here. Don't mind, Shade." She held out a hand towards William. "I'm Curly. What's your name?"

"Curly?" William's brow furrowed, glancing over the ebony ringlets that framed her round deep brown face.

"You don't look like a Curly." A boy chuckled. "More like a Tall." This soul was shorter than most but lean like a tree limb. "I'm Branch."

William's brow furrowed. "Will. I mean William. Branch is an...interesting name."

"He would be a William. He looks like a respectable fellow." A young boy crossed his arms, and William's eyes widened. "The name's Long—I will let you make your own conclusions as to why." Long held out his hand and although there was hesitation, William did whatever he could to keep his gaze upward on the completely naked soul and shook Long's hand.

Shade couldn't hide his giant grin at the shock worn on the new soul's face. "Come on, don't crowd him. He's just arrived after all. Will might want to stick with his name or pick another down the line. Until then, don't make fun—at least, not too much."

Some removed their old names, and even their wrinkles and scars when they arrived at the Waiting Place. They could do that here. Take on the age they were most comfortable or happiest. Curly, for example, had been in her late twenties at the time of her death but now looked closer to nineteen.

The others ignored Shade's request and began to pepper William with questions. While he seemed overwhelmed by the sudden barrage—and possibly still in shock from Long's nudity—he answered what he could hear. Darting a glance from one soul to the next, he yelped out one useless answer—*no, my shoes are not made from leather of a royal cow*—after another.

Deciding William would fit right in, Shade rose a few feet in the air. No one could beat this welcoming committee. They clapped William on the back as they moved in closer.

Melancholy filled Shade, but he pushed it away as the desire to brush wavy hair from a girl's desperate face hit him in his chest. *Damn it to all the levels of hell.*

"Are you leaving already?" Another girl, her green eyes shining bright, elbowed her way through the crowd until she was directly underneath Shade. Astari had a way of finding herself the center of attention and even now the others darted glances in her direction. It had happened to him at first too— and he might have made a mistake allowing her into his private quarters a few times. Definitely one too many. He'd ended things and kept his distance months before, but she still vied for his attention.

"I'm going to see Captain. Can you keep watch over William? Maybe show him around?" Shade always hoped she would find interest in another. William might detour her attention, even though she hadn't cast a look in his direction and kept that piercing gaze of hers on Shade. "Then maybe it is time for some games."

A cheer went as Shade rose in the sky. He flipped in the air, applause following him as he took off in the direction of the *Charon*. He wasn't looking forward to this meeting, but it was best to take the first step. Keep his brother off guard. And if he'd sent Taea, then his brother's curiosity could only spell trouble.

Shade crowed as he arrived above the *Charon*, doing a double flip in the air that was wasted on his brother. Eye rolls were all the immortal would get as reward. But Shade enjoyed annoying

Captain, so why not have some fun? He landed on the main mast beside the large white sail. "Ahoy, Captain!" he bellowed.

Taea waved at him from her perch on the helm of the ship. Captain brushed her off in annoyance. She flew away before impact, landing on the crow's nest at the top of the mast with a few curses spewed from her pert little mouth as she went. Shade smiled at the spectacle.

Captain clasped his hands behind his back and met his gaze. "I didn't want to speak to you."

"You sent Taea to check in, so figured it was best I did it myself." Shade crouched down, giving his best smile. Annoying Captain was the easiest way to get him to forget what he wanted to know.

Captain grumbled in frustration. "You returned and there was silence. No caw, no reminder of your annoying existence. There is always a welcome upon your return—an announcement." Captain's gaze thinned when all Shade did was shrug. "And you left three souls. You never leave so many at the docks."

"I do if the souls will be more trouble than good. One is headed to the Isle of Torment, if I had to bet. Don't want the murderous type in Limbo—not when we are trying to have fun."

"We don't need any type on Ananomí," Captain snapped. "In fact, the only reason the Waiting Isle exists is to dock the ship. And I've heard on good authority that you have turned the coins into a game. Only those who have been deemed worthy should have payment for crossing. No others should be on the shores. Instead, you make it a place of frivolous games and unnecessary shenanigans."

Shade shrugged. "Or, if they're lucky, they're ensured the right to cross, coin in hand. With all the troubles in the mortal world, not many have the means to do so. Your way would return the Isle of Waiting to a place of moaning souls and sadness. My way allows those in my care a chance to be judged."

Captain's jaw clenched. "The mortal world wouldn't be falling apart if you would take up your responsibilities again."

"This conversation is old, Captain. Let the immortals return and do their jobs. Stop using me as an excuse for not being able to control your realm."

Thunder sounded above, but Shade ignored the draw to look towards the skies.

A scythe appeared in his brother's hand. Smith shuddered, moving towards the stairs. If the appearance of the blade was meant to be a reminder of what Shade had left behind, it only made him more determined to never return. The scythe was as much of a manacle as the title he'd abandoned. Captain pointed the blade at Shade. "That doesn't explain why you didn't make your signature announcement."

"I was sidetracked. I have concocted a new game—it was at the forefront of my mind. Do you want to hear about it?" Shade hopped down to the next mast and straightened, resting his hands on his hips.

"No, I don't," Captain seethed. "And you've never been sidetracked. Not enough to miss something as important as hearing the cheers of your awaiting Lost Souls. Since I've been here, I know when you've left because you cawed. I know you've returned when you cawed again. It is like clockwork."

Shade leaned against the pole and tilted his head. "Like I said, I guess I was distracted."

Storm clouds culminated over Shade's head, gray and ominous—similar to the ones in Captain's glare.

"You know that your lightning does little to me," Shade scoffed, crouching down and resting his elbows on his knees. It would do Shade little good for his brother to find out what he'd been distracted by. The ridicule, the judgment—there was enough of that between them already.

"But it still hurts." Captain chuckled under his breath. Thunder rumbled overhead but Shade kept his ground. "Or maybe I should send the storm to Ananomí instead?" The clouds drifted towards the shore.

Shade tilted his head, but he kept concern from his features.

The souls may be dead, but even Captain's power could force them to the gates of the Isles of the Nekrós thanks to the scythe in his hand. The King of the Immortals didn't have the power to clear the island, but a few souls would be transported to the feet of the Judges. He couldn't let that happen. Not after the promises he'd made. The choices he had given them.

One step ahead. "It was difficult to see the sick today." Shade's expression didn't change, but he crossed his arms.

Taea gave an audible gasp but quickly covered her mouth to stifle the sound. She fluttered down beside him, settling on his shoulder.

"Oh?" Captain's voice was low, a warning that if Shade was lying, there would be repercussions. "And you've chosen to return to your place then?"

"No, I came here to beseech your goodwill and allow the immortals to return to their positions in the living world." Shade's mouth thinned, hiding what he didn't want to say. "Otherwise, the Isles will be brimming with the dead in no time. The mortals can't take it much longer."

Captain sneered. "It's a decision—one you made. I can't leave them untethered or they will wreak havoc on the mortal world again. Many of the dead here are from the war your insolence caused. If you stayed in your place, the immortals wouldn't have caused havoc, and I wouldn't have had to call them away. The blame is solely on your shoulders."

Shade opened his mouth to deny it, but Captain continued, "Take your place and I will take mine. And the mortal world's suffering will end."

"I didn't have a choice to be here then, and I won't choose it now. This tentative life I've created now is my middle ground. I'll send the souls to the dock when it is their rightful time. If there is more you want from me, then I guess you're stuck here forever. Synnefo must be in shambles right now with your absence." The mention of the mount with Captain's gilded throne only made his brother's expression darken.

"It wouldn't be if you stopped keeping souls on the Isle of Waiting and did what you were created to do."

Shade rolled his eyes. *Created*? As if he was nothing more than an object—a symbol of death. He was forced here. "I don't *keep* them. They aren't a collection—they just have more adventure within them and deserve the time to enjoy it."

"You can tell yourself that all you want, but in the end, Shade, they are *not* going to fill whatever it is you feel is missing. They're dead." The finality rang across the deck. Captain's head tilted down, his gaze penetrating his brother's. "And it's best you remember that."

Shade was like a spring, ready to bounce at any given moment, coils taut. Anger, frustration—annoyance that his brother could see what he didn't want to feel or think. That he craved connection when he'd been left as lost as those souls. Captain would have known this if it had been before his brother's had left him in Nekrós. They used to be close. All three of them. Another example that eternity was a long time.

"I know what they are. But they weren't always dead. Some deserve the chance to make the choice to cross when they are ready."

"Eternal rest. That's what you are keeping them from."

"That's your view. Not mine. And I don't think the souls are complaining either." He was pushing Captain's patience to a breaking point. He could see it in his white-knuckled grip around the scythe. That damned scythe that had once been his. He never wanted it back.

Lightning struck the mast, right at Shade's feet. Shade pushed off as it broke floating in midair as the beam fell and shattered on the deck. First Mate groaned.

Captain's gaze narrowed. "Get out of my sight."

Shade's jaw worked. He wanted to spew something back at Captain, but the truth was that he had done exactly what he needed to do and detoured his brother away from his first concern. He could never know about Kora. The young woman who saw him. Shade flew off, back towards the Isle of Waiting.

"You're getting sloppy." Taea huffed. "If you aren't careful, Captain will get what he wants."

"Not with your help. We always stay a step ahead together." Shade sped up. "Now let's have some fun. Race you." He didn't wait for an answer before he picked up the pace. Anything to leave behind the conversation, and the threats from his brother. And hopefully the memory of the mortal girl.

Chapter 10
Kora

Kora curled up in bed, wrapped within her blankets with William's teddy that he hadn't touched in years clutched in her grasp. Since her final unanswered request of the gods, she hadn't cried. No tears shed as her family visited his grave for the three standard days after his death. There were moments she thought her younger brother hoped William would wake. When his shoulders slumped as they left, an ache gnawed at her chest. For Kora, it felt like a waste to visit a body when she knew her brother's soul was gone—had flown off with a shadow. But she didn't say a word to her parents. There was no way she could break their hearts or their traditions more than she already had.

They needed this—to have the chance to say goodbye. And Kora couldn't take that away from them. Not when it should be her who was buried beneath the ground. Friends and family visited to offer condolences. Meager meals were brought, offerings of help in a time when food was a necessity.

But Kora didn't want to eat. And judging by the leftovers Nanny had sent off to other families, everyone else in the house held the same sentiment.

Even now, it was early evening, the sun headed towards the edge of the horizon, and Kora had only nibbled on a piece of bread at lunch and sipped at the stew placed in front of her to placate Nanny's worried *tsks*.

Fine. It was the only word she could utter when asked how she was doing. Void—a giant hole in her body. Yet, even with the knowledge he was gone, there was a taste of denial with a twinge of hope that he would walk in through the door at any moment.

But he wouldn't...because it was all her fault that he was dead.

As soon as she was able to form words, she'd broken down and told her parents everything that happened that night. As Mother cried in Nanny's bosom, Father held Kora close—even with her blood-stained hands. It had been easier to recount her guilt than it had been to tell the story to the officers who'd arrived a few moments after the doctor. Before they moved William home for continued care.

They hadn't blamed her. It made her feel worse.

If William hadn't stepped in. If she hadn't been there...

That fact hurt almost as much as the rest of the news. He could still be with them if—

If was Kora's least favorite word now. Because there was no way to go back and fix what had happened.

The book, *Botany and Gods,* sat on her bedside table mocking her. She'd turned off the lanterns, the moon's glow casting a shimmering river of light illuminating the simple cover. She'd tossed it there, hoping to forget its existence as the immortals had forgotten theirs. Her sacrifice and prayer had gone unanswered. But there had been that shadow...

A knock sounded at her bedroom door. Kora pushed herself up and flung her legs over the side of the bed. She stuffed the bear under the pillow and dropped the book into the top drawer of her bedside table as she snapped on the lantern beside her. Wallowing in the dark alone was one thing—but in front of others, it wasn't acceptable.

"Come in." She straightened her skirts as best she could. Not that, in her current state, anyone would care.

Mother poked her head in, her eyes rimmed with red puffy circles. After the wake, it had taken her a few days to even emerge from her room. Her wails during the wake had pressed against Kora's temples, beckoning unshed tears.

"Kora, we need to talk." Mr. Darling pushed open the door further behind Mother. "Is it all right if we both come in?"

"Of course." A sense of urgency pulsed through Kora, but she didn't move from her spot as dread slithered down her spine.

Mrs. Darling took the seat in the overstuffed chair in the corner of Kora's room. The moonlight peering through the window made the red circles under Mother's eyes more prominent. Wrinkles Kora didn't remember noting before stood out against gaunt skin. Father looked to have aged ten years overnight. Kora wondered if her parents would ever look as they did before.

Mr. Darling sat on the window seat with perfect posture, shoulders drawn back. "Your mother and I have talked. We've concluded that it's time for you and your" —he swallowed— "brother to see England."

With a sharp inhale, Kora straightened. "England?"

Mrs. Darling nodded. "Yes, we think it might do us some good to leave Greece. Maybe get a fresh perspective. You, Michael, and I will be leaving at the beginning of the month."

Kora's mouth opened partially, but Father continued, "I will join you at the end of spring—once they can confirm my replacement here at the Consulate."

"This isn't just a visit, you're moving us?" She looked between both of her parents, waiting for one of them to continue. Or break into a smile and say they were jesting. They must be. Nothing about this made sense. "Is it because of what happened —what I did?"

"You did nothing wrong, Kora. We've told you that. This guilt—" She shook her head. "You need to let it go. We don't blame you at all. It was an accident."

Accident was the last word Kora would use to describe the events of that night. The man—his intentions were clear. The authorities must find him soon and punish him for his crimes. "Then why do you want to move?"

Mother looked up to meet Father's gaze then released a long, drawn-out sigh. "Because it would allow you time to become accustomed to life in England before you're introduced into society during the next season."

Kora wanted to leap from her bed. "You cannot be serious?" Her voice rose an octave.

Father's gaze narrowed. "Watch your tone, Kora. And yes, we are serious. It's time that you settled down and found a husband that cares for you. No more of this talk about school. Your brother will also benefit from English society and the opportunities there. We didn't rush to this decision. It took careful consideration before we decided it was for the best if we moved. For all of us."

"Careful consideration? How is any of this considered? He's only been gone for twelve days. What are you going to do with William? Forget him?" This was where their memories were. This is where he still existed. Greece had been where he'd grown up. Where *they* had grown together.

The tears were already dripping down her mother's face and guilt flooded like a rush of cold water through her system.

Father had gotten to his feet, his hand resting on Mother's shoulder as he glared at Kora. "Stop this nonsense right now. We're your parents, and we decide what is best for you."

Kora broke eye contact and stared down at her hands. "I'm sorry. That was wrong of me." It hurt to say when it felt like a lie. To be paraded around for the first eligible bachelor to drag her into nuptials. When opportunities like school and studying botany would be a dream of the past.

"The famine hasn't hit England as hard yet. We will all have better opportunities." Kora heard her mother whisper 'be safe' on to the end of her father's words.

"This is all so much to take in." Kora finally braved looking up at them again. Her mother's aching heart on her sleeve. Her father's quiet resolve masking his pain. They said they didn't blame her for what happened, but how could they not?

"We understand. But you have some time. We can talk further in the morning."

They headed to the door, and her mother stopped with her hand rested on the doorjamb as she looked back at Kora. "We will find the right man for you. A thriving future. One you deserve."

She waited for the door to close before Kora began to pace with her hands stiff at her side, face fuming red. It wasn't appropriate, but she wanted to scream. Yell.

At about the twentieth turn about her room, her anger subsided enough for the pang of guilt to course through her again. She felt so lost.

Without William, who was she?

Not that she would take all of the blame for their decisions. They had sprung this idea to her at the most unexpected of times. There had never been talk about moving to England at any point in her memory. Greece was the place she had been born and never wanted to leave. Except for adventures to write about, of course. But only if she was coming back to the place where her memories of William were the strongest.

She slumped on the window seat and curled her legs into her chest as she laid down. Kora willed the tears to come but they didn't. *That* night drifted into her mind. Her brother's faded pallor. The doctor's and her father's words of lost hope. The shadow figure's messy copper hair, and the way his dark blue eyes —almost gray—pierced deep within her. Then he'd flown away with a shadow remnant of William at his side. Until they had disappeared. She hadn't mentioned it to anyone else and never would. Maybe the image had been a vision—a hope that her brother wasn't alone. That he was happy and no longer in pain.

Or maybe it was real.

Chapter 11
Kora

Kora stared at the temple as darkness clung around her. She would usually be worried about her parents discovering she had snuck out, but they were barely aware of anything since William had taken his last breath. Too caught up in their grief to notice much beyond their conversation the previous evening.

After the incident, it wasn't surprising to find the grounds empty. Even the beggars had moved on to other stomping grounds. William had not been the only victim. She had heard word of two others who had died while four others had been injured.

She didn't allow herself to glance towards the spindly cypress where William had pushed her out of the way. Had taken the death meant for her. If they had medical supplies. If there wasn't a famine...

He'd still be alive.

She had only one more thing she could do. One last touch of hope. Beseech those who were said to be gone. That night a figure had materialized before her. The immortals still existed. Could hear her.

Kora took in her surroundings. There was no one around except for her and Ariana.

Her friend glanced around the space. "What are we doing here? Your letter didn't explain."

Part of her had wanted to come alone. Another part knew she couldn't return without support. Ariana was always just that. "I'm leaving a sacrifice and making a request to the gods."

Ariana studied her for a moment before taking her hand. "I'm here for you. I know this isn't the right question, but are you all right?"

Kora swallowed, trying her best to ignore the heavy weight that had settled on her chest. "No. But I will be once this is over."

They entered the remains of Theileus's temple. The ruler of the gods. If Shade, the God of the Dead, had a temple, she would have gone there, but that wasn't an option. The remainders of stone pillars stood in a group, away from the one where she had once hidden behind. Without a roof and only pediment along the edges connecting the pillars, it was open to the starry night sky, humidity sticking to her bare arms. Mudbrick steps led up to limestone floors.

She steered them towards the middle and knelt, pulling the bag from her shoulder to remove most of the contents: one strip of dried meat, a potato she'd sliced into quarters, and three of the seven pomegranate seeds she had received the day her life had changed forever.

Ariana settled on her knees beside her. "What do you need me to do?"

"Be here," she whispered. "And help me place this just right."

One by one they placed each item in a decorative pile as best as they could. Kora repeated words of hope in her head. No need to speak further, Ariana reached into her pocket and removed the requested flint and matches and handed them to Kora who placed the remaining things from her bag—a few pieces of wood and some dried leaves—onto their makeshift altar. Things she knew her family wouldn't miss. A chance.

It took some patience and more flint than she expected, but she hadn't done this since she was a child when her mother had still relied on the gods' return. Once enough of a fire had caught, she concentrated on the ache and heaviness that weighed on her chest. Like a stone had replaced the space where her heart had once been. With a deep breath, she clasped her hands together, staring at the flames as they danced over her offering, barely cognizant that Ariana had stepped back, giving her space.

"I know it's not much, but almighty Theileus, please hear my plea. My brother is gone. He died—and I know you're still there. That you and your subjects have not abandoned us to a fate of pain and suffering. I saw him. One of yours appeared and took my brother's soul away. You must still care. Even if only a little bit, that's all I need. I beg of you—return my brother to me. Allow me to see him again. He didn't deserve this." A gasp rattled her chest as tears burned tracks down her cheeks. She bent over, trying to stop the pain that stretched from her heart to her gut and made her queasy. "Whatever we have done, I'm sorry. I'll do anything to have William back." She pressed her forehead to the cool marble floor. "Please."

A gust of wind rushed through the pillars, wrapped around the altar and fed the flames. Kora lifted her head, her eyes widened. And then just as quickly as the wind appeared, it vanished, and the air grew stagnant. The flame snuffed out. Ariana gasped, the moonlight and stars seeming to blink from existence.

Kora fanned the flames in an attempt to bring the fire back to life. But no coaxing would do. With the last of her flint and matches used, Kora fell to her knees, bruising bones against the hard stone. With a gasping breath, she let the tears fall freely. Cried like she hadn't allowed herself to do since she had whispered that last story to her brother. Ariana wrapped her arms around Kora who sank against her friend, letting her presence be the comfort it was meant to be.

"What did you see that night, Kora?"

She hadn't considered her words before. Hadn't realized her

friend would overhear. "A figment of my imagination playing tricks on me."

They walked back home huddled in quiet grief. Ariana took her to the steps, and Kora stared at the owl mosaic at her feet. "Thank you for coming."

Ariana wrapped her friend in a hug. "I'm here for you. If you need anything." With a quick squeeze, she padded off to her house next door.

Kora slid inside, careful to be quiet. The house felt empty. Too silent.

She made her way back to her room. Before she had a chance to change, a knock sounded at the door and Michael's quiet voice was called from inside. "Kora?"

He'd come almost every night now because he didn't want to sleep alone. Not that Kora blamed him. He wore striped pajamas, his hair a scraggly mess of thick blond curls.

Michael whispered, "Why aren't you in your pajamas? I came earlier and you weren't here."

She had forgotten about Michael. What if he had followed her like she had followed William? He could have been hurt too. She shouldn't have left. Even if the sacrifice had been her only hope.

"I needed to do something. It's all right, Michael." A lie, but Kora didn't care to elaborate further. Not now.

Grief etched her brother's brow. A change of subject was necessary. "Are you here for a story?" Kora had gotten into the habit of telling them again. It was as much of a comfort to her as it was her younger sibling.

Michael nodded his head, a grin spreading. "Yes, please."

Kora got into bed and patted the spot beside her. She should get into her pajamas, but that could wait. Michael nearly jumped onto her lap. "Once upon a time..."

By the time the story was done, Michael was curled up, his low snores the only sound. She didn't dare wake him as she rested her head against the headboard and looked towards the window, the base of the moon visible.

She breathed a long sigh and pulled out the book from her drawer. With a turn to the glossary, she went to find the pomegranate—a symbol of death and one of the reasons she had used the seeds within her sacrifice. The remaining seeds were in the pouch. Ignored. No desire to plant them when all hope was lost.

With the low lantern light, she began to read about the different symbols of the gods until she got to Shade and the Isles of Nekrós. With a turn of the page, a glossy illustration of a large pomegranate tree took up the entire page. Her brow furrowed as she read, her heart beating furiously in her chest.

It is said if a living mortal eats from the grove of pomegranates found within Nekrós, that they may trade places with any soul they have lost. All one must do is share the fruit with whom they want to trade places. Of course, only demigods have ever survived traveling to Nekrós and returned alive to prove this belief. Now it is considered a myth by many.

Kora read it again. Then a third time, her mind concentrated on certain words. *Pomegranate. Trade.* This was it. What she needed. Except there wasn't a clear way to reach Nekrós. A trip to the library might help. Or the university. Would they let her peruse their collection? Kora closed her eyes, exhaustion mixing with the heaviness of the day. Those were problems for tomorrow. Tonight, all she needed was sleep. She really should change first. But her eyes grew heavy. Her shoulders lax. And she drifted off to dreams—or nightmares.

Neither of them stirred as the hook on Kora's second story window turned and clicked open.

Chapter 12
Kora

Voices, unfamiliar and muffled, filled her room. Kora kept her eyes closed, trying to place them but they weren't her family. A dream—it must be another dream although it wasn't the usual nightmare with bloody hands and sharp knives. Then she heard a name—one she was certain was recognizable, but she didn't know why. It hadn't been spoken for years.

"Shade won't be happy about this," a female voice tinkled. "Most unhappy. To be honest, I'm not either."

"I wouldn't expect you to be." This one was male—masculine and harsh. "As far as Shade is concerned, he doesn't need to know logistics. And you don't have a choice. Unless you want me to tell your best friend the truth."

The female hissed, "You're blackmailing me?"

The man chuckled. "Why are you surprised? It's what *you* do best."

"Your plan hinges on your expectations of a mortal following your every whim, and you know they always want something in return. What are you going to give her?"

Kora scrunched her brow in confusion but kept still. Even if she wanted to see who was speaking and what they were discussing, something willed her to remain silent. Forced her eyes closed.

"Exactly what she asked for," the man growled. "Now go—I tire of you."

"I'm more tired of you," the shrill woman snapped back.

What she asked for? The sound of buzzing almost had Kora opening her eyes, but the man called out in a harsh whisper, "Behave. Otherwise, you won't like what I'll do to you. After all, there are some who deserve their fates."

Kora didn't move for some time, rolling what she heard over and over in her mind. A dream. A confusing dream. A cold sweat caused her dress to cling to her body. Even with her nightmares as of late, her heightened emotions had been there but not the sensation of reeds against her skin. The smell—like a new spring day tainted by ash.

She pinched her eyes closed tighter, willing herself to wake. Just a dream...

It was silent for some time, but the scent remained. With a shuddering breath, the pressure decreased from her head. A fogginess that she hadn't realized had been there lifted, and when begging her mind to wake, she slowly opened her eyes. Instead of darkness and her brother's blood, she saw a field of tall grass that bent with an occasional breeze. Orbs and silhouettes of light floated about and clung among cherry trees filled with pink blossoms. It was beautiful. A dreamy sunshine soaking her skin, bright but not uncomfortable or harsh. Kora couldn't remember ever being somewhere like this, but it felt familiar all the same.

Old temples, like the ones built for the immortals in Athens, dotted the distance. Some were crumbling at the edges. Another stood tall a few feet away, its pillars erect and sturdy. Gauzy fabric of whites and creams drifted between the columns. Kora sat upright, her attention lingering on the doorway of that particular temple, unable to make out the etchings along the top.

"Hello, Kora."

She jerked her head to the right—almost giving herself

whiplash from the movement—to find a man standing tall and regal above her. It must have been the same man she heard speaking because there wasn't another except the orbs lingering in the distance.

There was no denying that this man was handsome. From his easy smile, sharp features, and his immaculate attire with everything in its correct place. He looked like a captain from a ship with his hat and billowing overcoat, which only caused her to puzzle further. Why would she be dreaming of a sailor in the middle of a field with no sign of water in sight?

He must have taken a hint from her expression because his grin widened into a saccharine smile. "This isn't a dream. You're no longer home."

Kora couldn't help but smile back at the audacity of her mind to play such games on her. "Oh, and where am I?"

"Nekrós. Or Iroes—the Isle of Heroes to be exact." The man tilted his head.

She almost laughed but bit back the idea. "Oh, so I'm dead now? And who are you supposed to be?" Kora was curious where this dream would take her. It must have stemmed from the book on her bedside table.

The man stepped forward, his features more visible without the sun cutting across his face. He nearly took Kora's breath away. Sharp lines and perfect cheekbones defined by a rugged remnant of a beard that made those features more prominent. His eyes were a bright blue yet held flecks of darkness like the sky during a storm. "Captain. At least that is my name here. And I assure you, Kora, you're not asleep."

"How do you know my name? Or is that all part of the dream too?"

"As I said, it isn't a dream." Annoyance edged his tone, but his expression didn't change.

Kora didn't care though because she knew her body must be asleep at home in her bed beside Michael. You don't just wake up in another world. Those moments were only meant for nightmares, and with the beauty of this place, this couldn't be one of those.

"I assume you're meant to be the God of Sleep playing tricks on me?" It seemed like a realistic expectation for this figment of her imagination.

Instead of answering, a lightning bolt shattered the earth in the distance, gray clouds suddenly blocking out the once clear sky. They appeared from nowhere and the orbs in the distance scurried from view.

Kora's eyes widened, the hair on the back of her neck straightened with the zing of the currents in the air. She whirled around, looking at the storm brewing above her. Her flesh goose bumped, a shudder running down her spine. "This isn't a dream?"

The man sneered, transforming his once handsome features into darkness. "I can pinch you if you want to find out the truth."

"You're...?" She swallowed deep, knowing who could wield thunder. This couldn't be the King of the Gods. How? Why was *he* in the Underworld? "Theileus?"

"I don't go by that name anymore." His jaw ticked.

More questions filtered through her mind, but she couldn't form words to ask them. "But the gods have long abandoned us. What am I doing here?"

His expression softened. Captain twisted his fingers and a stump appeared behind her, the clouds above dissipating. "An answer to a request. Now sit."

Kora didn't need to be asked twice, especially since her legs had turned to jelly. She was here—her prayer brought her here. "Is this a gift from the immortals? Or am I dead?"

Captain folded his hands behind his back. "No, not dead. And a gift—not exactly. But I did hear your prayer about your brother."

The mention of William had Kora searching in the distance. "Is he here? Or did you send him back home? Have I taken his place?"

He shook his head at the hope in her voice. "No, what you ask is more complicated than a sacrifice and a request uttered on hopeful lips. But I'm willing to make a bargain with you."

"A bargain?" Kora's hands fidgeted. She looked down at the movement and stopped. An immortal wasn't going to take her seriously if she showed nervousness. She folded them in her lap and looked up at him, drawing her shoulders back with the movement, mimicking her father's confidence.

"Yes. You see my brother has decided he no longer wants to carry out his duties. He's the reason for our absence in the mortal world. He's the reason that the famine extends from your home and spreads through the continents. Instead, Shade frolics about, letting mortals see him while he and his minions collect souls. Souls like your brother."

Kora shot to her feet. "Did that shadow—that man—steal my brother's soul? Where is he?"

"He's on Anamoní. The place where souls wait to board the *Charon* in order to be judged. The problem is that he is stuck there until Shade allows him to pass. He manipulates the souls, coerces them to stay with him, and makes it difficult for them to reach their eternal rest." Captain's expression was grave.

Kora sucked in her bottom lip. "Then what am I meant to do?"

Captain chuckled. "You need to get Shade to take up his proper title, his rightful place, and allow the others to finally reach their eternal peace. If you do this, then I can ensure your brother is returned—and you may return with him."

The guilt that had gnawed away at her insides, the heaviness within her chest, lifted slightly at his words. "Wouldn't it make more sense for you, as the king of the immortals, to force him back to his position?"

He snorted. "I've tried. Even I've underestimated his ability. It has come to the point that either you help me, or I force the souls to cross. But to do that, I would have to consume my brother's power. That is not something I want to do because this is his realm. One or two souls forced to cross is one thing, but all the souls on Anamoní is entirely another. And if I do that, then your brother's soul will be stuck in Nekrós forever. The one benefit of him remaining with the Lost Souls is that I can still give you what you request."

"How do you expect me to do this?"

He perused over her body from head to toe. She didn't shy away, glaring back at him. "I think you'll find a way."

"If you're eluding—"

Captain laughed. "I wouldn't force you to do anything you didn't want to. All I'm insinuating is Shade has something you want. Your brother."

She stared at him. "Are either of you able to send my brother back to the mortal world? Or is this just a game of the gods?" Kora knew the stories. The tricks they played. Even if it had been some time since they had been seen.

"I cannot. But Shade can help. You need a fruit tree."

Her eyes widened. "The fruit tree? I read about it." And she laughed again. "This must be a dream then. No one discovers information about a pomegranate that could save a life and then happens to wake up in the exact place needed to do so." Kora shook her head as hope deflated. "A horrible, taunting dream."

"You read about the pomegranate?" His brow furrowed, considering her.

"Yes. The book said I needed the fruit from a tree in Nekrós."

"Interesting..." He considered her for a moment. "That is a coincidence. And this is not a dream—but maybe a sign that we are meant to work together. Only my brother can find what you wish. Make him help you, and we both get what we want. And your world can be saved in the process."

"I need the God of the Dead to help me?" That little flutter of hope emerged. Could this be real? She plucked a piece of grass and twisted it in her fingers.

Captain's mouth elongated into that smile. "Correct. And do not under any circumstances tell him or anyone that I brought you here."

Kora puzzled over his words for a moment, then stuck the end of the grass in her mouth. The bitter taste had her nearly choking. Real. It was real. She faced the immortal standing over her, trying to hide her shock. "Why not?"

"Because if you do, then you and your brothers will be stuck here forever. He won't help you."

She nodded and then stilled. "Brothers?" Kora's brow furrowed.

Captain twisted his wrist, and an image appeared in the space beside him. Michael was asleep against a palm tree, the fronds dancing on a breeze, white sand under him. It was not a place that Kora recognized. Fury rose within her, replacing the fear she'd felt before. With fists formed at her side, she stormed up to the man—immortal—recklessly invading his space despite that he was a god who held more power in the tip of his pinky than she could ever imagine. "Send him home right now."

"No." Captain looked down his nose at her. "Just in case you change your mind, or decide to give up, I need a little leverage."

"I'll help. I would have anyway. Not only for my brother, but for my world." She folded her arms over her chest. "We're suffering because of your brother. Now send Michael home."

Captain's brows rose and tilted his head to the right. "He's safe. As much as you'll be. As long as neither of you die within this realm—just like your own—then once you complete this task, you'll get what you want."

"He's just a little boy. This isn't fair." The idea of her younger sibling there frightened her. She'd already lost one brother. There was no way she would risk losing another.

Captain chuckled. "You may need the motivation. I don't want you to fall for Shade's manipulations. My brother is conniving and you're going to have to navigate pretty words and promises. Your brother's presence will be a constant reminder to keep your head on the task I've given you."

"Why do you think I can manipulate him if you've failed?"

"Shade saw you that night. You said it in your prayer." The

immortal straightened, and Kora didn't know how, but he seemed taller. "You're going to find out why and use it to our advantage."

"How do you expect me to do that?" She opened her mouth to ask more questions, but Captain raised his hand, silencing her.

"You seem like a smart girl. I know you'll figure it out." He snapped his fingers.

And darkness embraced her once more.

Chapter 13
Shade

It had been a few weeks since William's arrival. At least here on Anamoní. Back in the mortal world less time had passed, but he'd kept his distance from the Darling house. Worse, though, was that Captain had been too quiet. It worried him. Even if he made certain to crow extra loud at his every return just to annoy his brother.

There were more important things to do and contemplating Captain's need for control wasn't something he should ponder. She saw him. It was done—in the past, he told himself before his thoughts would drift to Kora. Nothing he could do about it now, and he would continue to keep his distance. It's not like he'd see her again. He'd told himself he'd stay away from her...but maybe he should check one more time. See if she still told stories filled with hope. Still had hope...

Damnation. He couldn't stop thinking of her. He pinched his eyes shut and shook his head as if that was enough to dispel her memory from his mind. Maybe it was time to think of a new game. Something to distract his thoughts.

Taea whistled near his ear. She'd been absent, surprisingly giving him space. "Did you go back to see her? You're only distracted after a visit to that mortal."

One time. One time he'd admitted it to her, and the pixie

wouldn't let him forget. "Come off it, Taea. Let's call the Lost Souls together for some fun." Shade gave his best smile. There had to be a reason she was still interrogating him on this particular subject, but with Taea it was best to let her get it out of her system until she grew bored and moved on.

She returned his smirk with a glare. "Every trip you return from you've dropped all the souls off at the dock. This isn't like you. Usually, you give them a choice. Why was this last soul different?" Taea crossed her arms over her chest, her wings beating rapidly.

"Because." He sped forward, not feeling the need to explain himself further and shouted over his shoulder as he broke through a cloud. "Race you to Camp."

Taea could never resist competition. She sped after him, a trail of pink pixie dust left in her wake. Shade laughed as she caught up, then with a flap of his arms, he nosedived towards the clearing, flipping in the air right before landing on his feet. He snorted as she came to a halt beside him, her skin a shade of burnt red. Whether it was from losing or frustration, he wouldn't dare ask.

The camp was nearly empty when he landed. At any given time, some of the beds were abandoned until new souls took residence. Others were favored and always taken. For the souls, sleep wasn't a necessity and neither was rest. They were safe on the island seeing as they were dead already. But most clung to the lives they had lived before and turned this clearing into a little neighborhood.

A figure broke through the trees, and Astari sashayed her hips as she strutted towards him. She could be another distraction. But her expectations from their dalliances had turned into more—even with his warning that it could never be so. It would be a mistake to go there again. He cleared his throat, glancing around the clearing. "Where are the others?"

"They went down to the beach. I hoped you would return." She folded her hands behind her back, accentuating how the grass skirt she wore brushed her knees. "They will be gone for a while. We could spend some time together. Just the two of us."

Taea snorted in annoyance beside him. He'd almost forgotten the angry pixie was there.

He tore his gaze away from Astari's hips. Yes, a definite mistake and not a temptation worth pursuing.

"Naw." He glanced in the direction of the beach. "I got plans."

Before Astari had time to respond, Shade shot off into the sky again. Not even Taea followed him.

He landed on the beach amid the group of souls who had been tossing a coconut around. A few dodged out of the way, others laughing as they wiped sand from their faces. Curly tried to shake it loose from her hair, her own expression a mix of annoyance and joy. She turned to William but spoke to Shade as she brushed sand from his shoulder. "Where've you been?"

"Where I needed to be." Shade winked at the soul. "I'm back now though." He rested his hands on his waist, a grin playing at the corner of his mouth. "How is it going, William?"

William shook his head from side to side, more sand dusting the air from his thick brown hair. "All right. I can't decide how I feel about being here."

Some of them said this in their early days. Shade hoped he wouldn't have to do much to detour the soul's attention away from those docks. There was something about the boy that told Shade he needed to stay a little longer. *Stupid, stupid.* "Ah, I get it. We can discuss it in a few days or so. No need to jump to rash decisions."

William nodded, though it was a bit uncertain. "But why deny the inevitable?"

Curly leaned into William's arm. "Because it is more fun here. Once you cross the Depth, then you're just at peace—and that's only if you end up in the Isle of Heroes or Contentment. Have you lived a good life? Otherwise, you might find yourself in torment forever." She rose her brow in question, lips curling up into a smile that had William shying away. Still, he gave her a boyish grin in return.

Shade could always rely on Curly to say the right thing.

Long was sitting on the ground, his lower body covered in sand. "It's rare that some want to move on quickly. But I've chosen to make the crossing. I've taken on a rather sedentary lifestyle in the past few weeks, and it feels time to make it official." The others quieted and turned towards the soul. None seemed surprised, so it must have been discussed.

Shade's brow furrowed, but he quickly brushed it off. "It's been many suns since your arrival." He darted a glance in William's direction. "I accept your decision, but as you know, you must find a drachma to cross."

"Hunt," Branch spoke the word in a whisper.

"Hunt," another added a little louder.

All of them began chanting as Shade's smile egged them on. Long stood amidst the hubbub, riling them up. Shade joined William who watched the calamity from the edge, taking everything in.

"All right, all right." Shade waved his hands in the air to get their attention. "A hunt it is."

The souls whooped and hollered in jubilation.

William peered at Shade out of the corner of his eye. "Hunt?"

The others began to run back towards Camp, leaving Shade behind with the soul. "Yes, when a soul has chosen to leave, we do a treasure hunt. There are two teams—the first to find the drachma must re-hide it for the second team to find. Most coins appear when they have need of them. As I told you, yours will when you're ready to cross." At this, William looked at his empty palms. Shade shook his head. "But the isle makes it a little more fun. You must hunt for them."

In the past, the drachma would appear easily. When the coins became harder to come by, fear and worry settled over him. Then he realized it was no longer necessary. They appeared on the island once the soul's physical bodies had been laid to rest in the mortal world.

Shade had attempted to rally Télose into allowing some of their arrivals to stay—to give them a chance to find passage, but he didn't always take Shade's offer. Those who didn't have loved ones or the means to pay for their passing were lost to the Váthos Sea. A fate no soul deserved—but there was only so much Shade had control over.

Shade pushed up into the air, just a few feet off the ground, and floated alongside William who trudged back to Camp. "I'll make sure you and I are on the same team. I haven't given you much of a tour of the island yet, although I know the others are capable. There are a few places where one can get trapped. One soul hadn't been found for a week after a hole he'd made on the beach caved in on him. Through all our searches, we hadn't considered to dig until one of the other souls remembered the last place they had seen him was at the beach."

"What happened to him?" William's eyes widened with concern.

Shade shrugged. "Nothing. He was already dead. Bored for a week of being encased in sand. Never did like the beach after that, but he still didn't cross over until sometime later."

Although William had been here for a while, Shade had kept his distance from the soul, attempting to dispel the last dredges of his thoughts of *her*. Brown hair. Amber eyes. Shade ran a hand through his hair, shaking his head to stop. It seemed time and distance weren't enough.

William worried at his bottom lip. "Is it worth waiting for others to come? Is that why some of the souls remain here? Are you able to tell when loved ones would arrive?"

"That's not how it works." Shade lowered to the ground. "I don't have control over *when* someone dies. Most of the immortals don't unless they have chosen to smite them. As you say, we aren't as open with our happenings in the mortal world now. Natural causes, accidents, illness or free will are the major cause of your deaths now. While life has stopped for those here, it goes on for the living." He glanced at the soul. "Why do you ask?"

"I guess I feel like I owe my family, particularly my sister, an explanation. She showed up before..." William's gaze remained downcast as his feet trailed in the sand. "I don't know how long she was there or what she overheard. I almost lost her that night. If..." William shook his head.

"She's special to you?" Shade didn't know why he asked. Kora, alive and well, shouldn't matter to him at all.

"Very. It's always been her and I. Until I pushed her away. There is something about having a twin that I can't explain. You have brothers, don't you? If I remember the stories correctly." William darted a quick glance in Shade's direction.

Stories. That was what the immortals' existence had come down to. Stories—not realities of the strength they contained. Instead, they *used* to walk among the mortals. Had been one with them. It was partly Shade's fault. At least that was what Captain reminded him of on the regular. Yet, going to the Isles of Nekrós was as much a prison sentence for him as it would be for any immortal.

"Yes," he replied when he realized that William was staring at him. "I have two brothers, and I'm the youngest." Until recently, he was the one who had been forgotten. Shade had only been given the time of day again when he decided he didn't want to follow his brother's orders anymore.

William nodded and stuffed his hands in the pockets of his pants. They had once been soaked with blood from an unhealing wound but now that he was here, the remnants of his past life were gone. "I'm going to miss them if I stay here, aren't I?"

Shade's jaw tensed. There was no sense in lying to him. "Until you go to lay at rest, there will be parts of you that will miss not only your life, but those you've left behind. Some have chosen to stay until their loved ones join them. Then they cross together. Others want nothing to do with their past. And some just want to remain on the Isle of Waiting to enjoy the time they feel they're due."

"But it's not just by chance that many are dying right now." He eyed Shade carefully. "Is it?"

Shade's teeth clenched. He didn't want to talk about the issues he was having with the immortals. "My brother has a viewpoint I don't share. He doesn't want to let the immortals do their jobs and won't listen when I say otherwise."

William sighed, his brow furrowed as consideration filled in his gaze.

Shade nudged him in the arm. "For now, try to have some fun. See if you can settle in. Like I said, we can discuss it in a few days. But your time was cut short—and it doesn't hurt to play a little longer. Not like the Isles of Nekrós is going anywhere."

William chuckled at this. "No, I guess not."

"That's right. Besides, with Long gone, it will make things less awkward soon. I might have to start requiring trousers, at the very least." It hadn't bothered Shade, but he knew some had grown up more modestly.

As he'd hoped, William laughed, and Shade joined in as they entered the camp. Already the teams were made, two groups standing on either side of a line drawn in the sand. Thankfully, Astari wasn't among them. Six against eight. Perfect. Shade could add himself and William to the opposite team. He patted Branch on the back as he stopped beside them. "I'm going to give Will a tour. That doesn't mean we won't hide the coins if we come across them though."

The teams cheered again, their voices carrying through the forest. Shade raised a fist in the air and silence fell. With a grin, he flipped into the air. "Let the game begin."

❧

SHADE LEVITATED BESIDE WILLIAM. So far, he'd taken the soul up to the outskirts of Pixie Meadow and to the Fairy Circle.

He explained that permission must be granted before entering their home. Then he headed towards the beach and the small island just off the shore.

"The tide in Skull Isle gets high during the late afternoon. Don't let the others trick you there or you'll be stuck for the night. Although, it can be a fun adventure…"

"It seems like there are many dangers here. Why do so many choose to stay?" William had picked up a stick off the beach and dragged it behind, creating a trail in the sand.

Shade almost laughed but thought better of it. "Because when the risk of death is gone, the dares are exciting for a while. Yes, it's a pain to get stuck in the caverns of Skull Isle, but it's both terrifying and thrilling to be dragged down into the lagoon. Think of it as a chance to exist without fear before you head to the Isles of Nekrós and just float about."

William looked up at Shade, his feet now hidden within the surf as the tide rose to his ankles. "Why do you get to fly and once we arrive the rest of us can't?"

There had been many similar questions throughout the tour. "Perks of being an immortal." He didn't mention that it was for ease of traveling from one of the Isles of Nekrós to the next. Not when he didn't plan to step foot onto the soil of the distant islands with their peaks and valleys barely visible in the distance.

"Also, if I've left the island for any reason, don't venture onto —" Shade turned towards the soul, surprised to find that he was no longer beside him.

William had stopped short, every limb of his body rigid. "Michael?" The soul ran past him towards a palm tree with a slumped figure against its trunk. "No, no!" William splashed as he rushed through the surf, desperation in his pleas. He broke free from the water and ran towards the forest edge.

Shade tilted his head, the thrum of heartbeats catching his attention.

Thump, thump. Thump, thump.

That was odd—nothing here was alive to emit such a sound.

William slid to the ground at the foot of a tree and that's when Shade saw him. William screamed, shaking the boy hunched against a palm trunk. The child didn't move at William's distress, his eyes closed. Shade's own shock at the sudden presence of the boy was enough to still him for a moment. How? *Thump. Thump...*

The last time he'd seen the boy, he had been curled up listening to one of Kora's stories before William had died. *How was he here now—alive?*

William's continued screams tore Shade from his shock. He was about to explain that, somehow, the boy was still alive when another heartbeat caught his attention. He whirled around. The sounds of life, familiar yet irreconcilable on Anamoní. There, just a few feet out in the surf, a figure lay prone on a lone flat rock jutting above the water. Tangled auburn hair covered her face. The hem of her dress was soaked from the waves that splashed around her. Shade knew who it was before he even reached her side.

His thoughts weren't enough to draw her here. There was no fathomable reason for her or the other living boy's appearance.

He swallowed as he bent over her body and brushed the hair from her face. Air caught in his throat. He stared at Kora, eyes widening. She didn't move, didn't stir as he wrapped his arms around her and pressed her against his chest. Still warm—alive.

In the distance, the white sails of the *Charon* floated towards the Isles of Nekrós. Captain couldn't bring the living to this realm. It didn't mean he didn't have tricks up his sleeve. But he didn't know about Kora. About the girl who saw him.

Shade flew back to William, whose wails magnified at the sight of his sister in Shade's arms. "No!" William buried his head in his hands.

"They're alive." Shade landed on the ground with her pressed close. "Both of them."

William wiped his face and looked up at Shade, his sniffling quieting. "What? But how are they here? Why?"

Captain, maybe. But even as Shade attempted to understand, he didn't have an answer. Taea knew he had visited their window once or twice, but she didn't know it was this girl. "I don't know for certain. But trust me, I'll find out." He nudged an elbow towards the sleeping boy and feigned ignorance. "Another relation of yours?"

"My younger brother. Will it kill them to be here?" William's eyes widened at the realization of his siblings' plight. "What does this mean?" He rushed to his feet and held out his hands for Kora.

His grip tightened around her. Then, with a deep breath, he released her into William's waiting arms. "What wouldn't be dangerous to you and the other souls will be for them. This is not a place for the living. We'll take them to my treehouse, so the others don't know about them just yet. Not until they wake and we can question them. I need to go meet with Captain."

"Will he know what to do?" William looked down at his brother, and Shade could see he was trying to ascertain how to carry their unconscious bodies.

Shade swallowed his desire to snap that Captain didn't know the answers to everything. Mouth thin, he shrugged. "Maybe." He turned and cupped his mouth. "Taea," he yelled loud enough for the pixie to hear. It wasn't often that she was far away. "Taea."

A few moments later, the sound of tinkling bells announced her arrival. "Do you know the meaning of this?" He pointed to the breathing mortals.

Taea gasped, her iridescent wings fluttering faster as she covered her mouth with a pale hand. Shade had seen her act—she wasn't very convincing—so her shaky hands told him she hadn't expected them either. "What is this?" She turned on Shade, her trail of dust and skin turning bright red. "Why are there living people here?"

"I don't know, but I don't want the others to find out yet." He didn't want more questions he wasn't prepared to answer. "We need some pixie dust to get them to my treehouse. Then I want you to stay with William and watch over them. Detour any of the others if they come snooping around."

Taea huffed but opened a pouch at her side. A rainbow of dust fell from her fingertips onto the boy. Once the pixie dust hit his skin, it shined before dimming and dissolving into his skin. After the last fragment disappeared, the boy began to rise. "You're lucky his dreams are happy," she said and added with a frown, "The others know better than to come to your treehouse unannounced. Where are you going?"

Shade lifted into the air and his gaze settled on the *Charon*. "To get answers."

Chapter 14
Kora

K ora blinked the sleep from her eyes. She sat up, stretching her arms wide, barely cognizant of the limited light coming through a small window.

Her eyes widened further and she almost fell from her bed. Not her bed, she realized with a gasp. She gripped the unfamiliar blue and green faded patchwork quilt lying atop her and glanced around. The textured walls were made of—bark? Wood. It was hard to tell in the dim light. Above her head, fabric hung from one side of the circular space to the other. She squinted her eyes at what looked like a hammock hanging above her head.

"Who are you?" A soft voice came from the dark.

Kora squeaked, searching the room for another person. "Who am I? Who are you? Where am I? Where are you?" Kora tried and failed to keep her voice from trembling.

"You're on Anamoní—the Isle of Waiting." The individual sounded close, yet no figure appeared within the room. "I'm Taea."

Kora swallowed and pulled the quilt up to her neck, uncertain of what to say or do. Anamoní? She hadn't died, had she? Her eyes began to adjust to the lighting, but she still couldn't find anyone standing amongst the sparse furnishings. "Where are you?" she repeated.

A flittering light illuminated brighter, zipping across the room to stop inches in front of her. "I asked you a question, and I still haven't gotten an answer. Who are you?"

A figure as large as Kora's palm with only an oak leaf wrapped around her body hovered in front of her. She looked human—short blond hair, a button nose, and small dark eyes—except for her size and the iridescent wings that flapped quickly from her back, catching the limited light.

Kora gasped, her eyes widening as she covered her mouth with a hand. "You're a—"

"A pixie. Yes." Taea pursed her lips and glared, reminding Kora that the pixie had asked a question.

And then the dream—no, not a dream—of Captain crashed over her. "My name is Kora." She swallowed as she tried to control her rising panic. "Is...is my brother here?"

"Kora?" The light around Taea tinged pink on the verge of red. "Your brother is William? He is. But why are you here? You're still alive."

"I...?" She didn't know how much she could say. There was something about the pink light that was off-putting. "I'm still trying to piece everything together." She gripped her head, steadying herself when the world felt like it was tilting. "Where's William and Michael—is he here?"

The pixie sighed. "Your siblings are outside."

Kora tossed the quilt off and rushed across the room, stubbing her toe on a footstool that sat atop a shaggy cloth meant to be a rug. She hissed in pain but kept moving until she reached the window. There were her brothers. William sat on a log beside Michael, who drew pictures in the dirt with a stick. She turned around, searching for a door. There had to be one. Her desire to rush to William was overshadowed by the fear of her reality and the guilt threatening to suffocate her. "How do I get to them?"

Taea's bright light fluttered next to her, drawing her attention away from them. "Can you help me? Can you help us get home?"

It was a long shot, especially since she wasn't certain who this little pixie was.

"Home? It's not that easy, otherwise you'd already be there." Taea seemed to consider Kora for a moment, her mouth pursed. "Are you here because of *him*?"

"Him?" She bit her bottom lip. "I'm here for my brother."

"But who sent you? Was it Captain? It couldn't have been Shade."

So, the pixie knew both Shade and Captain, then. Careful—she needed to watch how she went forward. Captain had warned her not to share his involvement. "I've heard there is a way to bring my brother back from Nekrós." She wouldn't mention how or who she'd heard it from. "I just need the King of the Dead to help me find it, then I can be on my way home."

Taea pursed her lips. "But how did you get here?"

Kora glanced around the room at the empty bed and lone table. "I...I don't know how. I just woke up here. I made a sacrifice?"

"To whom did you make this sacrifice?"

"To anyone who would listen."

The pixie tsked. "This will not please Shade."

Kora's brow scrunched. "I don't understand. Why won't he help me? Then I can be on my way." Keep it simple. Save William, get Michael, then return home as soon as possible. She just needed the fruit. Surely, Shade would help. Though he was the cause of her world's destruction, he couldn't be heartless. Otherwise, Captain wouldn't have brought her here.

Taea glanced out the window. "You will need to tell this to him once he returns." She regarded Kora again for a moment. "Poor girl. Stuck in the middle of a dispute among immortals."

This conversation was getting her nowhere, and she could hear the doubt in the pixie's voice and didn't appreciate it. "I don't want to be in the middle of anything. I just want to take my brothers home." She grabbed onto the back of a chair to keep upright, her legs wobbling as her current predicament settled over her. Not only was she bickering with a fairy, but she was talking about immortals. In limbo. While alive.

Taea sighed, the sound was as exasperated and annoyed as her expression. The pixie settled on the windowsill with crossed legs. "Shade and Captain are in a bit of a long-standing disagreement, and currently my friend is confronting his eldest brother about your appearance. Now, tell me more and let me see if I can help."

She considered her choices. If she told Taea more, maybe this would be easier. Would she even need Shade? Except...Captain had mentioned that the God of the Dead was the only one who could find what she needed. She frowned. But if this pixie was Shade's friend, maybe she would have sway over him. "Why would you want to help me?"

"It's not safe for mortals to be here. If I know why you're here and what you're searching for, I can look for it. The sooner you're home, the better. For your safety and your brothers'. Besides, Shade is my friend so he will involve me either way."

Was that true? Kora's head pulsed from countless nights of troubled sleep and the strain of her new predicament. "In one of my books," she began cautiously, "it mentioned a pomegranate tree in Nekrós. And the fruit from that tree could save those who hadn't crossed yet."

She kept Captain out of it. Taea might be offering to help, but Shade was the real problem.

The fairy thrummed her fingers against her arm. "I can help you get Shade's assistance." Taea smiled. "But you can't stay here." The pixie waved her hand towards the window and what waited beyond it. "Let me think. What do you know about this fruit?"

Kora opened her mouth, then closed it. "I don't know if I can trust you."

Taea chuckled, the sound like bells. "Smart girl. I might grow to like you." The look she gave Kora said that was the farthest thing from the truth. "If you change your mind, just let me know.

Shade will return soon. He won't leave you alone for long. In the meantime, are you ready to see your brothers?"

"Yes." Kora looked out the window again, watching her siblings huddling together. Death had separated her from her twin, and now only glass remained between them.

Kora followed Taea as she lit the way to the exit. She uttered a quick 'thanks' as she trotted across the room, tossed the door open, and stared at her twin. Michael stilled for a moment once he spotted her before jumping to his feet.

The sun heated her skin and stung her eyes before they adjusted to the light. Her gaze met William's and tears threatened. The first since that night in the temple. "Will?"

He ran across the little space between them and wrapped his arms around her. She gasped at the feeling of him. Whole. His scent was no longer the same. His skin cold. Guilt clawed up her lungs to her throat, his name a choked sound in a dry mouth. "William." Kora buried her head into his neck as he dragged her off her feet and twirled her in a circle. Tears dried and were replaced by laughter. She would save him. Find the fruit, force Shade to take his position, and then save her brother from this undeserved fate.

William set her down, holding her at arm's length. "Oh Kora, I have so much I want to say to you. So much to discuss and—" He shook his head and his smile faltered. "Why are you here? Don't get me wrong, I never thought I'd see you again until..."

She gripped both of his arms. "Never mind all of that now. What matters is that we're together. I've missed you." An apology caught in her throat. She'd prove how sorry she was once she got him home.

Kora released his arms and grabbed hold of his hand and squeezed it. "You're real. So far, we've only talked in my dreams. You even look alive." He looked the same, except more pale—his skin and hair having a faded pallor.

"Until I make the crossing, this is how I look. I guess...once you arrive here, you take on the form from when you were happiest." A sadness entered his tone. "How long has it been?"

Kora swallowed and kept her gaze downcast, unable to meet his eyes. "Almost two weeks."

He nudged her chin to meet his gaze, then squeezed her hand. Michael came up alongside them. "It has been longer for me. How are Mother and Father?" His eyes dazzled in the sunlight, but no tears came. A sad smile played at the corner of his lips.

She winced at the mention of their parents. "Not great, but they're trying. Like all of us." *But I'm going to fix this.* Kora wrapped her arms around him again, and her younger brother did the same. With the touch of his cool skin against hers, it only resolved her more. Even if Captain had an ulterior motive for bringing them here, Kora had her own.

When they finally let each other go, they walked back to the log and took a seat. She looked at the treehouse she'd just vacated. It was nothing like the lush forest that surrounded the clearing. The branches were bare, desolate. It looked like the remains of a twisted carcass that spread towards the sky.

William drew her attention from the treehouse. "I have to ask —do you know why you're here?"

She hated that she had to keep things from him, but for his life in return, she would. "I'm here to find a pomegranate tree that will save you. Allow you to come home." She looked at William for a moment and wondered if her brother would understand what she meant to do. "I left a sacrifice and prayed to see you again—and for your return. The immortals listened."

William's eyes widened. Michael jumped up and down in excitement. "Will's coming back. Yes!"

Kora grabbed her youngest sibling's hand, and he stilled. "We'll have to work together, and we need an immortal's help."

William looked at her quizzically, but she saw the hope in his gaze. "I don't think that's how it works, Kora. The gods have been gone for some time. And who is supposed to help you?"

She pushed her hair behind her ears. Or attempted to. She

would need a brush soon or it would become a nest in no time. "The God of the Dead. And this is a gift. A chance, William."

Taea cleared her voice, drawing all their attention upwards. Michael must have already met her, because he didn't seem surprised by the pixie. "I have a hard time believing you've not been sent here for other reasons."

Kora swallowed, but her gaze hardened. To put the world right again *was* the other reason. And the God of the Dead stood in her way.

"Why us, though?" William's brow furrowed, and he and Kora shared a look. "We're not special."

Michael scoffed. "Of course we are. I've been praying too."

William shook his head. Sometimes his pessimism was exhausting. Kora squeezed his hand. "I don't know but if we don't try, then we are already set up for failure. If anyone could find a way home, it's us."

"Kora," William sighed, running a hand through his hair. "It's dangerous for you both to stay here. This is a place for the dead, not for the living. Besides, what you are asking doesn't sound easy, otherwise anyone could do it."

Kora's voice heightened as she straightened. "It doesn't matter. I won't wait a week longer without you home. We have a chance, and we need to take it. This is it, Will, an answer to my prayers. You're supposed to come home, or we wouldn't be here. We just need Shade's help to find the fruit. Maybe that is why you haven't left the waiting place yet."

"I was going to." William's brow furrowed. "Soon."

Kora crossed her arms and tapped her toe, but fear outweighed her irritation. She could have been too late. "Then it's a good thing we arrived when we did."

William opened his mouth, then snapped it shut.

Kora was resolved. Had to be. Not just for her brother's life, but for so many others. "This is it. We can do this. Who's with me?"

Michael raised his arm, jumping in the air. "Me. I'm in."

William ran a hand over his face and groaned. "Fine. But it's not me you're going to have to convince in the end."

"Yes." Kora smiled. "We're going to find the fruit."

"Fruit?" A voice echoed.

Kora tensed and turned to stare at the young man before her. The same one who's shadow had whisked her brother's soul away. One that she thought she'd imagined loitering outside her window, listening to stories. She wanted to question why he kept her brother from crossing to the Isles of Nekrós, but after what she'd learned from Captain, that was a blessing she couldn't ignore. A mixture of hate and curiosity twisted in her chest as she bit her tongue and pinned a glare on him.

Shade looked her age, twenty maybe twenty-two, but she knew he was much older. He was as pale as her younger brother with light copper hair that hung over blue eyes as bright as the sky. His cream tunic was torn at the sleeves and hem. His calf-length pants were folded at the cuff. She thought she'd dreamed of him. Even after everything she'd experienced in the last few hours, she hadn't wrapped her mind around the fact that the shadow-turned-immortal existed.

A mischievous grin spread across his chiseled face with a dimple flashing in the left corner of his mouth. He had a slouched posture and unkempt hair—but was undeniably handsome, if she was interested in such things. As she analyzed Shade, his smile grew. There was no doubt in her mind who he was. Yet, she felt no fear, only awe. He wasn't just a collector of souls, but the God of the Dead himself.

Shade rested his hands on his hips as he landed in front of their group. "Hello, Kora. I've heard so much about you."

Chapter 15
Shade

S hade had been given all the proof he needed that his brother would be of no help by completely ignoring him upon his arrival.

He'd made a mess on the deck and nearly tore the sails to shreds to draw Captain's attention.

"You can stop with the temper tantrum."

Shade glared at his brother. "Why are there mortals on Anamoní, Cap? I know it was you and can only assume this is some ploy to force me back to the Isles of Nekrós."

Captain's attention drifted to the scattered tankards and the broken barrels littering the deck. "Really, boy. Such a mess you've created, and I can't understand a word you're saying." His mouth was a hard line, expression grim. "Explain."

"Two living mortals arrived."

Captain stiffened. "Living?"

Shade regarded his brother. It was impossible to tell when he was lying. Too many years practicing his political charms and two-faced charade. There was nothing to read. "Yes. Two very much alive mortals."

Captain rested his hands on the helm. "It seems you have some trouble on your hands. Who are they?"

Shade rolled his eyes. "The siblings of the most recent soul to arrive on the Isle of Waiting."

Captain's brow rose. "Oh, how interesting. How did that happen?" When that damn smile played at the corners of his mouth, Shade considered calling his power just to force that smug expression off his brother's face. Captain ignored him and moved around the helm. "Maybe there is a reason they're here."

It no longer mattered if he kept this secret or not. The last thing he expected would ever happen, happened. The mortal was there, alive. "She saw me. When I took her brother at his death."

"What?" Anger edged his brother's tone. "You let a mortal see you?"

"No." Shade glared. "You know I'm smarter than that."

Captain cocked his head, considering him. "If that's the case, aren't you curious why the girl could see you when you didn't allow her to?"

"You expect me to believe that you didn't know? That you have nothing to do with this?"

Gray clouds congregated above them, appearing from nowhere. Captain folded his hands behind his back as he settled himself at the top of the stairs. The sun was blocked out as his storm spread, and the newly acquired souls from the dock shrunk in fear. Shade's own power reached his fingertips, a darkness inked out around his body.

Captain glanced at the spread of Shade's power. "You're meant for this world, Shade. You can wield your ability and do some good for the mortals you pretend to care about. I know the truth—what you want." His eyes narrowed to slits as he glared at his younger brother. "It seems you have some work to do to find out why they are here. Those mortals' lives are in your hands. What are you going to do about it?"

Shade ground his teeth. Captain only thought he knew what Shade wanted. That was part of the problem—his brother never saw the full picture. "I'll find a way to get them back to the land of the living," he said before he shot off into the air.

"Only a pixie can return them home, and I've heard Astraea isn't here. Without her consent, you can't ask another pixie to take them to the mortal world. And you can't take them either." His brother's words followed him. There were limits to his power and he couldn't take any mortals out of Nekrós. "Think about it, Shade."

BEFORE HE HAD RETURNED to the treehouse, he went straight to Pixie Meadow to confirm Captain's claims. And unfortunately, the pixie was gone. As the Queen of the pixies, Astraea's permission was required for any pixie to leave the meadow for any other reasons beyond their job to change the seasons. After requesting that someone inform him upon her return, he took to the skies and flew back towards his treehouse.

Shade saw them before he heard them. The Darling siblings stood talking with Kora in the center, but her attention was directed on her twin. Taea had settled on a knoll of the log, watching as if they were a show for her own amusement. When she saw Shade, she took off and flew past him.

The pixie's trail of dust was tinged green. "Going to the meadow, will return soon," she shot over her shoulder. He considered questioning her. She had to know something. Was she working on Captain's orders? His brother was the most motivated for Shade's return.

But that trail of green was either jealousy or annoyance. Shade rolled his eyes, used to her mood swings, but he had enough to deal with. He thought she'd want an update on how things had gone with Captain. It wasn't out of the ordinary for her to defy his expectations though. He slowly circled overhead, watching the siblings below to see if any noticed him. Maybe if he made an impressive entrance, caught them off guard—frightened them?

"Yes." Kora's smile lengthened. "You won't regret this. We're going to find the fruit."

Shade's brow drew together. "Fruit?" He hovered closer, the opportunity for an entrance no longer at the forefront of his mind. Kora turned to face him, her eyes widening as he crossed his arms. He smiled at her, curiosity rising as his stomach coiled up tight, his attention drawn in by her inquisitive amber eyes. "Hello, Kora. I've heard so much about you."

She stepped back, off balance, and his arm flinched towards her, but he forced them to remain in place. William caught her and she steadied herself on his arm, releasing a long, slow breath. "You're Shade—the God of..."

Yet, there wasn't fear in her eyes. *Interesting*.

She trailed off, and Shade was thankful she didn't finish her train of thought. He cleared his throat. It was best to get right to the point. "I'm not certain how you got here, but I already have a plan to get you home."

William stepped forward. "Is there a way? Let's do it." He shot a look in his sister's direction.

Kora groaned. "No, not without you."

Shade stared for a moment, dumbfounded. "Him?"

Kora nodded. "Yes, him. William, my brother. There is a way to bring him back, and you know it. I prayed for a chance—"

Shade couldn't resist. A grin cracked, followed by a laugh. "Prayed?" he choked out. "No one prays to the God of the Dead. They curse me."

"It was a sacrifice. Are you calling me a liar?" The flash of indignation across her features. Her jaw tensed, fists forming at her side. The fire in her gaze was tinged with hatred. Directed at him. Nothing new there. Most didn't look at him with admiration.

But he wouldn't call her a liar. No one expected the God of Nekrós to listen. "What made you offer a sacrifice?"

"Hope. That even though you all seemed to have abandoned us, someone cared to listen."

He turned to Kora with a thoughtful expression. "I'll admit that I haven't heard prayers in decades."

Kora blinked. "Can the other gods?"

Shade shrugged. "One is more inclined to listen when everyone praises their name."

The girl glanced at her brothers, her twin silent while the youngest watched their exchange with rapt attention.

Shade landed on the ground, his brow furrowed. "What is this fruit?"

William pushed past his sister. The soul's shoulders taut, and Shade almost saw his face twist as he connected the dots. "Did you do this? You kept me and sent the other souls to the dock. Why?"

Shade tried to brush off the guilt that settled in the pit of his stomach. There was no denying that it was his fault, even if he didn't plan on Kora seeing him. But there was a reason beyond his own understanding why the young woman was here. He glanced in her direction. "I didn't do this." He waved at the soul's siblings in question. "I did have my reason for having you stay though—Kora saw me when I took your soul."

William groaned, covering his mouth.

A heavy pause spread through the group. "You didn't tell me." Michael was the first to remember words. "Kora?" he said with sadness in his voice.

Kora closed her eyes. "I'm sorry. I didn't know how to explain it. Besides, I thought I'd momentarily lost my mind." If she had ever seen him on his other visits, she gave no hint to it now.

Michael wrapped his arms tight around his sister and squeezed her waist. "We'd never think that."

William squinted an eye. "Well, maybe I would have...."

Shade cleared his throat, drawing the attention back to him. Where it should be. "It won't be easy to return them home, but I'll find a way. A pixie is usually required for such things, and the one I need permission from isn't currently on the island. But if—"

"No." Kora shook her head, and when William opened his mouth to speak, she shot him a glare. "Not until we find the fruit so I can take him home."

Shade's face scrunched up. He waited for them to laugh. To poke fun—whatever it was they planned to allude to the prank that must be in play. But no one said a thing. The first chuckle broke free, unbidden.

By Kora's pinched-up expression, she was not amused. "It's not funny!"

That only made him laugh harder. She stepped towards him, her arms crossed and squared up to him toe-to-toe. He met her gaze filled with fiery rage and he immediately stopped.

"It wasn't a joke." Kora didn't back away. "Tell me where the pomegranate tree is. The book I read told me the fruit can bring William home, and the only one who could find it is you." She jabbed a finger into his chest.

"It doesn't exist." Shade's expression darkened when he realized what fruit she was talking about. He hadn't seen the tree in nearly a century. "At least, not anymore." He frowned further when he realized her presence on the island was due to a flimsy story. A story she had oddly specific details on, considering it hadn't been seen in nearly a century.

William's sigh was filled with disappointment, and Shade realized the soul had been holding on to this with hope. Anger simmered to the surface. How dare she do this to her brother. He kept his attention on Kora. "Understand this now—there is no way for a soul to return from the dead. And you shouldn't be giving false hope that hurts others."

She glared. "What about that one I read about? The—"

Shade's bitter chuckle cut her off. "The Savior Myth. *He* was a demi-god. You're mortal. He also went into the depths of hell for an unselfish reason, so whatever you're thinking right now, it won't work. Things aren't the way they used to be."

"Why aren't you on the Isles of Nekrós?" Michael pointed a finger at Shade. "I thought you were supposed to be there."

Shade's jaw tensed. A prickle trailed along his spine where the Isles waited. Called to him. Even now. But his patience was waning with each of them. He looked at the one being who might listen to reason. "William, I'll find a way to return them home, so prepare your goodbyes." And he would—that wasn't an impossible feat.

Except agreement is not what he found in the soul's gaze. Instead, William peered at his siblings, sadness crossing over his features as he looked at Kora. "I can't. If there is a chance—"

Shade threw his arms up in the air. "Are you hearing yourself?" He rubbed a hand over his face. "This isn't a choice."

"What? Are you taking away our choices now? Need to collect more souls to keep on your island?" Kora countered, her eyes narrowing to slits.

Life. It flashed across her features. Vibrant. Powerful—like a sensation he'd never understand. A sense of hope. A need to fulfill as much as possible before an end. "That barb wasn't necessary."

"You know this isn't the first talk of the fruit? A pomegranate has been said to have magical properties over the living and dead."

Shade closed his eyes as he realized Taea had arrived. Her timing imperfect, as always. "Go away."

Taea landed on his shoulder, either oblivious to or unbothered by the anger in his tone. "Give them a chance."

"No."

"Why? Astraea isn't here. I just confirmed it, and you already did too. You might as well use the time to help them out." Taea leaned against his neck. "If anyone could find the pomegranate tree, it's you. You only *think* it doesn't exist anymore. It wasn't always a myth."

She was trying to appease his pride. This, he knew. But it was true that he couldn't send them home now, and he didn't doubt with the stubbornness visible in Kora's stance that she would look anyway. There had to be a way to make them see that this was a mistake, but in the meantime, he could entertain them. If anything, to uncover why she saw him, but also give him time to find a way to return the mortals home. Especially *her*.

"Here's the deal—we'll search for this nonexistent tree, but you have three days to find it. If we have found nothing at the end of those three days, you will both go home without a fight."

Kora shared a glance with William before all three siblings turned their back on him. If Shade hadn't lost all patience before, he had now. He crossed his arms, tapped his foot and glared at those who dared to shut him out. The three Darling children huddled together, arms wrapped over their neighbor as they began to whisper. The muscles in Shade's jaw tensed further.

After a few minutes—or very long seconds—they turned as one. "Ten days?" Kora offered.

"Hells no. Mortals aren't meant to be here. I have no idea how it will affect you. It's never been tested, so the shorter the better." Shade shook his head. "Four days."

"Nine. If you're just going to add a day, I'm only subtracting one," Kora shot back.

Shade tilted his head, taking in the ferocity in her gaze. He hated that it excited him. "Then we'll meet in the middle. Seven days. And before you attempt a counteroffer, you should know I will not agree to more. Seven days is a night for your world. Any longer and your family will be worried beyond belief."

"Deal." Kora held out her hand.

Shade stared at it a moment then side-eyed William. "Only if I make the deal with all three of you."

Kora's gaze thinned. William and Michael held out their palms. Shade shook each of them in turn before finally facing the strong-willed woman and took hers. Ignored the feel of her warm palm, slightly callused skin—and the flash of electricity that passed between them. Had she felt it too? "You have seven days. Stay near Camp unless you're with me or your brother. Most importantly, stay far away from the beach when I leave Anamoní."

Curiosity flashed in her eyes, but it was gone before Shade could decipher it. He tried to pull his hand away, but she tightened her grip. "Fine. But you must help us search," Kora added.

Shade almost choked on her audacity. "I'll help, but only

because this place isn't meant for mortals—it's dangerous." He stepped in closer, looking down at her. "You might think so, but this isn't a game." His grip tightened over hers.

Lesser mortals would have cowered, but Kora only glared. "My brother's life was never a game."

Shade wasn't going to fall easily for whatever she was playing at. Those amber eyes—the curly hair. Nope, he was stronger than that.

When William cleared his throat, Kora let go of his palm, but he was the first to break their staring match.

Her twin bit at a nail on his right hand. Of course, now he looked concerned—he'd already been told about the island's dangers. Did he only now comprehend what his siblings were in for?

Shade ran a hand through his hair. "It's getting too late to search today. We'll start tomorrow. Let's have you meet the Lost Souls and find a place for you to sleep."

"My siblings aren't sleeping at Camp with the Lost Souls," William snapped.

It was the smartest thing William had said all day. It wasn't that Shade didn't trust the others, but mortality was something many of them had lost a grasp of over time, which could put the siblings in more danger.

"Then, we can make a hut here." He was surprised when the words left his mouth. "But they need to stay with you when I'm gone. Understood?"

William nodded. Kora watched them carefully. "If we aren't starting today then the countdown begins tomorrow."

Shade couldn't understand why he had ever been curious about this hot-headed woman. Now, he wanted to send her back to the mortal realm as soon as possible. "If that's the case" —his smile widened— "I think it's time for a little fun."

William stiffened, but Shade didn't care. "Come on. Let's go to the Lost Souls Camp. Keep your reasons for being here to a minimum." He glanced at the youngest mortal. "Maybe stick with waiting for the pixie queen's permission to take you home. We don't want to cause chaos thinking they can all return home." Shade winked at Michael, and the mortal grinned back. A smile stretched at the corner of Shade's mouth, and he pushed off into the air. "Keep up, you don't want to fall behind."

Michael ran under him as Shade flew just a few feet over their heads.

"Michael!" Kora called.

A quick glance behind told Shade that everyone was following. He'd find a way to send them back soon, but for now he didn't need to concern himself with such things. There was no way they would find the pomegranate tree. Seven days would be over in the blink of an eye.

At least for him.

Chapter 16
Captain

Captain thrummed his fingers against his desk, staring at the pixie who sat poised on the edge of a book with one leg resting over the other. The lit lantern didn't let off as much light as she did. Captain hadn't been surprised when he'd found her waiting. Even if she didn't agree with his way of doing things, she'd want to be involved with Shade's return to the Isles of Nekrós. Anything to get the immortal away from the souls who distracted him. "It will work."

"Shade shall be unscathed at the end of this, Captain. If you can't promise me, then I'll go straight to him and tell him everything." She turned away, crossing her arms over her chest in a small huff and whispered, "Like I should anyway."

He knew she wouldn't. Not with the secret he held over her. "Don't threaten me. Shade has a duty to fulfill and an important one at that. I don't want to cause him harm so he's unable to do it."

Captain leaned back against his chair and steepled his fingers in front of him. He knew that the pixie hid something from Shade. Something that could be dangerous if not watched carefully. "You spoke to her—what do you think? Is she the one to draw him back to the Isles of Nekrós?" Even with his own certainty, Taea knew Shade best.

Taea laughed. "Kora seems like most other mortals I've come across. There is nothing special about her. You can use her concern for her brothers, but I don't think she'll have any power over Shade to force him to do anything you want. Shade has dealt with much more beautiful women." Taea flung her shoulder length hair behind her ear. "As far as I can see, you could have used Astari and gotten the same results."

"Ye of little faith." Captain's smile vanished. He knew little of the soul whom Taea mentioned but if she had been important, Captain would have already used her. "Sometimes the unexpected can surprise us all. Besides, I just need him to care enough to want to find the tree. To help her."

"How do you expect her to force him to do so? He must know what's required of him to find it."

Captain shrugged. "Not necessarily. How did he respond?"

"He said it didn't exist. That it was a myth."

So, he hadn't seen it either. Did it bother Shade not to have such power? "Don't worry, I have another plan in case I have to force his hand."

Her brows rose. "Would you sacrifice a mortal to get what you want?"

"There are always casualties in war." He drew back his shoulders. Hopefully it wouldn't come to that. "It's time this charade comes to an end."

"I think you're putting your faith in the wrong one. If not Astari, I could offer myself as bait." She peered at him with her mouth pursed. "I'm his best friend, after all."

Captain laughed, the sound a booming echo in the space. When his laughter subsided, he leaned forward. "Shade has no friends. He's selfish—cunning and wouldn't cross into the Isles of Nekrós for you because he knows you can get out. You choose to remain here. Besides, even I'm aware of his interests and curiosity of mortals."

"Then why do you think she will tempt him?" Her cheeks flamed red. As did the dust that sprinkled off her wings.

"Because," he began and chuckled mostly to himself, "he let her see him. There is a logical reason for it. So, let's see how this all plays out."

Taea rolled her eyes. "She better be gone at the end of this, or I'm going to make things more difficult for you."

"You'll help because you don't want me to tell him the truth about what you've done. He'd never forgive you. And you know that." His voice lowered to a dangerous level. "She'll be gone, and Shade will be in his rightful place. Just you wait. We have until Astraea's return. How long did they agree to?"

"Seven days." Taea pouted.

Captain titled his head. "You know Shade will be upset if he finds out you had a hand in this. Are you prepared?"

The pixie huffed and glanced out the window towards the Isles of Nekrós. "Don't worry, I can handle him."

Her gaze slid towards the islands in the distance. Captain turned to see what had drawn her attention.

Thick black smoke lifted from Mizéria, the Isle of Torment, but nothing was different about the view. A rumble shook the island. Its vibrations disturbed the placid water and rocked the boat. Captain's gaze thinned, his brow pinched in thought. When he turned towards the pixie, he snorted, realizing she had left. He'd need to watch her.

A knock sounded and he waved, the door sliding open. "What?"

"You asked for me to bring the box once she was gone." Smith cleared his throat, looking down at the floor between them.

"Leave it on the table and go. Don't disturb me." Captain waved away the soul, taking a seat in the high-backed chair beside the table. It had been too long since he had checked in on his subjects at Cloud Mount, Synnefo, and his absence would be noted. This was also the perfect opportunity to see if Halieus would deign to make an appearance.

Once the door clicked shut behind Smith, Captain picked up

the box and placed it in his lap before he removed the key from around his neck.

The lock clicked and the latch sprung open, revealing a gold rimmed monocle set in velvet. He picked it up, light refracting off the lens, revealing the mount he called home.

Captain closed his eyes as he settled the piece over the left one. When he opened them again, he was back within the landscape of Synnefo. A large temple of marble, trimmed in gold with ivy vines wrapped around the marble pillars surrounded him. He sat on his embossed gold and silver throne etched with ornate lightning bolts. A piece and fitting of his station. A few gasps, a couple applauses, and Captain's smile grew as silence spread through the room, and a modest group of immortals turned their attention towards him. Reverence and excitement visible on their faces.

A familiar chuckle, and Captain turned his head to find his brother striding up the steps. "Welcome, Theileus. It's been too long." Halieus's muscular body was on display for all to see. Not surprising since he took great joy in receiving attention. His shimmering green mermaid tail was gone, replaced with legs partially covered by a cream wrap that tied at his tan hip.

"King. Or Your Majesty." Captain pinned a glare on his sibling. "No matter how long it has been, I'm always your king." He should demand the same respect from Shade, but they each had their mind games. With Halieus, time had just made them wary. Neither trusted the other, and prior to his call for the immortals return to Synnefo, the two of them had kept their distance. Halieus remained in the water, Captain here. And Shade in Nekrós where he belonged. A realm for each. Responsibilities that they carried out on their own. There had been no need for any of them to interfere with each other.

Until now.

"Of course." Halieus grinned as he fell into a partial bow while the others lowered further.

Halieus was lazy and without an ounce of ambition. It didn't mean that he didn't enjoy pestering his eldest brother at every available opportunity. Not in the same way as Shade. No, his middle brother did it with an air of boredom. Halieus was one of the main reasons Captain recalled the immortals to Synnefo.

"Report." With this word, everyone straightened.

Herald stepped forward, carrying an ivory scroll wrapped with a strand of silver ribbon. "There isn't much to report, Your Majesty. The immortals have continued to follow your orders to remain within Synnefo unless it is to fulfill tasks you've allowed. After the incident with Sera and the war with the nymphs, your warning has been a constant reminder."

Everyone's gazes shifted to where the Goddess of War was shackled to a giant sculpture of Captain in the center of the veranda. She rolled her eyes at the sudden attention, rubbing at her wrists. "I got the point. No longer need to be chained here, Father."

Captain grinned. "But you're still fulfilling a purpose. Besides, what kind of father would I be if I let you go before your time? I said you were punished until I was able to return permanently. Either find a way to make Shade take his position or be the example you're meant to be." His tone and expression were sharp.

Sera groaned as she leaned back against the stone version of Captain's feet, folding her arms over her chest with a huff.

He turned his attention back to Herald. "And how is the mortal world?"

Herald cowered. As the messenger to the gods, Captain allowed him to visit the land of the living to check on their status. By the immortal's grimace, Captain wasn't going to like what he was about to hear.

"The mortals are suffering. Even with the shifting of the seasons and phases of the moon, things are not growing the way they should. It is causing distrust among the people. Some are being selfish, unwilling to share what they have, while others are starving and going without. It doesn't help that herbs and plants used for medicine are no longer available, so the sick are dying. Slowly." He swallowed. "And when I mean slowly..." He shook his head. "Many seem like the undead, My King. It's as if they are decomposing while still alive. Festering sores, illness, rotting skin —it's enough for many to believe we've abandoned them completely. By the time some die, their bodies are nothing more than skin and bone."

Even with the gossip he'd overheard from souls as they crossed, Captain hadn't imagined it would be that bad. His jaw tensed as he looked over the crowd of immortals—a few huddled together to discuss the information they'd just overheard. "Is there anything else?"

Herald shook his head.

Captain thrummed his fingers against the arm of his throne. "This is what Shade's negligence has caused. The Dikastés have given me some guidance, and I have our possible last hope playing out right now. But I need assistance to make the goal come to fruition."

He turned towards his brother. Halieus' shoulders drew back, head cocking under Captain's scrutiny. "What is it you need?"

"You're to come to the Isles. I expect you no later than tomorrow. We will discuss it further then." The others had grown quiet while Captain spoke, and they seemed to lean forward at his words. He turned back to them, a few stumbling a step at his attention. "Come up with an alternative plan. Or I'll have no choice but to drag every single one of Shade's Lost Souls into the Depth and call you in to force him into the bowels of Mizéria." He gave a pointed glare to the room. "Then one of you will have to take his place."

The shock written on the immortals' faces was nothing compared to the cacophony of murmurs. Captain raised a hand to silence them. "Since you've had time to consider this dilemma and have the desire to return to the mortal world, then I assume you'll have something for me soon." That threat would keep them busy and motivated.

"Yes, King." Most spoke the words simultaneously in agreement, many nodding their heads.

"Good." Captain leaned into the chair and glanced towards a goddess with long black hair in thin braids, and eyes of nutmeg rimmed with gold who sat at the bottom step of the dais. He inhaled a deep breath, wishing more than ever that his body was actually there. It had been too long since he'd touched another. Grinding his teeth, he stood and everyone who wasn't already on their feet did the same. They bowed, the goddess peering up at him while she did. Captain bit the inside of his mouth. "I'll be back soon."

He removed the monocle from its place. He'd forgotten to close his eyes though. His attention held on the golden goddess with her gaze snaring him until the brightness of Synnefo dimmed, and a sharp ache jarred his skull when she was gone. His dark quarters, the empty bed, and the rock of the boat were a sharp contrast to the bright mountain and the gorgeous immortal he'd left behind.

His fingers grazed along the edge of the glass, the gold cool to his touch. It was tempting to throw it in his anger, but then he'd not even get a taste of home, and without it he'd have gone insane long ago. This plan had to work.

The mortals needed them to return.

And he needed out of there.

Chapter 17
Kora

Whatever Kora was expected to do to ensure she and her brothers return home was going to be impossible with this infuriating immortal. Loathing was possibly too strong a word, but at the same time it felt right. She raced after her siblings through the forest so as not to lose sight of them. Large trunks, thick canopies overhead, and wildflowers sprinkled along the path. She wanted to slow down, take it all in and mentally cursed her brothers as well as that obnoxious immortal for racing ahead.

Even so, she noted the yellow daisies. Marveled at the thick ivy that curled around tree trunks of great oaks and cypress. Clumps of purple aster that grew beside white anemone. Plants she'd only seen in her books and only dreamed of breathing in their fragrant scents or imagined growing in her garden.

William kept only a few steps ahead and with the continuous looks he shot over his shoulder, she could see he was going to be protective. She wanted to yell at him not to rush her. Couldn't he see that it was gorgeous here? It had been two weeks without him, and she hadn't been in her garden since before—

Kora shook her head. She couldn't let herself think of then.

This was now. It was just as dangerous in the living world as it was here.

Shade howled as he ran, Michael echoing the call. This was an immortal? Why the gods wanted him to rule the Isles of Nekrós was beyond her.

At least she had finally made him see reason. It would be helpful to have allies if she could find one among these Lost Souls, as Shade had called them. Seven days may not be long enough, but she would take advantage of every moment she had. She searched around her for any fruit that may have fallen on the path. The ground didn't have the usual resemblance of a forest floor. No leaves or dry nettles clung to the dirt. Everything was bright. Cheerful. Unlike Shade's cypress tree they had left behind. Even so, she scanned the trees they passed for the bright red fruit.

She jogged through the forest, passing under the large canopy that blocked the lowering sun from view. Green leaves as large as her torso seemed to reach for her legs as she passed them. Suddenly, the forest broke away, revealing a clearing where the dimming sunlight blinded her for a moment. She covered her eyes as they adjusted. William gripped her hand and gently led her forward with ease. Then after a few blinks, she glanced about as a group of people—or souls, to be exact—sauntered out of their respectable lean-tos and others appeared from the forest's edge. They left squat houses and hammocks that dotted the perimeter of the clearing as they circled around Shade, their gazes glued to Kora and her brothers.

"Who is she?" A woman with straight sandy blond hair that touched her hips pointed at Kora. In contrast to the others, her hair was clear of knots, her skin clean, and she wore a cream wrap around her torso that clung tight to her feminine frame. Her brown eyes shot daggers of ice in Kora's direction.

Shade waved with a flourish at her and Michael. "It seems William's siblings have been sequestered here. Meet Kora and Michael." He rested his hands on his hips in that conceited way Kora was beginning to hate. Shade cleared his throat. "They are alive, and we must ensure they remain that way so they can return to the land of the living as soon as possible."

A girl with neat, curly black hair stepped forward in a cream shirt that contrasted her dark skin and reached her knees. "It's nice to meet you." She held out her hand.

Kora took it, giving it a shake and returning the girl's kind smile. "Likewise. And your name?"

Shade interrupted any chance of her answer. "That's Curly, this is Branch." Shade pointed at a short boy who was all torso with long arms and a childish smile. "And Astari." He waved to the girl with sandy-colored hair who continued to glare at Kora as though she was a grotesque creature. "And..." He continued rattling off names of the other twelve souls present too quickly for her to grasp. "Long just left us for the Isles of Nekrós while you were unconscious."

"Nudist," William whispered in Kora's ear, and she blushed.

"Where are they staying?" Astari had crossed her arms over her front, a pout forming on thick lips. "She can stay in my hut, and I can stay somewhere else." She turned her gaze to Shade, her expression completely changing into a small shy smile.

Kora resisted the desire to gag.

"They're all staying near my tree. Don't worry your pretty head about it, Astari." He turned away, and Kora was certain the only reason she paused before resuming her death glare was because he'd called her pretty.

Curly glanced back and forth then sidled in closer to Kora. "We'll watch over them, Shade. But what are the living doing here in the first place?"

Shade seemed to consider her question, a tick in his jaw the only evidence he didn't know how to respond or that he didn't want to. "Time will tell. No, your families can't come visit. This is..." He paused in consideration. "Not normal. But let's show them the fun of the isle while they're here."

A few mumbled under their breaths, whispering their disappointment. A spark of envy was visible in tones, and a few gazes of longing sadness. Kora stared at her feet, gripping Michael's hand and pulling him close to her.

Shade threw his arms into the air. "Let's have a bonfire tomorrow night and give them a proper welcome."

Whoops and hollers echoed the clearing, the sounds turning into a chant of Shade's name. His chest puffed up. With a smile, he clapped, and they all stopped with their rapt attention settled on him. "Prepare. I'm going to take our guests on a tour of the island."

The souls quickly separated. To do what, Kora didn't know. Michael started to follow Branch, but William held him back.

"I want to go." Michael pulled on his brother's grip. "I don't want to go on a tour of the island. Not now. I wanna play with the others."

William cleared his throat. "You should learn the dangers first."

Shade leapt up, levitating above the ground. Kora tracked the movement, her heart leaping. As much as it annoyed her that he placed himself higher than them, the idea of flying was intriguing. She turned to her youngest brother. "We need to stay together, Michael. You'll have your chance later, but let's explore where we are first."

"You say explore but all I hear is tour. Why don't I stay with them? They'll watch me." Michael tilted his head towards the others.

Branch stood at the edge of the clearing as the twins eyed each other.

"I don't care either way." Shade waited expectantly.

William darted a glance between his brother and Kora, then a last look at Shade. "I've had the tour. Why don't you go, and I'll stay?"

Shade didn't wait for an answer. He scooped Kora up unceremoniously and rose a few feet higher into the air. "Be back."

"Put me down!" She pushed against his chest, squirming in his arms.

William stomped his feet below. "Let her down now."

But the immortal just froze mid-flight. "I could drop you if you'd prefer. Might hurt—or kill ya. Or you could stop fidgeting and hold on."

She froze in his cradled arms, not wanting to call his bluff. With a glare, she wrapped her arms around his neck and pressed tighter against him. She tried to ignore the hard planes of his chest and the defined arms that were wrapped around her back and curled under her knees. "A gentleman should ask permission before he touches a woman."

"I'm not a gentleman." He grinned. "Immortals haven't asked permission for generations."

A flush coursed up her neck into her cheeks. "I don't care who you are. If you ever do that again without asking first, I'll make your time in the Isles of Nekrós seem like a holiday."

He tilted his head, his gaze darting over her expression. "I'm curious what you could do to an immortal..." His sky-blue eyes seemed to dance as he chuckled.

She bit her bottom lip. Truth was, she didn't know, but she'd take that knowledge to the grave. "Test me and find out," she snapped back.

"I'll remember that." His chuckle turned to a boisterous laugh as they rose into the sky.

Anamoní was vast. And breathtaking. Flying was another type of wonder that she'd never thought she'd ever experience. The air that slid across her skin. The view of the sky that never seemed to end and the lush land of the isle below. The feel of Shade's breath against her ear as he effortlessly carried her over the island. Not that she allowed herself to linger on *those* particular thoughts for long. Her grip on him had loosened slightly as they traveled, but his hold never faltered.

Without flying, the tour would have taken them an entire day or longer. To find the pomegranate tree seemed impossible in an eternity, let alone seven days. None of the trees they passed held signs of the red fruit. Many were unfamiliar to her, and she wished for a notebook to draw the white-barked tree trunks. Or the vibrant yellow flowers with black centers. More than once, she asked him to take a closer look, only to find that it wasn't the right tree or fruit. If she had known, she would have researched how the leaves and bark of a pomegranate tree looked. Learned more about the tree.

Shade landed at the top of a bluff overlooking the island from every direction and put her down. It wasn't the highest point, but it did offer a decent view. Already, he'd taken her over the white sandy beaches, along the jagged coastline where he pointed out Skull Isle—the jut of rock that was just off the coast of the main beach and from her viewpoint looked like a dome of smooth, gray rock.

Shade lingered over the small island. "The path sometimes connects to the isle depending on the tide. Don't travel there alone." He flew them over the lagoons where her eyes had widened at the water nymphs.

"The nereids aren't kind and will drown you if you get too close," Shade warned. "We've lost souls to their depths for weeks before they decided to throw them back on land. For mortals, it would be a death sentence. It's a game to them."

She could see a glimpse of the lagoon now, from her perch. "Why are they here when this is the place for the dead?"

Shade followed her gaze. "Have you ever met a nereid in the mortal world?"

Kora shook her head. "Of course not. There is nothing of the immortals left in the living world." *Thanks to you.* He might be kind now in giving her a tour, and patient by slowing when she requested, but she wouldn't be fooled. Her world was suffering because of him.

Shade's jaw tensed and gaze hardened as he looked away. He must know what he was forcing upon those in the living world with his selfishness. He had been there, retrieving her brother's soul. The dead. It was impossible to ignore the hardship and suffering and yet the immortal did. It sickened and disappointed her.

He settled his hands on his hips. "The nereids weren't always this way. They would guide sailors through rough seas. Then mortals began to hunt them. Force them to either guide them to treasure or hurt them through depraved forms of torture." Shade glanced at her out of the corner of his eye. "They asked me for protection, and I offered them the lagoon as a place to rest. The souls have been warned not to visit their waters, and I withhold the xéchase from entering. The nereids can return to the mortal world if they request it."

"You give them a choice but not the souls you retrieve?" Kora grumbled.

Shade laughed, the sound harsher than she expected. His gaze darkened as he faced her. "Who told you this?"

She shrugged, crossing her arms over her chest. "Did you give my brother a choice?"

He tilted his head. "No. If he asked me after a few days to cross, I wouldn't have denied him the option. I never stop them from crossing if I know they have had enough time to decide on their own." His brow rose, as did a corner of his mouth. "Are you really upset when you had a chance to see your brother again?"

Kora turned away, unable to answer him. Her impending move, and her parents' plan for her engagement filled her mind, but she tried to keep her expression blank. "I can understand that—allowing someone time to accept their fate." The idea of leaving Greece...she realized terrified her more than angered her. Her parents' plans *for her* were what truly had her frustrated. Another thing that would be fixed if she could just find this cursed fruit tree.

But he had mentioned something else. "What are the xéchase?"

Shade looked away, his expression darkening, and she swore

the island stilled. "The forgotten. Those who don't have payment to cross the Depth."

Kora swallowed, noting the sharpness of his tone. It was time to change the subject. She turned back to the view. "What's that over there?" Another bluff in the distance was covered in dancing grass and tall colorful mushrooms. Quite the opposite of the flat and rocky surface they stood on.

"That's Pixie Meadow. Maybe at some point I'll take you closer." Shade folded his hands behind his back.

For a moment, he didn't look like the playful immortal who'd scooped her off the ground, but she forced the thought from her mind. "You'll have to take me there to search for the tree."

Shade laughed again, and this time she could hear the mocking in his tone.

She resisted stomping her foot, her mother's voice in her head reminding her that *ladies hold their temper*. "You promised."

"I did, yes. But not even the souls are allowed in the meadow. I'm the only one who has permission, and I doubt they will grant it to you." He rose a brow. "And it depends on how well you take my warnings before I will ask them."

Kora's face heated. This may be more challenging than she expected. "You gave your word. If you don't help, I will do it without you even if it means going to Taea and begging for her assistance."

"Ah, Taea." Shade tilted his head in her direction. "You know, she's already caused trouble and trust me, she will only cause you more."

Kora bit the inside of her lip. "I won't give up easily."

Shade smiled, a dimple appearing on his left cheek as he rested his hands on his hips. *Hells*, he was conceited. That pretentious stance and the way the breeze ruffled his hair as if on cue. She was going to lose her mind working alongside him.

He glanced over the island. "I might not be all-knowing, but Anamoní is my home. I think I'd know if there was a way to return to the mortal world."

"That's beside the point." Kora needed to detour this conversation. He wasn't going to change her mind. "You said you would help me. If you don't keep up your side of the bargain, then I will stay longer."

Shade groaned. "I will. Begrudgingly. I'm not brushing you off. You need to understand that the tree hasn't been seen in a long time. It likely no longer exists." He crouched down in front of her before she could retort. "Now hop on, it's time to head back."

She crossed her arms. "That wasn't a request—more of an order."

Shade peered over his shoulder. "Well, you can either jump on or walk back. It should only take you until morning. I don't get tired, but you do." He stretched his arms in the air, and a blush filled her cheeks at the flash of his stomach while he feigned a yawn. "You'll need all the energy you can muster for tomorrow's search."

Kora's attention wandered and when she realized she was ogling him, she forced her gaze away from his defined arms flexing from beneath the tears of his sleeves. She groaned and took a step forward. This was more awkward than her mother's matchmaking dinners. She hopped on his back, wrapping her arms around his shoulders and clasped her hands around his neck.

"Hang on." Without any further warning, he jumped into the air, forcing her to tighten her grip as he wrapped his arms around her knees to hold her close.

"You're a fiend, have I mentioned that?"

Shade laughed. "I have a feeling you'll come up with more colorful words to describe me before these seven days are done."

With his arms around her, the feel of his back against her chest, she tried to concentrate on anything else. She'd never even danced this close to a boy, let alone had one carry her upon his back. Even the one kiss of her childhood had been rushed, no other touch but their lips. It had been the neighbor boy who was one year older than her. He'd bragged of being more experienced, and she'd dared him to prove it. As soon as their lips met, he had gasped, then turned and ran. The memory faded away as the sun hit the horizon, the light casting over the island.

The view was unlike anything she'd ever seen. Spectacular. And so green. Nooks and crannies of the island were in shadow, others still bright as though grasping hold of the last of the sun's rays.

Inlets of blues and greens curled in along the edges of the island, wedging within the grooves of lush grass and black shale. Snow melted into cascading waterfalls from the highest peaks that fed rivers zigzagging towards azure pools that led to the Depth. As they continued around the outskirts of bluffs with meadows of tall emerald grass shimmered in a light breeze surrounding them with floral and spring scents. Rainbows of color, prisms brought to life by the light and waves, curled and twisted around the island as the sun shifted and settled on the horizon. Large mushrooms in reds, purples and blues poked out between rocks. The Depth glittered in the distance, white waves crashing upon rocks like rolling suds against the side of a tub. A ship sat anchored in the distance. "What's that?"

"The *Charon*. The ship that ferries the dead to Krisí—the Isle of Judgment." He nodded to a dock that expanded out onto the Depth from the beach below. "That's where they are picked up from. Most of the other soul deliveries go straight there. I get the special cases. It's sad they don't all have the option to remain here, but then Anamoní would be bursting at the seams."

"You make it sound like a collection of stones or coins instead of souls—they used to be people you know? Alive, breathing. With families. Or does an immortal not care of such things?"

Silence expanded around them as though he controlled sound itself. No longer a rustle of leaves from the breeze or the wave of grass. The island stilled. Kora tried to see his expression but couldn't from her position.

"I do know," he finally whispered.

She was quiet for a moment, her mouth pursed as she considered. "Why did you decide to have William stay?"

His muscles grew taut underneath her hold. "I don't have an answer. At least not one that would make sense."

"Try?" She leaned in closer to him to hear his response above the breeze. "I'm glad he didn't go because there wouldn't be a chance to save him, but I'm curious as to why."

Shade sighed but didn't relax beneath her hold. "There was something about him that told me he was meant to stay."

She had a feeling there was more to it than that. She would find out.

Chapter 18
Shade

Mortal women were stubborn and difficult. What did Kora expect from him? For centuries, Shade hadn't lived or been in the mortal world for longer than a few hours. She had the audacity to call him a collector of souls. To assume he didn't understand they were mortals who previously had lives...

The two of them had flown in silence for the remainder of the tour except for moments when Shade had pointed out other dangers within the Isle of Waiting. Similar to those that he'd made clear to William—except for her it was the difference between life and death.

After they scanned the beach for signs of the souls, Shade headed towards his treehouse. William had been standing outside watching and waiting for them with thin eyes while his brother built a small hut beside the withered cypress. Concern flitted across William's expression as Shade landed. Before anyone could ask questions, he released his hold of her, and she quickly stepped back as he pushed off into the air to get away. From her. From the thoughts she raised, and the accusations she flung his way.

One question kept playing on repeat in his mind. *Does an immortal not care?* There was a time when one would never have questioned the gods. Either you served one and lived in reverence to them or you quickly regretted it. Few had ever looked towards the God of the Dead, though. Always believing he was something to fear and nothing more. When most did all they could to avoid Nekrós, one would think they would be more inclined to pay homage. But that wasn't the case.

Shade tried to clear his mind by flying over Anamoní. The beginnings of the bonfire collection came into view. The Lost Souls had already piled up a large number of logs and driftwood. There was plenty still to do—more fun to be had with the Lost Souls. No need to contemplate what the living world thought of him or the immortals. Even though Kora had said things that had hurt and angered him, he wanted to prove he was better than that. Better than the others. And it wasn't just because *she* was the one to make him question himself. Or was it? He'd listened to the stories at her window. About the gods. Her words had been filled with so much hope.

Shade did one last loop over the treehouse as the sun dipped further from view. William had set himself up against the front door—a hint that Shade wasn't welcome. The Darling mortals must be sleeping inside, making his refuge the last place he wanted to be. That would have to change. Now, he didn't want to poke the minotaur since Kora would undoubtedly want to begin the search as soon as possible. Shade stayed out all night, allowing the plans for the bonfire to draw him away from his thoughts.

A little before dawn, he landed in the clearing and frowned. Flowers had sprouted from the base of the tree beside William— blue lupines, similar to the color of Kora's dress. Never had he seen anything flourish close to the dead cypress, but he brushed off the thought as William pinned him with a glare.

Shade raised his hands as a sign of peace. "No need to wake them yet. I wanted to let you know that I'm going to check on the plans for tonight's festivities. Have Kora wait here, and I'll come back before we begin the search."

"Kora has one weakness—patience. So don't take long," William warned.

A snappy comeback was on the tip of Shade's tongue. One that would put the soul in his place. He swallowed it, analyzing William instead. The steady gaze, no question in his eyes or fear that he spoke such a way to an immortal. The other souls had never been so forward, but something about the way William carried himself reminded him of others long past. Bloodlines he hadn't seen in a long time.

He scoffed. "Don't worry so much. I know the deal I made."

❧

"GRAB a few smaller logs to keep the fire going," Shade called out to Branch. The soul hurried off to fulfill his request while Shade looked over the burning pyre. It was twice his height and four times his width.

"Here you are."

The eerily calm tone had him reeling around to find Kora with her arms crossed, her hair in a messy pouf on her head. A few loose curls added to the image of her frustration, along with a scowl across her beautiful face. Not beautiful—he couldn't think like that. Human—pretty face. *Damn him to hells*. Nope don't want to do that.

"Here I am." He tried to force back a smile even if her rigid anger only entertained him. "I told your brother I would come back soon. Did you not get my message?" It didn't work. His smile seemed to have a mind of its own which only made her flush red.

Warm amber eyes glistened with rage in the bright day. The same ones that had entranced him for a moment that fateful night. What was it about this girl that drew him? That she had somehow seen him then? Curiosity rose with each furious tirade she had when he should be more annoyed. Shade reminded himself of why she was here. Someone's version of a Trojan horse. Dangerous. Kora wasn't going to throw herself at him. She wasn't that kind of girl. He already could tell that. But it would be stupid to ignore why she was on the Isle of Waiting.

"The sun has been up for hours and so have I." She stopped a few steps from him and glared.

Over her shoulder, he spotted William and Michael waiting at the edge of the tree line. Her twin watched with his arms crossed over his chest. Michael, stick in hand, was bent over picking up a few more to add to his pile. If her brothers wanted to witness his and Kora's disagreement that was fine by Shade. A phantom sensation slid along his back, similar to the press of her body against his. *Trouble*.

"I had to oversee a few things here." Shade pointed to the heightened logs before him as if that was reason enough for his absence.

By her heightened agitation—her foot tapping—it wasn't.

"All right then, let's get started. Figured we'll begin along the beach." He pointed in the opposite direction of the nereids' lagoon and Skull Isle. "There are some reefs in that direction we can search, and there's a chance we might find something near the dock."

"Pomegranates grow on trees." She pursed her lips.

His jaw twitched. "I haven't seen the tree here—ever. We aren't in the mortal world. It could grow on a beach. Maybe underwater. Perhaps the fruit will be bobbing in the water by the shore. Do you know for certain?"

By the annoyed look on her face, she didn't have an answer for him.

Shade started walking without waiting for her, although she quickly caught up. He peered at her from the corner of his eye. "Do you have *any* idea where it could be?"

When Kora remained silent, he faced her to find her brow furrowed and her bottom lip between her teeth. He sighed. "You don't know, do you?"

"No. The author of the book didn't give specifics regarding the location of the tree. It's not like he lives here on the island like someone else I know. But you're delusional if you think it will be growing underwater or along the beach. The forest makes a lot more sense to search."

"You said that I'm meant to help you find it, then that means we're starting here."

Kora's shoulders slumped. "But the forest—"

"Is an obvious place traversed by many," he interrupted. "But, again, I haven't seen a pomegranate there. So, unless you have an exact location to start, then we are checking along the coast first."

A flush brightened her cheeks. "Fine. But only until midday. Then I choose where we search next."

He shrugged, then glanced at the cotton blue dress she wore. "You may want to change first."

"Do you think I'll be cold?" She gestured at the perfect weather—the same as the day before. It didn't change here. Not unless Captain threw a temper tantrum.

Shade ran a hand through his hair. Would she debate everything he said? "I just meant it might be easier to get around in a pair of pants."

She lifted her chin. "I'll be fine. Dresses haven't slowed me down before."

Shade could hear the defiance in her tone. "Don't say I didn't warn you."

They walked past the pyres and reached the reef in a content silence that neither felt the need to fill. The water that usually splashed against boulders had withdrawn into the Depth, revealing speckled rocks covered in holes.

Kora didn't wait but began her search with Shade watching her movements. The edges of her dress were already snagging on jagged stone and soaked from puddles. If it bothered her, she didn't show it as she moved from one spot to the next with ease.

Shade cleared his throat. "Are your brothers joining us today?"

She tossed aside stones. "I think William wanted to give me a moment to yell at you first without Michael overhearing." She squatted down, splashing water within the crevice. "No animals are here?"

He started poking about with a long stick he found washed up on the shore, using it to see if anything red stuck out. "No need to come to limbo. They head straight to the Eiríni—the Isle of Contentment."

She picked up a red sphere, analyzed it, but before he could tell her it was a berry, she tossed it behind her. "I miss the sounds. At home, I hadn't realized how much I enjoyed the chattering of birds or the bark of the neighbor's dogs. Sounds beyond humans —life. Even the wind barely rustles the trees." She shook her head. "It must be hard for them to get used to not having the noises of the lives they left behind."

Shade picked up a smooth red stone and turned it over in his palm before dropping it in a puddle. "You'd have to ask your brother. Most of them don't talk much about their lives before death. A few might talk about people—but emotions aren't felt as strongly here. At least, not after the passage of time. They don't *miss* things."

"What about you?" She peered over her shoulder, regarding him for a mere second before continuing her search. "Do you miss things?"

Shade considered the question—probably longer than he should have. What was he meant to miss? His father was a vile immortal giant who had only wanted power. When Shade and his brothers had been born, his father had always pictured them as his warriors for a cause. The one that kept him in power. That had changed. Then there were the others who had left him during his long existence—

While he'd been stuck in the Isles of Nekrós, he'd lost so much. But that wasn't a burden he had to carry anymore. Not that he was exactly free either. He couldn't leave the realm for longer than a night, but the momentary visits to the mortal world at least satiated his desire to witness life. He wouldn't admit that to her, though. "No."

The next stretch of silence yawned like the distance between them. A breath of relief slipped from between his lips. Her line of questioning was a tad more personal than he was comfortable with.

"So, how did you do it?"

Damn her. Another infernal question and he hadn't a clue what it was in reference too. "Do what?" His tone was without its usual playfulness. Time was running short and so was his patience. She was *dangerous*—and he was growing bored. He poked the stick into a few other crevices, trying to find something useful. This was a waste of time. But what else was he meant to do with her?

If she noted the change in his mood, she ignored it. "Leave the Isles of Nekrós?"

He froze. The stick stuck in between a crevice of stone. Captain had only asked him that question once. Probably because his oldest brother knew he wouldn't answer.

One corner of his mouth rose. "When you desire something enough, you find a way." He stepped further down the reef to get away from her inquisitiveness. But also to stop himself from saying something he shouldn't.

Her brothers joined them a few minutes later, and Shade saw it as a reprieve from *her*. That is until Michael began whining more than helping. Shade stopped and picked up a red rock that looked similar to a fruit. "Let's make a game of it, shall we?"

Kora groaned, casting him an annoyed glance before picking up another rock. "I doubt a game will help."

Michael clapped his hands, jumping up and down, his blond hair bouncing in his excitement. "What kind of game?"

Shade took the stick he'd been using to dislodge the stones and made a circle in the sand. "If you find anything red, place it here. Let's see how large of a tower we can create from them."

Michael immediately started to search, tossing aside rocks that didn't fit the description. William found a particularly large red stone and placed it in the center of the circle. "I found the biggest."

The youngest sibling gasped and started to find larger rocks. William chuckled, soon handing off his finds to his brother so they could make their teetering tower. Kora called over their excitement. "We're searching for a pomegranate. Just because it's red, does not mean we need to find everything red."

Michael ignored her, wading knee deep into the water to hold up a red rock with two hands. "Look at this one."

The rest of the morning they walked along the coastline until they reached the jagged cliffs, searching through pebbles and rocky shores. It was getting dark when they made it to the edge of the tree line, not venturing within just yet. Kora didn't ask any further questions regarding his past. It didn't mean he let his walls down.

"Do you see how difficult this task is?" Shade pointed to the ever-growing pile where William was currently placing Michael's most recent find on the top. "We've found hundreds of stones, even a few red sea pods that we've discounted as nothing. That doesn't count how many more there could be that we didn't come across." It was a long shot to make her see reason. He couldn't blame her for wanting to search when she believed it could save her brother.

She didn't look at the pile, ignoring it completely as she stared towards the tree line. "Maybe you know more about this fruit than you realize. Is there something specific that could be connected to both the Isles of Nekrós and the mortal world?" Kora's eyes widened with her speculation, filling with hope.

It was a look he could get used to. *No.* "Or maybe this is a lost cause."

She pursed her mouth. "Maybe *you* need to have a little faith."

Shade pushed off the ground and peered into the distance as the sun hit the horizon. The *Charon* a silhouette against the giant orb. "Well, maybe you and your brothers can check the rest of the forest tomorrow. Take Branch or some of the Lost Souls with you. Make it a game and everyone will help."

"What about you?" Kora stepped onto the path. Sand clung to the edges of her soaked dress. Her ankles were red from the drenched skirts chaffing against her skin. His fingers flinched at the urge to take away the pain.

Shade shrugged. "I'll check other portions of the island to decide where is best to search next. Maybe see if I can get some information."

"Shouldn't I come with you?" She hitched up the skirts of her ankle-length dress, her bare feet kicking up the sand as she walked.

"No need." He smirked. "I'm much faster on my own."

"Fine. I suppose we don't need you to search the forest anyway."

A crackle and the scent of smoke caught his attention. Up ahead, flames began to envelop the logs of the bonfire. After a day of work, he needed some fun. "Race you?"

She narrowed her eyes. "Only if you run instead of fly."

Shade lowered to the ground, his smirk growing. "On your mark..."

"Go!" She took off.

Shade couldn't help but laugh as he trailed after her. She was fast, but her dress caught around her legs as she ran, causing her to stumble before barely catching herself. Whoops and hollers behind them told Shade that the others had chosen to join in as well. Once he caught up with her with sand flying up behind them, he laughed. "I was going to do that."

She smiled at him. "I know," she said and then picked up her pace.

For a second, he considered letting her win. But where would the fun be in that?

Chapter 19
Kora

Shade won the race, but Kora told herself she didn't care. Enough time had been wasted on him. Especially after their lack of success today. Not that she expected anything when they were searching for a stray pomegranate in the ocean. More times than she could count, she'd attempted to lead them towards the forest, but Shade put a stop to it each time. He was more of a hindrance than help. After a while, she began to placate him by playing along. Captain had put her in an impossible situation.

The bonfire warmed the clearing, and some of the Lost Souls sat nearby thumping on drums made from hollowed-out logs and branches. Shade waited for her on the outskirts of the ring of Lost Souls congregating around the bonfire. "I won." His childish grin, dimple and all, had her skin prickling. It was disarming, giving him such a youthful charm for someone who was older than she could even fathom.

"Yes, you did." She stopped beside him, watching as some Lost Souls began to move to the beat of the drum. She searched for her brothers, finding Michael jumping up and down in the center of a large circle with those surrounding clapping along to the beat.

"Come on, join in." Shade cast a quick glance and a wink in

her direction, his arm brushing hers as he passed. The touch had her pulse spiking. She inhaled a deep breath when he disappeared among the Lost Souls dancing in a circle around the fire.

Ever since he'd looked at her that night, after her brother had bled in her arms, he'd burrowed into a little pocket in her thoughts. She'd never admit this out loud, but when her nightmares had twisted into a room coated in blood, his eyes had been a comforting embrace as she fought back screams.

But she needed to ignore her curiosity. Her concentration needed to be fully on the task of returning Shade to the Isles of Nekrós and getting her brothers safely home. To save the living world. Not on some insipid immortal attempting to manipulate her.

Running through the sand after spending the last few hours searching the reef and shoreline with no luck had been a welcome distraction. Even though she knew that they were looking for a needle in a haystack, she couldn't reign in her frustration with Shade's continuous doubts. Everyone's doubts, to be more specific. William had voiced his own, but she brushed them off as she had done the immortal's. It was shocking enough for her to be on Anamoní. Days ago, if someone had told her she would ever meet one of the immortals, she would have laughed in their face.

"What do you think of the fire?" Shade appeared at her side and playfully nudged her, something a boy hadn't done since she was a child. She hid her smile, knowing he watched her.

Careful. "It's fine." She tried not to let any of her conflicting emotions show. *Stay on task.* This mischievous immortal was attempting to detour her priorities. "When will you ask the nereids about checking their lagoon? Or the pixies about the meadow?"

"Relax, Kora." He grinned. "Tomorrow is another day. Tonight is for fun."

Her jaw flexed, but she gave him a saccharine smile. "I understand that. I'm a planner. It's in my nature. And we only have—"

"Seven days." He sighed. "I know."

"Don't interrupt me." She turned on him, fists formed at her side. "Listen—I don't need you doubting me anymore. You already admitted you could do anything when you want something bad enough. I don't know why you felt the need to abandon your post, and I don't care about why. But I do care about my brothers. That's all I want. Us to go home. Together. Maybe we are more alike than you think, because I would do anything to get what I want."

He blinked, his head cocked slightly as he studied her. She had just told off an immortal. Her heartbeat heightened with the drums as the two of them stood still, the dancing continuing around them. "All right."

"What?" She breathed as her brain caught up with her own words.

"You're right. I'll take it more seriously." He stepped closer, and she inhaled as she looked up to meet his gaze. Shade reached towards her, twisting an errant curl around his finger, then tucked it behind her ear as he lowered his voice. "But I'm going to tell you something you should also know—there is nothing more we can do tonight. You need to learn to live in the moment. Spend time with your brothers. Because you don't know what tomorrow will bring."

She knew that truth more than she wanted to admit. "Do you see my brothers?"

He rose up in the air and peered above the crowd. "I see them, yes. They've joined in the dancing. Ah, your twin just saw me. He's heading this way."

"Which direction?" She peered around the festivities, searching for William in the throng of dancing souls.

He pointed to her right, and she turned on her heel before stopping to look up at him. "He's in the other direction, isn't he?"

His face contorted, holding back laughter. And to think she was about to thank him for his help. She stormed in the opposite direction and almost ran right into William.

"This is exciting, isn't it?" William righted her, his hands gripping her arm to help her catch her balance.

Kora sighed at his tone. "I guess so." As she looked at her twin's merry face almost the same shape as her own, her thoughts drifted back to the day's lack of success. "I wonder if I should keep looking. There is light from the fire to search along the beach." One day was already gone. Only six days left, and this island was massive. She could find a way to spend time with her brothers, like Shade recommended, while still searching for the fruit.

William took her hands. "No, I declare that you must have fun now. After an entire day of looking, we deserve it."

Before she could consider arguing, he was already pulling her in amidst the crowd. The beat of the drums lulled her in until she was moving along with the rest of them, the fruit momentarily pushed to the back of her mind.

After a few songs, her brothers attempted some footwork that had most of them snorting with laughter. Kora took a seat to watch the hubbub of activity. Sweat glistened on her brow and her feet ached from the day of treading over the sand. Shade had risen in the air a few feet above the others and had started a ridiculous game of hoops and sticks with dried vines weaved into circles.

William sat down next to her. "You're staring."

Kora broke her gaze away and glanced at her brother. "I was watching, there's a difference."

"I know the difference. I've seen the difference. You were staring. Should I be concerned?" William leaned in, his voice a near whisper.

"About what? An immortal?" She purposely turned her back to Shade, smiling up at her twin. "I'm watching to understand him better. Because no matter how I look at it, if I want you home, we need his help."

He sighed. "It's just not proper. If Mother and Father knew."

"Knew what? That we were in the Isles of Nekrós? We aren't in Athens anymore, William." She glared, attempting to keep her voice low as the beat of the steady drumming heightened on the opposite side of the bonfire, drawing a few of the other souls towards it. "I can handle myself. I don't need you to watch over me."

This is what had gotten them to this point, after all. Because he had wanted to protect her when she didn't need it. Yes, she should be grateful that he stepped in, but his life was just as important as hers.

William lowered his gaze to the space between them. "It's not that I don't appreciate what you're wanting to do for me. I...I just don't want to get my hopes up. And I worry what could happen to you—"

She turned a sharp glare his way. "If I have a chance to bring you back, would you expect me to turn around and leave you? Or try my best?" A vision of her blood-stained hands flashed through her mind, and she looked at her palms now as though the image would appear.

"I'm so sorry, Kora." He pulled her close, dragging her in for a hug she wanted more than she dared admit. It wasn't the same though. There was no heartbeat. No warmth. He didn't breathe with her. A lump formed in her throat.

Alive. She needed him home. "If you mean that, then help me find the pomegranate. Don't doubt our hope."

He sighed, giving her one final squeeze before pulling back. "We will do things your way. But you must understand that I feel guilty you're here in the first place."

"You shouldn't," she murmured and thankfully he didn't hear. She spoke up, her attention drilling into him. "I'm here for you, not because of you. For a reason. We've been blessed with this chance." The bite she wanted to instill in her words was lacking.

William pulled back and looked over her expression. "Tomorrow, the three of us will search. You tell us what to do."

Kora nodded. "The forest. Or should we check Skull Isle?"

"Not without me." Shade strutted towards them and sat

down beside Kora with his arm pressed against hers. She tensed at his proximity and looked down at the sand between her feet to hide the heat that rose to her cheeks. "It might be too dangerous depending on the time of day." He chuckled. "Don't want anyone alive to die here."

William's jaw tensed. "Understood."

"You do as you plan in the forest." Shade crossed his arms. "But we talked about this—this is a party. It's time for fun, not business."

"I know." Somehow, she had to manipulate a god to get what she wanted. She had gotten him to listen to her before, she could do it again. There had to be a way to turn the games around on him.

Before she could delve more into her scheme, Michael passed by with his hands gripped tight between Branch and Curly. They had created a circle around the bonfire that twirled about as they chanted and danced. He grabbed William's hand as they passed.

Kora laughed as her brother was dragged away.

"Come, Kora." Shade held out his hand with a smirk daring her to comply. "Live a little."

The way the corner of his mouth rose brought a smile to her own lips. William's earlier accusation caused her to hesitate—but only for a moment. She took his outstretched hand, smooth and cool to the touch, and allowed herself to be dragged along with the others.

They sang songs she'd never heard before. Branch began to build a sandcastle with Michael, and they all jumped in to help. They snacked on berries from a basket that a soul had plucked from bushes. None of the berries tasted the same—some like toffee, others like chocolate or vanilla. Each one brought a million sensations to her tastebuds. Her twin laughed as Michael's mouth puckered on a lemon one.

The sun was long gone when William cleared his throat. "It's very late. Probably best to get some sleep, Michael."

Before William could stand, Michael jumped to his feet. "You'll have to catch me first." He darted towards the trees.

"Michael!" William rushed after him, heavy steps sending sand flying at Kora.

She raised her hand to protect her face from sand, but it never hit. When she opened her eyes, Shade stood beside her. He twisted his wrist, and the sand fell from where it was suspended in the air.

Kora pushed herself up from the ground where they had built a messy sandcastle. "Thank you," she mumbled before meeting his gaze.

Shade shrugged, his expression serious. "No problem."

They stared at each other for a moment, and Kora considered detouring the conversation back to the fruit when Astari stepped beside Shade. "What are you two doing?"

"Nothing." Shade pointed at the sandcastle he'd helped Michael and the others build. "Besides this anyway. Just finished."

Astari wrapped an arm into the crook of Shade's, straightening as she looked down her nose at Kora. She turned to Shade and smiled. "Dance with me? Or would you rather head back for the night?"

Kora cleared her throat, heat climbing up her face. "I'm going to find my brothers."

Shade paused mid-step and looked up at the sky. "Duty calls." Tuck, a Lost Soul with hunched shoulders, chuckled at Shade's words before skipping off. Shade snorted then patted Astari's hand, removing himself from her hold. "I'll return by morning, Kora." He shot up into the sky. "Everyone off the beach. I'll be back." A caw echoed after him as he disappeared into the night.

"Where is he—"

Before Kora could finish the sentence, Astari stood nose to nose with her. "He's mine. You're not dead."

Kora's brow furrowed, confused by the soul's words and the sinking feeling in her stomach. What was with everyone tonight? "First of all, I've never laid claim to anyone. Second, I'm just working alongside him to find a way home." The lie slid off her tongue as easily as water down the throat. "Whatever is between the two of you remains that way."

Astari inched closer, forcing Kora to step back. The waves just missed her heels as the tide receded from the beach. "Shade is an immortal—you're still breathing, so he has no need of you."

"I don't understand what you believe is happening..." Laughter echoed, but if anyone noticed Astari's anger, no one interfered as they headed towards camp. She considered calling for help, the manic expression on Astari's face making her stomach clench and throat dry, but she could handle this.

"I believe that I'm telling you your place." The soul turned to walk away, letting her threat linger between them.

Kora should have kept her mouth shut. Her mother raised her to not bicker or fight in public—but her mother wasn't here. "Is your relationship so tenuous that you feel the need to threaten the new girl for spending time with the God of the Dead?"

Astari paused and glared over her shoulder. "You're not new. He'll send you home as soon as he can." Her tone was sharp, anger lacing each word.

Kora kept the truth to herself. "Then what's your problem?"

The soul advanced on Kora, the surf bubbling against her ankles. "You're my problem. Just watch yourself." She pushed her shoulder with one hand, sending Kora stumbling backwards. The cool water lapping at her calves unbalanced her. Kora fell on her butt, the soul laughing down at her with her arms crossed over her chest. "I'm dead, mortal. What can you do to me?"

Kora should walk away. She should ignore the temptation. Just as she should have ignored the young men who showed up at her home dressed to impress and talked down to her. Astari was just like them. Kora splashed water at the soul who gasped, wiping the salt and sand from her face with a growl. "You lit—"

Her eyes widened as she looked at something over Kora's shoulder and screamed. For a moment, she thought it was a new tactic, but then Astari stepped back once. Twice. Before Kora had time to get to her feet or react to whatever scared the dead, a tug yanked her around her waist as a flash of lightning hit the ground behind Astari.

With a queasy stomach, Kora waited as her eyes adjusted to the bright lights. Wooden boards instead of sand and water were under where she laid sprawled flat on her back. The night sky glistened, stars dancing above. A lone cloud moved across the moon. She flinched and lifted her hand to find a splinter in her palm when the click of boots caused her to still.

Captain loomed over her with a sinister grin spread across his face. "How are you faring, Kora?"

She groaned at her aching backside, pushing herself up to a sitting position. "Been better." The ship—the *Charon,* if she remembered correctly—teetered at the swell of a wave. The vessel looked as though it had seen a season too many. The splinter in her hand wasn't the only one piercing from the paneled floor or rails—a few cracked—and the deck below was visible through holes in the boards. It was a skeleton ship, through and through.

"Making friends with the souls, I see. You may want to win them over to your side. At least, if you want to gain my brother's trust." He held out his hand towards her.

Kora considered whacking it away, but her dress was soaked through and that splinter throbbed. She took his palm, and he pulled her to her feet. In the dim warm light from the lanterns that hung along the rail, she was able to see the fleck of wood between her skin and removed it. "You know, this mission you've given me is near impossible." *Shade is impossible,* she bit back.

The immortal glanced her over, taking his time to peruse every inch of her body. It was unnerving. Her arms wrapped around her chest, aware of how her wet dress clung to her body. Captain flicked his wrist, and a gust of air dried her clothes and boots. She swallowed, still uncertain. "Thank you."

He smirked, leaning forward slightly. "Can't have you catching a cold."

She blinked in surprise. "I didn't think you'd care."

"I care about my investments, and if they pay out. You're currently one. Can't have you dying too soon, can I?" Captain leaned against the stair rail. "That's why I'm checking on your status. It's been a day."

"As I said, this is near impossible. Shade's smart. I spent most of today looking through stones and searching along the coast for fruit he denies exists. He's only promised me seven days to find it, or he plans to send me back."

His jaw ticked. "He'll need the Queen of the Pixies to send you back. I'll make sure he doesn't have her permission until all hope is lost. As for the fruit, the tree travels without any way to determine its next destination. It's said that the tree makes itself available at a time of need, and you need it. No matter how much you want it, only the God of the Dead can find it. Shade is your only hope. You must stay with him, or he might purposely *overlook* what you seek. Don't let him fool you into thinking he cares. He won't make it easy for you, but the pomegranate will give you what you want. And I get what I want in return. This is the deal I offered you."

"I know, but is there something more helpful you can give me?"

Captain pursed his lips as he considered her question. "The tree might not be on the Anamoní. It could be found on the other Isles of Nekrós."

"What?" Her mouth fell open. "I've only been with him for a day, so why would he take me to the one place he doesn't want to go?"

The immortal tilted his head. "Ask him for a tour of the other isles. A quick fly over. You will need his trust to get him to do it."

"I still haven't been able to figure out which one of you is more impractical..." Kora grumbled. Captain was being vague. Shade was incorrigible. With only six days left, how was she meant to save William? The world?

He snorted. "I've lived more centuries than you can imagine, girl. I've seen wars tear families apart, empires crumble and yet it has never been this bad in the world of the living. Nothing this widespread. It's not just your brother you're saving, but so many others. I know you can handle this. He's curious about you—use that."

Kora pinched her eyes shut for a moment. "I'll do what I can. For people like me—and my brother." She sighed and thought about her brothers. Of Ariana back at home. The loss of the future she longed for. "If there is anything else that you can help me with though—"

He smirked. "Then I'll call you again."

Before she had a chance to say anything further, he flicked his wrist and with another flash of light, the boat was gone, and she stood with the surf splashing at her ankles. She tried to catch her balance but fell backwards into the water again. As she started to compose herself, screams wracked the air.

She fumbled to her feet with her soaked dress wrapped around her legs and obstructing her movement. "What—"

Shadows moved through the darkness, nearly invisible in the dwindling light of the bonfire. Souls scattered, screaming—trying to escape from figures grabbing hold and dragging them towards the water while others tried to battle off the creatures that looked like darkness personified.

What was happening?

Something hit her side, breath nearly stolen from her lungs by the impact. She whirled around to find Branch between her and one of the shadows. "Out of the water!"

He pulled her from the surf and tugged her up the beach towards the trees. "Hurry, we need to get—"

Another scream from behind them had Kora tentatively looking over her shoulder. She searched the surf, her gaze snagging on blond hair. Astari was being dragged by two shadows towards the sea. Without thinking, Kora twisted from Branch's grip and ran towards her.

It was hard to run in the sand, but her movements faltered as Branch's shrill voice called for her. "It's too late."

She didn't listen. All she knew was that the soul was terrified, and she couldn't leave someone like that. Not even if they were dead—or horrible.

Kora didn't know what she was going to do, but as she ran by the bonfire, she grabbed one of the logs with embers shining on the end. She swiped it at the first shadowed figure who hissed, stepping back from the heat of the branch. As others clawed towards her, Kora swung at the second shadow holding the soul as Astari let out another scream and fought against the creatures.

Kora hit the other, the log going through its body—or at least, what was best described as a body. It hissed, and a maw of jagged rotted teeth screeched in her face, causing her to gag from the scent of decay. With another swing, the creature let go of Astari who ran towards the beach.

"Go," Kora yelled.

Twisting around the shadow, Kora ran after her when something cold grabbed hold of her arm. The creature let out a high-pitched screech, letting her go as it stared at its hand before darting towards the water.

A quick glance around for the hidden enemy showed more of the souls fighting back and rushing at the shadows with the burning branches. Kora aligned with the others, her own log still in her grip. Once they made it to the line of trees, she whirled around with the others who were searching the sand for the monsters. Hunched over, she gasped for breath, looking down the line of souls who stood with her, but the shadows were gone. She dropped the log and stomped out the last of the embers in the dirt at her feet. "What—what were those things?"

"Kora?" William was at her side a breath later, pulling her in for a tight hug. "Where in the hells did you go?" He pulled back, his gaze scanning her body for injuries. "You were in the water, then you were gone."

Branch rested his hand on William's shoulder, his eyes penetrating her skin. "We thought you'd been taken by the xéchase."

"Xéchase?" She remembered Shade mentioning them. "Those were the Forgotten?"

"They are the souls that don't have payment to pass. They are left to roam Váthos for all eternity. They are lured by unjudged souls and want to force us into the sea. Shade usually can keep them at bay but lately…" Branch glanced at the others who huddled close, a few searching the beach warily.

Kora finished the sentence for him. "He's lost control?"

"Not exactly. They only come when he's not here. That's why we must stay off the beach when he leaves to collect souls. We were lucky none were taken tonight, but we dallied too long after Shade left."

A few of the others nodded in agreement. Astari pushed through the crowd to stand beside William. She held out her hand to Kora and swallowed, her eyes holding sorrow Kora could almost feel. "Sorry…about before. Thanks for saving me. You didn't have to."

A snide comment stuck to Kora's tongue. It would take a little longer for Kora to forgive the soul, but she could at least be civil. "You're welcome."

Astari gave her a small smile, then turned away and headed down the path towards the Lost Souls Camp.

"Where's Michael" Kora's eyes widened as she took stock of the crowd. He wasn't with them.

"Safe." William nodded. "He went back to Shade's cypress with Curly. The others and I were at the tree line when we heard the first scream. By the time I got back down here, I'd lost sight of you." The others followed Astari back, but William took a step closer, lowering his voice. "Where were you, Kora?"

"I fell in the water during the chaos." Lying. Now she was the one keeping things from her twin. That's what got them into this trouble to begin with. But it was the only way. Shade couldn't know she was working for Captain, and to say it out loud would mean she might never gain the immortal's trust.

William trailed behind, and Kora slowed to walk with him as

they trudged through the brush along the narrow trail to the treehouse. She was exhausted, her legs heavy and knees weak. Her drenched dress clung to her, and goosebumps pebbled her skin. She rubbed her arms for warmth, but her muscles ached from swinging the heavy log.

William wrapped his arms around Kora's shoulder, drawing her close. "I don't care about the pomegranate. You scared me tonight. Please, Kora, abandon this quest and go home. Let's get you and our brother out of here as soon as possible."

She fought back threatening tears. Fear, shock, and her impossible task—it all mixed with grief. How could he ask her to leave him? But how was she supposed to force an immortal to do anything? She looked down at her feet, unable to bear facing him as she fought to pull herself together.

Captain's words about not only saving William but the mortal world too repeated in her mind. What her twin had been hoping to accomplish with the believers at the temple who had been unable to protect him, she could do now. She broke free of his arm. "I'm not giving up. We're here for a reason, Will. You might not believe that, but I do." There was a bite in her tone.

He was smart enough not to utter another word as she stormed towards the treehouse. She closed the door behind her, and spotted Michael curled up, obliviously snoring in the bed. She sat down on the floor, taking a blanket bundled up at the edge of the bed, and wrapped it around her body.

She let the tears flow, stifling her sobs so she didn't wake her exhausted brother or alert William who undoubtedly was right outside the door. She wiped her eyes, took a few long breaths, then curled up in the bed beside Michael. He nuzzled into her with a small sigh of contentment. She breathed in his childish scent of dirt and sweat from a day of fun.

Tomorrow was another day, and she had a lot of searching to do if she was going to prove everyone wrong. It was time for them to realize she could do things on her own. Here, she didn't have to be the meek woman everyone expected her to be at home. Now, all she had to do was trick the God of the Dead into trusting her.

Chapter 20
Captain

Captain twisted a coin over and under his fingers, watching as the sunlight refracted against its shiny surface, creating an orb of light that danced against the wall.

A knock sounded at the door. They were already on their way to the Isles of Nekrós with a fresh batch of souls, so Captain had settled in his quarters. "Enter."

Smith scuttled in and gave a low bow. "There is someone here to see you, Captain."

His brow knitted together. Captain could count how many times Shade had ventured this close to the Isles of Nekrós on one hand. "Who is it?"

"Your brother. The King of the Sea."

Captain straightened, dropping the coin into the pocket of his red coat. "Send him in."

Before Smith could respond, the door flung open, revealing Halieus in the midst of the dim sunlight. Shirtless with a pair of linen trousers hanging off his hips, he swung his head to force his dirty blond shoulder-length hair out of his eyes. "Even here you demand to be treated like a king."

"Of course." Captain's jaw flexed. "I expect respect. You

should remember that." He nodded to Smith who scurried from the room.

Halieus chuckled as he moved around Captain's quarters in an arc, staying along the edge of the room as he examined the space. "Looks like you've settled in."

"I didn't exactly have a choice. You do realize how many years it's been?"

His brother picked up a rock that held down a map on Captain's desk, then peered over his shoulder at him. "Forty-nine years, seventy-one days and twelve hours. Give or take a few minutes." The grin that stretched on his face made Captain want to throttle him. Not that it would do him any good.

"I offered to come here before. You could have kept things running in the mortal world, and I would have handled this place just fine. Besides, if anyone would have settled in with this position ferrying the dead, it would have been me." Halieus put the rock down haphazardly on the corner of the map, then took a seat in an overstuffed chair. He removed a golden watch from his trousers and clicked it open. The tick-tock was silenced with a snap of its cover before he slid it back into his pocket. "That is what those in Synnefo have chosen as their alternative to forcing Shade to the depths of Mizéria. Let me come here in your stead and see what I can do."

There had been a time when Shade had been considered the most responsible of the siblings. He used to have Nekrós running like a well-oiled machine. That was hard to believe now. In the past, he'd stood strong and ran the realm with precision while Halieus had stuck his nose into the business of the living. Some of the things the Sea King had done were unforgivable in the eyes of many—hence why Captain had been forced to keep him on a tight leash. And he certainly wasn't meant to lead the Underworld. It would be turned to ruin and there were *things* within the depths of Mizéria that couldn't be let out.

There was a reason Captain had trusted Shade, in the past, with such an important responsibility.

Captain tilted his head in consideration, watching his brother carefully. It would be a bad idea—disastrous—to let Halieus take over. "Why do you want to come so badly?"

A flutter, a flash of light, a twinkling sound, and iridescent wings came to a stop in the center of the room. "She's returned," the pixie announced.

Captain growled. "Now isn't the best time, Taea."

She glanced over at his brother. "Oh. I see."

"Still playing all sides, Little Pixie?" Halieus jeered.

Taea stuck her tongue out and turned towards Captain. "What is Fisher doing here? I thought his stink wasn't invited?"

Halieus snorted, the corner of his mouth lifting. "I didn't change my name to these modern terms. Not all of us have forgotten the past."

Captain sighed. "His presence is not your concern right now. Who is this *she* you referred to?" It couldn't be the girl. He'd know.

"Astraea. She's come back from the mortal world. If Shade finds out..." She shook her head.

"Then he won't find out. I expect you can control this situation and keep Shade away from the pixies. They don't leave their valley to travel over the island, correct? Or has that changed?" Captain ignored Halieus who tapped his toe in an annoying succession.

"No, he'd need to go to her. I'll do my best to delay him from receiving word." The pixie took a seat on the edge of Captain's desk, crossing her legs and glaring at Halieus. It was as though she had chosen a side, and it wasn't *Fisher's*. "Now, why is he here?"

Halieus stopped the tapping mid-step and glared. "I was asked to come. And because the two of you still haven't been able to change Shade's mind, I'm offering myself in Captain's place."

Taea rolled her eyes and turned to Captain. "You can't seriously be considering this? He would never get a single thing done. If you thought it was chaos before your arrival, leave it in his hands and it will be worse."

"Thank you so much for the vote of confidence," Halieus grumbled. "You can't take the word of a two-timing pixie over mine."

He stated it so matter-of-factly that Captain couldn't help but laugh. Never would he trust either of them—not the pixie with dark secrets and an even more dangerous past, nor his brother who was meant to be his equal. "My plan is working. Shade will return to his role and all will be well."

Taea and Halieus shared a look that he couldn't decipher. But he brushed the curiosity away. "Taea, you're excused. I need to discuss a few things with my brother."

The pixie lifted her nose in the air. "Fine. I can tell when I'm not wanted."

As she rose in the air, Halieus sent an obscene gesture her way. "I would hope you can tell when he outright told you to get out."

Before Captain could comment, the pixie huffed, turning a dark shade of red before she zipped out of the room.

With a twist of Captain's wrist, he closed the window behind her to deter any curious ears. "Any news from Synnefo? Have the others come up with any *other* ideas?"

"Nothing to report. Except we are getting closer to summer, and the season seems to be fighting the change and instead...reversing." He went back to tapping his foot, which Captain made conscious effort to ignore.

"What do you mean?"

"It's been cooler. An unexpected storm that brought havoc to the continents. People were appreciative of the water to help their crops grow and fill wells—until the rain brought more catastrophe. There have been worldwide tsunamis and floods. The people are either cursing us or pleading for our return. They can't take much more of this." Halieus shrugged. "I hope this plan you've put so much weight on actually works."

"It hasn't been this bad for the mortals since our father ruled Synnefo." Captain's arms flexed.

Their father had once ruled all. The dead, the mortal world, the waters and Synnefo. Too much power and it had corrupted him. He saw his children as a threat to his reign and planned to restrain them and strip them of their immortality. Captain had been the first to escape. With their mother's assistance, he had raised an army to free his brothers. Shade had enacted the final plan, tricking their father into the bowels of Mizéria where he had been imprisoned ever since.

"Some of the mortals blame me, Brother. I'm meant to assist the water. Bring rain. If this continues—if I hear one more curse..." His gaze thinned. "Maybe that's why you need me here. To deal with this. Otherwise. I'll—"

"You'll do nothing without my order," Captain warned.

"If you have everything under control, then why am I here?" Halieus picked up a spyglass from the table beside him. "Or did you just want company?"

"If I were to ask anyone to be here for companionship, trust that it wouldn't be you." Captain considered the immortal before him. "I need more eyes on the Isle of Waiting. Taea can only see so much and since I'm unable to step foot on the island, it would make more sense for you to see how things are progressing."

Halieus's brow rose. "You want me to spy on him? That's all? I thought you'd want me to lure him towards the isles or something?"

"I don't need you to lure him anywhere. He'll go to the nereids soon, and I want you to be there when he does. After, you're to report back to me what you've seen." Captain kept Kora's presence quiet. The reveal would be much more exciting. Besides, he didn't want his brother to question his choices. "Do we have an understanding?"

"Let me get this straight. You sit here in the comforts of your ship and still get to order me around?" Halieus got to his feet, flecking a speck of imaginary dust off his trousers.

The air crackled, a shiver visibly running down the immortal's spine as Captain's power emanated around the room. "Don't question me, Brother."

Halieus flung his long hair out of his face again. "Fine. I'll go. If Shade doesn't arrive in the next few days though, I'm coming back here and demanding answers."

"We shall see about that." Captain's words trailed after Halieus's retreating steps. His brother snapped the door shut behind him. The King of the Gods looked out the window in time to see his brother dive overboard, his legs melding into a long, spiked tail. The thick hide of a crocodile curled over his shoulders just as his head morphed into the reptile, and he hit the water with a splash.

A corner of Captain's mouth curved into a smirk. He almost wished he could be there when Halieus caught sight of the mortal who would be Shade's undoing. Taea and Halieus may have doubted his plan, but Captain knew he was on the right track.

Soon. Very soon, Shade would be wearing the helm of his title once again. And the mortal would receive the answer to her prayer.

Chapter 21
Shade

Shade overlooked the clearing from the highest branch of his favorite tree. The thick leaves hid him from the souls below who were content with the game they'd created involving an old net made from twine and twigs, and a coconut. But Taea knew where to find him.

"You remembered to signal your return." She landed on his knee and sat down, draping her legs over his. "No girl to distract you this time?"

"Ha. Ha," he deadpanned. The crow had started out as a way to announce his absence or return. The Lost Souls used to mourn his exit and cheer his return. Now they did it because they were safe again from the threat of the xéchase. He'd heard about last night's attack from Curly and Branch. Another attack. Another moment he'd been unable to protect them.

She leaned back on her arms, kicking her feet gently in the air. "Did all the souls get dropped off at the docks?"

Shade nodded, resting his hands behind his head as a barrier against the rough bark. "Didn't need more to deal with. Figured two living mortals was enough."

"Or was it just a particular mortal who has kept you preoccupied?" Taea pursed her lips, drawing Shade's attention to her and away from the brown-haired girl talking with William and Curly below.

They had just returned from searching the forest along the stretch of beach, and judging by the siblings' expression, they had about as much luck as Shade had. "Have you seen a pomegranate tree?" It had been years, and he hadn't even thought about the fruit tree until Kora mentioned it. The fruit had damned him to this place and had once saved another, but he never had needed to search for it before now.

Shade was aware Taea kept in contact with Captain as their liaison and might let something slip. While he trusted her the most out of everyone on the Isle of Waiting, it didn't mean he wasn't careful.

Taea shrugged. "There have been whispers, but I've never seen it. Maybe Astraea knows more?" Taea tilted her head at him, her brow raised.

"I haven't received word that she's returned from her duties in the living world yet. Until then, there isn't anyone I trust in Pixie Meadow. I covertly asked the nereids. Or attempted too. I think I'll take Kora there soon. If anything, a mortal might draw their curiosity enough to get some information from them."

"Did you hear about Astari?" Taea straightened.

Shade stilled. "Hear what?" He peered down at the camp below and found the soul settled on a makeshift chair on the little porch outside her hut. Her arms were wrapped tightly around her as she watched the others. "What did she do?"

"It's not what she did per se..." Taea dangled the bait in front of him, her mouth a pout as though she had the most important gossip within the Isle of Waiting. Well, she usually did.

He waited for a moment but when her gaze trailed off into the distance, he knew he was going to have to ask. "What happened, Taea?"

Taea smiled, biting at her bottom lip as she met his gaze. "She and Kora had a fight on the beach. Before we know it, the xéchase attack and they don't know where Kora is."

He jumped to his feet. Taea tumbled over herself, wings saving her from plummeting headfirst into a branch. "What? Where did she go?"

She pursed her lips before recounting the events. "So, Kora's gone. Astari's running, and chaos took over the beach." Taea rose until she was even with his face. "No one knows who started the disagreement, but words were overheard about Kora being alive and possibly throwing that information in Astari's face—after the latter told the mortal she cared about you." The pixie tsked. "Trouble is caused with their presence. It's too bad you made this agreement with her."

"You don't have to trust her, but she and I have an understanding." He'd made that decision, and so far his instincts hadn't steered him wrong. "What concerns me is who interfered, and did they have control of when the xéchase attacked?" He glanced over his shoulder to the ocean, at the *Charon* in the distance. His brother claimed not to know how the mortals had arrived. But if Kora was in the water...

"That's what concerns you? Not that your souls could have been taken away?" Taea blinked slowly. "This girl is sidetracking you, manipulating you. Mark my words—"

"Enough." Shade's jaw twitched. Taea's reaction reeked of jealousy. He knew she was protective of him, but this was pushing it. "I know there's a reason she's here. I'm not stupid." Anger pulsed, mixing with the chilling power circulating through his body. "Have some faith in me, Taea. Mortals and immortals are never a good mix. History has proven that point, and I've observed enough of my family's antics to know better. Once the seven days are over, they are going home, and we'll never see them until their deaths."

And whatever draw he felt for the young woman would end with her absence. Not many came to the Underworld out of curiosity or interest in the immortal who presided over death and decay. It was a lonely existence.

Taea rolled her eyes. "Hopefully she doesn't drive any of your souls away before that happens. Otherwise, the Isle of Waiting might not be the same place you've worked so hard to create."

"They aren't *my* souls."

Taea shook her head, clicking her tongue in disappointment then settled on his shoulder. "The Kora girl is dangerous. You might want to keep an eye on her for the sake of the souls, if not for yourself."

Before Shade had time to comment, Taea leaped off and flew out of sight. He rubbed his temples, trying to relieve the pressure building in his head. As much as he hated her nagging, Taea was right—the young mortal was proving to be dangerous. Not just for her reason for being here or the schemes of the god who brought her here, but because Shade couldn't deny he was drawn to her. Even if she annoyed him, they'd also had fun last night. A memory of her dancing among the souls, her cheeks red from exertion and the smile on her face that dazzled. Shade pinched his eyes shut to dispel the thought.

William broke away from Camp, tossing a stone back and forth between his palms. Shade flew down and landed beside him, the soul barely reacting to his sudden appearance. "No luck?"

"Did you see the new rock towers on the beach? The others have created torches and built them within the piles we created. They are planning to light them for a party tomorrow night. Most have started to help just to make more all the way down the shoreline. There are smaller versions of the piles along the path in the forest made up of so many red objects that I don't think anyone would have noticed otherwise." William tossed the rock with his brow furrowed and mouth in a taut line. "Is she crazy for having this hope?"

Shade would never say she was crazy. At least not out loud. "Do you blame her?" Shade bent over and picked up a stone and tossed it into the gentle waves of the sea. "I saw her that night by your side, William. She would have done anything she could to keep you alive then, and would do so now."

"But at the risk of her own life? What about Michael? The

living shouldn't be in Anamoní, and you know it. She's just so stubborn..." William's shoulders slumped.

"I do know it." Shade's jaw flexed, and he sighed. "I'm taking her to the nereids tomorrow."

"What?" William stopped mid throw and turned with the rock in his hand now pointed in Shade's direction. "You said that place was dangerous. I'm already dead, take me instead."

"She needs to realize some of the dangers beyond the xéchase. You said so yourself—she's stubborn. If she doesn't go herself, do you think she'll be satisfied? Do you trust me enough to keep her safe?"

William lowered his arm and pinched his eyes closed. When he opened them again, his expression fell. "If anything happens to her—"

"Nothing personal, but your threats mean little." Shade snorted. "My goal is to have all of your siblings returned home in five days."

William nodded and turned his attention towards the sea. Shade followed his gaze and breathed a deep sigh. His brothers had called him selfish for leaving the Isles of Nekrós. If they could only see him now...

During the night, William had rested at the foot of the bed. Souls, like immortals, didn't require sleep, but that didn't mean they couldn't take a nap or get some shut eye from time to time. Shade had settled within the hammock above them. He preferred that spot anyway. The soft snores and heavy breathing were enough of a distraction from the girl with soft brown hair who curled up in his bed. Michael's unfinished hut was one of their priorities today but by the size of it, the younger Darling sibling was making it for only himself when it had been meant for both living mortals.

When he realized he wasn't going to sleep, Shade took off and searched along the edges of the camp for any signs of trespassing before returning to the treehouse. He sat waiting at the Darling boys' makeshift fire pit with a stick in hand.

The previous evening, he'd spoken in detail with Branch regarding what had happened at the bonfire. It sounded like Astari had made her annoyances known to the other Lost Souls regarding Kora's presence prior to the attack. Now, she was quiet and withdrawn. That alone was enough of a reminder to keep his guard up around the mortal. Obviously, many thought of her as a possible weakness. Her presence was the ultimate game, and one Shade wasn't going to lose.

The door to the treehouse popped open and Kora stilled in the entryway, her hesitant gaze meeting his. He heard her heart speed up. The sound entranced him for a moment, until he turned away. "Did Will tell you we are going to the nereids today?"

"Yes." She swallowed, smoothing her tattered dress that was changing from pale blue to brown. He should talk to the Lost Souls about getting her some other clothes. "Did you find out anything yesterday?" She moved in beside him, his attention remaining on her torn and tattered hem. When he looked up, he swallowed, watching as she gathered her hair into a ponytail and tied it back with a blue satin ribbon.

"No one knew a thing, and I didn't find a pomegranate tree. Tomorrow you should search the mountains with the other souls." Shade headed towards the beach where he would take off with her. It would send a message to someone who might be watching from his ship.

"What about you? You promised to help me." Kora had to jog to keep pace with him.

Shade stopped in the midst of the trees, the trail overgrown. He should stay away from her when they weren't searching. He was already going to be spending too much time with her, and it was proving a problem. "I am helping. There is more I can do alone, and we can cover more ground if we split up."

"You're the key to all this." Kora grabbed his arm, pulling him around to face her. His skin tingled at the contact. Familiar and bold. "I know it doesn't make sense but please, I need you to stay with me." He stilled, not realizing how close they would be. The smell of sea salt and spring flowers curled around his body as Kora released her hold of him. "Would you leave us to search this entire island alone? We don't know it like you do."

Shade diverted his gaze. Looking at her caused his senses to go haywire. He wanted to look at every nuance of her face, touch that little curl that always seemed to curve around her jaw. Damn it to hells, he needed to control himself. "I'll take you to the dangerous locations."

She sighed. "All right. And what other places will you take me to?"

"Skull Isle. We'll need to be quick. When the tide rises, water fills the cave, and that's the last place for a mortal to be. We can go there tomorrow. And if I can, I'll ask for permission for you to speak to Astraea after she returns." Once they broke through the tree line, he stopped and looked out towards the sea at the *Charon* bobbing on the water.

"The pixie queen?"

"Yes. She's also the head of their council."

Thankfully, that was enough for the mortal to quiet down and stop with the questions.

He turned towards her, and without a word, scooped her up and took off into the air. Her arms wrapped tightly around his neck. Her body pressed against his, and a small squeal escaped.

He chuckled softly, daring a glance in her direction. "I won't let you fall."

"You could be more polite about it. Let me know before you're going to sweep me off my feet." She glared.

It was adorable that she thought she was menacing. Especially with the way the breeze blew through her hair and the wonder in her eyes when she relaxed in his arms. Nope—his mind shouldn't be drifting to such thoughts.

Shade's expression went blank. "I'm the last one you want sweeping you off your feet. But I'll warn you next time." He smiled. "Maybe."

Kora mumbled a few choice words under her breath. Indiscernible even with her proximity.

"What happened with Astari last night?" He wondered what her side of the story was, although he'd told himself on multiple occasions that he shouldn't care. *Immortal. Dead. Mortal. Souls.* The words circulated through his mind on repeat.

Kora remained quiet, and he was curious if she'd even heard him. Then a warm breath curled against his ear, and he swallowed deeply, ignoring the way the sensation shuddered down his spine.

"Astari was angry with me and pushed me into the water. There was this flash of light, and I think I hit my head or something. Thankfully it wasn't too deep, or I would have drowned. When I opened my eyes, there were those *things* on the beach."

Shade's grip tightened around her body, jaw clenching. She was keeping things from him—he could tell by the way her voice wavered. "I'm sorry I wasn't there. That flash of light might have saved you, it seems."

Her gaze met his, but her mouth remained shut. Her expression near unreadable. Almost.

Chapter 22

Kora

Kora rested against his chest and tried to ignore the hard lines of his body pressed against hers. Shade's grip shifted slightly around her, and he cocked his head, peering down at her. A playful smile curled his lips but before she could ask what he was thinking, he swooped down at top speed. A scream escaped her, followed by a loud whoop of joy when he twisted her in a corkscrew through the air.

Shade laughed, his cheeks flushed as he evened out. She batted his shoulder. "You fiend."

He laughed harder. "You enjoyed it."

She hid her smile in his shirt, only to breathe in his floral and spicy bergamot scent. "I did, but don't for a second believe that I thought that was your intention."

His dimple deepened, as did his smile. "Nice to know that you aren't so wound up you can't have some fun. I won't lie and say that I didn't expect you to squirm from my hold."

"Would you have dropped me? Just to annoy me?"

Shade met her gaze. His blue eyes sparkling, but a seriousness settled in his expression. "Never."

Kora turned away from his intense gaze, taking in the treetops they flew over. She couldn't help but search for the red fruit among the branches. He didn't fly too high over the canopies, and she mentally thanked him since it allowed her a chance to look. "So, tell me about the mermaids."

He came into a landing on a bluff overlooking the lagoon and set her down. The grass tickled her calves, a few bushes dotting the landscape, but otherwise no trees. His hands lingered around her waist until she found her footing. She didn't move away, staying close, enjoying the flutter of his fingers against her body. Then she realized what she was doing and looked at her feet, biting her lip and willing the heat not to rise to her cheeks.

Shade cleared his throat and stepped back, his fingers tracing her waist before they fell away. "They prefer to be called nereids or water nymphs." His tone hardened. "You must stay clear of the water's edge. They won't hesitate to drag you down into the depths. Mortal or soul—they won't care." Shade rolled his shoulders—such a mortal thing to do. "Ready?"

Shade started along a path that led along the bluff's edge and headed downward towards the lagoon. Shade handed her piles of bright purple berries from nearby bushes as they walked.

"Blueberries?" She rolled one around between her index and thumb, taking in its indigo skin and sweet scent. This wasn't like the berries they had eaten yesterday. Those had looked like raspberries but had tasted like every delicious thing she could think. The last time she had any type of berry was when she was a child. They had died off nearly eight years before.

"Maybe. I wouldn't exactly know."

"Oh." She recognized the melancholy in his voice. She shouldn't have, but she pitied him a little.

"Haven't had food in the mortal world in a very long time, so I don't remember much."

She held out one towards him, but he waved it away. "You need food more than I do. The berries here are all safe to eat and should sustain you."

"I thought you might want to try one."

He came to a stop and stared down at the berry in her

outstretched hand, then back to her. "I'd never really thought about it. Never had a need too."

He grabbed it, and she held another up. "Cheers."

This, he seemed to understand, and he smiled, dimple and all as they tapped their berries together before popping them into their mouths. Juice burst over her tongue, sweet and tangy, and unlike anything she had tasted before. "Delicious."

He nodded in agreement. His attention sliding to her mouth and she swallowed, suddenly aware how close they were. Shade reached up his hand and brushed his thumb against her bottom lip. "You have a little juice right here."

Her mouth opened slightly, and he stilled. The world itself froze in place as she held his gaze.

A breeze brushed the stalks of grass against her calves, and she stepped back, Shade's arm falling to his side.

She gave him a small smile, and he cleared his throat, stuffing his hands into his pockets and continued on the path. The sun had hit the center of the sky above. Her feet were beginning to ache in her worn-out boots and the fabric of her dress had gotten itchy and stiff between the sand and ocean water as it scratched and rubbed against her legs. "How much further?" Kora asked.

He peered over his shoulder. "We should reach the lagoon around noon. I'd fly us in, but they are particular and *dropping in* is not going to make them more inclined to help." His gaze softened as he glanced down at her feet. "I'll talk to Curly to find some other clothes for you. I'm surprised William hasn't considered it."

With a brief nod, she continued a step ahead of him. Their earlier tension flattened out at the reminder of her brother. The reason she was here—to save him. Not for the one who caused the world to fall into ruin. Because of his selfishness. Although...she was starting to wonder how true that was.

Or were those doubts part of his mind games?

He caught up to walk alongside her. "Drachma for your thoughts?"

"You." Might as well be straightforward.

Shade's brow rose and a smirk played on his lips. "I like this—and what are you thinking about me?" He puffed up a bit as he slowed to a stop.

"You don't seem selfish. Yesterday the souls were telling me stories that proved you genuinely care." It was true. Curly and Branch had traded tales of how much Shade did to make them feel as comfortable as possible. It was opposite of what Captain had said. "Why did you abandon your post and curse the world to famine and death?"

If he was surprised by her abruptness, he hid it well. Only the flex of his jaw showed any reaction. "My brother pulled the gods from the mortal world. I can say it over and over again, but it was never my intention to cause hardship for the mortals." He glanced down at the ground between them, and she became aware of the strands of hair grazing her neck that had fallen free during the flight. "Have you ever felt completely alone?" He shook his head. "Like someone made your decisions for you and you had little say?"

She didn't answer, even if she was faced with those similar emotions regularly. Mother's countless dinners with eligible bachelors. Fulfilling her parents' expectations for her. The move to England she didn't want. How many times she mentioned her desire to go to university only to be scoffed at or ignored.

Shade continued, "I'd spent a lifetime with figments of what humanity used to be. The only occasional visit I had was from Télos, the God of Death, and my brothers. I was cut off from the mortal world. Left here. And after centuries, I needed to escape."

Kora was tempted to hug him. To tell him she understood how he felt. But she hadn't lived centuries of loneliness—the bleakness she saw in his eyes right now. He seemed careful, pragmatic, boisterous. But there was another side to him. Did Captain understand him? Consider Shade's reasons?

Before she could delve further into those thoughts, Shade turned and continued on. They walked in silence until reaching a fork in the road, and he nodded towards the path on the right that widened slightly and led them further down. "The lagoon has only one entrance and exit. Jagged cliffs curve around the inlet." He pointed across the way to sheer rock that made up the mountainside with a near vertical drop. "The point where the bluff meets the mountain is blocked by a waterfall that feeds the river and lagoon before it reaches the ocean. Otherwise, we would have to swim the Váthos to reach it. Not the best idea with the nereids and the xéchase. We have to go up and around the lagoon then follow down on the opposite side to reach our destination."

Kora followed behind, thankful for the change of conversation as his response to her question only confused her more. She couldn't relate to an immortal. That was unfathomable.

"Why are you really here, Kora?"

She inhaled, caught off-guard by his direct question. "I'm trying to save my brother." Her stomach twisted with guilt. "If I hadn't gone that night…he might still be alive."

Shade stopped abruptly, and she almost ran into him as he turned to face her. He was so close. Too close. Vulnerability shuddered through her body, but she continued in a quieter tone, "I knew he was keeping something from me." Kora remembered the tension in the crowd that night before her world had fallen apart. "I didn't expect the attack. Maybe if I hadn't been there, William would have gotten out. Instead, he protected me. He saved me and lost his life." She held his gaze, unable to turn away from the truth.

Shade swallowed, and she saw the battle in his eyes. His hand rose to hover near her shoulder then fell, and he stepped back to put distance between them.

Kora let out a shuddered breath. "The truth is that I'm not ready to talk about it. He died in front of me. I should apologize, but what better way than to do everything within my ability to save him?" She shook her head, brow furrowing, and she looked down at the space between them. Couldn't look into those ocean blue eyes as she admitted her guilt. "This is my chance to prove myself and find out what I'm capable of. The guilt has been eating me alive. And it breaks my heart to think I was the one who held his hand, helpless, as I told him a story—watched him bleed in my arms. Had to say goodbye when it should have been me in his place."

Shade stepped closer, his fingers brushed her jaw and slid under her chin, forcing her gaze to meet his. "It's not your fault, Kora. And I know William doesn't have a single regret about his choice that night. Fate has a way of dealing their own blow, but death wasn't ready for you yet."

She jerked her head in an attempt to break his stare, but Shade didn't let go of her chin. "Don't back down now. Because I'm telling you the truth—not placating you with words you want to hear. It's not your fault that William is here. The goal is for you to return, unharmed, to the living world. You're meant to live. To be a reminder to all who he left behind that William had been a blessing. He needs you to return home and do that for him."

Her eyes were clear as they bore into his, and he took his point home. "Because they love you."

Kora inhaled deep but didn't break their stare. She wanted to believe him. Knew he meant those words. But it wasn't that simple. Shade dropped his hand to his side, and she suddenly became aware of how close they were.

Immortal.

He stepped back. "Come on."

This time she stepped in alongside him as they walked, shoulder to shoulder. "Thank you," she whispered.

"Sometimes we need others to remind us of what we can't see."

She shouldn't be enjoying his closeness, but she did. And maybe he did too. "Is that why you left the Isles of Nekrós? Because others didn't see you?"

His jaw flexed. "In the Isles of Nekrós, there isn't anyone *left* to see you."

The pixie came to mind. The one who seemed protective of him. "What about Taea?"

Shade's shoulders drew back. "Not always." He gave her a half smile. "Before her was Raz." There was something inexplicable in his tone. "He was my pixie, born from my first laugh."

"First laugh? I thought that was a part of the myth?"

He shook his head. "Every pixie is born from a god's first laugh. They are wholly their own, but there is a sense of camaraderie that always remains between them. Taea's god bored her. Or so she says. Then she showed up here, looking for Raz."

"What happened to him?" A note of concern audible in her voice.

"He left," he whispered. "Why wouldn't he though? No one wants to stay with the dead when there is so much living to do. That's when dealing with the souls in Nekrós became more difficult."

Kora reached across and squeezed his hand, then quickly let go. "I'm sorry."

He nodded and continued forward again. She didn't press the matter further. Instead, they followed the twist and turns of the path and dodged long trunks or pesky brush that tried to prick their skin.

Chapter 23
Kora

They reached a small river that flowed down from the top of the highest peak. "This leads to the waterfall that feeds their lagoon." Shade pointed upstream towards another fork in the path. "We can cross from that log there."

She let him take the lead as they reached the crossing point. "It was nice to not rush around. I saw more of the forest by not flying." And had an opportunity to search for the pomegranate. Unnecessary, really, since the only trees were growing near the lagoon.

Shade chuckled. "You don't like to fly?"

"It's not really me doing the flying, it's you. Although it's the closest I'll probably get to the real thing." She smiled. "I used to lay on the ground in my garden and watch the birds fly overhead. There was a part of me that wished to join them and see the world from their viewpoint." Her mouth puckered at a memory that settled in her mind.

"What is that look for?"

She winced. "Well, it's a little embarrassing."

He paused. "We all have embarrassing stories. Maybe one day I'll share one of my own."

She considered the proposition. "Fine." She sighed. "Once I was changing when I saw a flock of pigeons flying into my garden from my window. I'd recently planted my first experimental seeds of squash and eggplant. Without thinking, I ran down the stairs and out the door. I scared the birds away. Just in time for them to poop all over me from fear."

Shade laughed, his head tilted back. "Where?" He stuttered out the word, trying to stop himself from snorting. "Where did it land?"

She couldn't contain the giggle. "Well, that's the worst part."

He watched her, his mouth quirking. He wasn't doing a great job at suppressing a grin.

"I hadn't finished getting dressed. I ran out in my chemise and drawers. The neighbor was as shocked as I was as reality had come back to me. His eyes were so wide and his daughter started laughing. So, I walked back inside, covered in bird droppings."

This time when he laughed, he tripped over a log and fell into the grass causing a fit of fresh laughter. She stood over him and attempted to keep a straight face but failed as she joined in. It *was* funny. Now.

When he quieted, he laid still in the grass and looked up at the blue sky. Kora sat beside him with her legs stretched in front of her and leaned back against her arms. "I haven't laughed like that in a long time," she admitted.

"Neither have I," Shade agreed, a smile across his face. "Not a true laugh anyway."

She analyzed him, her gaze discretely sweeping over his body. A breeze danced over the grassy knoll, and she inhaled the salty scent of the air. A reminder to concentrate. On other things. Not him.

"Come." Shade pushed himself up to his feet. "We need to climb down now. Ready?"

She took his outstretched hand. "Ready." He pulled her to her feet, her body filling with static as she brushed against him to catch her balance.

They walked single file on a narrow pathway alongside sharp, sheer rocks. She tried to ignore the dangers and kept her attention on her footing, but it was hard to do. Kora's heart leapt to her throat as her feet slid on the stone, her arms flying out, but Shade caught her around the waist before she fell over the side. Their eyes met, his arms steadying her. She bit her bottom lip, and he stilled, his gaze sliding over her mouth. She breathed in deep, wondering what his lips would taste like.

He swallowed. Deeply. "All right?"

She nodded, and he stepped away. His hand grazed hers again, and she relished in the feel of his skin against hers and steadied at his touch.

At the last curve, the path evened out to a small beach set against the slate wall they'd just traversed. Long boughs of leaves hung over the water in odd angles and tree trunks broke through the rock to offer shade over the pristine waters. The lagoon stretched out before them in hues of teals and navy. A flat stone in the center jutted above the water in layers.

Kora gasped as she spotted the figures on top. Two nereids were sunning themselves. The first was laid out on the top stone, hands behind a head of long red hair with their scaled orange and yellow tail waving up and down. The second was curled around the stone's edge at the bottom, braiding their thick lilac hair.

"They're beautiful," she murmured.

"And will drown you in the next breath," Shade reminded. "Stay near the wall."

Kora pressed herself against the slate and watched as Shade waved a greeting. "Good day."

Red Hair turned around onto their stomach and scanned Shade. They raised up on their arms to jump into the water when they tilted their head in Kora's direction. "What brings you here, Immortal?"

"I need a question answered." Shade crossed his arms. "Before you swim away again." Shade had explained that they frightened easily, but with Kora's presence, their curiosity might be enough to ensure they remain a captivated audience. At least long enough for him to barter for information.

Purple Hair dropped the unfinished braid and peered over Shade's shoulder at Kora. "Who is that?"

"Never mind her." Kora didn't intervene, letting Shade take the lead. "I'm here to ask about a pomegranate tree."

Red Hair rolled their eyes. "You're meant to be the ruler of this realm—is there something you don't know about in your own domain?"

The second slid into the water, disappearing from view before resurfacing at the edge near Shade's feet. "Don't poke fun, Andromeda." They pinned their gaze on Kora. "Do you like to swim, Little Human?"

Shade bent down to Purple Hair's level. "She doesn't want to now. Would you like to do me a favor and check the depths of your lagoon for a tree?"

Andromeda scoffed. "Magna, don't listen to them." They pinned a glare on Shade. "We have orders not to help you."

"From whom?" Shade grimaced.

"From me." Another appeared from around the rock in the center of the lagoon, blue scaled arms crossed over his bare chest. He kept his attention on Shade, but Kora pushed further against the rock wall, the stone now biting into her back. She didn't want to be in his viewpoint as every part of her body screamed at her to hide.

The new arrival glared. "At least not until you've answered a few questions of my own."

Shade pinched his eyes closed and rubbed his temples. "What are you doing here, Halieus?"

"What? I can't come to visit my brothers? Thought maybe it was time for a little reunion and to find out what trouble you'd been causing now." Halieus grinned, shaking his head and causing his blond hair to slide behind his shoulders.

Brother. Why was the King of the Sea here? Kora swallowed, uncertain what to do with herself. She didn't know much about him except that he lorded over all water. It seemed he was another brother Shade didn't look forward to seeing.

Magna swam back towards the center rock and slid upon it, dipping their tail in the water with a predatory gaze on Kora. Shade shifted his position in front of her, and his brother tilted his head from Shade to stare at her.

The smile that stretched across his face made Kora's stomach churn. "Who are you?"

"None of your concern," Shade bit out.

"Can the girl not speak for herself?" Halieus chuckled. "I didn't picture you choosing such a submissive consort. Maybe I was wrong about you—"

Kora would not be talked about that way. "Not a consort, thank you very much."

"Then, what other reason would a human be here?" Halieus cocked his head, his gaze leering over her. "Alive."

Kora gave a placating smile. "We need information. If a pomegranate tree happens to be in the lagoon, it would be wonderful if you could fetch one of the fruits, please."

Halieus's head fell back in laughter. "Fetch it? Do you know who I am? I don't fetch." He snorted, catching his breath with a hand on his chest. "This fruit—what is it you need it for?" He turned to Shade with a quizzical look. "And what is a mortal doing here? Alive."

"Good question. Not one you get an answer to," Shade snapped.

Kora moved in a step beside Shade, sticking close enough to feel his skin against hers. Now that she had already been seen, she wasn't going to hide behind him. "I have need of it."

Shade kept his expression neutral as Halieus considered her explanation. The nereids chuckled under their breaths as Halieus's gaze narrowed. "Interesting. And who gave you this quest?"

Kora pursed her lips.

"I see." Halieus's smile darkened. He stepped out, treading water until his body rose above the surface. "This is an interesting turn of events."

Her eyes widened as Halieus walked on water, his scales turning to skin—and thankfully a wrap appeared—although it left little to the imagination with its mid-thigh length and hip slit. The immortal stopped in front of Kora. "Would you like to go for a swim? You could join me in my domain instead of staying here in Nekrós. The Depth is vast and as beautiful as you are." He took hold of Kora's hand and pressed a kiss on her knuckles.

Fear transformed into a simmering rage and had Kora tearing her palm from his grip to slap Halieus across the face. "Don't ever touch me again."

Halieus stilled and stared at her. Shade stepped into the space between Kora and his brother. "You heard her."

With anxious splashes, the nereids disappeared. The Sea King clenched his teeth, a dangerous calm stretching over his stone-like features. He straightened and drew back his shoulders. "There's no tree here. Leave now."

Shade pointed to the water behind his brother. "Search for it. This is my domain, not yours. Here, the waters belong to the dead."

"This is not yours anymore, Shade," Halieus spat out. "You've abandoned your post, therefore it's free range." A grin spread over his face. "Maybe it's time I took over. There is enough water here for me to gain control, don't you think?"

"Out," Shade ordered. "We are asking the nereids for help. The ones I protected and you ignored. You shouldn't be involved. Or here."

Electric currents sizzled in the air, tension building as the two immortals glared, Shade's hands fisted at his side. Kora inhaled, the air stuck in her lungs. A darkness edged between the two gods and seemed to seep from Shade. A new side to the playful, mischievous god of Nekrós.

He reached for Kora. "Then I'm taking—" Suddenly, Halieus was flung back. Shade appeared behind him, and his finger flicked upwards. Pitch black hands protruded from the water, grasped hold of his brother, and forced him into the depths. Kora's eyes widened and she reached for Shade but stopped herself, noting the power exuding off him like ink.

"Stop," Halieus yelled, fighting against the limbs and appendages that pulled at him.

"Don't. Touch. *Her*. Ever. Again." Shade didn't back down, his concentration solely on his brother.

Was he losing himself to this power? Consumed? Kora gripped his arm, and Shade faltered, the black ink shifting to gray. "Shade," she whispered, and pressed her palm to his chest, a thrum rumbling at the contact. A sense of awe and curiosity had her giving him a small shake. "You can stop now."

Shade blinked and his power cooled, stilled. The hands fell away from Halieus who was half submerged as the darkness evaporated. "Find me the fruit, Halieus. Or I'll call them back."

His brother glared with his long hair tangled, and scratches that marred his chest and arms were already beginning to fade.

Kora took a tentative step forward. "This fruit is all I need. Please? Or next time I won't stop him."

Halieus's brow furrowed, his gaze assessing as it slid over her body. "No." He sunk into the water and out of sight.

Kora fell to her knees with a gasp, the sliver of hope she'd had gone again. Shade dragged her away from the edge. "Not so close. Just because we can't see them doesn't mean they won't grab you."

"Can you do that again? Call them back and make Halieus help?" Kora asked.

He shook his head. "No. Not when I can't see him." Shade assisted her to her feet and ran a hand over her hair. "But I have other means to get what we want. Come along."

They walked along the edge of the lagoon, Shade careful to keep Kora on the thin strip of beach and as far from the water as possible. When they reached the mouth of the lagoon, Shade called upon the shadowed hands again. They began to build a wall from stone and rock, cutting the access of the Depth to the lagoon.

"How?" Kora asked, watching with her mouth agape and eyes wide.

He didn't answer right away, concentrating on the task. When they were nearly done, water no longer flowed into the lagoon with the dam barring its path. Shade held out a hand and she didn't hesitate as she took it. He pulled her close and wrapped an arm around her waist before scooping her off her feet and pushing into the sky. "I have power over the dead. Just those who are on Mizéria or those within the Váthos who never had payment to cross."

Kora's grip around his neck tightened. "Those were the forgotten that we saw the other night?"

Shade nodded. "Does that frighten you?"

Kora's mouth parted, and her eyes searched his face. "They did that night on the beach but not this time. Not as much as I think they should. Your control over them was different."

The truth of her words and his closeness had her heartbeat quickening. He had to feel it. Her body must be betraying her. But if he knew, he didn't comment.

Chapter 24

Kora

Shade had dropped her off before disappearing into the trees with nothing more than a nod as a goodbye. Kora watched him fly away, left alone at the treehouse with only her thoughts for company. Her brothers must be with the Lost Souls, wasting time looking for a fruit only Shade could find. These were the moments when she felt guilty that she hadn't told her brother the truth about the pomegranate. But after all that took place with Halieus, and her confusing feelings over Shade, she didn't want to be alone with her thoughts.

A strong embrace, corded muscle, firm body—heat. She blushed and buried her face in her hands. It was his words that had made her take a longer look at him. The laughter that had bubbled out after he stumbled. Not the immature recklessness that he usually succumbed to, but the joy she'd seen written on his face. His admission about always being left alone—she couldn't blame him. The pain was written all over his face and in his tone.

The way he had said it so plainly, for a moment, she believed him.

"It's not your fault."

With a groan, she pushed up to her feet and stormed down the trail towards the Lost Souls Camp. Anything would be better than wallowing in guilt or thinking about a certain immortal. Not when her brother's life was on the line. When her home was on the line.

When she reached Camp, it was nearly empty. Except for *her*. Astari sat on a porch, rocking in her chair. As Kora broke through the brush and their eyes met, the soul stopped and stared.

Kora skidded to a halt, uncertain where to go. "Um, do you know where everyone is?"

Astari sighed. "Yes, they'll be back soon. Your brothers and the others went to search along the outskirts of Pixie Meadow."

"You didn't want to go with them?" It was awkward to talk to the soul after the incident. They hadn't been alone or even attempted to interact since the attack on the beach.

Astari shook her head. "No. I've been thinking and contemplating a lot."

She looked so sad. Lost even. Kora inhaled a deep breath. "Listen, nothing has happened between Shade and I. Really, he's just helping me search the island for a way to return home."

"I'm aware of this supposed fruit. Sounds like there is more to it, but what do I care?" Astari snapped her mouth shut, then dropped her chin to her chest. "I'm sorry. You just bring out this other side of me."

"I've noticed."

Astari bit her bottom lip. "It's not that I'm upset about Shade. I realized that I don't even care about him like that anymore. All I wanted was his attention, and I wasn't getting it. He'd left me behind a long time ago." She shook her head. "The thing is I never expected anything from him—not when I'm dead. But I kind of have you to thank you for the fact that I've realized something."

"Oh?" Kora took a tentative step closer.

The soul nodded. "I think it's time for me to cross. Honestly, I think I was meant to a long time ago, but I was too scared."

Her steps brought Kora to the base of the porch. "Are you sure? Maybe after all this is over, that will change."

Astari laughed. "No, it won't change." She smiled at Kora.

"And I've never felt so free until I admitted that to you right now." Her smile widened. "I'm ready."

Kora saw a lightness in the soul's expression she'd hadn't seen in the short time she'd known her. "Then what do we do? Don't you need a coin?"

"I do need a coin. Do you—" She swallowed. "Will you help me find one? If we come across the others, then we can ask for their help. I would love to work with the souls one last time before I cross. For so long, I've been staying away from them, and I want to have a little fun before I go."

Kora swallowed, suddenly self-conscious. "Are you sure you want my help?"

Astari stood, fixing the grass skirt she wore. "Yes. If you want to, that is. I wasn't very kind to you and—"

"You've apologized. We can move on now, don't you think?" Kora smiled back at the soul. This was something tangible she could do for someone. Support Astari with this choice. She wondered then if this was how Shade felt? She pushed him from her thoughts before he could settle there and stepped backwards towards the path. "Come on. Let's start looking, and maybe we'll catch up to the others."

The two of them rushed into the forest, searching under shrubs and kicking over rocks, the late afternoon light slipping through the canopy to enlighten the path and plants.

As she searched for the coin, Kora couldn't help but search for the pomegranate tree too, although she knew without Shade there was little chance of finding it. The island had started to feel smaller with each passing day. Somehow, she needed to talk Shade into taking her to the other Isles of Nekrós. But that was a thought for later.

Astari grumbled about how many places they had found the coins in the past, berating herself for staying on the isle for so long. "I don't know why I was denying the inevitable. I hadn't been having fun for a while now."

Kora spotted something glinting right off the trail and

reached into a bramble, careful not to scratch her hand. She froze. The plant expanded, parting away from her arm as if allowing access. She removed her hand quickly, and the plant moved back into place.

What just happened?

Astari's voice brought Kora back to the present. "When I first arrived, it was a relief. No rush to be judged. Didn't have to worry about eternity. Just adventures and making friends. Even Shade was a perfect distraction from the idea of death. But that was fun too. Easygoing. Gave us freedom we never really had. In the end, Shade was just an excuse to stay."

"Why do you think you waited?" Kora absently hoped she didn't sound toying as she stared from her hand to the plant. Was the island enchanted?

Astari climbed down from the tree she'd been searching. She wiped the dirt off her hand and scrunched up her face. "Is it strange to say that I was frightened of eternity?"

Kora considered the answer. "No, not really."

The soul laughed, a genuine sound that held sunshine and happiness. "It's forever. I know I'll be on Contentment. I had a decent life and nothing extraordinary happened to place me anywhere else. The idea of just floating around, no longer feeling anything beyond a restful quiet made me uneasy. But I think I've come to realize that I was due."

"Sounds like a healthy outlook." Kora smiled absently. "When it's my time, I hope I feel the same way."

She considered testing the plant again, but Astari was already walking further down the path and the search for the drachma was meant to be fun. She had enough on her plate without adding any more mysteries.

"I don't think Shade would want you to cross over."

Astari's matter-of-fact tone had Kora stumbling. "What? Why? I thought it was your decision to make. We are usually fighting or annoyed with each other. Besides, it's obvious he just gets bored. I wouldn't keep his attention for long." She didn't want his attention. Kora shook off stray thoughts, and nearly smacked herself in the face when she realized she was rambling.

The soul smirked. "There is something completely different in his gaze when he looks at you. He looks like he could be consumed by you. He's never looked that way at me. Or any other soul. Maybe it's because you're alive."

Before Kora could ask what she meant, a crack of a branch startled her.

"Hey, what's going on here?" Curly broke through the trees, her gaze pinned on Astari.

Kora was thankful for the interruption. Especially now that her thoughts had drifted back to territory she had been attempting to escape.

"What are you two doing out here?" William appeared, his wary gaze shifting between them and his eyes narrowed on the blond soul.

"I've decided to cross over." Astari smiled. "Kora and I were searching for a coin."

"Hunt?" Branch pushed through the growing crowd. "Are we having a hunt?"

Kora giggled as Astari shook her head. "Not exactly. But if you want to help, I'd love to have you all join in. I know I've been distant for a while now. It would be nice to spend time with my friends before I go. I'm not rushing it, but it will be soon."

Curly wrapped an arm through the crook of Astari's elbow. "Let's do it."

The boys chanted 'hunt' and began their search. They made it to the beach and spread out, staying near the tree line. With Shade present somewhere on the isle, they should be safe. The sun was reaching towards the horizon when others began playing a game of tag while they looked, prolonging the task. Sometime later, Astari screamed with delight and held up the coin covered in seaweed, the last of the sunlight glinting against its surface. "I found one."

The group whooped and hollered. Branch, Curly, and a few

others tackled her to the ground, her grip tight on her prize as she fell laughing under them.

William came up beside Kora and wrapped an arm around her shoulder. "This was fun."

"It was." She nudged him gently with her hip. Michael trotted over to them after disentangling himself from the mess of souls. "Can we do that again?"

Her twin bent over and pulled Michael into his arms. "Another time. Now, we should head back to Camp."

Chapter 25
Shade

The following morning, Shade had settled at the fire pit. Michael snored peacefully from the hut he had finished the previous day. He'd arrived to find William sleeping with his back against the door of Shade's treehouse, and a curious bush of green leaves that had grown around the base of the trunk. Blue buds peeked from long stalks, and he glanced over the bark of the tree itself and pursed his lips. Was that new growth on the trunk? What was happening to his home?

He nudged William who was on his feet in a breath. "You were sleeping."

William ran a hand through his hair. "Old habits die hard."

Shade only nodded. "You can head to the camp or inside if you want. I'll wait here." He waved towards the fire. "When she wakes, I'm taking her straight to Skull Isle."

William's shoulders slumped. "All right." He headed inside and gently closed the door behind him.

Shade waited like he said he would, his mind wandering to Halieus's presence. Prior to Captain's appearance and settling on the *Charon*, the Sea King had been the last of his brothers to visit him in Nekrós. That had been at least a century ago. Halieus had asked him questions about the Isles. How things were faring. Were the souls behaving. As if souls did anything but float around in contentment or suffering depending on their location. It had been a strange conversation then and upon thought, still was now. Especially since that *check in*, he hadn't returned.

Deep in thought, he jumped slightly when Kora emerged from the treehouse, caught off guard by her sudden presence. A yawn escaped her as she stretched, his quilt surrounding her in a shroud as her arms held it aloft. Need permeated to the depths of his core. At the way her dress hung against her skin. The peek of her finger-combed hair in a mess, looking as though she'd been thoroughly caressed during the night. He wanted to be the one that caused that look of contentment. Of want. Desire. All the things he should never ask for.

"Morning." He cleared his throat. "I think you might need new clothes. I'll ask Curly today."

"No rush. My dress is still in one piece, at least." She sat down on the log across from him, his quilt wrapped around her shoulder even though the temperature was always the same— never too hot or cold—just right. Her hair framed her face, and those amber eyes danced with light from the fire. Her ribbon was tied around her wrist today, and he wanted to reach out and touch the smooth satin.

Damn! He ran his hand over his face and turned away.

He felt Kora's gaze on him. A warm caress. "I didn't know I could catch an immortal off guard. I didn't mean to frighten you."

His shoulders slumped. All the hope that she would ignore his blunder gone. When did he get so discombobulated? That wasn't like him. "I was deep in thought. That's all."

"I didn't know you were capable of deep thinking." Her smile widened.

"Oh. Am I supposed to appreciate your assumption?" He frowned, trying to hide that he did, in fact, appreciate the fact that she assessed him at all.

She laughed, and he knew he shouldn't enjoy the sound. "I didn't mean it that way. You always seem so spontaneous."

He tilted his head, a small snort escaping. "I'm immortal. There is plenty of time to think—and then to make it seem as though it's from off the top of my head."

Kora bit her bottom lip. "Well, what were you thinking about?"

You. But he forced the thought back as soon as it popped into his mind. "Are you ready to head to Skull Isle?"

Kora smiled, and a warmth he hadn't known before expanded in his chest. He didn't name it. Couldn't allow himself to.

"Yes." She stood up and headed for the treehouse. "Give me just a minute to put the quilt away."

"You also might want to mention to your brother that we are leaving," he suggested.

She turned to glare at him. Any excitement that had previously existed in Kora's expression gone. Her lips formed a thin line, and slow and steady, she met his gaze with a piercing one of her own. "You know how you allow others to make decisions for themselves? All the same for me," she said with a curt tone.

Shade stepped around the log he'd been sitting on to put more space between them. "It's polite."

Kora rolled her eyes. "Since when have you been polite?" He opened his mouth to object, but she turned on her heels and stormed towards Shade's tree. "I'll tell him."

When she appeared again, her expression had darkened a shade further. "Let's go." She crossed her arms.

"Do you want me to fly you?"

Her mouth tightened before she nodded. They flew in silence as he curved with the land below towards Skull Isle. When the rocky opening of the cave came into view, he cleared his throat. "When we get there, I need you to listen to everything I say, do you understand?" Shade tried to ignore the warmth that had spread through his limbs and skin at every point her body touched his.

"I'm mortal, not incapable," Kora grumbled.

Shade sighed. He should have been prepared for her response.

"You do know William and I are concerned you'll do anything, even if it's dangerous, to save him."

"Of course I'll do anything for him, but that doesn't mean I'm not thinking through my actions first," she scoffed. "And do you really expect me to believe the God of the Dead is concerned about me—a mere mortal?" Her mouth was a thin line as she glared.

A desire to make her smile moved through him, but he knew now wasn't the time for sarcasm. "No, I don't think you believe it. But you should. I'm here, aren't I? Giving you the chance you want."

"You said free will was important to you? I guess I'm trying to understand why you are making me feel like I need to prove that I'm capable." There was a hint of venom in her voice.

Shade considered her question. She smiled, a sensation tickling his neck at the sight, and he knew she thought she'd outsmarted him. "I've never doubted your gumption or drive. But I also want to protect you from heartache and loss. You have a rare chance to be with your brother when you thought him lost forever. Yet, instead, you're here with me. Maybe this gift—this fruit you seek—is more about the chance to ask the tough questions. How he feels? If you have any reason to feel guilty."

Kora went stiff in his arms. "You know how he felt?"

Shade nodded. "I know the stories of every one of the dead that arrive on the Isles of Nekrós. I know how your brother felt —" He stopped short. There were things he should never share, and specific experiences were one of them.

"How..." She cleared her throat. "How did he feel?"

"That's his story to tell. You should ask him." His voice dropped to a whisper. "While you can."

He didn't meet her gaze, feeling it penetrating his skin as he landed at the sandy entrance that led to the cave. The land was flat, a large rock in the center of the small island formed the shape of a human skull—a dome of stone with cracks and fissures. Jagged stalactites hung at the top of the cave like teeth, and two large gaping holes were above the mouth allowing in light and gave eyes to the monstrosity.

Kora bit her bottom lip. "Do you really think a tree can be found in a cave?"

"There is more in there than you can imagine." He winked and she blushed. It was cute—the way the pink brought out her freckles. *Damn it to hells.*

Shade cleared his throat. "Where are the others searching today?"

"Curly mentioned that they might explore the western mountain ridges." Kora took a seat and began untying the laces of her boots. "I think Curly might have an interest in my brother. Is that common?"

He turned away, watching the water brush against the rocks, anything but the way her nimble fingers worked at the knots. "It happens sometimes. Most just look for companionship and friendship. With Curly's story, I wouldn't expect it though—but I've been wrong in the past. She's a good soul. One of the better ones."

"So not your type then?" It was the first time she even broached the subject. "Unlike Astari, that is."

Shade stiffened and sliced a glance in her direction. "Astari is complicated, but our...relationship has been over for some time now. When you're dead, there is a loneliness that wraps around you here on the isle. Finding comfort in mortal practices can help. Even for me." His gaze grew distant even as he looked in her direction, a darkness edged around him. Love—a figment of his imagination. Desire wasn't though...and she was eliciting a touch of that now with her line of questioning, making it difficult not to cause her to flush further in response. See if she'd play with him.

Kora stood up, brushing the sand off her backside. "You get lonely surrounded by all of this?"

"Does that surprise you? Death is my friend—the dead are my responsibility. They aren't one and the same. Not exactly a place for fostering relationships or strong emotional connections. Especially when everyone leaves at some point."

"Then, why are you here and not fulfilling your responsibility? It's not like you're in the mortal world—you're here on Anamoní." Kora's tone held more curiosity than judgment, but the question caused him to jerk back a step.

"Like I said—complicated." He started walking, not looking to see if she followed. The sound of her feet against stone as she jogged to catch up informed him of her location.

The problem was that even if Kora was working for Captain, and if they didn't have immortality to contend with, Shade believed she wouldn't be complicated for him. Exasperating, stubborn—definitely. Uncomplicated hadn't worked out for him though. Easy hadn't been an option since Raz, his pixie, left. After a lifetime of friendship, and just like that the pixie had abandoned him. Like everyone in his life had. Why expect that anyone else would be different?

Shade stopped right before stepping into the water, and she did the same. "The tide will be out for a little longer."

"Is it going to be dark in there?" Shade liked that every emotion showed on her face—fear at the forefront.

"Don't worry, it's all handled." Shade cleared his throat and grinned. "After all of this, you aren't scared of the dark, are you?"

She whirled to face him. "I won't pretend like this nightmare isn't real and hide from it. Not when there is a chance the pomegranate is there. So no, I'm not scared of the dark."

Her amber eyes danced with fire. He'd struck a nerve. "I know. Otherwise, I wouldn't be here with you now."

Her mouth snapped shut. He brushed past her—a touch he played off as accidental. Yet, he was becoming addicted to the action, to the sound of her heart skipping a beat. To take the chance to inhale a breath of her scent of wildflowers.

Gritting his teeth, he waded towards the rocks that led into the mouth of Skull Isle.

Chapter 26
Kora

As he ventured in, a part of Kora considered staying in place to see what he did and if he'd even notice. But she wouldn't be obstinate. Not when time was limited. The water swirled around her lower calves as she stepped deeper into the surf. It took her no time to reach the first of the stepping stones where Shade was jumping from one to the next. She pulled herself up onto it, then turned, drenched up to her knees in the water. "I thought you said the tide would be low."

"It is. The land within the cave is higher than it is here. You'll see." Shade held out his hand, and she took it before he hauled her up. Her foot slipped on the wet rock and his other whipped out to grab her hip, settling her while she caught her balance. "Got your footing?"

She stilled and stared at his hand curving over her waist. It was familiar. Comforting. A warmth permeated at his touch. She wouldn't allow herself to meet his gaze. He quickly withdrew his hand, and she swallowed. "Thank you."

He let go of her other hand and took the lead. Each step was a small hop, nothing too far but the rocks were slick from the salt water and algae. She slipped again, her leg plunged into the surf, slicing against the stone. A hiss broke from her lips as she eagled her arms, then gasped as she started to fall into the water before

Shade scooped her into his arms and flew them to solid ground. "Everything all right?" he asked as he carefully put her down.

She pulled up the hem of her dress up and looked at her leg. "The rock cut my ankle. That's all."

He looked down at the crimson blood dripping down her calf into the frothy water at her feet. He froze, staring at the injury. "What should we do?"

"Nothing." She shooed him forward. "I can take a closer look once we get to the opening."

Shade swallowed, then turned away with a nod. "I can—" But he stopped immediately when she glared.

With one last leap, he reached Skull Isle before turning to face Kora. She jumped across and he caught hold of her, ensuring she didn't fall again. "Take a seat and brush the sand off. Infection can happen if you aren't careful."

Kora's brow crinkled as he tore a portion of the sleeve from his shirt. The act revealed a tan muscular bicep that had her averting her gaze. Propriety. Something she needed to hold onto. Not the memory of his defined arms wrapped around her as they flew. Or the way he held her hand. The touch strong and warm yet light and gentle.

He held the torn piece of cloth out to her. "Hold this." She glanced down at the fabric in his hands before sitting down. He crouched and cupped water in his hands and used it to wash off the cut. Kora winced at the sting of salt water but didn't move. Wasn't even certain she was breathing as he added, "The cavern is deep and stops at a lagoon. If there is a chance the fruit is anywhere in here, that's it."

She hissed again as he washed the sand free from the cut as best he could. Shade used the hem of his shirt to wipe off the last of the grime and blood that was already beginning to cake her skin. When he finished, he took the cloth back and wrapped it like a makeshift bandage around her leg.

Through all of this, she tried to ignore the sensation of his fingers brushing against her. The way his gaze slid over her exposed skin. A final check to the knot he'd made, and he nodded. "There you go. It should keep the worst of things out until we can get it cleaned up at Camp."

"Thank you." The words were a whisper. Their eyes met. Instinctively, she bit her lip, and he tracked the movement.

Shade cleared his throat and straightened. The corner of her mouth lifted into a small smile, and he returned it.

Holding out his hand, she took it, and he pulled her to her feet, teetering slightly. From the injury, of course, not his touch and close proximity. His brow furrowed and glanced down at her injury. "Is it all right?"

She held out her leg for him to get a look. "It's holding. Really, it's fine."

"Good. Can't have anything happen to you under my watch, or I'll get a stern talking to from William."

"Why do you both do that?" The words rushed from her mouth.

His brow furrowed. "Do what?"

"Underestimate me?" Like everyone at home. Her parents. Society. All those men paraded through her dining room.

"Trust me when I say that it's not that we underestimate you. It's that we know how much you're willing to give."

She swallowed as that playful smirk of his appeared again, then he turned and continued into the skull's maw.

The two walked beside each other as they ventured deeper into the cave. When darkness began to encompass them, a light curled around the corner. Warm and bright. When they turned, a torch waited, and he pulled it from the wall. "We put this here a long time ago. I can see in the dark, but I assume you cannot?"

"Does it ever go out?"

He winked, a smile leading to his dimple. "No. Magic."

Kora blushed and looked down the cavern, hoping he didn't see the pink on her cheeks. "How am I going to find anything when we get deeper? There isn't nearly enough light from that one torch."

Shade's smile widened. "You'll see."

Kora was trusting this immortal beyond reason. The further they walked, the more uncertain she became. Darkness was not her friend as it was Shade's and even with the torchlight, she soon had to hold his hand just to feel less alone. It was terrifying and foreboding. The walls were pressing in on her from all sides, and a damp, musty scent causing the cavern to feel hauntingly dangerous.

He started chattering about a few of the Lost Souls, and Kora concentrated on his voice. "Branch has been here the longest, and I think he's waiting for his family. He was close to his siblings and if one passes on, he'll join them. He and Smalls were close before she left…"

The stories continued, and she found herself calming to the rhythm of his voice. He crouched down at one point, and she followed suit, the top of her head just missing the lowered ceiling. She inhaled a sharp breath at the sudden compactness of their path.

"Just a little farther," he reassured with a squeeze of her hand.

It was little comfort as her heart raced faster against her chest. Panic was beginning to overtake her senses when a glimmer of blue and green became visible beyond the torchlight. "What is that?"

"Almost there and you can see." He peered at her, most of his face hidden by shadow. "I think you'll like it."

Shade lifted the torch as the cave's ceiling rose, and they stepped into a deep cavern. Kora's mouth widened in awe as she turned in a small circle, taking in the colors around her that illuminated the space. In the center of the cave was a lagoon with glowing blue and green water. From what, she couldn't tell. But more importantly, in the middle of the water stood a large tree with thick branches of leaves that hung down, hiding its trunk from view. Hope rose, a smile spreading as she scanned the boughs. And just as quickly as her heart raced with excitement, she swallowed back disappointment when not a single fruit was visible. "Is this it?"

Shade moved around the lagoon, the path only wide enough to walk single file. "I don't know."

Her eyes widened at the green and blue light that illuminated the water and spread along the walls of the circular cavern. A musty scent mixed with salt and a touch of florals. "What is emitting that light?"

"Algae." He led her to the cavern walls and pointed to the bioluminescent particles stuck against it. "See?"

"I've never seen anything like it." Her eyes widened at the small plants stretched against the wall, the ground, and that floated in the water. "Intriguing."

Shade shrugged. "I don't know how it glows in the dark, but I guess that's just the magic of Anamoní."

She peered into the water, and the floating particles reflected light onto the walls and ceiling of the cave. "It's beautiful."

"It reminds me of star clusters throughout the sky when I'm flying at night." Shade raised his gaze to the ceiling above.

Kora found herself glancing at him. "I'd love to see that someday."

Their eyes met. His darkening slightly as they lingered, and she blinked, turning away from the desire to have that look—his intensity—always directed at her. Despite his lean body, the way his copper hair dipped over his brow, or the chiseled face and dazzling blue eyes, danger lurked around him.

Shade wasn't a young man—he was an immortal. It was best she remembered that. Even if he was one of the most intriguing beings she'd ever encountered. The task Captain had given her itched at the back of her mind. Suddenly, she realized how close he was. That her hand was still in his. The feel of his skin warming to her touch. The scent of bergamot wafted from him, wrapping around her. She grabbed hold of a stray curl and wrapped her finger around it to sidetrack her thoughts. Last night, she had taken a dip in a small spring and was able to scrub off a layer of grime, and Astari had gifted her a comb that helped untangle her frizzy hair. She wondered if he noticed and then just as quickly, she reminded herself she shouldn't be thinking like that.

He grinned as if he knew where her mind had wandered off to. Heat rushed up her neck to her cheeks.

The algae began to glow brighter, pulsing along with Kora's quickening heartbeat. Shade tilted his head. "Hm, it's never done that before."

She searched the space, glad to have a reason to look away from him. When her body relaxed, she pushed back her growing feelings. The algae dulled to its normal glow.

He shrugged and turned back to the water. "That was strange." They shared a glance before Kora quickly looked back towards the tree. Shade was quiet for another moment, then said, "I don't see a fruit, but let's take a closer look at this tree."

She barely heard him as she edged closer to the water, scanning the tree. A plunk sounded to her left. Kora scanned the water, searching the rings on the water for a circular object but it quickly sunk into the dark abyss. "Wait, what's that?"

"I'll look." Shade released her hand, walking along the edge to the place where they had heard the sound. "I think it was a fruit."

"Like a pomegranate?" Her eyes widened, and she ran her fingers through the hanging leaves.

Shade was quiet and when she turned to face him, she found him watching her with a quizzical expression. The look worried her, so she shrugged, calming her expression to one of disinterest. "If so, it could be what we seek."

"Only one way to find out. You check the branches, I'll check the water." Shade stepped towards the edge of the lagoon and pulled his shirt off over his head. His shoulders and chest flexed as he tossed the shirt aside. Pronounced, cut abdominal muscles shifted as he stretched, his trousers hanging low on his hips. And she took it all in—even though she knew she shouldn't. He was breathtaking.

She inhaled deep, feeling her lungs expand as she fell silent.

Her face flushed, every inch of her skin suddenly warm. That's when she realized he wasn't moving and slowly her gaze slid up to find him grinning, dimple and all.

With a roll of her eyes, Kora crossed her arms. "Aren't you going somewhere."

When he dove into the lagoon, his chuckle followed him. Kora rushed to the edge and peered into the water, trying and failing to see past the glow.

"Concentrate," she hissed at herself.

Turning into a blubbering girl was not going to help her save William. Since when did anyone turn her into an open-mouth guppy? He was the cause of her world's decay. Not one to fawn over.

With a huff, she tied her hair back with the ribbon from her wrist as she circled the lagoon, pushing the cascading leaves aside to search for any sign of the red fruit.

Time seemed to pass at a snail's pace and gave her too much time to think. About him. About the way he made her body react. How her mind became blank in his presence. It was when her mind wandered to his shirtless torso that she realized how long he'd been gone, and warning bells went off in her mind. Instinct urged her to jump in, but she reminded herself he couldn't die. At least not by drowning. Right?

When the algae brightened again, as if in time with her pulse, she stared down at her hands. Her mind was playing tricks on her. Or was it the lighting shifting? Was she the cause? Like before with the vines? Or was it magic?

A sudden bubble popped on the surface of the water, and she turned her attention to the lagoon. Preparing in case she needed to find him, she pulled at the edge of her dress, and it was halfway over her head when the sound of splashing water froze her in place.

"Uh, what are you doing?"

If Kora had been red before, now she felt like she was on fire. She hastily pushed her dress down, then covered her face in her hands. "I—" She tried to find words to explain herself, but they got stuck on her tongue. "You—"

She peered through her fingers and caught sight of Shade floating out of the water and onto shore. The smirk—his dimples—told her that he knew exactly what she was thinking. "Well, this is all I found." He held out an bumpy orange fruit. "It's not a pomegranate."

"An orange." Kora inwardly thanked him for the reprieve. "Are you certain there is nothing else?"

He shook his head, droplets splashing and sliding down his skin, sidetracking her once again. *Really, Kora,* she inwardly cursed herself. Shade picked up his shirt and tossed it over his head. She swallowed, trying to ignore how his wet translucent shirt clung to his skin and showed off the defined muscles of his torso.

"If you feel so inclined to check, then after you. The water is deep so don't know how far you'd be able to dive. I searched the floor and looked for any crevices. There was nothing else but shells and rock."

With a grumpy sigh, she reached for the torch he'd left hung at the entrance of the cavern. "Fine. Then where else could it be?"

At his silence, Kora looked up as the seconds passed without a response.

Shade stared in the direction of the opening with a look she had never seen him wear. Then he turned to her with alarm and grabbed hold of her arm. "We must go. Now."

Chapter 27
Kora

"What is it?"

He ignored her question, pulling her onto his back and flew towards the exit. The torch extinguished as it clattered to the floor.

Darkness enveloped her, and if she had been anxious with the light, she was now petrified without it. He didn't put her down as they reached the narrow portion of the cave, and she pressed closer to him as her body thrummed with fear. Although it was already dark, she pinched her eyes shut, trying to hide from the pressure surrounding her as Shade raced through the passageway.

She couldn't bring herself to ask him again for an answer—until she heard a sudden whoosh.

Water sprayed over her, but she forced herself to keep her eyes open. "The tide rose." It was more of a demand than a question and still Shade ignored it, flying them onward. The narrow tunnel finally widened again, and she gripped tighter to him when a chilling wave crashed into them.

"Hold on," he ordered as another splash walloped the side of her body. "Whatever you do, don't let—"

His sentence was cut short as another wave crashed over them. With a scream, Kora tumbled from Shade's back. She inhaled a lungful of water, struggling for the surface and just as she breached, another wave toppled her. Jagged stone cut into her skin, and her head banged against rock. She sputtered, coughing up salt and brine as she tried to stand but before she could find her feet, another wave felled her, forcing her on her knees. She was able to inhale a gulp of fresh air before she was pulled back under.

"Shade!" she called, when she broke free, unable to see him as the water receded. She searched for him, her arms wide and sliding through the water. "Shade!" she screamed as loud as she could before another wave hit her, pulling her down and engulfing her in salt water.

Her head pounded from the impact as she was crushed against the cave floor, and then carried further into the cave. Darkness beckoned, but so did the promise of air. With aching muscles, she swam to the surface, sputtering for air and gasping for breath when she reached it.

Where was Shade? Her eyes adjusted to the darkness. She couldn't see anything but waves and the cavern walls. The smell of salt and dank stone. Her ears rang with the echoing splash of water.

Something rammed into her, and she screamed, batting it away until she recognized the copper hair of the bobbing body. She grabbed hold of Shade and held him unconscious in her arms as they floated on the surface of the water. Her stomach plummeted, her strained muscles fighting her as she held his head above water. Kora swam to the entrance, another wave beginning to swell blocked her escape. She gripped Shade tighter, then instead of attempting to fight the tide, she turned and let it take them.

They were dragged deeper into the cave. Kora caught her breath as they traveled through the narrow pass, the water gently lapping them back towards the tree. When they reached the entrance to the lagoon, the water dropped to ankle level as she dragged Shade out of the water as much as she could. Soaked, shivering, and terrified beyond belief, Kora shook Shade by his shoulders. "Wake up," she demanded.

Images of her brother's death smudged against her current predicament and played on her mind. With shaking hands, she searched his torso for any injuries. Tears swelled as she pressed her ear to Shade's chest. Nothing—not a single sound of that heartbeat she recognized. "Shade, you can't—"

He couldn't die. Could he? Not an immortal. There was no way she killed an immortal. She ran a hand over her face, and the sensation of the water momentarily reminded her of William's blood on her hands. No—no she didn't kill someone else.

She pressed against his chest, trying to force air into his lungs. Ariana had shown her what to do if there was a drowning victim. At sea, it was good practice and could be the difference between saving someone's life. With another round of deep compressions, she pressed her head to his sternum again, but no sound welcomed her. Without thinking, she tilted his chin up and his head back, then breathed a gentle lungful of air into his mouth.

Before she could pull away, lips formed against hers. She pulled back with a gasp, covering her mouth to see Shade's eyes were opened and the most mischievous grin tilting his lips. "So, all I had to do was become unconscious for you to want to kiss me?"

There was no denying the flush that rushed from her neck to her cheeks. She batted his arm. "How dare you? Your heart wasn't beating. I was worried something had happened and was trying to help—not kiss you."

He leaned up on his elbows. His eyes dazzling shades of colors. "Excuses, excuses. Besides, you know I'm immortal." He winked.

She jumped to her feet and kicked his arm out from underneath him, causing him to fall nearly on his head.

"Ouch." He rubbed his back. "Don't hurt me or I might need another kiss."

"I'm never going to help you again!"

"Don't say that, Wildflower. One shouldn't make promises they can't keep."

Kora rolled her eyes and started to search the lagoon illuminated by the algae. Water still came in through the opening in increments of ten counts. Not a lot, but enough that she kicked up water as she searched for an exit. "What do we do? We can't stay in here." She wrapped her arms around herself to ward off the chill.

"You're cold to the bone. Here." Shade was beside her within a breath, a hand held out.

She pulled away. "What are you doing?"

"I'm going to warm you. I just need to touch you. If you'll allow me."

She opened her mouth and almost let slip that Captain hadn't needed to touch her to dry her clothes but stopped short. She nodded and placed her hand in his.

A warmth, not that all unfamiliar to every time he touched her, grew and expanded through her body. Her dress didn't completely dry like Captain had done, but her body itself was no longer freezing.

Shade tilted his head, his gaze like a caress as he looked at her from head to toe. "Are you all right?"

She released a breath. "Yes, I think so."

There was a softness she hadn't often seen in his expression as a wave of dizziness nearly had her knees buckling. Shade scooped her off her feet. "I could tell something wasn't right. Where are you hurt?"

In her haste to help him, she'd forgotten about the hit to her head, the deep cut on her leg that now stung from the salt water, or the new bruises already blooming against her sides. "My head."

He carried her to the highest point of the cave and took a seat, keeping her within his lap. "Will you show me where?"

She knew she should be squirming from his hold and putting as much distance as possible between them, but she didn't move. "Here." She touched the side of her head and winced at the discomfort, removing her hand immediately.

He was gentle as he examined the location with deft fingers. "No blood, but there is a bump."

She shifted in his lap and took time to look him over. "Are you all right?" She asked, grazing a finger over a cut at his temple. "I didn't know immortals could bleed?"

Her fingers lingered along his hairline, and his breath caught.

"We can be injured, yes. I'll be fine," he whispered. He didn't move or remove her from his embrace. She swallowed, resting her hands in her lap. Every limb hurt, but not as much while she was in his arms.

"I'm sorry." He brushed the hair from her face as he scrutinized every inch of her. "I thought we had more time. I didn't consider how long it would take for a mortal to walk."

Even with all the aches and pains, she pierced her eyes to his. "Don't use my mortality as an excuse ever again."

Shade stared at her for a moment, then nodded. "I should have taken your needs into consideration. I'm sorry."

"Apology accepted," she mumbled. "Except, how do we get out of here?"

He chuckled. "We don't. The only way to do so before the tide recedes would end in you drowning." He nodded towards the lagoon. "That would take us to the Váthos, but you'd have to hold your breath way too long."

"How long until the tide recedes?"

Shade's nose wrinkled. "A little before sunset."

Kora's jaw dropped. She pushed off him, ignoring the small pang to her head. "That's hours away. How can we search elsewhere for the pomegranate?"

"That's what you're worried about?" Shade leaned against the wall and stared up at her. She was suddenly very aware of the soaked dress clinging to her skin and every curve of her body.

"And what should I be worried about?"

He shrugged, a pang of disappointment in his eyes gone just as quickly as it appeared. "Nothing else, I guess. Not how worried your brothers will be. Or that you're stuck in here with me for hours."

She rolled her eyes. "I'm not worried about you." She began

to pace, splashing water slightly as she felt the walls slowly closing in on her. The cold once again permeated her body.

"Oh, but I have been told that I can be quite annoying. I ask difficult questions, or maybe I'll just leave you here when I get bored."

She stopped and turned on him. "You wouldn't," she said with bite—even with certainty—but inwardly she hoped she was correct.

"No, I won't leave you," Shade chuckled, leaning his head against the stone and watching her raptly. "But I will ask you again. Why did you kiss me if you knew I was an immortal?"

"First of all, I didn't kiss you. I thought you needed help. How was I supposed to know you weren't in need of assistance?" She crossed her arms over her chest and glared at him. "You might as well forget about it because it's never happening again."

"Have you ever been kissed properly?"

Her mouth fell into an 'O', and her eyes widened. He smiled, his dimple appearing. He was such a nuisance. "That's an inappropriate question."

"We have already discussed this. I'm not gentlemanly or appropriate." He waved a hand at the cave. "We are stuck down here for a few hours and I'm bored. So, unless you have another way to entertain me..." he trailed off, his eyes sparkling with mischief.

"You're despicable." She pursed her lips. "It's none of your business, but I have been kissed before."

"That's not what I asked. The key word was *properly*."

A shudder coursed through her body. Because of the cold air, of course, not the way he said the world *properly*. Full of insinuation. An unwanted blush rose to her cheeks, and she seethed that his question affected her so much. But then there was that...curiosity. The way he had tasted like sea salt. How soft his lips were against hers. There wasn't much she could compare it to. Her last kiss had been with the neighbor boy three years prior. A stolen moment behind the shed after she'd overheard her mother discussing Kora's marriage prospects with her father. There had been a moment when she needed to control the situation. Thought she could. And Nicholas had been an appropriate choice. Friendly. Kind. Safe.

He'd died six months later from influenza. Another soul gone too soon. She never loved him. Didn't even have a crush. But she missed his demeanor and friendship.

"It was a proper kiss if that's what you mean."

"It's not." He leaned forward, the little light coming in from a small crack above cast him half in darkness and made the mysterious immortal look a little dangerous—like temptation. "Did you feel anything with him?"

"Like what?" She shrugged. "He was a boy. It was a kiss. Just a chance to say I had tried it once. Not like you who have kissed hundreds."

"I haven't kissed hundreds," he whispered. "Sure, I've spent time with the dead, but that isn't the same."

"Astari would feel differently."

"No, she wouldn't. It's a habit from a life long gone. There was never a time she truly cared for me—and none of the others ever have been more than a passing fancy."

She remembered Astari's words. Her admission that Shade was a distraction. "Well, then the mortals when you were—"

He shrugged. "Two."

Her fists tightened with fabric of her skirt. "Why are we discussing this?" And why was she feeling jealous?

"I've thought about it."

"Thought about what?"

"Kissing you." He rested his elbows on his bent knees. "Properly."

A breath of air escaped her lungs. Her lips parted, her gaze falling to his mouth. She wondered if he could hear her heartbeat because she was certain it echoed throughout the cavern that suddenly pulsed with light. But she was wrapped up in him. His heated look. She swallowed, considering all the moments she had yearned for him to be closer.

He stood, slowly, the movement languid and hypnotizing. "Have you ever thought about it, Kora?"

"You're just playing with me." She stepped away from him. Uncertain. Nanny had told her the stories of the womanizing gods. But...none of those stories had ever been about the God of the Dead.

"I do like to play with you, that's true. But not about this. I *shouldn't* be playing with you about this."

"What is *this*?" The words came breathier than she'd hoped, betraying her.

He took unhurried steps with his hand clasped behind his back until he stopped in front of her with only an arm's length between them. "I haven't figured it out yet. You keep drawing me in unlike anything I've experienced before. And as you are aware, I've been around for a long, long, time."

Involuntarily, she took a half step closer to him. "But you annoy me. Frustrate me." Made her body thrum with a want she never knew could exist. That last part she tried to muffle even in her thoughts. And failed.

"That's how all the good stories start."

"Do we have a story?" She closed that last bit of distance between them now, looking up into his eyes.

His hand reached out and traced a path with his thumb along her jaw. His other hand rested along her throat, her pulse spiking beneath his fingertips. "We have a story, Wildflower. Is it a tragedy or a happily ever after?"

She thought he'd pull away then. That he'd make the decision to stop, but he didn't move as though waiting for her to make it for him. Maybe she should answer his question, but was there an answer yet? "So, are you going to kiss me properly?"

He leaned in with his gaze holding hers, looking for any sign that she'd stop him. Because she knew he would stop if she asked. Without a doubt. But she didn't want him to. It was more than curiosity that had her gripping his arm, her other hand resting on his chest to feel that heartbeat and the strong lines of muscle.

He brushed her cheek with his thumb before sliding it along her jaw and tilted her chin up slightly. A wisp of his breath curled against her skin as he gently pressed a kiss to her cheek. Her eyes fluttered closed, her lips parting slightly. Shade's mouth curled near her ear as he whispered, "Is that what you want?"

Yes.

More than anything else in that moment. Or the next. Or any after.

But she couldn't put words to it, so instead, she nodded.

"Even knowing what I am? Who I am?"

She pulled back until she held his gaze. She saw it in his eyes. The vulnerability. The expectation that she'd walk away from him. "I thought you died. That scared me. But you—you and all you signify doesn't scare me. You're more than an immortal trapped alone in eternity. You're a dreamer."

There wasn't a chance to continue her thought. To tell him what she saw in him—his desire to be seen as more than the God of Nekrós. To be valued for more than his power over the dead.

Because his lips pressed against hers and were all consuming. Each caress of his tongue was like being brought to life again and again. He wrapped his arms around her, and heat coursed through her body. Each swipe of his tongue was a welcomed taste filled with want and need. Consuming her as though she was the air for his lungs.

"You're shivering." He kissed her again, sliding down against the wall and pulling her into his lap. She curled against him, her hand resting on his chest as their lips met again. Warmth spread through her core. An ache in her center.

He dropped his head, catching his breath. She was nearly panting, her hands grasping his tunic. Wanting to pull him closer.

"Kora."

"Shade," she breathed.

"You shouldn't say such things to me."

"Why?" Kora twisted his shirt in her grip.

"It undoes me. You undo me. I'm trying to be better. For you. And—" Instead of finishing his thought, he leaned in and pressed a gentle kiss to the corner of her mouth. Her cheek. Then another to her forehead before he pulled back with a serious expression. "I still can't give you your brother."

William.

She broke his stare and from his hold. "That's not why I wanted to kiss you." Because despite everything, she knew the truth was that she had wanted to kiss him for a while. Had felt the draw to him at each graze of his skin against hers. Not that she wanted to admit such things out loud.

"Maybe not the sole reason, but it's part of it. And I don't want that between us." As though he remembered himself, he dropped his hands away from her. She stood and began to pace, her drenched dress and hair like a bucket of cold water against heated skin.

There were secrets she kept from him. Lies between them. She was going to betray him. For her brother. Her home. The world.

"Kora, I know this is not ideal, but I can keep you warm. I don't want to find out the hard way if you can become sick here."

She looked down at her hands to find them shaking and turned to look at him sitting against the wall with a look of vulnerability and concern.

"All right." She knew she shouldn't but for this moment, she let herself fall into him. For warmth, she told herself. When they walked out of this cave, she would keep her distance again.

The evidence of his want was there. When he wrapped his arms around her, she realized how cold she had been without his touch. He rubbed her arms, generating heat, and the shivers slowly subsided.

"Tell me a story, Kora." He kissed her temple. "Please."

"You first," she whispered, uncertain where to start.

He rested his head against the wall and stared towards the ceiling. "My story is a tragedy. It began with a mother's love and a father's greed. She assisted in saving my brother's and I from his prison, kissed us on each of our heads, then left. We never saw her again. The first in a long line of goodbyes."

She was going to ask more when he tightened his hold around her. "I only thought that I was meant for tragedy..."

"Until?" She couldn't help but ask.

Shade looked down and an ageless hurt had settled in features that usually only held mischievousness and need. "It's your turn to tell a story. I'd prefer a happily ever after though, please."

So she did. One of warriors. Of women fighting for what they want. Of the gods happy among the people. With twisted vines of ivy, great big trees casting shade, and gardens filled with fruits and vegetables.

She didn't know if she ever had seen the King of the Dead as relaxed as he was at that moment. Head reclined against the wall of the cave, his grip firm and comforting around her body. Her head rested on his chest as she whispered dreams. She considered bringing up a trip to the Isles of Nekrós, but guilt gnawed at her. Realization had dawned. Shade wasn't the only one to blame for what was happening. It hadn't been her desire to be placed between warring immortals, but she knew one way or another, she had to force one of their hands. For her brother. And her people.

And the idea of doing that to Shade after the words they spoke. The kiss they shared...

Captain may be right that his brother was manipulative, and she'd fallen for it, but it was more than that. *He* was more than that. Somehow, she'd have to make him find the fruit.

But her heart wasn't as agreeable as it had been before.

Chapter 28

Kora

I t was late at night when they returned to Camp. They had stopped at a pool of fresh water so she could clean her wounds. She noted that Shade's fingers had twitched more than once to help, but he kept a safe distance between them.

After he landed in the clearing, Kora was clutching her already aching head when William ran towards them and screamed, "Kora! What the hells, Shade? What happened to her?"

She was a little wobbly when Shade put her down but was able to stand on her own. "Nothing too bad. Just a little scratched up and achy after the tide tried to drown us."

"Drown you?" William's expression darkened. He whirled on the immortal, stepping closer to tower over the god. "You said she'd be safe with you. Promised—"

"William, I'm okay. It wasn't his fault." When she stepped between the two of them, Shade's jaw clenched, and a darkness swirled around his clenched fists that hung at his side. "Things got out of hand, but everything is fine." Kora gave Michael a reassuring smile, and his bottom lip stuck out in response.

"Are you sure?" William wrapped an arm around her waist. Even with the short nap, the aches and pains from the tumble against rock and wave had begun to intensify. "We need to get you some rest."

"I'm good. Promise." Kora rested an arm around his shoulder. Michael tugged on her skirt. "Did you find it?"

She shook her head, unwilling to put words to their lack of success. It was disappointing, to say the least.

The young boy groaned, and then turned towards Shade with lifted brows. "I think it's unfair that Kora gets to fly all the time."

William chuckled as he nudged his brother with his foot. "Michael hasn't stopped complaining about that all day." He glanced at Kora. "And we finished the hut today. I'm a little concerned that we didn't make it large enough for you."

"She can continue to stay in my tree if she wants." Shade snapped his mouth shut as if surprised he had spoken aloud.

Michael laughed, pointing at William whose mouth had fallen open in shock.

The immortal crouched in front of Michael. "Let's rectify that. Want to go for a ride?"

The boy squealed in delight as he clambered onto his back. They shot off into the sky, leaving William speechless, and Kora attempting not to laugh at her brother's wide-open mouth. He looked like a cod fish, but she knew it wasn't the time to poke fun.

Kora stared at Shade and Michael's retreating form.

"Is he safe doing that?" William mumbled under his breath, but loud enough to hear. Kora opened her mouth to answer, but William sighed. "Not like we can stop him now. Come on. Let's see if you can fit in the hut. Then we don't have to take Shade up on his ridiculous offer."

"It's not like Shade stays in the tree often." Kora's muscles ached, but she couldn't complain to William, or he'd never let her out of his sight again. She started to twist from his hold, but his grip tightened around her waist. "What?" She looked up at him with confusion.

"Are you considering staying in his house? In his bed?" William's eyes widened. "It's asinine—"

"It isn't, though. I've been sleeping there the last few nights, and it hasn't been a problem. Besides, you've been in the treehouse. Is there room for the two of us? Michael could move into the treehouse too. We aren't staying forever. Besides, you sleep at the foot of the bed anyway."

"You know Michael won't agree. He made this for himself."

"Either we tell him what to do, or you can deal with the current sleeping arrangements," she countered.

William huffed. He dropped fisted hands to his sides and turned on his heels to storm in the direction of the hut.

When they reached the clearing, Kora bent over and climbed inside the hut, ignoring William's narrowed gaze as she tried to lay inside. It was too short. The rectangular space obviously built for Michael's shorter frame. Either she slept at an angle, eliminating space for her younger sibling, or she would have to sleep curled up in a ball. Neither choice was optimal.

William pulled back the rag they'd constructed as a door and glowered down at her. "Fine. But if you're staying in his tree-house, then I am too."

"Then who is watching Michael?" She rolled her eyes, pushing him aside and crawling out of the hut. "Sleep by the door for all I care. It's not like anything is going to happen, Will. Or do you not trust me? Or know me anymore?"

Her words had their desired effect—her twin's expression crumpled. He ran his fingers through his hair and groaned out a few curse words. "I get it, all right? I'm just worried, and you can't blame me for that. No one else is here to watch over you."

"You already watched out for me. That's how you ended up here. If you'd stayed home like you were—" Her face brightened, the heat rising up her neck to her ears. She snapped her mouth shut. William's gaze fell between them, and Kora pinched her eyes closed. "I'm sorry, I didn't mean it."

"Yes, you did." William rubbed the back of his neck. "We should talk—about that night."

She wasn't ready for the truth. Not until she had saved him. Then they could talk. Kora grimaced and turned away to face the lupine bush that had blossomed beside the doorway to Shade's treehouse. It was a welcoming sight among the wilting tree. She frowned.

Her gaze slid up to the bare branches. Was that a leaf budding? Out of place, yet not. A sudden hunger filled her. A desire to see more flowers and a garden grow around the tree. A loud sigh reminded her that William had broached a subject that felt too daunting to explore. Not when she already felt guilty for his death. Not when she was working against Shade. It was too much to bear. "There is nothing to talk about."

"Obviously there is. Kora, I don't regret how things happened." William took a step closer. Her shoulders tightened at his proximity.

She ignored the sensation. "No. You made a choice, and it ended your life. You chose to fight for the belief of the immortals. To take a stand." Kora lifted her head and turned to him. No matter how much her guilt stung, she was here for him. To save him, this time. If they stayed on this conversation too long, he'd find out the truth. He had a knack for making her break, and she couldn't allow that to happen. "All that matters now is that we can change things."

"But what if that's not how it works?" William sighed. "There's a chance that this tree doesn't exist. I know it. You must know it too?"

"If you don't say something positive right now, then I'll force Shade to let me stay longer." He was so infuriating sometimes. How could he not see that this was his chance? And why were they still having this same conversation? When had he lost all hope? Was it before or after his death?

William's eyes widened. "That's not..." When her glared sharpened, he relented. "Fine. I'm thankful I saw you again. I never thought I'd have another chance to hug you or talk with you. Or even fight with you, for that matter." He held his hands up in surrender. "Now please don't threaten me any further. I don't think my soul can take it."

Kora folded her arms with a huff. William took advantage of

her distraction and pulled her tight to his side. "Let's just promise to make the best of this situation. Maybe have a little fun. Play a few games and create new memories that can last a lifetime? Just in case."

That was something she could agree to. "Only if you promise to believe in me. I have enough doubt surrounding my life." Kora's gaze thinned.

William squeezed her a little tighter. "You shouldn't. It's not that I doubt you. I'm just worried about you and Michael being here. You're my baby sister."

"Same age," she ground out, pointing between the two of them. "Twins, Will. Seconds don't count, only days."

"Seconds can sometimes mean the world." He pressed a kiss to the top of her head. "And you have to make me a promise too."

Though part of her thought it was best she kept her mouth shut, she asked, "What?"

"That we will have a talk about that night. One way or another—whether it is here or in the mortal world."

She knew she shouldn't have asked. "There is only one option, Will."

"Always the optimist." William released his hold and looked up to the sky as a whoop sounded above.

Shade lowered to the ground, Michael giggling as his feet touched the earth. "That was the best thing ever."

The immortal chuckled, ruffling Michael's hair. "Glad you had fun. Well, I'm going to do a glance over to see if a new tree popped up." Kora tried to not take it personally that he didn't look her way as he spoke. "Kora should get some rest."

Before she could say anything, he shot off into the sky and tightness gripped her chest. Maybe it was manipulation. Did he know he had planted a seed of doubt? Was he using her too?

Her youngest brother pointed to the hut. "Do you fit?"

She swallowed, trying to dispel her thoughts as she turned to her youngest brother. "No."

Michael guffawed sarcastically. "I thought for sure you would. Oh well, guess that means I get it all to myself."

William's right eyebrow rose. "We thought it was best if you slept with us in the treehouse."

Michael groaned, stomping his foot. "Aw, come on. This is an adventure, and I want to sleep in it. Please?"

Both twins laughed at his adorable scrunched-up face. Kora pulled him in tight for a hug and hid her wince as he pressed against her bruised ribs. Another reminder of her mortality. "I suppose so. As long as you behave."

When Kora let go, Michael's grip on her tightened. With sad eyes, Michael glanced between them. "Do you think Mother and Father are worried about us?"

This time she couldn't hide her wince, but thankfully William had crouched down to their brother's level. Her twin shrugged. "Not when you get home. From what I understand, the pixie will take you back to the morning after the day you left. It will be like it never happened."

"Then why don't we just return before your death and change things?" Kora asked, perking up. Then he would never go to that meeting, and it would be like his death had never happened.

William ran a hand through his hair. "I asked. Time is still passing. That's why the seven days and no more, remember?" He gave Kora a pointed glare. "That's also changing fate. My fate. And that is not something we have control over—neither do the pixies and certainly not Shade. That's why this fruit—" He stopped short as if the promise not to be negative rang in his ears as it did hers.

Kora sighed. Exhaustion mixed with new aches as her body caught up with the experience at Skull Isle. She was going to feel it tomorrow. "Maybe we have been given a miracle, a chance to change fate itself." She knew it even if her brother didn't hold hope.

"Hey there." Curly appeared from the path, holding a pile of cream fabric in her hands. "I've brought something for you to change into, Kora."

She held out the clothes for Kora who took them with gratitude. "The pants might be a bit tight—they are on the smaller size—while the shirt may be a tad large."

"I'm appreciative either way." Kora held the garments against her chest, thankful for them. Her dress had grown scratchy and uncomfortable over time.

A few steps behind, Astari appeared. "We are also heading down to the beach. I'm planning to head to the docks tomorrow, so tonight everyone wants to have a little bonfire."

"Is it safe?" William asked, searching the skies.

Curly smiled. "We wondered the same thing, but Shade is here. And if he crows to announce he's leaving, then we will cut things short."

William returned her smile, his shoulders relaxing a fraction. "Sure—if Michael wants to go."

"Of course." Michael wiggled out of William's arms and grabbed Astari's hand. "Let's go."

Astari smiled down at Michael. "We can find some of those berries you liked so much."

As the two of them ran off towards the bushes, Kora watched their retreating forms. "I think I will change after. Let me go put these down." After she placed them onto the bed in the treehouse, she returned to Curly walking backwards toward the path. "Let's go jump some waves?"

William chuckled as Kora came up alongside him, hands stuffed in his pockets. Then, without warning, he ran towards the beach. She and Curly hurried to catch up, only to reach the water just in time for him to splash them both in the face.

Before they knew it, the sun had disappeared. Their bellies were full of berries. Kora sat in front of the fire, thankful for the warmth since her dress was still damp. Branch began to regale them with what he swore was the best story to ever be told. He claimed it was truth, but they all called him a liar when he bragged about every maiden in the land trailing in his wake, begging him for a kiss.

"Kora should tell a story." Michael pulled himself into her lap, his little body warm against her. "She's the best at it."

The others huddled in closer, pleading eyes pinned on her. "Will you tell us one, Kora?" a few mumbled while others begged.

Kora glanced at William and suddenly her hands were clammy. Her heart raced. The story she told him—the last story she'd ever thought she would tell him—flashed into her mind. William tried to smile at her but couldn't. Almost as if his own thoughts had followed the same line as hers.

Michael tapped her nose. "Please?"

She wiped her hands on his shirt, tugging him closer as she did. With a deep inhale and slow exhale, she collected herself. William would be home. Alive. Soon enough, everything would be as it should be. She'd make it right.

"There was a maze that had a surprise in the middle. But it was guarded by a monster..."

As she continued her story, the others inched closer. Some settled their chins on their hands, staring in rapt silence. Others leaned onto their neighbor while they listened. Kora spoke, and their attention never faltered as they gasped at certain points or laughed at others.

When it was finished, Michael prompted another sandcastle and many of the Lost Souls joined in. Kora stayed close to the warmth of the fire as the sun disappeared behind the horizon. Some sang songs, and Kora laughed along as they made up dances. William sat down beside her, and her heart eased at the smile on his face.

A groan—loud and foreboding—brought them to silence. It sounded from a distance, out towards the water. "Will, did you hear that?" Kora shifted her legs in the sand. Her limbs had fallen asleep, and something about that sound made her think that she would need them awake and ready.

"I don't know." He started to his feet, placing himself in front of her. "Michael?"

Their brother and the others came back to the fire, carefully watching where they stepped. Branch had a tight grip on Michael's arm until he broke free and ran to Kora.

A few turned slowly, peering over their shoulders into the dark abyss. All Kora could see was the moonlit waves as they licked at the shore.

"What was that?" Michael curled deeper into Kora's lap, making it even more difficult for her to stand.

Kora's grip tightened on her brother. "Nothing." She looked at William. "Right? Shade is here still. He hasn't left Anamoní."

One of the souls stood up, taking a few steps towards the water before stopping near the shore. He scanned the distance, and Kora wondered if he saw more than she did. The soul sighed and turned back towards the group. "I don't see any—"

A scream cut his words short before he disappeared into the abyss.

Everyone rushed to their feet as the darkness thickened. The moon was snuffed out by an unnatural blanket of clouds. William grabbed Michael from Kora's arms. A few souls started rushing back towards the camp when another moan came from behind.

Branch, only visible by the dimming firelight, grabbed hold of another soul's hand. "We—we're surrounded."

"I can't see," another soul cried. "How do we get back?"

Kora bent over, grabbing one of the logs from the fire. They were mostly embers now, but it was better than nothing. "Hurry, let's get away from the water. Stay close together."

The others huddled in, a few more taking logs. Kora grabbed hold of William's elbow. After all this, she wasn't going to lose either of her brothers again. They slowly moved up the beach. Kora's breathing was heavy, and her heart raced as silence spread around them.

A roar—another scream from behind—and chaos broke.

They weren't just shadows this time, but flashes of indistinct figures. They were pieces of skeleton—torn flesh wrapped in seaweed. Hands as black as soot reached out and grabbed hold of Curly's leg. Kora jabbed it with the embers, and it screamed, turning its terrifying face in her direction with an eye hanging from the remains of a socket. The creature let go of Curly, but with harsh steps that didn't align with its body, it came for Kora much faster than she expected. She nearly tripped as she moved back, forcing Michael behind her.

The creature was nearly on her when she sent a pathetic attempt at a punch to the creature's remaining jaw. It howled, grabbing tight to its crumbling face as Curly came from behind, raising the torch Kora had dropped. "Run!"

Kora worried about her friend only for a moment before she remembered Michael was there. But as she turned around to rush him away, his screams echoed in the night. A splash of water had her whirling towards the beach. She saw the creature carrying him and sprinted towards the waves, barely visible in the limited moonlight. Where was Shade? He hadn't left. Why were they doing this?

She made it to the creature and Michael at the same time Astari did, the soul right behind Kora. She waved a burnt stick, and Kora stepped back as her friend barred the xéchase from disappearing into the water. Kora reached out and yanked on a flailing Michael who fumbled, nearly falling into the ocean. The creature turned, about to rush at Kora when she grabbed its arm, trying to free her brother from its hold. Before she could think about the way her fingers sunk into the corpse, it yowled in pain. Kora didn't think twice, just placed her other hand on its hand and it immediately dropped Michael. She grabbed him, pulling him away from the water and turned for Astari. But three had her. The xéchase dragging her towards the water, one at her ankle. Another her torso, and the third her arms.

"No!" Kora screamed.

She put Michael down. "Don't let go of my skirt." She reached for the creatures. Lunged for them. They dodged her touch, and Astari reached out her hand. Kora grabbed hold—pulled. Tugged.

Michael pulled on her from behind, trying to help break the soul free. Astari screamed, kicking and attempting to free herself, but the corpses held tight. Michael screamed. Cried.

"You're slipping." Kora tried to tighten her hold. "Astari, don't let go."

Astari's gaze slid to Michael, then back to her. She stopped fighting. Met Kora's gaze. "Thank you."

She let go of her hand, and Kora scrambled for a hold. The xéchase dragged Astari into the water. Kora cried out, reaching for Michael and pulled him into her arms. Made one final lunge for the soul when one of the xéchase turned on her and roared in her face. Spittle and salt coated her as she turned her back to the beast to protect her brother. William appeared the next second and dragged her away from the water as she tried to go for Astari. "There are more, Kora. We need to get out of the water."

"She needs our help!" Anguish twisted her gut. How could this happen? It was all so fast. Again—she couldn't help again.

William grabbed her arms and shook her. "For Michael."

Her youngest brother was sobbing, gripping tightly around her neck. William nodded once, took Michael and they ran.

Chapter 29
Shade

Shade had considered staying with Kora until the others returned but she knew the dangers and wouldn't want to be coddled. If he had stayed, he might have done or said something he'd later regret. With only four days until their deal was over, he knew it was time to check in and see if Astraea had returned. The longer he ignored it, the worse it would be.

He flew over the canopy of trees, the forest floor invisible from his viewpoint. When he was outside of the Fairy Circle of redwoods, Taea flew in front of him. "Where are you off to?"

Shade came to a stop, levitating in mid-air. "To see if Astraea returned. I need to talk her into taking Kora and Michael home."

"I'm certain she'll help, but I just came from there and she hasn't returned yet." Taea brushed her short hair over her shoulder. "Has the mortal realized there is no reason to stay? I'm proud of you for resisting her charms."

Shade rolled his eyes. He hoped Taea didn't try to pry further into the reason his heartbeat quickened at the thought of Kora's charm. The kiss he couldn't stop thinking about. "No, she hasn't given up. Our deal is almost done."

She huffed. "You aren't any fun anymore. Ever since Kora arrived, you'd rather spend time with her. The Lost Souls have noticed it too. Why do you think Astari wants to leave? She's changing you, and I'm worried—"

"I made a deal." Shade's voice lowered to a warning tone. "And you know I don't back out on my promises."

"Oh, so running Nekrós—"

He cut her off with a growl. "I never promised to do that. I was forced. There was no request, only an expectation. You know this."

"Yes, and I know you. Don't you see how dangerous this girl is to you? You're letting a mortal get under your skin. A *mortal*." The way she bit the last word out like a curse had Shade stopping short.

He glanced her over. "You've stepped out of line."

"No, I haven't. Someone needs to tell you the truth. You're going to fall right into their trap, and you'll only have yourself to blame. I should take her and the brother back now. Get this over with because obviously you can't stomach it." Taea's body turned bright red, her dust a tinge of crimson.

"You'd be breaking the pixie code. They would never allow you on the council if you did such a thing." The pixie council did their best to stay neutral, especially with concerns between mortals and immortals. They didn't ruffle feathers. Except each other's.

"Hells to the council," she yelled. "In the end, they're useless to me anyway." Taea sped up, heading towards Camp.

Shade raced ahead of her, the pixie forced to a stop by the impact of his power—a wall of darkness blocking her path. She rubbed her nose, glaring at him.

Shade straightened, drawing his shoulders back and his power curling with them. The last of the sunlight dimmed to darkness behind him, disappearing with his magic. "You're banished from Camp."

"What?" Taea's eyes widened.

"Until the mortals return home safely, when our deal is done, then you may return. If I see you near them or Camp prior to that, then you'll never be allowed on the isle again. Do you hear me?" He glared at the pixie as his words seemed to register through her shock.

She tilted her head, mouth set in a sneer. "Fine. You're going to regret this, though." With those last words, she turned and flew as quickly as her wings could take her towards Pixie Meadow.

Shade continued to hover, watching until her dust disappeared. As night encapsulated the island, Shade breathed a long sigh and closed his eyes.

Taea was his friend. She may often annoy him, but he always accepted her opinion when she spoke her mind. But this—something was different. They hadn't always agreed on everything, but there was danger in the way she spoke. In the actions she was willing to take. He turned back, continuing his flight towards Camp. It was getting too late now to see the pixies anyway. They never appreciated evening visits unless he brought a gift, and he didn't have one now.

A glimmer of light glinted on the beach. Firelight. The souls must have put together a little celebration of sorts. Usually, he would fly straight there and join in, but he didn't feel like it. Didn't know if he could handle the idea of being near that distracting young woman. There was no doubt that Taea was right about that. But he hadn't become so infatuated that he didn't remember she had a mission of her own. One he couldn't agree with.

Shade took a deep breath and began to fly the circumference of the island. It had been some time since he'd toured the outer mountain peaks. You could never be too careful when Halieus was loose in the realm.

He considered Halieus's presence and if the nereids were ready to talk. If Shade could break his final ties of the realm, he would. But could he leave it to his brother? At least with Captain, Shade knew it would be well cared for—that the souls would be treated with respect. The same couldn't be said if Halieus presided over the dead. Not that his middle brother would be able to stomach it anyway. Not with the restrictions taking such a title would have on his lifestyle. It was difficult enough for Shade who could only leave for one night, and only when he was called to retrieve souls.

With this thought, he realized it had been a while since his last tug to retrieve the dead from the mortal world, and he hadn't missed it. Hadn't missed escaping the realm nor seeing the world of the living. Had Kora changed his viewpoint in such a short time? No, it was because he was worried—about her and Michael. There were many other reasons that had nothing to do with her.

The sunlight had completely vanished by the time he had finished, and he headed towards the treehouse. The fire on the beach had dimmed to a warm glow of embers—Shade's gaze narrowed. It wasn't one fire anymore but speckled over the beach. A closer look revealed figures darker than night shifting between the flames. Embers waved through the air. A scream followed.

Hells.

He flew as quickly as he could, the rush of his power tingling against his skin. The xéchase. They weren't under his control. He grasped for his power. Trying to call them away, but it was as though it was just out of reach. How?

Without a second thought, he swooped down to the beach to a cacophony of screams. Souls fought, swiping blazing branches at the creatures. Shade called his power, attempting to gain the control that evaded him. But it fought back. Away from him.

Kora. Her name pressed against his mind, and he sent waves of darkness at the nearest creatures, knocking them towards the water. They were more than shadow this time—their grotesque forms bent and jagged as they shifted or crawled. Like a herd of sheep, some scattered, but others pressed together as the Lost Souls created an arc beside him. "Where is Kora? Michael?" he yelled to the nearest soul.

"There." Branch pointed.

Kora had a cowering Michael at her feet. A few of the scattered xéchase moved closer as she waved a fiery log, keeping them back. William was at her back, protecting her other side.

Shade roared.

Everything stilled as he held out his hand and his scythe flickered into existence within his grip. It had been so long since he held it, called upon it, and the control returned. Just as quickly as the scythe appeared, it was gone. But the power remained, and he forced the Shadow Souls back to the water with a wave of darkness.

His chest rose and fell in succession, anger pulsing in time with his magic. A few wailed, others gripping tight to each other in comfort from the fear of what could have been.

"Everyone to me," Shade called, trying not to concentrate on the sound of Kora's heartbeat hammering within her chest. She was alive. All was well. As she grew closer to him, he turned to Curly. "Find out how many—" He swallowed and shook his head. "How many we lost."

She nodded. A sadness evident in her expression as she began to count the souls present.

"I thought they didn't attack when you were here," William stated curtly. "They could've been lost to the Váthos." The soul glared at him. "They need to return home *now*."

"Hells, Will." Kora's voice was filled with spitfire and rage. "We'll stay away from the beach unless Shade is here. Don't you dare—"

"Quiet." Shade was surprised when Kora actually complied. He took a deep breath, shifting his attention towards the young woman. Tears had trailed down her cheek at some point. Her hair was a frizzy mess, and a decent bruise already bloomed on her shoulder where her dress was torn, revealing bare skin. It was a mistake to have looked at her. His rage urged him to head towards the sea and destroy them all.

"Are either of you hurt?" He nodded at Michael who was gripping tightly onto William's arm.

Kora glared at him. "This is because of you. You've lost

control. Astari was dragged away by those monsters. They were more than just shadows now, Shade. Why is that?"

His jaw clenched, but he didn't speak.

Curly trudged up beside him. "We lost three."

He pinched his eyes closed. "You're certain?"

She nodded. "Lilac and Figuero were here but are no longer accounted for. And she's right—Astari was dragged in too."

They were souls who had arrived just weeks before William. "Thank you. We'll remember them tomorrow. Head back to Camp." They did what he asked, putting distance between themselves and the beach.

Kora didn't move, her gaze pinned on the water. Shade noted that William had stopped a few feet away. She swallowed, and Shade reprimanded himself for noting every curve of her body as she moved. "You have a way to fix this. To save not only your world, but my own. I didn't think it before, but now I know it's true. You're selfish."

"Yes."

She lifted her chin.

"I am selfish. For wanting a choice in my own life. A life that never ends. For wanting friends—even if they no longer live and breathe. For giving up a power that could stop all of this." He dropped his voice to a whisper for only her to hear. "I am selfish. I let you stay, because I wanted you near even if only for a blink of my time. I shouldn't have."

Her shoulders lowered as she looked him over, and he thought he saw her fingers twitch before he met her gaze again. She swallowed. "I have to find the fruit. Please...please don't listen to William." Her pleas held a twinge of her anger.

He moved to stand in front of her. The need to touch her, to brush the hair behind her ear and to feel her warm skin against his to remind himself she was fine built within. But it wasn't only William's presence that stopped him. "You and I have a deal. Understood? I'm going to give you every chance I can to save your brother. But you will have to understand that I'm not going to change who I am."

She wiped away the tears that had streaked her cheeks, staring at him for a moment before blinking away any remaining ones from falling. "Understood."

She didn't look at William when she passed him, resting her arm around Michael's shoulder and steering him away. The plants rustled nearby as if moving on a non-existent breeze. Shade stilled, watching them as they bent towards the mortal.

He shook his head and turned his attention to William. "There are four days left. I'm going to find out when Astraea will return. It should be any day now." After what had happened, Shade would need to have a little fun soon, or he might as well return to the Isles of Nekrós. "If you haven't already, I'd prepare for the fact that we won't find the fruit, but that she won't give up on you." The words came out harsher than planned.

William dropped his gaze.

"I'm sorry." Shade winced. "But I thought it best for you to prepare. I'll take her back to the nereids tomorrow. We just need to wait for the pixies to grant permission, and they can go home soon. I'll remain nearby to be certain they remain safe otherwise."

He ran a hand through his hair, uncertain what to do next. "Maybe you all need a little fun. Some time to make good memories. Tonight should not be how you remember your time together."

William's eyes widened. It seemed he understood what Shade was trying to say because he nodded his head. "Will I remember? After I cross the Váthos?"

Shade sighed. "It depends on what isle you end up on. Memories are what your soul will hold onto. But if you are filled with bitterness, then you will be plagued with it if you end up on the Lýpe—the Isle of Regret. If you are on Eiríni, then yes, you will have memories of those who you've left behind. But only the good ones."

William nodded, looking past Shade towards the dark abyss of the Váthos. "I'm not going to stay after they leave. I don't think I can."

Shade only nodded. "It's your choice."

He turned and leapt into the air. He hoped he gave William the chance to accept the truth. To play, enjoy his time with Kora and Michael. It was something no other soul had been given before—an opportunity to spend time with their loved ones and voice all the things left unsaid. A proper goodbye for a life cut short. Something he hadn't been given a chance to do either. Those who left him rarely said goodbye. Only his mother had said a proper farewell. His brothers...Raz. Shade pinched his eyes closed, blaming the air for causing them to sting.

He'd return Michael and Kora home so he could forget the way she'd looked at him today, and the pain that bubbled to life when he almost lost her.

Chapter 30
Captain

The scythe materialized into Captain's hand. He held it tight as it fought his hold for a moment before he let go. Captain thought it might disappear as it flickered. But it remained. The power of the dead had been drawn away—a desire to return home—but only for a moment. It was rare his brother touched on his power, but in the past few days that had changed. He smiled, and the scythe disappeared. Waited for the next time it would be needed.

Captain's plan was working.

"It will never work." Taea sat on top of the spoke, looking longingly towards the Isle of Waiting. "He's too smart, and you're just wasting your time."

The pixie could be clueless to the realities around her. "He sent you away until the mortals are gone. What about this plan is not working?"

She huffed, crossing her arms over her chest, her dangling legs swinging back and forth. "He was just upset. It's not like I meant it when I said I'd take them home."

Taea hadn't wanted to explain why she was here instead of the island but based on her attitude it wasn't a social visit. After some manipulation, she'd finally given a short explanation. Captain rolled his eyes. "If you had, you'd have had more than my brother to contend with."

The pixie shrugged in response. "You said to keep him away from Astraea. I was doing what you asked."

"At least you succeeded with that. If she knows how to find the fruit, it could have ruined my plan."

If looks could hurt, then she was making a real good attempt at harming him. Stronger villains had tried and failed to take him down. She flung her short hair behind her ear. "He probably already knows what happens if he finds the fruit and is just buying time until the deal is done."

"It's fine if he knows. There are more important tasks I expect the girl to accomplish. She isn't even aware of it all. Yet." Captain smiled to himself.

The door flung open, a splash of water with it as Halieus entered. The last of his scales disappeared from his body as he slumped into the nearest chair. Naked and annoyed. Captain's jaw flexed, annoyed that Halieus dare sit in *his* chair on his bare ass.

Halieus glared back "What the hells made you think it was a good idea to involve a mortal?"

"Oh, do you suddenly care for the living, Brother?" Captain sneered. "You've treated them like objects since the beginning of time."

Halieus rolled his eyes. "It would just have been nice to be prepared when a breathing girl shows up at the lagoon—then slaps me."

Captain couldn't resist bursting into laughter, and the sound boomed against the walls. "I like this woman. She's got more spit-fire and spunk than I gave her credit for. You probably deserved it."

Taea nodded in agreement, fighting her own smile.

His brother wasn't as amused though. "If Shade hadn't been there—"

"You would have done nothing," Captain interrupted. "She's

here to fulfill a purpose. A means to an end. She will receive what she wants when this is done."

"And what is that?" Halieus's brow furrowed. "What is it you will give her? We deserve to know more about this plan of yours. Because if you don't care that Shade knows about the pomegranate—"

"Spying at the door again?" Captain snapped. As long as Halieus doesn't know the truth of the pomegranate's use, Captain wouldn't care that his brother had a little information.

"You've not been exactly forthright." Taea shrugged. "Do you blame him? If you want our help, then we need more information."

"Right now, you're banished from his side and have very little use to me." Captain enjoyed the color draining from the pixie's face. "As for you, Brother, stop asking questions and watch the story unfold. You can share with the others on Synnefo about my prowess."

"While I've been here, I've been slapped and pulled underwater by the damned. I'm not at all impressed with your prowess." Halieus crossed one leg over the other.

Captain met the glares of both of his companions. He needed to appease them, or they would be more likely to betray him. Even with the information he held over Taea, he couldn't guarantee that was enough to stop her tongue.

"Shade will forgive you." Captain shrugged. "He always does, Taea. So, chin up. Return to the island. Make a ruckus with the pixies about how sorry you are. They will ensure he will take you back sooner and give you a chance to spy. Remember, in the end, you'll be the one on Shade's shoulder. No other."

"I know." Taea's wings fluttered for a moment, the iridescent colors catching in the lantern light.

"I don't understand why you'd want to live in Nekrós anyway, Taea?" Halieus's nose scrunched up at the thought. "On the ship there is the water and the views."

Taea sliced a gaze in his direction. "Water and I don't mix. Besides, I was fine on the Isles of Nekrós before."

"Oh?" Captain asked.

She shrugged. "Trying to look at the positives. It's you who I'm forced to work alongside, not Shade. He's a choice. You're an annoyance."

"Well, when you easily give me leverage to force your assistance, whose fault is that?"

Taea turned red and stuck her nose up away from him, eyes closed.

Halieus chuckled. "What did he catch you with, Pixie?"

"None of your concern." Her nose went higher into the air.

"Is it enough to tear your relationship asunder?" Halieus didn't know when to stop sometimes.

With a menacing glare, she faced his brother. "He and I have an understanding. Both of us are tied to things we don't always appreciate or want."

Captain leaned in closer. "I have a feeling that your light blinds many from a darkness within you."

"You don't know what you're saying."

"Really? Because I think it was more than greed and jealousy that forced you to kill Shade's pixie so you could insert yourself by his side. I've had plenty of time to think about it." His smile widened as her eyes did. "Is that what or who you're tied to? Do you have alternative plans? If Shade ever found out—"

Taea pushed off from the spoke and flew at his face with a finger pointed at his nose. "I'm already helping you get him to the Isles of Nekrós. If you think you can threaten me, then I'll go straight to Shade and tell him your plan."

Captain was aware that Halieus grinned like the conniving prick he was as he watched their disagreement unfurl.

"So your supposed best friend can turn you away forever with the truth I lay at his feet? I don't think so." He grew serious and concern edged Taea's features.

She tilted her head and the tick-tock of a clock echoed in the space. The sound both familiar and not, caused goosebumps to rise along his skin. The past—his father's cruelty darkened his mind.

Taea leaned forward, ignoring the sound. "Remember Captain, sometimes you ignore the truth that's right in front of your face. Shade won't return to the Isles of Nekrós for a mortal, and you don't need to pretend to care about anyone but yourself." She flew out the open window and disappeared.

Captain sighed, running a hand over his face. The pixie was dangerous for such a little thing. Something wasn't right with her. But for now, he needed to concentrate on the task at hand. He'd take care of her later. Or better yet, Shade would.

"She's a spiteful little thing, isn't she?" Halieus's foot bobbed up and down.

Captain ignored him. Shade would take his place within the Isles of Nekrós soon enough. The scythe—the power of the dead —was calling for him. Preparing him.

Soon.

"I'm returning home." Halieus stood, a wave of his head forcing his hair away from his eyes.

"You're giving up already? How many days has it been? One or two?" Captain thrummed his fingers against the arm of his chair. "You're not leaving yet. I still need you."

"Why? The nereids are angry. He's blocked off the lagoon from the river. The xéchase are surrounding it, so I can't help them. In the end, he'll get what he wants, and they'll be searching the waters for this non-existent pomegranate. I assume you have her searching for the fruit. Why?" Halieus asked. "You didn't tell me everything when you asked for my help, and I don't hold enough power here to best him."

"I don't need you to best him. I need you to observe and report back to me. Next time he comes to the lagoon, you don't need to interact with him or the girl. Understood?" Captain glared at his brother. "Don't test him, Halieus. I need him pliable for it all to end."

"I'm going to laugh when this all comes apart." There was a promise in Halieus's words, but Captain knew it wouldn't come to fruition.

"And I'll tell you 'I told you so' when I succeed. After he has the nereids search the lagoon, come to me, then we'll discuss your return to Synnefo. I'll be making a visit soon as well. You've met Kora, and I think you'll have to agree with me that she doesn't give up easily." He smiled, attempting to picture the slap as Halieus's nose scrunched up in disgust. It would have been a sight to see.

"Does she know what she's giving up?" Halieus started for the door, scales already curling over his body and around his ribs. "It's not just her life on the line. I told you, I can't take the mortals' curses much longer."

Captain stood, following his brother. He needed to make sure he was off the ship. The sniveling fool would stay and make himself at home otherwise. "I'm not like you."

Halieus peered over his shoulder. "I wouldn't count on that." Then he jumped over the rail, his legs forming into a tail. He'd be able to swim the Váthos without any interruption—he would be sure of that.

He considered having a little fun, then decided against it. He still had need of his brother.

Of both of them.

Chapter 31
Kora

The sun was barely coming in through the little window. A hint to the lateness of the day when she was finally able to sit up without sending her head into a spiral. Everything ached from both the incident on Skull Isle and the attack last night. A good enough reason why her body had resisted waking early this morning. Sometimes being a mortal really wasn't all it was cracked up to be.

Her head pounded slightly at the sound of a knock at the door. "Come in."

Shade entered, his eyes downcast. "The nereids are ready to talk. If you're up for it, or I can head—"

Kora rushed out of the bed, smoothing her skirt down and ignoring the unsteadiness in her ascent. The scratches on her legs from the rocks stung as the fabric brushed against them. She fumbled slightly but hoped he didn't notice. "Yes, of course I'm up for it."

She caught the small smile playing at the corner of his mouth. He cleared his throat. "Your brothers went with the souls to search the cliffs. No luck to speak of yet."

Kora bit the inside of her mouth. It was a good idea, even if it hadn't yielded the results they wanted. "Thank you."

They hadn't spoken after she'd yelled at him. Her. Yelled at a god. Not that she regretted it, but there was a touch of awkwardness between them now.

Shade nodded, then glanced at the pile of clothes. "You didn't change?"

She looked down at her attire—the torn blue dress that was turning shades of brown. She would need another bath soon. Kora bit her bottom lip. "I will."

As if he could read her thoughts, he ran a hand through his hair. "Curly can take you to bathe later. If you want."

Her cheeks flushed. "Yes, please."

"We can arrange that." He nodded towards the clothes. "I'll give you a moment."

Once the door was closed, she changed into a pair of linen pants that clung to her legs and waist, and a loose white button up that she was certain had once belonged to a young man. Kora had never worn pants before and was surprised at how much easier it was to move in them, although a little self-conscious about wearing them in public. She was amongst the dead though, so there wasn't a better time. At least she didn't feel as dingy as she had before. Surprisingly, they had located a pair of boots that fit her feet.

"Ready." She stepped into the late morning light, feeling more like herself than she had in days.

Shade swallowed as he held out a hand. "Fly?"

As she grasped hold of his outstretched palm, she nodded, that same rush of warmth ran through her limbs and into her torso. The memory of the way he held her the previous day in the cave, and how his lips had felt against hers sent a new wave of...something she couldn't pinpoint.

He held up a small pouch. "Did you want to see how it feels to really fly?"

Who was this in front of her? Was this the immortal all along or had something changed? "What is that?"

"Pixie dust." He shook the bag. "Think a happy thought and it will allow you to fly until you land."

Kora's eyes widened. "Really?" Her gaze narrowed. "Or is this a peace offering?" Maybe by mentioning it, they could go back to the way things were.

He grinned and slapped hand to his chest dramatically. "Aw, Wildflower, I'm wounded."

At the nickname, heat rose from her neck to her cheeks. To distract him, she reached for the bag and nearly swiped it from his hand.

He pulled the pouch away. "Not so fast. You need a happy thought first."

"You mean beyond the chance of flying."

He chuckled. "Yes."

She closed her eyes. And unbidden the first thing that came to her mind was another kiss. With him. For him to wrap his arms around her.

She snapped her eyes open. "William returning home. Of course."

"Of course." He opened the pouch and turned the contents over in his hand. "Think about your happy thought." There was a knowing grin on his lips as if he knew where her thoughts had been. "And hold onto it."

She concentrated on William. Home. A happy world. Then he blew the dust from his hand, and it swirled around her.

Kora's heart leapt as she rose slightly. He took her hands, holding her. "Keep thinking happy thoughts."

Focusing intently on her brother, she only rose a little higher. "Is this right?"

Shade moved in closer, his lips brushing her ear. "Think of something happier."

That alone had her swooping up higher into the air. Shade laughed, keeping up with her. "Whatever made you soar—hold onto it."

Kora looked down, her eyes widening at the distance of her feet from the ground. "What do I do?" She wanted to let go of his hands and wave her arms like a bird. That's not how he did it, though.

He let go of one hand. "I'll show you."

Shade taught her how to move with the wind, to shift her body in the direction she wanted to go. Soon she was horizontal, flying beside Shade as they flew towards the lagoon. Kora cleared her throat, trying to think about anything but her hand still gripped tightly in his.

"Do you think, if Halieus hadn't been there, that they would have helped us?" Kora ventured.

Shade shrugged. "Maybe. For the most part, they are flighty creatures and prefer to be left alone while here. They wouldn't have meant to hurt you if, by chance, they'd dragged you under water. I didn't want to test that theory—not with you."

The way he said those last words made her heart flutter. *Don't be stupid. He's not worth the thought you're putting towards him—immortal or not.*

"I'm sorry about last night. If I'd known about the attack, I would have been there sooner."

"We don't have to do this." The word rushed from her mouth.

"Astari didn't deserve that end. If I'd been there—"

"She didn't, no." There was that guilt twisting in her gut again. The soul had saved her and Michael. For that, she would always remember her. "Is there a way to find her?"

"At one time."

Part of her wanted to ask. To make him confirm that he didn't have the same power he'd once held. The control. And somehow make him take it back.

But then there was the side of her that understood how he felt. "I want to go to university." She didn't know why she said it, but she was aware that Shade's head tilted towards her. "It isn't common for women. My mother wants me to marry." His grip tightened slightly on her hand. "That's what proper young women do. But it's not what I want. Not yet."

"And what do you want to study?"

"Horticulture. I want to find a way to grow plants and the herbs we need for medicines and food."

He breathed a long sigh. "I see it, you know? The way the world has shifted and changed over the years. It was slow at first. Captain didn't call back everyone to start. It was when Sera started the Greco-Turkish War that he felt the need to call them back. That was the beginning of the changes."

"After so much time away from your post, why did you not want to go back?"

"What's Ovid's saying?" He smiled, though it was fake. "The harvest is always richer in another man's field." He waved to the view below. "It's hard to give this up."

Kora looked at the landscape below.

The pristine waters. The expansive green mountainside. Even the ship leaving the dock with new souls aboard. She'd considered herself a dreamer like him, but now she was here—even if it was not by choice—flying with an immortal. It was more of an adventure than any dreamer could imagine.

Her goal flashed through her mind. Would he hate her for helping Captain? Look at her differently? How could he not. But also, how could she not continue forward? "Is there a way to have both?"

"There wasn't before. And I'm scared—" He snapped his mouth shut.

"You can talk to me if you want," she whispered, the air stinging her eyes.

He met her gaze. "I'm afraid to find out if I will be trapped again. If I return."

She didn't know what to say and before she could fathom what he felt, Shade began their descent. So much different from the past experiences where her stomach had felt as though it would rather be out of her body. Had her near-death experiences changed his outlook this much? For an immortal who'd lived centuries, it seemed unlikely. But she couldn't unsee the changes in such a short time. Maybe they wouldn't last, and he was still in the apologetic stage.

He landed at the spot where the water fed the lagoon, then he assisted her on their landing. When her feet touched the ground, the pixie dust stopped working as the weightlessness she'd had moments before disappeared. When he let go of her hand, her fingers flexed and she missed the feel of him. She turned away—from both him and her thoughts.

The lagoon was different than it had been on their last visit. The water level was much lower, and the rock where the nereids had been sunning themselves on just a day before was now gray and dry. Upon the boulder sat the same two nereids and from the sneer on their faces, they were not happy with the changes.

Shade gave her a half smile. "Stay here."

Kora nodded, taking a step further from the water's edge and closer to the rocky formation at her back. Shade sauntered towards the lagoon with his hands folded behind him. He whistled at the sight of the nereids, shaking his head. "Such a shame. What's happened here?"

The nereid with red hair—Magna, if Kora remembered correctly—snorted in disgust. "You did. If you think we don't know it was you—"

"Hush!" Andromeda cut off the other's tirade. They turned to Shade, and Kora saw the hate flashing across their expression. "Give us back the water, Immortal."

"I'm afraid I cannot." Shade shrugged. "I need to search the lagoon, and without your help I must do it alone. Which means I need to empty the water from your home. Should only need a few more days by the look of things." He turned to walk away, and Kora was worried that another day would be wasted.

"There is nothing here that you want," Andromeda snapped. "Nothing important enough for your little mortal anyway. If you don't watch her closely, we might grab her when she least expects it. How would you like that?"

Darkness seeped off of Shade and with a snap, encapsulated them all. Kora gasp as her back pressed against jagged rock.

"Touch her and die. Do you understand me?"

She couldn't see Shade, only the sound of his voice echoing in the darkness. This was the third time she'd witnessed his power and again, she wasn't afraid. What that said about her concerned her almost as much as the fact that she trusted the immortal.

"Yes," hissed Magna. "Now, quiet your power before *they* come."

The black dissipated, and Kora's heart raced against her chest as Shade came back into view. The mischievous young man no longer stood before her. Shade looked more like the immortal of legend—he stood straight, shoulders back, chin held high, and fists formed at his side. Shadows emanated off him in waves that shimmered in the sunlight. He looked foreboding. Taller. Sharper and more sinister. It took her breath away.

"We'll look for this tree. What fruit is it?"

"Pomegranate."

Kora bit her lip. "Should you check?" Captain had made it clear that Shade was the only one who could find the tree.

He peered over at her. "I don't feel comfortable leaving you alone here."

She tapped the rock beside her gently with her knuckles. "I'll stay away from the water."

He glared at the nereids. "Will you allow me entrance without hindrance?"

The two shared a look before nodding. Magna tilted their head. "As long as you free the water, we will let you pass. I'll tell the others." They dived into the water, their tail splashing against the water's surface.

Shade turned his attention to Kora and his gaze darkened as he examined her from head to toe, momentarily lingering on her lips. He took a step closer, and her body thrummed at his proximity. "You'll stay here? Won't try to save me again, Wildflower?"

She licked her bottom lip and didn't ignore the fact his gaze tracked the movement. "Don't give me a reason to need to save you."

He leaned in. "I just need to know that if I do this, that you won't risk yourself for me."

He rested a hand by her head. She inhaled. Wanted to draw him in closer until his body was pressed against hers. Then she remembered their last kiss and how they had decided that things couldn't happen between them. "You said we shouldn't be doing this," she whispered, immediately wishing she could erase the words.

Shade blinked, stepping back. "I'm sorry. You're right."

That's not what she meant. She wanted him to take it all back. To say he didn't regret the kisses they shared the previous day. Tell him that she didn't agree with his assessment. Even if she should. Before she could say anything, he reached that arm that had been so close to her over his shoulder, muscles tightening and flexing as he pulled his tunic over his head.

He tossed it aside and turned to dive into the water. The nereids hissed, and she shifted her attention to the lagoon as their shimmering tails disappeared below the water. Would they interfere? Should she be worried?

She remembered the power that he contained and forced herself to count her breaths.

She was alone. The silence near deafening without the sounds of birds. Woody liana vines wrapped around the brush and trees that hung over the lagoon. Kora tilted her head, staring at the nearest branch. Wondered.

She raised her hand towards the wide green leaves and held her breath as the vine slowly shifted. The leaves untangled from a thick conifer and reached towards her.

And then it touched her. Kora gasped.

"Are you alone?"

Kora jumped, dropping her hand and her connection with the plant. Her attention darted towards a man who appeared at the edge of the water. Not man—immortal.

Halieus glanced at the vine and then back to her. "Do you have a secret, Little Mouse?"

"What do you want?"

Halieus pushed off from the edge of the water and as he did, his alligator tail shifted as air touched his scales. Eyes wide, Kora diverted her gaze to his face as his naked body sauntered towards her.

"If you're here, where is your bodyguard?"

Kora kept her attention on him. Shade was vulnerable within the Sea King's domain. Or so she assumed. "You ask a lot of questions."

"Because I'm not getting a single answer." He kept his gaze pinned on her. "What are you, Little Mouse?"

"Not a mouse, for one thing. I'm a mortal. And I'm here for a fruit."

"A lot of very important gods seem to think differently." Halieus tapped his chin. "Do they know you can do what you just did?"

"None of your business." She didn't even know if it was her. This was a realm she would never fully understand.

Halieus chuckled. "So, that's a no. Don't worry, it can be our secret."

She didn't want him to dwell on that—or ask further questions. Let him think he had something important. As it was, she had no idea what had just happened. So what if the plants reacted to her? She'd always had a green thumb before the famine had destroyed the crops. Her new skill likely had something to do with the magic of the isle. "Why are you here, Halieus?"

"Most would be more polite. Especially when you're the reason the lagoon is currently suffering." A dangerous grin. "Is that what he's doing? Is my brother looking for this insufferable tree for you right now?"

"I think you should go."

"You think I fear him? He's given up too much to be considered a threat. Did you know that Shade was once the smartest, most strategic one of us all? It made him dangerous. A threat to Thei—" He shifted quickly. "Captain. Now look at him. Shade's nothing more than the cause of the destruction of worlds."

That was why Shade was sequestered here? Did Captain send him to rule Nekrós because of the threat of Shade's power? How deep did their disagreement go? "Shade isn't the only one at fault. You all need to learn that there is more to each other than the power you possess. The only one I think who is willing to try to change is Shade."

Halieus tilted his head, and when he smiled again, his teeth were sharp—like a shark. "You are brave. I'll give you that."

"But...?"

"You also have a death wish." Halieus shifted, and before she had a chance to dart away, his hand wrapped around her throat. Kora gasped for air. He pinned her hard against the rock as she fought for breath. Pressed his body into hers. She could feel every sharp edge. Every angle. She tried to swallow. Scream. Halieus tilted his head, considering her. "He's not here. And you have pushed the line one too many times. Do you know what I do to those who annoy me?"

Kora's eyes barely had time to widen at the sudden appearance of a shadow behind Halieus before the god was flung off her. Shade, dripping wet and shirtless with a red fruit in his hand, stared down at his brother. Halieus fought against Shade's shadow as it pinned him to the ground. "I warned you." Shade tossed the fruit in the air and caught it, Kora's gaze jumping from it to him. "I said to leave her be. You just couldn't listen."

Then the xéchase clawed from the lagoon like a decaying specter. Pitch black skeletal frames, sharp claws with long nails, and pointed teeth that chomped as they crawled on all fours. Kora gasped, pressing herself against the stone. They weren't monstrous as they had been the previous night, and Shade had control of them now. Halieus attempted to run but the creatures grabbed hold of him. The immortal sent water gusts at the xéchase, but they ignored each attack. His curses echoed through the canyon as he was dragged into the water. Then with a flick of his middle finger towards Shade, Halieus's body turned into water. Kora gasped at his ice-like form before the shape dropped, and water splashed, the xéchase disappearing into the water with him.

"Are you all right?" Shade's gaze caused pin pricks against her skin. She faced him and nodded. Words lost. Kora's hand lingered at her throat, trying to find words.

"I hope I didn't frighten you." He levitated towards her, stopping a few yards away with his brows drawn together.

Kora swallowed. "No, you didn't."

"Good." He tossed her the fruit, watching her carefully. "Do I need to track down my brother?"

Kora thought about Halieus's response to seeing the plants move. She needed to test her theory to understand. Experiment a little more. "You showed up just in time." Part of her wanted to see how he'd respond, but she shook her head. "Is this it?" She recognized the fruit—an apple. "This isn't a pomegranate."

Shade sighed. "No, it's not."

"Another dead end?"

"Seems that way. I'm sorry, Kora."

She bit her bottom lip, trying to figure out the best words to ask for what she wanted. What Captain wanted. It hurt her that she was betraying Shade, but after all this, she needed to save William. All she could hope was that Shade would understand. "Will you consider taking me to see the other Isles of Nekrós. Maybe it is there—"

The turn of his head in her direction was slow, methodical. "You want me to take you to the Isles of Nekrós?"

She wanted to wilt away under his scrutinizing gaze but wouldn't allow herself to do so. For her brother. "Yes."

"And you really think the pomegranate will be there?"

The truth... "I don't know. But if we don't look, I'll always wonder."

He turned away, shoulders tight. "I'll think on it."

"Thank you." For now, she would accept his answer. Afraid if she pushed too hard, he would grow suspicious of her motives.

"Wildflower?"

Kora looked up and met his gaze. "Yes?"

His eyes tracked over her face and down to her neck. "He hurt you." Darkness edged once again. "Left a mark on you..."

A scythe began to materialize in his grasp, and Kora reached out, grabbing hold of Shade's tight fist. "You stopped him." She held his gaze, searching for the playful immortal in a sea of midnight. "I'm safe. With you."

His expression softened—but only slightly. The form of the scythe disappeared before it could fully form. The darkness in his eyes edged away, turning blue once more. "I'm always too late for you."

She reached up and cupped his jaw. "Or just on time." He leaned towards her, closing his eyes at her touch.

The nereids breached the surface, interrupting the moment, and Kora dropped her hand and turned to face them. Gills flapped as they adjusted to the air before closing to breathe through their lungs. Kora hadn't seen the transformation before, but was transfixed by it. Even when Magna glared at her.

She gave a half smile to the nereids. "Thank you for allowing us to search your lagoon."

The nereids jumped back into the water without response, ignoring her appreciation.

Shade headed back the way they came. Kora followed, remaining near the rock formation.

"You will free the water?" Magna called after him.

Shade reached the mouth of the small river and with a few wisps of darkness, water flowed in a burst towards the lagoon. "Next time, don't make things more difficult, and I won't be forced to take such measures."

They had stopped paying him any mind, already splashing about as the dam broke away and the water level increased.

Shade turned to Kora. "Are you ready to return? Or would you like to search along the coast here?"

She was about to request they continue their search when her throbbing head made her realize how tired she was. "I don't think I can."

"I'll take you back and have Curly take you to bathe. You're going to need your energy for tomorrow."

"What is it?" Anticipation rose. Did he have an idea? Something that could actually help?

"I don't want to say yet. Not until it's confirmed."

He flew them back to the clearing and dropped her off at the edge of the tree line. As he prepared to take off, Kora saw a flicker of wings disappear from view. Was that Taea? She'd heard that Shade had forbade her from returning. Although she didn't know the details and assumed Shade had his reasons, Kora felt bad for her. This was her home too. "Shade, should you lift the ban on Taea?"

He tilted his head for a moment, and then turned on his heels. "No." He took off before she had time to question him further.

It may be for the best, but she was concerned that the pixie's absence was more dangerous. There was something about the liaison that concerned her, though she didn't know what.

She broke through the trees and entered the clearing. Her brothers were outside of the treehouse, and a small fire blazed in their fire pit. William slid over on the log he sat atop, patting the empty space beside him.

"Any luck?"

None of them answered her, their gazes piercing the dancing flames.

"We can't give up." She had to raise their hopes just a bit. There was still time and portions of the island unsearched.

"Instead of concentrating on such matters, why don't we have a little fun?" William stood, resting his hands in the pockets of his trousers.

"Fun?" Kora blinked at his offer. "What do you have in mind?"

Michael rushed to his feet in anticipation. "A campout. That would be fun. We can make a fort and—"

"No." He chuckled and caught his breath, patting Michael on the back. "Not a campout. At least, not yet. Let's go build a sandcastle. We'll leave before the sun sets and stay near the tree line. It will be safe there."

Michael shivered. "Are you sure?"

Kora glanced at William, the light shining in his eyes, but she could see his sadness barely hidden. One she never wanted to see again. Maybe this was exactly what they needed. She got to her feet. "Of course we will be. Together." She tagged William's back. "You're it!"

She ran, leaving them all in different versions of flabbergasted as she rushed towards the beach. Before she exited the clearing, she heard their laughter following behind her.

By the time Curly found them, Kora was covered in sand from head to toe. They had left a pile of shoes nearby and the boys' shirts hung over a nearby branch as they took turns burying each other's feet and legs in the sand.

"Do you still want that bath, Kora?" Curly laughed when Michael dumped a pile of sand onto William's head.

Kora peered at her brothers, debating leaving them behind. The sun was setting soon. She stood, trying to remove the sand clinging to her body and clothes. Michael was breathing heavily from laughter and the day's activities. "Give me a minute."

She called for her siblings, and they turned to face her. "It's time to head back, don't you think?"

Michael groaned in response. William laughed, scooping Michael up in his arms. "She's right, and you know it. Why don't we plan to do this again? Tomorrow?"

Kora nodded, trying not to think about the fact that they only had two days left. If Captain failed her—if she failed... "Yes, I think we should."

"Do the rest of you need to know where to bathe?" Curly ruffled William's drenched hair. "Not that you need it, but you might want to take Michael down to the pond at some point."

William shrugged. "We found the pond yesterday, and he took a dip. I'll take him again tomorrow to clean up."

"That doesn't sound fun," Michael pouted. "I only like it when Mother or Nanny bathe me."

The mention of their home sent a twinge down Kora's spine. She kissed his forehead. "Maybe not, but you stink."

"Just as much as you do." He grimaced, pinching his nose. Kora pushed Michael's shoulder, and he pouted. "When are we going home? I miss Mama and Father."

William and Kora shared a glance, and William's grip tightened on his brother.

"Soon." Kora ruffled his hair. "Before you know it."

A corner of William's mouth rose, but it didn't reach his eyes. Uncertainty lingered in his expression. So much remained unsaid between them. After last night's conversation, she hadn't allowed herself to consider how he'd feel if she were to succeed. Kora turned away, not wanting to see his doubt. "Lead the way, Curly. I need to smell as fresh as roses by the time this is done, so they can't throw it in my face anymore."

Even William chuckled a little.

Kora and Curly walked in silence towards the Lost Souls Camp. Once they reached the other side, they followed a wide trail through the forest in a direction Kora had not yet traveled—away from the lagoon and the mountains towards the western side of the island.

"So, what is this tree, really?"

Kora gulped, not expecting the question. She peered behind, glad to see they weren't close to the camp anymore. "I thought it was a game that Shade had created."

The soul peered at Kora with pursed lips. "Shade has been spending a lot of time with you. He's never done that before. And all your brothers talk about is this fruit. I doubt it's just part of a game."

Kora veered the conversation away. "I figured Shade spent a lot of time with new arrivals. Besides, we aren't meant to be here, and he's trying to help find us a way home."

Curly chuckled. "Aye, he wants you to return home. But not for the reasons you think."

She stopped mid-step. Curly continued down the path before realizing Kora had stopped, and then turned around.

"What does that mean?" Kora asked.

The soul sighed, her mouth curling up on one side in a sad smile. "A lot of times, we get lonely. It's expected on an island with such small numbers. We're dead. All of us know that. But it doesn't mean we don't feel the need for companionship. I haven't been here the longest, but I've been around awhile. Shade has filled that need of companionship for other souls. That was all it was between him and Astari. A need to not feel alone. Unfortunately, Astari didn't realize what many of us already know—it's not forever. Just like the souls who cross to the other side together, they may stay by each other's sides, but they won't feel the need for connection anymore. Here—we do. Shade may want to feel that as well, but he's different than us. And not just because he's immortal."

Kora's brow furrowed. "All right, but what does that have to do with his reasons for wanting us to leave?"

"He's never had such an interest with anyone before. I'm not saying it's because he's selfish, but why would he want to connect with the souls when they're eventually going to leave? At first, we thought he stayed close because you were mortal and he wanted to keep you safe. But now..." She shrugged. "Maybe it's something more than that. It might be a weakness he's not willing to confess."

Curly began to walk again, and it took Kora a moment to gather her thoughts before she followed. "There is nothing to confess. I'm mortal. I don't even think it would be safe to call him a friend. Besides, we're leaving."

"Are you sure you want to?"

Kora bit her bottom lip. *No.* She wasn't sure. Not that she'd ever say that aloud. Here things were simple. Easy. But her goal was to return home with her brothers. With William. Alive. That's why she was here. For him. For her world. For those suffering and dying. Not for an immortal. She needed to remember that. Even if guilt was eating away at her for one reason or another...

"I don't blame you for not having an answer to that question," Curly said, interrupting Kora's thoughts. "I can see your confusion when you look at him. The way you don't want to say goodbye to William too. Do you know why I haven't crossed yet?"

Kora shook her head, wishing she could tell someone the truth. That she wasn't going to say goodbye to her brother.

"At first, I thought it was because I feared the unknown. Then I realized it was because I wasn't finished with my purpose. There hasn't been a time that I hadn't wanted to be a mother. Here, I'm able to be that for so many when they've needed it. I died in childbirth with my little girl."

"I'm sorry." Kora remembered all the times she had thought the idea of being a mother more burden than blessing. It had nothing to do with the act itself, but with the expectations society would place on her—to halt her dreams and focus only on her child. But this soul had once wanted nothing more than to hold a baby in her arms.

"It's all right. Shade checks in and said my daughter and husband are doing wonderful together. Maybe I'm waiting for them. To see her as I had dreamed of before I passed. But until then, I wait and fulfill the need I have here. There might be a purpose for your presence as well."

Kora opened her mouth to ask what the soul meant when a small pond came into view with moonlight reflecting off the water. The last place she had bathed had been more like a puddle of clean water that had reached her waist. This place offered a chance to soak her entire body.

Curly smiled. "It's beautiful, isn't it?" She patted Kora on her shoulder then turned. "I'll wait over here to give you some privacy."

"You don't have to stay. I can find my way back." Kora began to untie the laces on the boots.

"I know, but Shade asked me to." Curly winked.

Kora could only nod. When Curly was out of sight, she stripped off her clothes. Once in the water, relaxation was replaced by the many thoughts brought on by Curly's words.

Chapter 32
Shade

Shade had sat upon the canopy of the tree and watched as Kora broke through the brush below, her brothers trailing close behind before they had tumbled onto the sandy beach near the forest. He grinned at their play and the laughter that echoed through the trees. It was nice to see her relax. To let her guard down and enjoy herself. For a moment, he considered joining them, but he knew that he wasn't needed. The Darlings needed this. A memory—a moment—that most never get to have.

Besides, William was annoyed at him. It had been evident by the glares he'd received when he brought Kora back. Although he had tried to be a perfect gentleman or at least follow Curly's advice in an attempt to achieve such a title, it only seemed to infuriate William more. It probably didn't help that she was injured or in peril most of the time either. He felt guilty for what had happened with Halieus. Shade should have known his brother would've been a continued threat and shouldn't have left her alone.

But William was right—Shade needed to watch how close he got to her. Immortal. Mortal. God. Mortal. They couldn't be more opposite. She still had a life left to live—to return to. Shade wasn't meant for warm touches and didn't deserve a heart like hers. It was foolish of him to even look at her as anything but what she was—off-limits. He needed to ignore the flutters that grew in his chest at her touch. The small glances. The smiles and laughter. The all-consuming kiss. A kiss unlike any he'd ever had before. And she wasn't frightened at the power he possessed.

Even Astari—all the others—balked at the darkness within him. Kora had almost seemed intrigued by it. He shook his head, turning away as the siblings began to build a sandcastle. They'd be safe near the trees. William and Kora would remain vigilant, and they were far enough away from the water to be safe from any danger that lurked within.

Shade took off into the sky and searched along the horizon for the silhouette of the sails.

The *Charon* was visible in his peripheral. He turned in the direction of the ship before deciding against it, heading toward his original destination. It must have been the moment of seeing the siblings at play. Sentimentality was lost on his brother. There had never been a chance for such a relationship, and there wasn't going to be one now. Their youngest moments together fraught with dark memories of their father. A jealousy that he was certain his brother's felt towards him because of his relationship with their mother. And certainly not with everything that stood between them—a wall of stubbornness separated them, and it would take more than a few words to tear it down.

Along the southwestern mountainside, little twinkling lights came into view. The sun was edging towards the horizon and as darkness thickened, more of them appeared, brightening the meadow they inhabited. But he didn't fly straight to Pixie Meadow.

He banked along the edge, then landed amidst the thick trunks of the redwood trees. Bushes and flowers sprouted amidst the giant trees that created the Fairy Circle. The entrance to Pixie Meadow.

While he was welcome to enter at his leisure, he came to the Fairy Circle out of respect. It was one portion of the island that he didn't allow any others to go without careful consideration. Not only was his permission needed, but the permission of the Pixie Council. Taea had striven to achieve a role on the council but was —to her disdain—always denied. It entertained Shade how flummoxed she became. By now, he'd expect she'd be used to it. The council had strict rules, and according to them, she didn't meet their standard requirements. To be considered, the pixie needed to be born by a ruling immortal's first laugh. Mostly because they were the wisest of the pixies, having lived the longest, but also because they could lead over spans of time. It was rare for a pixie to die, especially one of the immortals.

Taea wasn't born of Shade's first laugh, but because their relationship was so close-knit, she had hoped it would be enough to gain her a place on the council. It wasn't. She wouldn't speak of her lineage, and he always wondered who she had come from but hadn't asked. He had given her the privacy she deserved.

Shade settled on a rock that rested in the center of the circle, looking towards the cover of thick branches and needles. Patches of the dark blue sky broke through, giving a glimmer of the last light of the day that made the space glisten.

It didn't take long for Astraea to appear. Her red tulip skirt brushed her ankles, as did her cascading pale pink hair. "To what do we owe this honor?"

Shade smiled as the pixie settled on his shoulder, crossing one leg over the other. "You're back."

"Yes, it seems there have been some needy immortals as of late." She pinned a glare on Shade. "Trouble is brewing—I can sense it. Which makes me believe you want something from me. Otherwise, you wouldn't have deigned to visit." She gripped his tunic from her perch, the feel of the fabric bunching under her little fists rubbed against his skin.

"True. I apologize, but do you prefer me to leave you be?"

Astraea rolled her eyes. "Smart, yet so full of mischief. One day you'll surprise me, I suppose. Maybe that will be tonight. What is it you came to ask?"

"Have you seen a pomegranate tree?" It was best to get straight to the point. Any attempt to go around the truth would only lead him here anyway. The pixie didn't like her time being wasted.

Astraea pursed her lips. "Why do you ask such things when you already know what you seek?"

Shade sighed. "Because I hoped I was wrong."

"I assume this has something to do with the mortals who have suddenly appeared on the island?" Astraea brushed her fingers against the petals of a flower. When he opened his mouth, only to snap it shut, she flung her hair over her shoulder. "I hear things too, King. Please don't consider me inept even if we choose to remain separate from the going-ons upon the island."

"You've been gone. I didn't know what you'd been made aware of already. And I don't need more unnecessary drama. Least of all from you."

"Fine." Astraea waved a hand in the air. Her incandescent wings cast rainbows from the dwindling daylight. "Since when does the King of the Dead doubt himself?"

Shade rose above the ground. He made sure to keep the surety in his voice. No need to have Astraea question him further. "My deal with the mortals ends in two days. After that, will you be so kind as to return her and her brother home to the living world?"

Astraea tilted her head. "You didn't bring a gift for such a request."

"I—" He knew better. "No, I didn't."

"I want to meet this mortal. That is the gift you will give me. Tomorrow. Bring her here. I must speak with the young woman who is causing you to grow soft." Shade held back his annoyance. He had a sense of respect for the pixie, and he knew her heart was in the right place. Even if her tone was harsh. Especially when he had hoped to bring Kora to see her. "Watch how you speak to me, Astraea." His voice low, the warning left between them. "I wanted to give her a chance to save her brother. It wasn't an easy loss for her—she blames herself. She needed closure and this allowed it."

The pixie waved her hand with a scoff. "I can assist with their return tomorrow, if necessary."

He knew she would question him further, but he didn't care. "I won't go back on my word. They have two more days."

The pixie groaned. "I like you, King. Always have, but sometimes you're so frustrating." She tensed for a moment. "I've been hearing things. Talk of strange happenings since their arrival to the island."

"Such as?" Shade folded his hands behind his back. He hadn't spoken of his observations to anyone else.

"The plant life—strange growth not seen here before."

Shade cleared his throat. "It seems as though the plants are reacting to them."

"Explain."

Shade told her about the lupine growing at the base of his dead tree. How the algae had brightened at Kora's presence. Astraea's mouth pinched closed in thought. "Interesting."

"Care to elaborate?"

She laughed haughtily. "Maybe I will after I meet her. Really, King, you would think by now that some questions are unnecessary. Do you forget who you speak to?"

"I obviously need to visit more often." Shade grinned.

With a pop, she transformed to the size of his hand. She flew forward and patted the top of his head. "Maybe, but don't rush back. Unless she's with you."

Shade rose higher in the air, chuckling.

"Oh, and be careful," she called after him.

Shade waved. "I always am. Don't worry, I have things with Captain under control."

"I wasn't talking about him."

Shade whirled around, but the pixie had already flown away.

By the time Shade returned to the treehouse, he chose to ignore the pixie's words. Even if he had overanalyzed what exactly she had referred to his entire flight. In the Isles of Nekrós, there was nothing he needed to be wary of unless it was Captain's plan.

A reminder of why Kora was here. There were signs. Her disappearance in the water was no coincidence. And her mention of visiting the other isles wasn't either. Her presence was to distract him. But what was the final phase to this plan?

Because he knew it was his brother's doing that the mortals had arrived. That he had high hopes for the Darling children.

He landed in the clearing, at the entrance of his home. The lupine that had sprouted beside the trunk of the tree had sprouted flowers in shades of deep blues and purples. His hand was on the handle when a brush of cold touched his shoulder.

"You know, I like to rest too." Shade turned to face William, the soul standing with his arms crossed. "I might not need it, but it does help my mood."

"She's sleeping in there." William's gaze was clouded, and Shade recognized the warning in his tone.

Shade sighed. "I'll sleep in the hammock." He turned to go inside, but William grabbed his bicep.

"No, I don't think you should." He pointed to the hut where quiet snores sounded from the sleeping boy.

Shade's anger rose, but he bit back the taste of the power that spread through him. He glanced down where the soul dare touched him "I've done all I can to ensure you and your family are as comfortable as possible. For the past five days, I've assisted in searching for a fruit that can't be found."

He paused, almost expecting the soul to balk at the certainty in his tone, but William didn't react. Maybe he had already accepted the truth as Shade had hoped he would. "What do you think I'll do from a hammock that I couldn't have done in the many times we have been alone together?"

William blinked in surprise, pulling away. "You wouldn't have—"

Shade ran a hand through his hair. "Exactly. Not then and not now." Except kiss her. He wouldn't repeat it, though. Even if it was constantly on his mind. "She's mortal—living and breathing,

William. I'm aware of that. How many stories have you heard about my dalliances with the living?"

William's eyes widened for a moment, swallowing hard. "None."

"Exactly. That's because no one wants to tie themselves to the God of the Dead, and I would never force anyone to. Least of all a mortal." His heart pitter-pattered against his chest at the thought.

None had chosen him, and he didn't blame them. They only left him. Mortal or immortal. Dead or alive. Pixie. He'd accepted long ago that his fate would be finding friendships with only those here on Anamoní—companionship with souls not ready to pass on. This was it.

The soul dropped his gaze to the ground.

"Now, may I go to bed?" Shade didn't really need his permission, and William had to know that. This would be the last time he would let the soul have this strange idea of equality. Otherwise, it would be time to go to the docks.

"I'm..." He looked up and met Shade's gaze. "I apologize for my assumptions. The stories of the gods are infamous. I shouldn't have—" He stumbled over his words, but Shade only shook his head.

"Good night, William."

"Night."

Shade stepped inside, slowly closing the door behind him. He glanced over Kora's curled up form in his bed. The scent of fresh flowers rose from her and surrounded him. For a moment, he allowed himself to close his eyes and inhale her scent. But only for a breath. Then he silently rose to the hammock that hung above. He rested his head back on his arms and stared up at the ceiling. There was a small hole in the wood that opened to the night sky. When he closed one eye, he could see through it—like a spyglass to the outside world. He drifted off to sleep, dreaming about what the living world had once been for him and what it could be no more.

Chapter 33
Kora

Kora hadn't tried to listen in on the conversation between Shade and William the previous night, but bits and pieces had traveled through the door. After Michael had fallen asleep under the stars, Kora helped William move him into his hut. She had trouble falling asleep even though she had pretended to be when Shade entered. While she was grateful that her twin was still willing to look out for her, she was also embarrassed. As the god had said—she was a mortal.

Their kiss must have been nothing more than that. A moment that she wouldn't regret, but that was over.

Basically a nobody.

Well, he hadn't said the last part, but it was close enough. It shouldn't bother her. For many reasons but particularly because she was here to take William home. Yet, there had been a tone of melancholy when he spoke to her brother. Unless the God of the Dead had manipulated her? Or maybe she saw the truth for what it was. That Shade, although mischievous and a bit selfish, cared for others. Mortals. After her conversation with Curly, she had a better understanding of why some chose to stay on Anamoní.

Now that she knew Shade better, she was having a difficult time keeping her end of the deal with Captain. Guilt gnawed at her. But for William, she'd do it. For the mortal world, she would.

Wasn't that what she was doing with her parents before all of this happened? Doing everything she could to appease them. For most of the night, she had spent her time over-thinking and replaying their conversation in her head.

By the time she had finally fallen asleep, she knew one thing to be true—there was no way she'd fail. Time was running short. If she didn't find the fruit now, she'd go to the King of the Gods himself. Somehow. It was going to be difficult enough to talk Shade into taking her to the Isles of Nekrós. But it was her last hope.

Which meant she slept like the souls on Mizéria Isle.

Nightmares plagued her, forcing her awake at odd hours of the night. At one point, she was certain someone was rubbing her back, soothing her with reassurances she didn't quite understand. If it wasn't nightmares waking her, she'd toss and turn until she had to unwrap her limbs from the blanket.

When the morning light blinded her from the little window, Kora sat up and stretched her arms. She considered lying back down and trying to sleep again, but she couldn't afford to waste daylight. The treehouse was otherwise empty. Even though she knew Shade had slept above her, the hammock hung vacant. She exited to the clearing, her eyes slitted to block as much of the sun as possible.

"You sleep all right?" William sat on a log near the dead fire, drawing shapes in the dirt with a stick.

She plopped down beside him, picking up another twig, and began to do the same. "No. You?"

He shook his head. "I don't need much sleep anymore. Not that I don't rest when I can. It's a hard habit to break. Which is weird, but I'm getting used to it. I just lay there most nights and stare at the stars. They sure are pretty."

"Oh." Maybe she should have stayed with him last night, but then he would have wanted to talk. Kora hadn't even asked him about what it was like to be a soul on the Isle of Waiting. "Food?"

"Nope, not a necessity either. Just something to enjoy from

time to time, but I don't ever feel hungry or a desire to eat." He stopped and held up the stick.

She glanced over at the line drawing of the island's mountainside and valleys. "I haven't seen you draw in forever."

"Well, Mother and Father said it was a waste of time."

Kora bit her bottom lip. "Just because they said such things didn't mean you should have stopped. You have talent."

William swallowed. "I'm not like you, Kora. Never was brave enough."

"What does that mean?" She blinked in surprise. "I was the one that kept quiet and sat there while they brought the next most eligible bachelor to dinner. Watched in silence as they dismissed my aspirations."

"But you still dreamed, and you still tried. All those experiments in the garden." The words were a mere whisper. "They didn't take that from you. You studied, read books, and followed your interests even though they said otherwise." He shrugged. "I just stopped drawing when they said it was a waste one too many times. Gave up and moved on to what Father wanted from me."

She almost asked him if that was what had pulled him away from her but thought better of it. Not now. "Well, when we find the pomegranate tree, you'll have a chance again. And I hope you plan to do things differently."

William's shoulders slumped and he turned to face her. "Kora—"

"Are you ready?" Shade landed, interrupting her brother.

She ignored the immortal, trying to see if she could decipher what William meant to say, but his face fell blank.

Resigned that this conversation would need to continue later, Kora stood, brushing the dust from her backside. "Where are we going?"

There was trepidation in his expression, his mouth a thin line, brow furrowed. "We're going to fly over the isles."

Kora jumped, her hope rising. "We are?"

"I'm coming too." William stood beside her.

Shade crossed his arms. "You can't. There is only one way the dead can enter the Nekrós, and there is no way back. You'll have to stay here."

"It's all right, Will. This is our chance. I know the tree is there." Kora grinned excitedly. She thought it would be a fight to get him to take her.

"It's not all right. He's taking you to the home of the dead. If something—"

Shade sighed. "We aren't landing. We'll search overhead." He pinned a glare on Kora. "Understood?"

She resisted the desire to continue jumping up and down. It would be more than enough. There was no way they would miss the tree. Once there, she'd find a way to get him to land. "Of course."

Shade stepped away from William. It was then that Kora realized how close the two had come together, the space between them narrow. Even though, in certain situations, William seemed to tower over Shade, now the immortal looked taller than her brother who cowered beneath him.

But not in fear. Instead, a sense of understanding was in his expression. "Are you all right, Will?"

Her twin forced a smile. "Fine. It's fine. Be careful. Fly safe and when you're back, let's chat."

She nodded. "I would like that." Especially since she'd have the fruit.

"Pixie dust?"

"Not this time." He held out his hand towards her, and she stepped in closer to him. "I need to keep you close this time," he whispered.

Even though she had loved to fly alone, she couldn't deny the anticipation that moved through her at the thought of him holding her.

He maneuvered her on his back this time, and she wrapped her arms around his neck. As Shade took off, Kora looked over her shoulder and watched as William headed towards the Lost Souls

Camp with his shoulders slumped and hands stuffed in his trouser pockets. What had she missed in the conversation the previous night between her brother and the immortal?

Kora held onto Shade's shoulders as they flew over the beach and out towards the Depth.

The water rolled in waves below as they passed swells and suds. Shade curved towards a stretch of land that separated the Isle of Waiting from Nekrós. Kora gripped hold of him tighter. "What is that place there?"

"Krísi. That is the entrance to the Underworld for all the dead. It's where they will face the Diskatés and be placed on the proper isle." Shade flew along the edge of the large sand bar. She hadn't noticed it before with the pinnacles and lava of the Isles of Nekrós in the distance.

"So, we are just going to fly over it then? Is it that simple?" A shiver ran down her spine as the scent of sulfur and singed earth hit her nose.

Shade chuckled. "Not exactly, no." He banked back towards the Isle of Waiting. "You're going to need to hold on real tight. Whatever you do, don't let go. Promise?"

"Is this just an excuse to keep me close?" She couldn't help but ask and felt his shoulders tense in response.

"Don't tempt me, Wildflower. I'm trying to behave as it is."

"So that was it then. One kiss was all you wanted?"

Shade slowed and tightened his hold on her thighs. For a brief moment, she closed her eyes, enjoying the sensation of his grip on her. Resisting the desire to ask for more. She was thankful fabric was between her and his touch. "No, Kora. It wasn't all I wanted. But you will be going home. As much as I want more—we can't. You have a life to return to." There was sadness in his voice, and Kora swallowed, gripping him tighter in comfort—or because she wasn't ready yet to let him go.

"Why do I need to hold on?" She swallowed, that shiver turning to a flip-flop in her stomach.

"Because you're about to get wet and if you don't hold on the

Shadow Souls will have a chance to grab you." He rose a little higher in the air.

Her arms tightened further around his neck. Her legs gripped his waist like her life depended on it—which it did. "Are we going in the water?"

"Yes. It's the only way for someone like you to reach the Isles of Nekrós. I can't exactly walk a living mortal through the Gates of Judgment without causing a ruckus."

"You didn't say anything about this." But she had no time to ask anything more.

Shade plummeted, and her shrill screams could probably be heard all the way back on Ananomí Isle. Right before they hit the water, she took in a deep breath of air. The water was shockingly cold as they plunged into it. Kora pitched her eyes closed, clinging onto Shade as he jetted through the water. Lungs burning, legs aching from their tight hold, they broke the surface just when Kora thought there was no end and took a big gulp of fresh air.

Catching her breath, her body shivered again but not because of the chill of the water. The sight before her had her eyes widening in shock. "Wait. How?"

Before her was the Isles of Nekrós but, instead of the scent of death and torment she had expected, there was nothing. The air was stagnant, without breeze. The water like glass.

"What you see from the *Charon*, the Isle of Waiting, even from Krísi is a mirror image of the real Isles of Nekrós." Shade slowed, then straightened so she could take in the expansive view before her.

There were four islands in all, and each was as distinct to their name as one might expect. "But it doesn't smell and there is no sound?"

"No. Well, not unless you're over the isles themselves. The reason for this is to deter anyone from getting too close. It's also so those on Eiríni are not hearing the sounds of Mizéria. Not that they could if they wanted to. There are two points of entry—the Gates and a pathway within the Váthos Sea that connect the image to the truth." Shade wrapped his arms around the crook of her legs and headed towards the western island.

"This is Iroes Isle." He hovered over the island with gorgeous pine trees, fields of wildflowers and cascading waterfalls that surrounded temple-like structures with gauzy material hanging between columns. It only made her think of her first conversation with Captain and guilt bit at her. "Where the heroes and most noble go to rest. I'll get closer for a better look, but I can't touch down. We'll take as long as you need."

"Why can't we land?" Kora fidgeted on his back, wishing to jump free of his hold. A shiver stole over her but just as quickly she felt it, it was subdued with his touch warming her as it had in the cave.

"It's too dangerous." Shade's voice grew grim and serious. "We will know the tree when we see it. There is no need to get closer."

"I tried mentioning that to you before, but you insisted on searching every nook and cranny." She had tried to fight him on it, but he had deflected with his own logic. Stubborn immortal.

"That was when I was annoyed and wanted to keep you busy. Things have changed." Shade lowered until they were just a few feet above the highest treetop. He flew slow and steadily.

"Changed how?" Kora ignored his confession and searched the landscape, hoping that some of the trees would stand out to either of them. He with whatever ability he had to recognize what they searched for, and herself with the information she had from Captain.

Shade sighed. "It's..." He shook his head. "I just realized why it was important you had a choice. That's all."

She had a feeling that there was more to it but didn't push. They'd admitted so much to each other. He frustrated and infuriated her. But as she'd gotten to know him, it was becoming more difficult to assign blame to him. The lines between what she needed, what her world needed, and the feelings of an immortal were blurred. And she couldn't falter.

Figures in varying shades of colors created a rainbow as they floated among the trees. They weren't distinct, just outlines of the people they once were. She remembered them scattering when she and Captain had first met. "Are those souls?"

Shade nodded. "They are. It's the final essence of a person. What remains after living in the mortal world and being judged."

"That's what awaits my brother?" Kora bit her bottom lip. Maybe it was different for them, but she couldn't imagine William no longer being complete—whole. Not that, from how he explained it, he was whole now anyway. Unable to delve deep into emotions and cry, no body to cling to, sleep and food no longer a necessity. It was a half existence—if that.

"It's what all mortals become at some point, but there's a reincarnation option for those on Iroes and Eiríni. Eternity is a long time," Shade said with a touch of melancholy. He curved around a waterfall and pond similar to the nereid's lagoon. It would have intrigued her if she hadn't been so intent on finding her brother's chance to return home. But there was no pomegranate tree. Or any tree that bore red fruit. Once or twice, she asked him to lower closer to the trees for a better view. She noted their locations, wondering if she should ask him to bring her back here if things didn't pan out on the other isles.

"Everything seems so much more vibrant and brighter than I expected," Kora observed, hopes still high as she admired the bright wildflowers, shades of green and the multitude of colors that reminded her of her brother's favorite artist, Monet.

"Because of the dead?" His voice was gruff.

Her cheeks flushed. "Not exactly. But the stories make it sound like the isles were muted and devoid of color."

Shade glanced over his shoulder. "That's because most think of death as a curse."

She pressed her lips together, uncertain what to say in response.

"We'll head to Eiríni now."

"Where the good of heart rest?"

Shade nodded.

The island was a little less ornate than its neighbor, but similar with the occasional structures and fewer wildflowers and trees. The tranquil fields were broken up by sparse wooded areas of cypress and birch trees. There was a steady calm and a relaxing breeze that spread the scent of freshly cut grass.

Kora breathed a deep sigh. "Does anything stand out to you?"

He shook his head, curving once more around a group of trees with sweet-scented pink blossoms. "No. Most trees don't sprout fruit here."

Shade pointed to the next island. "That's Lýpe."

Desolate. Desert. The isle could be summed up in those two words. Where the sad and broken-hearted lived with their regret. Great sand dunes curved upward, but other than a few patches of dried grass, there was nothing else to account for. The orb figures here were just as depressing as the landscape. They moved slowly, hunkered over as if they held the weight of the world on their shoulders.

Kora remained silent as they flew over the island. Shade dipped and curved with the small hills, searching every divot but there was nothing there.

"Ready to move on?"

Kora bit her bottom lip. "Yes, but do you think there is even a chance the pomegranate tree is on Mizéria?"

"Scared?" He slowed as they headed towards the easternmost island.

"It just seems like a fruit with the ability to save a soul wouldn't be on the most dangerous island in Nekrós."

"I promised I would leave no rock unturned. If you prefer, I can come back without you and search on my own?" Her grip tightened and he chuckled, the sound vibrating against her chest. "I was only jesting, Kora."

The sound of her name on his lips took her away from the putrid torment of sulfur and ash coming from the nearing island. "Let's get it over with."

"Sometimes it helps to look at the island for what it isn't."

Lava curved around stone and the wasteland that made up the island. A volcano hiccuped, flaming lava sputtering upward. There were no orbs in sight. "It's so quiet."

Shade's grip tightened on her legs. "That's because I muted the sound. For Lýpe and Mizéria, the noises are enough to give you nightmares."

She leaned in closer. "Thank you."

He only nodded as they flew over the island. Not a single tree in sight—not that she expected there to be one amidst flames and destruction. It was a dark, dismal place. A gray cloud hung over it, blocking any hope a sunny day might bring. Shade took them over a large volcano near the center of the island. It was dry with no sign of lava, but it looked more foreboding than all the pain surrounding it. "What's that place?"

"The deepest levels of torture. Where the most deserving are sent and...the prison holding my father." He curved around the opening—it was a dark pit, fathomless and desolate. Magma made up the walls of the abyss.

"Your father?" Kora narrowed her eyes, trying to see the bottom—to this prison he claimed was there. All she saw was curling smoke and darkness. "That's where he is now?"

"After my brothers and I were freed, we needed a place for him," Shade replied noncommittally. "He would torture us, allow us to heal, only to be torn apart again. He always said that he must keep us under control, or we would rise against him. We were a threat he couldn't allow to run free. Theil—Captain, that is—and I had planned to overthrow him. He wasn't a great leader. The mortals were suffering. The gods were either deteriorating or running rampant. Somehow, he found out."

His hold tightened on her legs. "It wasn't until the three of us reached an age when our powers were at their strongest that Halieus and I helped Captain escape. He found our mother and the two of them worked together to get us out. I am meant to be my father's jailer for eternity. I can't remember how much time has passed now."

"I...I can't imagine what that was like." Kora considered the pain Shade must carry from his scars, but then to have to spend his life overseeing the immortal who caused them... She and her parents didn't always agree, but she couldn't deny that she knew they loved her."I'm sorry."

"Don't be. You didn't have anything to do with it."

"Doesn't mean it wasn't traumatic," Kora whispered the words, but the immortal must have heard them.

"I ignored it for a long time. Suppressed it. Raz recognized that I might not be as okay as I'd pretended. If it wasn't for him, I would probably be more damaged. He was a great listener, and gave even better advice."

"You miss him still. After all this time?" She could hear the heartbreak in his voice. Wanted to reach out and comfort him.

"The loss of someone you cared for never goes away. It might lessen, but it's always there. He left, not that I blame him. I like to think he's happy now. Even if I couldn't be enough for him."

"And your mother," she whispered, asking the questions she wanted to before. "Where did she go?"

He was quiet for a moment, as though deep in thought—if she didn't know him better. When he spoke, it was with a slight frown. "She had spent a long life fighting giants and dealing with my father's tantrums. When she knew her children were safe, she decided she was no longer needed. She felt it was her time to rest. All we know is she is still out there somewhere. Maybe she watches, maybe not. If she does, it is in the mortal world as I've had no sight of her. If my brothers have seen her, they haven't told me."

Kora didn't know what to say. It was obvious that he was hurt by his family's absence. She nuzzled into his chest. "If I could choose—"

"Please, don't finish that sentence."

She snapped her mouth shut. Of course, he was right. She was returning home soon. And she should be concentrating on William. There still was no sign of the pomegranate to save her brother. Had Captain abandoned their agreement? Since that night, she hadn't seen or spoken to him. How could she force Shade to the Isles when she couldn't get him to touch down?

Instead of saying what was on her mind, she kept it simple. "I'm glad Raz was there for you while he was. What about Taea?"

"Taea didn't arrive until after Raz left. She had come searching for him because the two had been friends. He'd never mentioned her to me but with the knowledge she had of him, I knew it must be true. She helped me try to locate him until we both decided he didn't want to be found."

Shade veered away from the island. "I'm sorry, Kora. I don't think the pomegranate tree is here."

She bit her bottom lip, tears stinging her eyes. No. She couldn't give up. "Can we go over one more time? Please?"

Shade was quiet, but then nodded. "Once more, just in case."

Neither said much as he flew them over each island. Nothing. He didn't seem to be drawn towards the tree as she had hoped. Unless he was pretending. Another fact to consider. Hopelessness settled within her chest, because if Shade couldn't find the tree and she couldn't make him return to the Isles, then how would she save everyone? "And you're certain we can't land?"

His muscles grew taut under her. "Yes, I'm sure."

She looked at the distance again between her and the ground. There would be broken bones, at the very least. Shade had been careful to maintain deliberate distance from the ground as if he knew the direction of her thoughts. She berated herself for not considering a back-up plan sooner. Instead, she'd concentrated solely on finding the fruit. Now, she had no plan. That had to change. And quick. Despite the way the immortal made her feel and the guilt for forcing him to return to the Isles. She couldn't blame him for not wanting to be here. Yet, if she didn't find a way, then William would be stuck here, and she would do anything to prevent that.

Chapter 34
Shade

Kora was contemplative as they broke through the water and returned to the other side. She remained quiet when they reached the island. Shade didn't interrupt her thoughts, letting her come to her own decision on how to move forward. It wasn't until they reached the coastline that she broke the silence.

"Can we fly over the Isle of Waiting?"

Shade could hear the disappointment in her voice. He hated that he was the one who took her hope away. But William would agree. Fate had spoken.

"I can do you one better. Not only will we fly over, but we'll go to Pixie Meadow. Astraea would like to meet and granted you access."

She emitted a small gasp, and he worried that he was giving her another touch of hope soon to be broken. He wondered if this would be enough for her to realize she'd done her best. Not everything could be controlled by sheer will and determination. Some things still didn't work out. He wished it was the case and not only for her.

As Shade flew them over the island, Kora twisted on his back for a peripheral view to continue her search. He almost felt bad for not telling her the truth about the fruit. But he'd always hoped she would talk things through with her brother. To get the closure she needed. And there was still time. Even if they only had one day left.

They reached the Fairy Circle and before his feet even had a chance to touch down, he felt the tug towards the Meadow. Astraea was ready for them. But he waited, turning to face Kora. Her arms were wrapped around herself, and he noted the vulnerability in her eyes. He let the pull lead them through the great redwoods. As they crossed, Kora's jaw dropped in wonder.

"How?"

Shade chuckled. "Magic."

"I've walked near those trees many times and caught a glimpse when we flew over it, but it didn't look like this." The awe in her voice made him smile.

"No, it wouldn't. You must have permission to enter."

Before them a meadow glittered in the sunlight. Pixie dust was sprinkled on the edges of every surface, making the space glisten with each shift of air.

As they landed, Kora smiled at the different flowers that danced in the cool breeze floating over the meadow. "I've only seen tulips in books." She crouched down and took in the scenery. "There are even orchids here."

He let her take her time as she continued to take in her surroundings. "Hydrangeas. Is that a bush of bougainvillea?"

"I wouldn't know. But tell me about it."

She spoke in that storyteller's voice, listing off different species and talking about how they usually relied on different soils or the sunlight to survive. "It must be different here?"

He winked at her when she met his gaze. "Magic?"

"It's beautiful magic. I could stay here all day." She blinked and swallowed. "Except...William."

He recognized the moment was over. When reality resettled on her shoulders, and he wished to relieve some of the pain. "Stay on the path and follow me. These are the pixies' homes."

"Homes?" Kora searched the ground, careful to place her feet exactly where he stepped. He held out a hand when she nearly tripped, and she quickly took it for balance. "Where are their homes? Now I'm terrified I'm going to smush them."

Shade pointed towards the plants. "They are in the petals of the bluebells or the tulips. Some live in the logs and others have created homes from stone."

The flowers bent towards her as they passed, opening slightly. Fairies flew from them, annoyed by the sudden movement. Even more so as pixies poked their heads from behind leaves or peered from beneath branches. A few exited from a cluster of daisies, levitating above the flowers and watching as she walked. He noted the way the flowers seemed to follow her, as though she was their sunlight. Astraea hopefully would have answers. Kora was unaware of what she was doing as her eyes took in the multitude of colors.

Shade was unconcerned with any of the pixies, though, and they him. He remained on the small, dirt-packed trail that forced them to walk in single file.

"It's beautiful," she breathed.

He glanced about and grinned. "It is, isn't it? The most colorful location on the island."

When Shade stopped, she almost rammed into him, but he didn't let go of her hand. She was warm to the touch, and he remembered how soon she would be leaving. That he would no longer hear her heartbeat. No longer breathe the scent of her, yet his bed would be tainted by her memory. An ache in his chest forced him to put those thoughts aside.

Mortal. Alive.

Reasons why anything between them should be forbidden.

Shade took a seat on a large stump and patted the space next to him. "We wait here."

"For what?" She settled beside him, still taking everything in with a wide smile and curious eyes.

"Aw...here is the reason for all of the excitement."

The small voice caught Kora off guard, and she jumped as the beautiful pink-haired pixie stopped in front of her. Shade couldn't help but grin at her reaction. Astraea was in her human-sized form, which was still a few inches shorter than Kora.

"Kora, this is Astraea." Shade stood and looked back at Kora.

As if the recognition of Shade's deference was enough, Kora stumbled to her feet, snapping her mouth shut in the process. The pixie's wings fluttered a bit at the sudden movement. Kora bit her lip. "You're much taller than I expected."

Astraea laughed, the sound as delicate as tinkling bells.

"Magic," the pixie whispered. "You caused a bit of a breeze on your arrival. The flowers appreciated your presence, my dear." Astraea's lips pursed for a moment, and she looked Kora up and down. "It's lovely to meet you."

"I'm happy to make your acquaintance as well." Kora gave an awkward curtsy.

Astraea smiled. "I hear that you were brought to the Isle of Waiting unexpectedly?"

Kora nodded. "Yes, but I know it was to save my brother." She pointed at Shade. "I don't think he agrees."

Shade held up his hands. "I've been assisting you this entire time. Don't turn things on me."

Kora grimaced. "Sorry, that was wrong of me. Shade has been a big help."

"That can wait a moment." Astraea folded her hands in front of her, tilting her head at the mortal. "Do you know what you are?"

Shade took a double take. His brow furrowed in consideration.

"Uh, a mortal woman?" Kora looked just as puzzled as Shade felt.

Astraea glanced at Shade then back towards Kora. "There is immortal blood within you. I've now seen proof."

"What?" Kora's mouth parted.

Shade considered the evidence and chuckled at the words being spoken aloud.

How had he not realized? The signs—the way the flowers and algae reacted. The unexpected growth of the lupines by his treehouse. The treehouse itself. He peered at the woman beside him and couldn't help it, he chuckled again. "Of course, you are. That makes perfect sense now."

Kora shook her head, her brow furrowed in thought. She began to pace. "No, that really doesn't make any semblance of sense."

Astraea held out her palm, waited for Kora to still long enough to take it before grasping her hand with both of hers. "You have spring within you. The flowers react to your presence. I've heard tales that plants have sprouted where none had deigned to before. Because of you—of your presence. Are you saying you haven't noticed?"

Kora glanced between him and Astraea. "Yes." She sighed. "I didn't think it had anything to do with immortal blood. I thought it had something to do with the magic of the island."

"That's understandable."

"That doesn't make sense though. My brother died, and I doubt my parents have any semblance of power." Her tone heightened. "And they are my parents. I know it—Mother and I—"

Astraea hushed her. "They are your parents, my dear. The blood within you is old but it has survived and passed through your family. The reason you nor your family have shown no previous signs of magic was because you had no connection to an immortal realm."

"Until now," Shade breathed. Even if he had an idea of why she was here. Did her presence have a deeper meaning after all? Or was it all by chance. "What does this mean?"

"It could mean she needs to learn to wield her power, or it could mean absolutely nothing at all." Astraea squeezed the young woman's hand. "It's a lot to take in, I know, but there is a chance this will mean very little. When you return to the mortal world, you may not be able to touch on your power at all."

"So, I will lose it once I leave here?" Kora blinked, glancing around the meadow. Her eyes widened as she took in the view. The flowers were all pointed in her direction.

Shade reached for her free hand and took it. "We'll figure it out." As soon as he said it, he regretted it. He already knew the truth—he needed to stay away from her after she left. Maybe Taea... "It's rare that immortal blood is awakened since mortals don't usually visit any other realms outside the living anymore—"

Kora cut him off. "What about Will? He died? He's my twin, so wouldn't he have this within him too?"

Astraea's expression softened. "He died prior to coming here. And having immortal blood doesn't mean you are, in fact, fully immortal. It may extend your life a good ten to twenty or so years. Maybe longer if—"

"You're lucky," Shade finished for her. Astraea seemed to think better of saying what was on her mind, and Shade was glad of it. There were secrets only the immortals should know.

Kora flopped back onto the stump, staring at nothing.

Shade gave her hand a squeeze. "It doesn't change anything. Not really."

"What about Michael?" She blinked at him. "Does he have powers, too?"

Astraea and Shade shared a glance. The pixie's wings fluttered, and she breathed a sigh as she took a seat beside Kora. "We don't know. Once you return, I hope you don't mind if I check in from time to time. I'll personally escort you home and all of this will remain between us. The other gods need not know." Her glare pierced Shade's skin, but he only nodded. It's not as if he owed them anything.

"But what about William? I prayed—I know Michael and I were brought here for a reason." She swallowed. "Is there a pomegranate here? One that can bring my brother back from the dead?" Kora scanned the meadow, and he knew she had already seen the truth. There wasn't fruit here. Not the tree she sought.

Astraea shook her head. "I don't know what you were told,

but that is not what the fruit was used for." She breathed a heavy sigh filled with annoyance.

Kora bit her bottom lip and tears welled in her eyes. He wanted to take away all her pain and had to resist the urge to pull her in close. To fix everything.

Astraea patted the mortal on the shoulder. "Spend time with your family. Enjoy it. I wish I could offer some form of solace, but sadly there is nothing I can give."

"Time," Shade added. "You had the gift of more time with him. Take it while you can."

Kora pinched her eyes closed, and when she opened them, all tears were dried up. "Can we fly over before we go back?" The resolve in her tone evident.

Shade stood, letting go of her hand. He stretched out his fingers, they were tight after gripping hold of her for so long. Already, he missed the feel of her skin against his. *Not helping.* "Of course."

She stood up and faced Astraea who had done the same. "Thank you for your guidance and insight. I guess we will see you soon."

Astraea dipped her chin. "I wish I could offer something more..."

They started along the path they'd entered, Kora leading. Astraea grabbed his arm. "Does she know what finding that tree would mean for you?"

Shade shrugged. There was a very good chance she did. Especially if she was here on Captain's behest.

Astraea sighed. "Tread carefully, King. Be gentle with her. There is much pain."

"I will." Shade glanced down at where the pixie held him. She still didn't let go. "Is there more?"

"Yes. I don't think I need to remind you that whatever you may feel is a bad idea. Especially under these particular circumstances."

"The warning is unnecessary, Astraea."

"Good." She searched his face, her eyes scanning every exposed part of him, and must have decided he wasn't fully lacking since she let him go. "I will see you the morning after tomorrow, King."

The corner of his mouth lifted. It was all he could muster. "Until then."

Chapter 35
Shade

The sun was falling towards the horizon as Shade flew Kora from Pixie Meadow. His tunic and chest were wet from her tears as he carried her, but he said nothing. Kept his mouth shut tight. She deserved every feeling and emotion, and he wouldn't pry now. Although he had told her the truth from the beginning, he knew the acceptance of losing her brother was fresh. This was no need for an 'I told you so'.

Instead, he flew towards one of the highest peaks along the valley, overlooking the forest and the entire island. He sat down in the center of a rather large boulder, still cradling her in his lap. She peered out from the crook of her arm and inhaled a deep breath. "Why are we here?"

He didn't know how to answer the question, so he pointed at a clearing in the distance below, still visible in the diminishing light. "That's the location of the Lost Souls Camp. When I came to Anamoní, there was nothing here. Souls had no clue that the island existed beyond the dock they were delivered to. A mist hung over the land, casting it invisible to all the new arrivals, so they didn't attempt to travel through it and couldn't if they tried." He'd flown over it more than once. But there had never been anything beyond the low hung clouds and a chill.

"They were forced onto the shores and to remain near the

dock. The souls would board that rowboat, which took them to the *Charon*." He pointed to the boat below tied to the dock where souls waited. Smith had been a necessary addition, because with Shade's withdrawal from his title, the rowboat no longer traveled on its own. "I'd arrive at the ship, collect their coins then fly away, and the *Charon* would start off towards Krísi Isle. If someone hadn't been able to pay, they waited upon the beach, hoping for scraps until they became a part of Váthos Sea itself."

When she didn't interrupt, he continued, "I was tired of flying over this unused island but never allowed to land upon it. The power of my ties to the Isles of Nekrós were too great. Until one day, it snapped. As if the chains holding me in place were broken. There was this tug and then it all went lax, and it wasn't just me, but the Isles of Nekrós also seemed to breathe a sigh of relief."

Shade looked down to see if she was listening. Kora was glancing out over the island, her gaze distant and glazed, but she placed her hand against his chest. The touch of her warm skin against his heart made it flutter, and he took it as enough of a hint to finish his story. "I was flying over and then I saw a tree. It was the only thing that looked dead on the island, with its spindly branches that curled and twisted upward and out without a single leaf. I flew closer to find that it had an opening at its base and curiosity called to me. Somehow, and I never understood why that day was different, but I was able to land. And this time, when my foot touched down, the mist evaporated. After a while, I realized I could talk to the souls and some chose to stay. I spoke with a few of the other reapers and found I was able to go to the mortal world, if only for the night."

He decided it was best not to linger on that subject. "What I didn't do was go back to the Isles of Nekrós. Part of me fears that if I do, I'll be trapped. But another part of me forgot the place completely. No need for responsibilities—I thought I finally had been given a reward for this power I had."

"Do you mean to say that today is the first time you've been back to the Isles?"

Shade's shoulders drew back. "Yes."

"Why?" Now she looked up at him. "For me?"

Hells, she was so close. Her breath mixed with his. Her eyes still misty from crying. Her lips—he brushed the tears from her cheek with his free hand. Not letting her go while stopping the direction of his thoughts. Astraea was right. He needed to remember his place. "For you to gain some closure. Yes."

Kora swallowed, then turned back to the view.

He followed her gaze to stop himself from staring at her. "I never wanted to return. At least here I had a new purpose. One I could get behind. Instead of being hated, instead of just over-seeing the dead, I could give some of the souls a bit of hope and fun. Make certain they knew they weren't alone. That I was there for them even if they had to say goodbye to their loved ones. Even if they are meant to cross, I wanted to give them a choice." A choice he hadn't always been given. But also, he had never made his frustration and loneliness known. He was angry and had been for a long time. But he'd never explained himself to anyone. Until now. Would things be different if he'd allowed his brothers in before? Instead of putting up walls and pushing them out.

Kora squeezed his hand. "You aren't hated."

Shade looked down at her, meeting her gaze. "How couldn't you hate me? I can't give you the one thing you want." Would she ever understand if she found out the truth?

She released her hold, and rested her hand on his cheek, brushing his skin with her thumb. "Because I've seen who you truly are. And I learned long ago that I can't get everything that I want."

He didn't move, scared she would turn away. Stop touching him. He wanted to tell her he understood how she felt, but he couldn't form the proper words. To have her look at him that way —even with tears staining her cheeks—she was the most beautiful gift he had ever been given in his entire existence. Yet, he could never make her happy, let alone be anything but a reminder of what she'd lost. He was the first to turn away. "We should head back. Your brothers will worry."

"I need time, Shade. It's still so fresh—like a new cut, or the loss of a limb." Kora sniffled.

"You're strong. I saw the fire and hope within you that night. It was the first thing I noticed about you. It won't always be easy, and it will take time, but even with all that's happened, you've had an opportunity most have only ever dreamed of."

"What is that?" Kora peered up at him, large puddles of tears settled against her lashes.

His own eyes misted at the hurt she felt. He couldn't remember the last time he'd cried. But staring at her now, he wished he had the power to take all her pain away. "The second chance to say goodbye."

Kora nodded and snuggled in closer to his chest. "Do you mind carrying me still? It feels nice."

He should decline. Her skin against his was driving him mad. She was going to leave. Like his mother, his brothers, and even Raz had. At least, this time there was a good reason he was being left behind.

"Of course." He took off into the ever-expanding night sky, holding onto those last moments of having everything he could ever need.

When they returned to the treehouse, her brothers were waiting in the clearing around a campfire. From the damp state of Michael's clothes, they had spent a good part of the day playing in the water. At first, William had run towards them, his gaze narrowed, mouth pursed. "What happened?"

But one closer look at Kora, her tear-stained cheeks and pouting bottom lip, and he softened and held out his arms to cradle his twin. Shade slid her gently into his waiting arms. His hands and chest immediately felt empty. William spoke in hushed tones as Kora clung to him, and Michael reached for her hand. Shade knew this was a moment for them—an intimacy he shouldn't dare interrupt. Already Michael was beginning to cry, not yet understanding the moment but feeling the anticipation of what was to come.

Chapter 36
Kora

Kora remained numb, even as she and her siblings had huddled together on the log meant for two. They kept the conversation light, allowing her time to think. To plan. Michael had curled up in William's lap, both pressed in close beside her.

William's arm wrapped around her shoulder, tugging her into his side. "We have one more day together, Kora. Let's make it a good one. I know it hasn't been the outcome you hoped for, but I still wouldn't trade these past few days for anything."

Kora stilled. Not once had she doubted. Captain had meant it when he'd given her the option. She'd never lost hope, and only had one thing going for her now. The sacrifice—it couldn't have meant nothing. And if she wanted to save William, she'd have to do what the King of the Immortals asked. She needed to get Shade to regain his title. Even if he ended up hating her, he had to see reason. If anything, for the people of the mortal world.

William released a long, exasperated sigh. "I think tomorrow we should go to the pond. What do you think?"

Michael burrowed further into William's lap. He'd cried when William had explained he wasn't coming home. If William wasn't already dead, Michael's tight grip on his brother's neck may have sent him to his grave. "I'll always remember the time on the beach, making the stone towers, the bonfire, the sandcastles—those were all fun times."

William ruffled their youngest brother's hair. "Yes, true. All good memories." He cast a look in Kora's direction. "You holding up?"

She nodded. Those words made the numbness tingle under her skin. *All this time, she'd never lost hope.* And she wasn't going to lose it now.

"Kora?"

The sound of William's voice brought her out of her thoughts. "Hm?"

"I asked if we could talk privately." He peered down at Michael. "Besides, I think some of us need to get some sleep."

"Yes, bed. That's what I need." It was all up to her now, and she had little time to fix this. There had been a mistake when her brother died. She was here because fate had intervened. "We can talk tomorrow if that's all right? I—" She breathed a heavy sigh. "I'm exhausted after today."

William stared at her, but she diverted her eyes to brush off her pants and held her hand out to Michael. She knew William would notice she was hiding something if he saw her face. "Why don't we all have a proper sleep out under the stars tomorrow?"

"Yeah, that's the perfect way to end this adventure." Michael beamed up at her. He darted a glance towards their eldest brother. "Please?"

William chuckled. "Sounds like a good idea. Get some sleep and we'll have some fun tomorrow." He touched Kora's shoulder. "But we really need to have that talk."

"Tomorrow." She turned on her heels, dragging Michael to the hut. Right now, she had other things on her mind. One last chance she had to save William. He'd do the same for her—she knew it.

Dead. The word was so final. No going back. She needed to be sure. To have exhausted all options. Shade said he wouldn't touch down on the Isles of Nekrós, so that must be the key. If she could just make it to the islands…it hurt her chest, her heart aching at the idea of betraying him.

The truth was that the sight of the dock while she and Shade had sat on the bluff spoke volumes about what was happening to her world. There were at least seventy souls who waited to be rowed to the *Charon*. The dock was full. If Shade was right that seven days here was only a few hours in her world, then many were dying while she was tempted by an immortal.

She'd also seen it in William's gaze. He'd already accepted his own death. From the way he spoke, he had a long time ago. He'd always been a pessimist.

But she was the optimist, and she couldn't give up. Not yet.

Chapter 37
Shade

Shade shot up into the sky.

He reached the top branch of the highest tree, the heaviness in the pit of his very being expanding as wide as the distance from the mortal woman. Every muscle in his body willed him to turn back and be by her side. There was nothing he could do for her now, and he hated that almost as much as the power she had over him. No other had ever made him feel this way—he didn't deserve it. Deserve her.

Maybe he did deserve the pain.

He stayed away well into the night, not wanting to intrude on the siblings' time together, but also needing space to get over the feelings bubbling up inside.

Time gave him some perspective. Not just about Kora but the future, and he knew he should keep his distance from the mortal world. At least, for a little while. Until he was no longer drawn to her. The temptation to visit her would be too strong. Astraea had mentioned she'd check in on Kora and Michael to ensure there weren't any lasting effects from their stay in Anamoní. He'd allow one last visit to the world of the living, and then he'd stay put for a while. Until she was no longer clouding his thoughts. He couldn't lose himself. Couldn't allow Kora to change him that drastically. This was what he had wanted. Freedom.

Shade walked with fists formed at his side towards the clearing. Resolved. Certain. This would be his final look upon them. Then he'd stay with the Lost Souls until Astraea arrived the next day.

William sat at the fire pit, stroking the logs with a stick. "Hello, Shade." By the distance in his tone, the emotion was still thick.

"Did you talk to her?" Shade tried to keep his voice light-hearted.

William shrugged. "A little. She went to bed about an hour ago." He nodded towards the hut. "Michael fell asleep shortly after."

The fire highlighted the sadness in the soul's expression. Even if he couldn't cry, this was a moment Shade wished William would let some of his emotions out.

"Is she sleeping inside?" Shade started towards the treehouse.

William grabbed his arm as he passed, stopping him. "I wanted to thank you first. Even though I know you had doubts, you still gave her a chance. I might not always agree with your tactics, but I appreciate what you did for my siblings."

Shade's jaw tensed, and he met William's gaze. From the grip on his arm, he knew—could sense it. There had once been a touch of immortal blood within William. It was gone now since William wasn't connected to his body, but within his soul was a strength beyond his size. "I wish I could have done more for you."

The soul chuckled, releasing his hold. "I can say a proper goodbye. My family was here, and I'll get the closure I need. I just hope she won't carry the burden of my death any further."

Shade smiled now, some of the heaviness released from his shoulders. "Good."

William took a seat again and went back to staring at the embers. Shade headed towards the treehouse, uneasiness growing inside him once more. He pushed open the door and stared at her quiet form, curled up within his blankets. How long would it take for them to stop smelling like her? Would he care or would it be his own version of torture?

He hunched down, squatting beside the bed. Then stilled. Something wasn't right. His brow furrowed as he listened.

Silence.

He swore under his breath as he tore back the blankets, and his stomach plummeted. No—no. She didn't. Wouldn't have.

Racing from the treehouse, he locked eyes with William. "She's gone."

The soul jumped to his feet and tore past Shade. He could hear William tearing the bed apart, a blood curdling roar breaking the air. The soul rushed at Shade and grabbed him by the wrists, getting William to face him. "You saw nothing? She didn't pass you?"

William shook his head. "No, nothing." His eyes widened. "There was the sound of rustling." He pointed with his finger in the direction of the bushes leading to the beach. "Over there. But I didn't think anything of it."

Shade let go of William and stared in the direction the soul had indicated. "She wouldn't."

"What?" William shook Shade. "What wouldn't she do?"

Shade rose into the air, and William's hold pulled free with the expanding distance. "I'll find her. Stay here with Michael."

Without further explanation, he flew towards Váthos and for the first time in a long time, said his own prayer that he was wrong.

Chapter 38
Kora

It was late at night when she stole from the bed. She didn't know how she had passed by her brother unseen. Or how she had made it to the beach. It must have been far enough from morning because no souls waited for the *Charon* on the dock, but the rowboat was tied to the wooden pillar. Waiting. Beckoning as it bobbed with the gentle surf.

Her opportunity.

It took some maneuvering to carefully enter without flipping it over. She hadn't spent a lot of time on rowboats. When she and William were younger, they had gone on holiday with her parents prior to Michael's birth. He'd done most of the rowing. Mother claimed it wasn't a lady's job, but William had allowed her to try when they were far enough from their parents' watchful eye.

With a few failed attempts, her limbs seemed to remember what she wanted of them. With each skim of the oars in the water, she wished she'd brought a torch along with her. Something beyond the moonlight to guide her to the gate she needed to cross into Nekrós. Once she found it, she would use the pouch strapped to a belt at her waist. He'd left the pixie dust hanging by the door to the treehouse. She recognized the pouch from the time he'd taught her to fly alone. It had tempted her since she

297

noticed it lazily discarded on the crooked hook embedded in the tree wall—too easy to steal.

Kora had paid close attention to the locations and distances of the water entrance when she and Shade had returned from the Isles. It wouldn't be too difficult to navigate, she hoped, even if her viewpoint was different.

Eiríni had been closest, and she decided she would fly over the island first before landing on the Isle of Heroes. By then, she had no doubt that Shade would realize she was gone and come searching for her. She would be ready for him. Would have to make him see reason.

Her arms ached, pain permeating into her shoulders and chest from rowing as she neared what she hoped was her destination. The water shifted, changed, and that's when she noticed a rippled pattern, like the makings of a whirlpool up ahead. That had to be it.

She put the last of her strength into rowing, forcing the oars to pick up speed. Right outside the whirlpool she stopped, letting the rowboat be taken by the gentle swirl and pulled the oars back into the boat. With a deep breath, filling herself with resolution, she removed the pouch from her belt.

A groan sounded from nearby. Kora stilled, searching the space around her. But besides the turn of the boat, there was no movement. No sign of where the noise originated. She gripped one side of the boat, scanning the distance. Nothing.

Maybe it was best to use the pixie dust now. Problem was, she didn't know how long it would last in the water.

Another moan had Kora turning quickly, looking behind her for evidence she wasn't alone. Maybe it was her mind playing tricks on her. Wouldn't be the first time. But something in her gut tightened, warning her. They sounded vaguely like the xéchase, and it would be suicidal of her to ignore it altogether.

She waited for a breath. Two. Her heart picked up pace in her chest. A scrape sounded along the bottom of the boat. Kora inhaled deep.

The boat rocked sharply, and a gasp broke from her lips. *No. No.* She fumbled to get the pouch open wider, her fingers suddenly felt too large and the tie too small.

A hand, dark and sinister, curled around the side of the boat. Before she could scream, the boat capsized. Water burned her lungs as she opened her mouth to catch a breath before she was plunged under.

Limbs forced her down, a shrill screech as they let go suddenly. She waved her arms, her grip still tight on the pouch of pixie dust. As she breached the surface, she spit out water and gasped. Just as quickly as she filled her lungs with air, she was pulled back under by her pant leg. She kicked with her other foot, squirming. When the fabric shifted and the xéchase touched her flesh, they hissed and rushed away again.

They couldn't touch her skin.

On the beach, she remembered their reaction but hadn't connected it to her flesh. With that realization, she made it to the top again. With the belt at her waist already loose, she kicked off the pants but there were too many buttons on the shirt, and she couldn't dare let go of the pixie dust.

The xéchase circled her, and she had no doubt they were planning their next move, biding their time until she tired. What the *hells* was she to do?

The water dark already, the moon nearly invisible, she cried out as the creatures opened their dark maws with jagged remains of teeth bared as they screeched a sound that had her clutching her ears.

A plan. She needed a plan.

Not giving herself a moment to overthink it, she removed the ties and turned the pouch over her head. Clumps of shimmery blobs fell to her shoulders, nothing like the vibrant dust it had been before. It was too wet.

"No, no." *Happy thoughts!* She tried to think of something but in her current predicament, nothing came to mind. Kora bit her lip, turning in a circle, searching for the rowboat. If she could get it upright before the xéchase attacked again—

There. She swam, her sore arms protesting the movement. Each kick propelled her closer and when she reached the boat, she attempted to heave it over. But nothing made it budge. She wasn't strong enough.

Kora cursed as another creature brushed her leg. She kicked out, but she missed making any impact. They were testing what they could do to her. She tried to pull herself up, but the seam in the center of the bottom of the rowboat didn't allow enough of a handhold for her exhausted limbs.

Think. Think.

The water inked to black. They moved in closer. The xéchase darkened the moonlit water into a fathomless pit. The creatures brushed against her skin but didn't hold on. It was as if they were playing with her.

Then a head broke the surface, hair like moonlight, torn in patches. Kora's eyes widened as the head rose higher, remnants of skin clung to bone, and a grin appeared that Kora couldn't explain away.

"Astari?"

The xéchase who had once been a friend, screamed a horrible sound and lunged for her.

Kora cried out as she tightened her hold onto the boat, trying again to pull herself up when a rageful roar broke above her. The monsters grabbed hold and with a scream, she was pulled under.

Kicking, fighting, trying to free herself, they held tight over the sleeves of her shirt. Her lungs burned, her head aching, her body failing her. But she couldn't give up. Not yet.

A firm grip took hold of her arms, and a powerful burst surrounded her, forcing the xéchase back. Only one held onto her arm, their hold tight and unflinching. Kora's vision was darkening along the edges. She needed air.

Another wrapped their arms around her and pulled, jerking her to the surface with vehemence. She gulped a lung full of air.

The surge of power had knocked the xéchase off her body. She looked up, gasping for breath as Shade's face came into view. He was no longer the mischievous immortal she knew. Instead, he *was* the darkness, unchecked and rampant. A black tunic of scaled armor spread over his shoulders, down his chest and torso. It hugged his body—a protection unnecessary for an immortal. He was the God of the Dead. Terrifying in all his power. Yet, captivating. The authority he exuded even with her in his arms, the scythe in his grasp... A part of her brain told her to be afraid. But she wasn't. Not in the least.

The monsters broke the surface, screaming and clawing for her. The strong one that hadn't been deterred jumped from the water, and Kora sent a sharp kick to their face. The xéchase screamed, scraping her leg as it fell back into the water. The immortal pulled her close to his chest and whispered, "Don't look."

High-pitched screams echoed in Kora's ears, but she didn't dare peek to see what was happening as she buried her face in his chest. The sound of sucking, tearing—the agonizing pleas that followed in their wake were unfathomable as he turned his back. It was best left for the imagination. He didn't say a word as he flew her towards Anamoní.

Chapter 39
Captain

Captain smiled as he drummed his fingers against his desk. A knock at the door only made his smile lengthen. "Come in."

Smith opened the door, setting a jeweled cup down on the table and walked away without a word. This plan involving Kora may have been far simpler than he'd expected. Even if the pixie glowering at him from across the table didn't agree.

"I heard Halieus left," Taea pointed out.

Captain leaned back in his chair and shrugged. He pierced her with a look. "He proved his worth, that's for certain. Halieus was able to garner enough information and now I know. It's time."

"Why?" She sat, one leg resting over the other knee, on a brass piece that held the corner of a map in place.

"The scythe was called home. It's near, but I can't reach it. As if it's waiting for Shade's decision." Captain leaned forward, pinning her with a glare.

She rolled her eyes. "It was the heat of the moment, nothing more."

"Did you not feel it? I think the entire Isles of Nekrós felt the thrum of his call—the power he used. For her." Captain chuckled to himself. "What do you think he would do if we activated the next phase of my plan? If it involved keeping Kora safe, I have no doubt he would do anything."

"She's human. Don't you think he'd let her die if he cares about her so much? He's a selfish immortal just like the rest of you, and he doesn't want to be chained to the Isles of Nekrós. But if she's there—just as you promised..." Taea unwrapped her arms and leaned back on them to prop herself up. "If she dies, he gets exactly what he wants. Her and his freedom."

Captain stood, ignoring her little jab. It wasn't anything he wasn't used to. The pixie was angry, which wasn't surprising considering her jealous streak. "When it comes to mortals, he's never been like us, and you know that. And that's what I'm wagering on now. I tried to treat him like every other immortal under my control. Honestly, I should have thought of this sooner. Of course, it needed the right touch, and I believe Kora was the perfect mortal to do the job. Otherwise, why wouldn't he let her die at the hands of the xéchase? They would be the perfect scapegoat if he was as selfish as you believe."

Taea scoffed. "Just so you know, when this doesn't work, I get to say I told you so."

Captain donned his coat, fixing the collar to make sure it was straight. "Ye of little faith. For someone who claims to know my brother, you certainly aren't well versed in his ways. Just you wait."

He headed towards the door, placing his hat on his head. "Be ready. I want a report tomorrow on their antics. If I'm correct, it should be a very eventful day." She groaned and he heard the tinkling of bells as she began to fly away. "Remember, Taea. You wanted this too."

"That's what you think."

Captain's brow furrowed as he stroked his chin. "When will you learn that he'll never be yours?"

The pixie flew out the window, and Captain knew that if anyone could ruin his plan, that small pixie would be the one. But they had a deal—and if she didn't want Shade to know the truth of what she'd done, then Taea would continue to play along.

Chapter 40
Kora

Shade didn't take Kora straight back to Camp. As the sun hit the horizon, he landed deep within the forest, put her down, and began to walk. Silent. He was angry. She could tell by how his shoulders were drawn back, his chin high, and the fact he wasn't willing to look at her.

Every one of her senses were heightened. She jumped when a leaf crackled under her foot. The metallic scent of blood stung her nose and eyes. The brush of a branch made her body shudder. After some time, they stopped and she sat down against a tree, the bark tore into the skin at her back. She looked down at her arm and moaned at the scratches marring her skin from the xéchase's sharp nails. She still only wore the oversized shirt that clung to her thighs and was thankful that she hadn't managed to shrug it off as Shade crouched in front of her, his mouth a thin line. "How do you feel?"

With a blink of surprise, she realized that there was no pain. Just a small ache remaining in her head from exhaustion and the inhalation of water. "Better. Just a little weak and tired."

He glanced over her from head to toe, scrutiny in his gaze.

"What happened? To them?" Kora bit her bottom lip.

As they had walked, the scythe had disappeared and the armor had dulled as though it was slowly dissipating, not wanting to let go of him but finally it had. Even with the absence of the darkness and armor, there wasn't an ounce of the playful immortal present. His voice was filled with gravel. "What happened? I should be asking you what happened. What made you think that you should go into the Váthos Sea, Kora? Why?"

Tears stung her eyes, but she had shed enough of them lately. He had every right to talk to her this way. But before she could say a thing, he continued, "You risked *everything*. Your own life! How do you think William would have felt if you died?"

Darkness settled under his eyes and permeated around him. "Did you consider what this could do to anyone else? What your choices might cause?"

She lowered her eyes to the space between them. "What happened back there?"

"I wiped them all out," Shade roared.

Air caught in Kora's throat as she met his gaze. Astari had been among them. But the soul had already been lost. That wasn't the girl she had known. Either way, she would keep the knowledge to herself. There was no reason for Shade to feel more guilty than he already did.

He looked her up and down, then began to pace. "What did you think would happen?" He shook his head, gripping his hair in his fists. "They would have killed you."

Her chest ached. This wasn't what she meant to have happened. "I had to try. I wanted to search the Isles of Nekrós on foot." The words didn't come out as forceful as she wanted.

Shade's teeth clenched for a moment as he regarded her. "He belongs here, Kora. For him, there is no going back." He ran a hand through his disheveled hair.

Kora couldn't bring herself to look at him. Her death would have been a waste. She deserved for him to speak to her this way after what she'd done. "Just because you don't have something you're willing to fight for doesn't mean I don't. My brothers are my family—I love them."

Shade leaned closer. "You. You're what I'm willing to fight

for." He held her face in his hands, his lips close to hers. All she had to do was lean forward and they would touch. Tears stung her eyes, and she so desperately wanted to get lost in his touch. To apologize for everything she had done and was doing to him. To claim him for herself. He blinked and looked away. "I never said you didn't care, but if you want to survive and return home, then you need to realize the truth."

Kora scoffed, shaking her head to break the momentary trance he had her under. "That he's dead? Trust me, I know that now." She forced back the tears again. "The truth is that I would take his place in a heartbeat. He died—for me! It should have been me."

Shade lifted her chin with his finger until her eyes met his. "No, Kora. It wasn't meant to be you. The Fates don't make mistakes. Death comes when it's time. You didn't do anything wrong that day."

The tears couldn't be held back anymore. Gods, after wanting to cry, now she couldn't stop, and she was sick of it. She rushed to her feet. "No." Kora shook her head. "There is a way to change that fate. He said it, so it has to be true, which means that I'm meant to be here to save William."

"Tell me, Kora." Shade stood slowly. "Tell me what Captain told you."

Kora inhaled a sharp breath that hurt her lungs. "You knew?"

He stared at nothing, before turning that piercing gaze on her. "I figured it out."

"I'm sorry." In all the moments when she'd convinced herself of her reasons and brushed off her guilt for betraying him, she hadn't expected he'd already known. "But for the world, for others like my brother, I had to try."

"To make me go back?"

She nodded. "It's not just for my brother, Shade. It's for my people." His jaw clenched and unclenched, so she continued, "How long did you know?"

"Does it matter?"

"Did you know before you kissed me?" Her hands tightened to fists.

"Yes."

"And you kissed me anyway?"

"And have been tempted to do it again since."

She gasped. Wanted him to say it again. And again. "I wish you would."

He didn't move. Didn't blink as his silence willed her to continue. With a long sigh, she told him everything. "Captain told me the pomegranate would bring William back to life. That if I got you to find it and return to the Isles of Nekrós, then my prayer would be answered."

She waited for the backlash. Her gaze searched his for a reaction, a bated breath held in her lungs in preparation of the surge of anger, power, something. Shade only considered her. With a deep breath, she gasped. "Wait—Astraea said it wouldn't do as I wanted. Does that mean...?" She couldn't bring herself to finish the question.

"Yes. There was once a pomegranate tree."

"You knew where it was this whole time?" Kora's heart hammered against her chest.

"Yes and no."

"That's not an answer." Anger coursed through her. "You had us investigate the island over and over. What for? A game?"

"I haven't seen any signs of the tree in decades. Would you have been satisfied without searching every corner and crevice? You don't run away from a challenge. Well, unless it's learning to live without your brother, it seems."

She cursed him under her breath. That had been a low blow. As far as she knew, all he'd ever done was run away. "William is my best friend. My brothers...they are everything worth fighting for. After all of this, he deserves to return home."

"That's not how it works. No one owes you anything. Nothing is promised in life, and you should accept it." It was as though he spat the words at her.

Kora brushed off her hands on her torn water-logged shirt, knowing she showed more skin than was acceptable. Shade was immortal—he'd seen it all before.

With a lift of her chin, she met his steely gaze. "Oh, but you're wrong." She held as much venom in her words as he had tried to send at her. "Death. Death is a promise life keeps. It's something mortals either welcome or fight as long as they can." Her shoulders drew back.

Unaware how she had gotten so close, she realized she was flush to his body. Something else crossed his features, the pompous immortal shrunk a little under her glare as Kora continued. "It's something you'll never get to feel. Instead, you will remain here in all the glory of the dead. But they have felt—lived, lost and gained. You'll never have the knowledge or understanding of what real living is like. Because for you, there is no end."

She turned on her heels, ignoring the bite of the forest floor against her bare feet, and the ache in her throat from her screams. Before she broke through the brush, she whirled around to face him again. "And you're jealous. I can see it. You wish to live like those souls you collect. The way you watch them tells me everything about why you keep them close and regret their choice to move on. Because they can." A brush of a breeze whisked her hair up behind her. "Now take me back to my brothers. I know they're worried sick about me."

Shade didn't move, staring at the ground at his feet. With a heavy sigh, fists formed at his side. "For those like me, death is an adventure that can only be imagined. Yes—I envy those who live not knowing if tomorrow is promised. Before, I thought you were one of those such mortals. Yet, you're wanting me to give everything to mortals who curse me. You blame me for your world's plight, but don't look at those who cause the gods' absence. All for your brother?" Shade's tone was stagnant. The truth plain and simple. "You want to think I'm selfish, but I'm not the one with ulterior motives."

Her shoulders slumped. "William was trying to change the world. Maybe he can make a difference."

Shade blinked once, his mouth a thin line. "So could you."

She wondered if there had ever been a time he had looked so serious in his entire existence. He sighed and shook his head, accepting her silence. "If you're brave enough to try, you can do great things. Because to live is an adventure too, if you're willing to fight for it."

Kora hated that he was right. Shade crossed the distance between them. For a moment, they stood in silence, a breath of space between them. "The only way I could ever find the fruit is if I take on the mantel of God of the Dead. Are you asking this of me?"

She didn't want to lie to him. Not anymore. "Even if you put William aside, my feelings aside, don't you realize what you're doing to the world? The mortals suffer—"

"Because of Captain's choices," he said. "It's him who withdrew the immortals. If anyone is to blame for the problems in the living world, it's because my brother cannot control what he is meant to rule, so he put these damned restrictions on them."

"Is there a way to make Captain see reason?"

Shade laughed, a bitter sound that grated. "I've been trying for years. He is stuck in his ways and doesn't like his authority questioned. He thinks this is the only way."

She blinked at his words and realized how true they sounded. Not all the weight should be born on Shade's shoulders. Others were to blame. "Then yes, it is selfish of me, but I want William to return. I want the world to be a better place, and you just said I could do something about it. If you went back, then the world would be right once again."

"Maybe. But is that what William wants?" Shade asked the one question she knew he already had the answer to.

"I—" There was no way to finish that sentence.

"That's what I thought. If I were to do this for him, when he already has accepted his fate, then who am I really assisting, Kora? Will has a right to know and weigh in on your decision. Don't you think?"

Emotions, many of which she couldn't pinpoint, rolled through her body. Frustration, guilt, disappointment...all because of the truth laid at her feet.

Shade was quiet for a moment, and she knew it was for her benefit. He held out his hand toward her, and she stared as he spoke, "Your brothers are terrified. We should get you back."

She nodded and took his hand, expecting to be hauled over his shoulder as he had done so often, certain all decorum was gone. When he gently wrapped an arm around her waist and looked down at her, her skin flushed under his gaze. She swallowed deep as he searched her face.

She should look away. But at the feel of his touch, cool against her skin and the firmness of his body alongside hers, she couldn't. Even with her bare legs—the shirt doing little for protection—he was careful where he held her.

He met her gaze. "I might not understand how it is to live with the promise of death." There was sadness in his expression. "But I do know they are worried about you. Like I was. And they might be worth living for. Even William," he whispered.

There was no comeback. No quick-witted words on the tip of her tongue. She had made an immortal worry about her and didn't deserve any kindness now. But maybe there was an understanding that each of them had made mistakes. Things they couldn't take back. He waited until she had her arms wrapped around his neck and then he pushed off into the air.

The rising sun kissed her skin as they broke through the canopy of trees—away from the forest. She hated that Shade was right. That she couldn't control everything. There were things she had to live for. Her brothers. Her parents. The future she had wanted and would fight for. And maybe this immortal who tore the world apart for her.

They were quiet for some time. She had so many more questions to ask. "I'm sorry." As they reached the edge of the clearing, the words spilled from her mouth. Shade had maneuvered her onto his back as they flew, her lips near his ear. "I said some things I shouldn't have."

"Yet, they were true." Shade hesitated before lowering to the ground. "You shouldn't apologize for speaking your mind."

Kora blushed. He was the first one, other than William, to tell her such a thing. "Still, I shouldn't have been deliberately hurtful, and I could have said it in a much nicer way. Especially after everything you've done for me and my brothers. I didn't mean for you to have to wipe out the xéchase."

Shade shrugged. "They probably were thankful for it in the end. Better than spending eternity lost in the Depths. Although, if I could have, I would have wanted to ask their permission first." He peered over his shoulder and winked. "But I would do it all again. To keep you safe." His last words were a whisper.

Her mouth clamped closed at his admittance, and she squeezed him a little tighter. As he touched the ground, she realized she didn't want to let him go. During her six days on this island, he'd been a constant. He wasn't scared to tell her what he thought yet didn't admonish her for being herself. Even when he'd known the truth about the fruit, he hadn't stopped her and stood beside her during the search. "Shade, I have to ask. If you knew about Captain, why didn't you say anything from the beginning?"

It wasn't until he set her down, still surrounded by the foliage and trees of the forest that he answered. "I wanted to know if you trusted me. And, selfishly, to spend time with you. Besides, it gave you time with William." He brushed a finger against her cheek.

She gasped. "Shade..."

Her eyes met his. Kora thought about the time she had seen him at her bedroom window what felt like a lifetime ago. She almost asked him what he had been doing there, but then his gaze dipped to her lips.

They remained close to each other, with her body pressed against his. She lifted her chin slightly, saw the bob of his throat—and he stepped away with a shake of his head. She opened her mouth to say something. What, she didn't know, but anything to make him stay. To ask him what he was thinking. Did he want the same things she did? To feel his hands on her skin. To be wanted, needed. To feel alive after being confronted with death.

"I can't make promises—"

"Kora!" William's voice brought her back to reality and cut Shade off as her siblings tackled her to the ground. Her bruises and bones ached under their weight, but she laughed as she hugged them, holding them tight.

"Where did you go?" Michael asked with a tremble in his voice.

William stood, helping her to her feet and held her at arm's length to look her over. "Are you all right?" His eyes widened as he noted the scratches and there was no doubt that bruises were already forming.

"I am now." She pulled them in for a hug and couldn't resist a look over their shoulders for the immortal. Shade was gone, but she wished he had stayed.

"What happened?" William tilted his head, his mouth pursed.

"That's a story for later." She shared a glance with William. Before he could pester her further, Michael pulled on what was left of her shirt.

"We came up with a plan for today but waited for you." Michael's muffled voice continued with the plans their brother had made—no doubt to try to sidetrack him while she was missing.

"It sounds wonderful." She kissed the top of his head. "Let's do it."

They broke free, and Michael tagged William. "Race ya." He took off towards the trail that led to the pond.

William gave Kora a smile over his shoulder. "Later?"

"Yes." She nodded. "This time, I promise."

William followed in their sibling's tracks, leaving Kora to trail behind. She glanced through the trees, searching, hoping Shade would reveal himself. But he didn't.

Chapter 41
Shade

Shade watched from a distance, ensuring they made it to the pond safely. Even though Kora searched for him, he stayed hidden within the trees. He needed to be sure Astraea would be ready to take them home tomorrow. The way Kora had looked at him—he'd almost broke then. Almost took it all back and kissed her again.

He could live with the heartache of never touching her again —she hadn't lived her life enough yet to know the possibility of what the future could hold. He had things he needed to finish before they said goodbye. But he'd be selfish. She had a life to live, and he wouldn't interfere with it. Not when he couldn't promise her anything.

Shade flew over the Lost Souls Camp and spotted the others in the middle of a game. Curly turned towards him, but he veered away from her curious glance. The soul saw more than he wanted her to.

He landed on the stump in the middle of the Fairy Circle. "Astraea?"

The pixie arrived in a breath, this time as large as the palm of his hand and settled on his knee. "Is it time?"

"Tomorrow. I will need you to meet us at the Lost Souls Camp to take them home. Today they will spend time together and say a proper goodbye." Shade wanted this for them. They already had so much extra time others hadn't, but it was the gift he could give.

Astraea regarded him for a moment, searching his expression. "I worry now more for you than I do for them."

Shade shook his head. "I'm being careful. I won't return to the mortal world for some time, and you said you would check in on them."

She considered him for a moment. "And you won't ask this of Taea?"

How could he explain? There were things he needed to discuss with his friend first before he brought his grievances to Astraea. He owed Taea that much. "No, I don't think I will."

Astraea, thankfully, just nodded. "I'll meet you at your tree tomorrow morning with two others that I trust with my own life."

Shade sighed. "Thank you."

Astraea rose off his knee and hovered in front of him. "If there is something about Taea I should be made aware, please don't keep your concerns to yourself."

He should have known she'd pick up on what he wasn't saying. "I promise I will if there are things to share."

Astraea pursed her lips, but nodded before she flew away.

Shade rose into the air and flew out of the circle. With a flip, he landed on the outskirts. He forced a smile to his face, whistling as he settled himself against the trunk of a lone tree. The silly pixie preferred solitude and had claimed it as her own. It was the only place he could think she might be staying while she was banished. "Hey, Taea. I came to talk," he called up to the branches.

He waited for her to appear and wondered if she was even present when a flicker of light caught his attention. It came from above one of the boughs—a hole in the main trunk of the tree. "I've missed you." Even with all the things stacked against her, he couldn't lie.

"You should miss me," she shot back. "I've always been by your side, and you sent me away."

He closed his eyes, trying to call that playful side of him. It wasn't coming—he'd have to fake normalcy. "Come out, please."

She flitted down from the tree branch, her wings flapping behind her in quick succession like a hummingbird and allowed her to remain centered at eye level. "Why now?" She peered at him out of the corner of her eye.

"What do you mean? I meant it—I missed you." He gave her his best smile, trying to exude the happiness he wanted to portray.

Taea narrowed her gaze. "I've known you for almost a century. Tell me what's wrong. We're friends, after all."

He considered the offer for a moment, but harping on it wouldn't fix the problem. It would only infuriate Taea. There were other, more important things he needed to do. Like get on with his existence—whatever that meant. "You don't know what I've had to deal with. The nereids and I continue to have problems. There have been a lot of difficulties with the xéchase."

Her eyes widened at the mention of the souls. "What happened with them?"

"I'm surprised you hadn't heard." He was glad that curiosity still reigned over her interest.

As Shade flew towards Camp, the pixie on his shoulder, he filled her in on the bare minimum of what had happened. Nothing about his feelings, the fear, or the desire he fought.

"You know, it's probably for the best," Taea chimed. If she was disappointed or surprised, she didn't show it. That alone made him appreciate that she was here.

"I know, but there was a better way to deal with all of this." He banked along the side of the nereid's lagoon, taking the long way.

She pushed off his shoulder and flew beside him. "Everything will all go back to normal tomorrow."

That was what Shade was afraid of. That his life would never be the same again. Shade flew along the back end of the island, searching for nothing while pretending to look at everything. Taea wasn't fooled. "What of the girl and her brother?"

Shade's brow furrowed. "Tomorrow things will go back to normal, so I need you to be on your best behavior until then. Understood?"

The pixie grinned and gave a mock salute. "Yes, sir."

He would be watchful, just in case. Her jealousy, for one, had gotten out of control. He would protect the siblings for one more day, send them on their way, and then ensure the pixie didn't cause any further harm.

"Maybe we should have another bonfire—tonight before they leave. A celebration of their return home and things going back to how they should be." Her brow rose in question.

Shade nodded woodenly. "That sounds like a plan. Tell the others to start preparing, and I'll pass on the news to the mortals."

"Are you all right?" Taea tilted her head.

He smiled, the one he used most often to disarm others. "Of course."

Taea stared for a moment, then sighed. "If you say so." She took off into the sky, forcing him to follow. "Race you back to Camp," she called over her shoulder.

It took sheer will for Shade to pick up speed and even give the race a half of an attempt.

Taea beat him, but not by much. He left her there to gather the group for preparation and went to find Kora and her brothers. When he broke through the trees near the pond, the youngest was the first to come running. Kora stayed back a step with William.

"I've gotten you a way home for tomorrow. How does that sound?" He kept a levity he didn't feel in his voice. "Before you leave, the others thought we would throw a bonfire in your honor. Give you a chance to spend some time together but also a chance for the others to say goodbye." He kept his gaze averted from her.

Michael danced on his tiptoes as if he was about to burst from excitement. William looked from his younger brother to his twin. "What do you think, Kora?"

At the sound of her name, Shade's attention was drawn towards the young woman. She met his gaze, a flush rising in her cheeks. Gods, she was beautiful. So much so that he nearly forgot that he didn't need to breathe. He shouldn't be thinking about her this way. But he couldn't, didn't, turn away. Soon enough, there would be a clean break between them, and he'd do as he always did. Go on from one day to the next.

Kora broke the stare first and smiled at her brothers. "It sounds lovely. A nice way to say goodbye to the friends we've made here." She peered at Shade for a moment, but long enough for Shade to remember himself. He ran a hand through his hair and turned back to William.

If William noted the moment playing through Shade's mind on repeat, he didn't comment. The soul swallowed. "Yes, let's do it tonight." He sighed. "How are they getting home?"

Kora's expression dropped, and Shade fought off the urge to wrap his arms around her. Why was it harder when they were now so close to goodbye? Shouldn't it be easier to not miss what he never had? "Astraea and a few trusted pixies are ensuring passage."

Shade knew that his brother may attempt to interfere. "Let's keep this quiet. I haven't told the others when you're going home. Just in case." Silence and secrets were best. Captain may be watching over the Isles of Nekrós, but he didn't hold the power of the dead. It would be Shade's first order of business to get them all back into line.

The memory of the shadow of his scythe forming in his hand flashed. It had felt right at home in his grip. But with it came the responsibility he hated. The power it beheld was stagnant—lost between the master it wanted and the one it was stuck with.

"Shade?" He'd turned to fly away when her voice caught his attention. With a glance over his shoulder, he met Kora's gaze. "Thank you again."

His jaw flexed and he nodded before he took off.

Taea broke through a tree and met him midair. "What else have I missed?"

"I've told you everything," Shade quipped.

Taea laughed sinisterly. "Then why did you rush away from her? Why did she blush?"

Shade batted her away, and she zipped out of reach with red dust trailing behind. He pierced her with a glare as they flew. "I know what I am, Taea. Forget what you think you've seen. And lay low until then."

Taea flew in his path, forcing Shade's attention at her words. "Maybe this was part of her plan all along, and you're falling right into her trap?"

Shade ground his teeth and pulled to a stop. "That's enough, Taea."

"Think about it, Shade. Maybe she's just using the truth to gain your trust." She shrugged. "All I'm asking you to do is be careful and remember that a mortal doesn't have to change your focus. That's all." She started flying towards the treehouse, leaving behind a trail of purple dust.

Vindictive. Dangerous. Some of Taea's comments settled in the back of his head, jumbled and confusing. He rubbed a hand over his face—he had other problems to deal with. Taea's possessive jealousy could wait.

Chapter 42

Kora

Immortal blood was one of the many things on Kora's mind as she followed behind her brothers. She noted when the plants seemed to turn towards her. The way the dirt almost jumped to cling to her skin.

Most of her concern was for William, though. The heartache at losing him again. At least this time she'd get to say a proper goodbye. Even if a huge part of her was determined to stay. William had reminded her that she longed for adventure and maybe England could be just that. But without William? When she was the cause of his death. No matter how much she had listened to Shade's words, she still felt guilty. And the anger. Less so at Shade, but at the King of the Gods who seemed to have abandoned her. It was better to concentrate on that instead of the immortal she'd been tempted to kiss. He had said it shouldn't happen again. But she knew he cared. And part of her wanted to explore what that meant.

How could they though?

She failed. Not only William, but her world. There had to be something she could do. That *Captain* could do.

William slowed to a walk beside her. "Michael and I found a small waterfall we've wanted to show you. How does that sound? Go for a swim and maybe a little rock jumping?"

"Rock jumping?"

"You'll see." He grabbed her hand. "Are you sure you're all right?" His gaze lingered over one of the scratches on her arm.

Kora pulled her hand from his hold. "Yes, I'm sure. I did something stupid, Will. Everything is better now, and I don't want to taint this time with you. So please, can we just talk about fun things? Make memories that I can hold onto for a lifetime without you?"

William turned his head towards the path and nodded. "Yes, we can do that." He stuffed his hands in his pockets. "Can I tell you a secret?"

Kora nodded, uncertain if he was going to delve further into a conversation she didn't want to have with Michael within earshot.

"Selfishly, I wish you could all stay with me. I'm a horrible person for even saying so out loud, but even though these last days haven't exactly been easy, I wouldn't trade them for anything." He stopped short and looked at her. "Always remember that. Please?"

She sniffed back the threatening tears. It would be impossible to say goodbye to him tomorrow. "Are you going to stay on the Isle of Waiting for long?"

He shrugged, then started walking again. "I don't know. This was everything I could have never imagined. A chance to see and spend this time with you. Staying here might no longer be a necessity."

They followed the twist and curves of the trail upward past trees and brambles. Thankfully, they weren't going in the direction of the nereids. Kora didn't want to deal with them while having to keep Michael away. The sound of crashing water pulled her out of her thoughts. William pulled aside a rather large branch, revealing a beautiful waterfall that fed a decent-sized lake. She had only ever passed over the place and moved on when no fruit had been visible. Now, a rainbow cast by the sunshine hung over the water as it hit the rocks at the base of the falls.

"It's beautiful. This is such a great find." She stepped near the water's edge, her eyes wide in wonder. "Even prettier than the pond I bathed in the other day."

Michael stepped in beside her, hands resting on his hips and a sense of pride in his stance. It reminded Kora of Shade. Her eyes fell to the tree line to see if he'd followed them. He wasn't hiding in the branches or at the top of the trees. She didn't feel him—the power that he seemed to emanate was absent.

A push from behind, and she was suddenly pinwheeling in the air. As she hit the water, she was thankful she'd changed into a pair of torn trousers and tucked in a flimsy tunic after she'd cleaned her cuts. Kora swam to the surface, her brothers laughing from land until William pushed Michael in. Her brother's splash flooded her, and she turned away laughing. Michael took a gasp of air when he breached the surface and gave her a boisterous smile.

"You better get in here," she snapped at William, sending a large splash in his direction. She pulled Michael into her arms and his legs wrapped around her middle as she treaded water.

William laughed as he took a few steps back before running as fast as he could towards the pond. He jumped, tucking his legs into his chest as he flew in the air. The splash he created engulfed them both.

From there, they wrestled and swam after each other. They laughed. Smiled. Forgot all the worries, fears and sadness that tomorrow would bring.

After some time, William climbed onto a boulder beside the waterfall, then stopped and looked down at the depths below. "Ready?"

Kora was tempted to call him down until it hit her—he couldn't get hurt. The reminder of reality settled again on her chest. Each breath of air scratched her throat and lungs, and she forced back tears. She hid it all behind a smile as he counted to five while Michael whooped and cheered him on from the water.

When William pushed off the rock, she held her breath as he splashed, sending droplets all over the stone surrounding the lagoon. Kora didn't wait for him to rise again. She pulled herself out of the water and made her way towards the boulder. As she climbed, Michael patted William on the back, congratulating him on his stupendous feat.

"Ready?"

The others turned, and William's eyes widened in surprise. A grin played at the corner of his mouth, and he nodded. "Go, Kora!"

She lifted her head up until the sun dusted her face with its warm glow. Her arms spread wide. Like flying. A thrum of power slid over her skin, and she knew Shade was nearby. Watching and always protective. But he wouldn't intervene. He'd let her live.

As her brothers counted down, she opened her eyes, took in a deep breath and pushed off the rock. Air rushed through her hair. Wind pressed against her skin. Water streaked against her as she followed the waterfall down. She closed her eyes, taking in one more breath of air as she broke the surface.

And as she splashed and swam upwards, she knew that the leap was the first of many she'd need to take if she wanted to live her life.

When she breached again, her brothers hollered her name, and Michael asked to take a turn. They found a lower rock for him to jump from and cheered him on as he took his leap. William nudged her. "You seem happy. Not too worried about returning home and the move to England?"

Kora chuckled. "For the first time, no. If I can't change Mother and Father's mind, maybe I can force Oxford to start taking female students."

Her twin laughed, but it wasn't in jest. "If anyone can change Oxford, it would be you." She smiled wider. He winked back.

Kora shrugged. "Maybe." And maybe there was a way to make the King of the Immortals change his mind too.

William cleared his throat, casting a quick glance at their brother. "You know, we still need to talk."

She wasn't ready. "Not with Michael here. Tonight, after the bonfire or first thing in the morning."

He just smiled. "Fine. Remember, I made a promise I don't intend to break." He swam towards the edge. "Come on. Best we return to Camp and see how things are going with the bonfire preparations."

Kora waded out of the water, wishing she had brought something to change into when she caught sight of a pile of clothes nestled under a nearby tree. She trotted over to it, picking up a few tunics and some trousers. They weren't the best fit for any of them but would be much better than the soaked garments they currently wore. The rustle of a tree caught Kora's attention. *Thank you*, she mouthed. She turned back to the others, holding up the dry clothing. "Come here. Let's get changed."

"Can we still sleep under the stars tonight?" Michael, unaware that a sense of decency was necessary, immediately began to strip out of his clothing.

William tousled the youngest boy's hair. "I don't see why not."

"I'm going to go into the forest so I can change," Kora shot over her shoulder.

The others barely paid her any attention as she slid behind a rather large bush and began to slip off the drenched attire. The scratches stung a bit, and she grazed her finger over the raised flesh. It would be a constant reminder of what she would lose here, but also everything she'd gained. Shade had said life was an adventure. There was no way she was going to waste away and not live. Somehow, she'd make her parents see that. And Captain too.

Chapter 43
Captain

The sun had set on the horizon. The pixie's light directed Captain's attention towards her as she landed on his knuckle.

A sparkle alight in her eyes, her mouth downturned. "You're right. He's ready."

"Are *you* ready for this?" With a little difficulty and far more concentration than usually necessary, the scythe appeared in Captain's hand. A grin stretched across his face.

The pixie turned to stare towards the isles in the distance.

She turned to meet his gaze. "Yes, are you?"

There was no need to answer her question. He'd been ready from the first day he'd set foot in this abysmal place.

Chapter 44
Kora

That evening, the bonfire's flames reached up into the sky. It always surprised Kora how much driftwood the souls could find to create these masterpieces. This one was even larger than the first bonfire—a feat that impressed her.

She wrapped her arms around herself. Not to ward off a chill, but the thoughts that kept consuming her mind. Soon, she and Michael would leave. This was not only her last night with William, but her last chance to talk with him—to discuss all the things she had wanted to ignore. It also meant going back to a life planned out for her. A plan she didn't want. She wasn't the same girl as the one who had arrived seven days before. This Kora had spoken her mind, stood up for herself, and fought. And when she returned home, she wanted to continue to be that young woman. Maybe, just maybe, her parents would see reason. See the opportunities available for her beyond a loveless marriage and running a household. Those were dreams for some, just not for her. Maybe, in time, it could be part of her future—but it didn't have to be the reason for her entire existence.

Then there was the famine...

The immortal came back to mind. The way his gaze had dipped to her lips. The heat of his touch, the intimacy of his presence. She kept searching for him, feeling his presence but not seeing. An ache settled in her chest at his absence. It was hard to admit that she missed him. Yearned for him and more than just for that kiss, but to hear him admit he felt the same way. She cowered in on herself as the others sang and played drums, her brothers dancing about. William and Curly were swinging in circles, giggling, with smiles on their faces. She felt like she was on the outside looking in.

"Are you all right?"

Kora snapped upright at Shade's sudden appearance beside her, and that all too familiar flush rose to her cheeks. Damn her body for betraying her whenever he was near. "Fine, thank you." The words didn't sound as natural as she'd hoped.

Shade chuckled. "You don't have to lie. I can tell when something is wrong."

A faint smile rose. A dimple appeared at the corner of his mouth—the mouth she wanted desperately to taste again. "How was I to know if you noticed me at all? You haven't been around since this morning."

She waited for him to deny it, but he only sighed and ran a hand through his hair. "I thought it was best I stayed away." He didn't turn to her, keeping his attention on the revelers as he spoke. "I'm an immortal. You're mortal," he whispered, almost as if he was telling himself more than her.

The firelight danced over them, casting shadows that moved and quaked with the music. "I understand you're trying to protect yourself, but you don't have to." Why did she just say that? She almost slammed her palm to her face, but Shade's chuckle stilled her.

"I don't need protection. It's you I'm keeping safe." His voice was deep, and her senses heightened at the sound of it.

She whirled on him, but he remained still with his hands clasped behind his back. Anger pooled in her stomach alongside a need she couldn't quite name. "Me? Have you even asked me what I do or don't want?" She kept her words sharp but low, not wanting to attract unwanted attention. "It seems that an immortal is making assumptions. That you're making the deci-sions for me."

Without another word, she turned on her heels and stomped off towards the forest. Maybe she had done enough celebrating. Or, at the very least, she should step away and clear her mind. Later, she'd find William and have the talk he'd so desperately wanted. Right now, she needed space.

"Where are you going?" Shade kept pace beside her.

Kora snorted. "You don't have to come with me. The dangers don't crawl into the forest, Shade. You're here. I think I can make it to the treehouse without you. I'll come back later." Each step kicked up sand that she hoped sprayed him. With her luck, it probably just fell off him though. Stupid immortals.

"They weren't the only dangers, Kora. There were others that were in front of your face the entire time."

"Then why are you following me if you think you're so dangerous?" she shot back.

He kicked off the ground, cutting her off just as she reached the door of the treehouse. "Because I don't want to leave things this way. No matter how many splitting headaches you've caused me, I don't want you to go without saying goodbye."

"So that's it? You just want to say goodbye?" She flung her arms up in the air. "So long, farewell? Then why don't you just say it already—especially since I've caused so much harm."

"Damn it all to hells. Can you stop making everything diffi-cult?" He ran both hands through his hair. "You infuriate me."

"Yes, well the feeling is mutual," she spat back. "So go ahead, tell me how you can't wait for me to leave. That you won't miss me at all and good riddance. Then you can go back to your life ambition of playing games."

Shade straightened, and Kora's shoulders slumped in the process. She dropped her head into her hands to cover the rising embarrassment. Why did she always have to take things too far with him? He hadn't deserved those words. But he angered her so easily.

He held out his hand, and she caught sight of it through the cracks of her fingers. "Goodbye, Kora. It has been truly an honor and a pleasure to have met you." Kora looked up at him, dropping her hands as he continued, "The Isle of Waiting will never be the same without you." When she met his gaze, he inhaled. "I won't be the same either."

Maybe it was the truth in his words, or the way his face had softened with a lingering sadness in his eyes, but she reacted without thinking. She grabbed his shirt with both hands, tugged him towards her, and pressed her mouth against his.

With a gasp, she pulled back, her eyes wide. "I'm sorry. That—"

He cut her off with his lips, a sigh breaking as their mouths met again. Shade wrapped an arm around her waist, pulling her close. His other hand cupped her jaw as he deepened the kiss.

Her warmth melded with his, her body pressing further into him. For a moment, she began to overthink where her hands were, but then she let instinct take over. She fumbled with the knob on the door, pushing it open behind him, and backed him gently through the doorway. He didn't resist, instead his movement became more frenzied. His touch held a need she wanted to explore as he turned her body with his and pressed her against the wall of the tree. His hand roamed along her side, pulling at the hem of her shirt until the warmth of his palm was pressed against her skin.

Her breath quickened, her senses rising with his touch. A feeling she didn't plan to ignore. Kora leaned into him until their bodies nearly melded together—him pressing back and she still didn't feel like he was close enough.

"Tell me to stop," Shade whispered between a kiss. "Please." His mouth trailed to her neck, then the crook of her throat

"Do you want to stop?"

"No, never. But—"

She heard the plea in his tone, met his gaze and cupped his jaw with her hand. "You're Shade. The God of the Dead. The King of

Nekrós." He tried to look away, but she held him in place. "I don't fear you. I don't deny you." She kissed him again. "And I choose you."

She wanted this. "Please, don't stop."

His lips were on hers in an instant, his tongue parting her lips, and she opened her mouth in response to his touch. She tasted him—sunlight at dusk that filled the forest. The freedom of flight. It was all encompassing, and she never wanted it to end. His fingers pulled on the end of the ribbon holding back her curls, and the cool touch of satin grazed her throat. His hand twisted into her hair as she deepened their kiss. She gripped his arm, aware of his taut muscles and soft skin. It was the first thing that felt right since she arrived.

Kora reached out, found the door, and closed it. Shade pulled back slightly, following the movement as his chest rose and fell in quick succession. "You tell me when you've had enough."

"All of you," she breathed. "That's enough."

"You leave tomorrow. I can't see—"

"Shade, I've made my decision."

"No—I mean how am I meant to walk away. If we cross this line" —he swallowed— "I'm still an immortal tied to this realm. You're human, meant to live. I want to make every promise to you, but I can't."

"I've thought about staying," she whispered the words as her gaze fell to his chest.

"I've thought about asking you to."

The truth hung between them for a breath. Two. She finally looked up to him, and he rested his forehead against hers, pinning her in place. "I can't be selfish with you. You're meant to live. If you've taught me anything—"

She cut him off with a kiss before pulling back slightly to make sure he heard her words. "We both always have choices made for us. This can be one we make for ourselves. I choose you. And if you choose me too, we can both be selfish."

He picked her up, her legs straddling his waist. Lips against her throat as she arched into him and for a moment he held her there, a small groan escaping between heavy breaths. Then he turned and carried her to the bed. He sat her on the edge and as he kneeled before her, she peeled his tunic over his head revealing the defined plane of his chest. Kora grazed her fingers against his toned abdomen. "I've never done this before," she whispered.

"We'll go as slow as you need." Longing shadowed his features. "I can't have you hate me, Wildflower."

"I can't hate you. I've tried."

He chuckled, the sound cut short as she began to unbutton the front of her shirt. She expected her fingers to fumble, for her palms to sweat, her hands to shake. But they didn't. Not even as he reached between them and his touch took over the movements until each button was undone. Her lips parted when he grazed a finger along her ribs where a few bruises remained. Then, on the one near her clavicle, he leaned in and pressed a butterfly kiss to her skin.

She closed her eyes, pressing into him as his mouth moved down to her breasts. Took a nipple into his mouth. Sucked. A gentle nip that had her gasping. This was all new sensations, but she only wanted more. Her breath rattled in her lungs as her fingers threaded through his hair. She gripped his locks tight, pulled back slightly until her mouth was on his again.

He laid her down on the bed, following her with his body. His fingers fumbled with the hem of her pants while she attempted to touch all of him. He shifted so she could shimmy off the trousers, and she followed his hard length with her palm. He growled at the friction until he stood and removed his pants too.

Both naked, she leaned on her elbows as he stood before her, and they took each other in. Their gazes slid over every angle, dip, and curve until their eyes met. She swallowed as she took in the need and want evident in his expression.

"You're beautiful," he whispered.

"So, I've been told." She blushed at her forwardness, but the words had been used by many before. She had no reason not to believe his.

He chuckled as he braced himself over her, her back flushed with the bed. "Then let me be more specific."

His fingers traced lazy circles along her thigh. "The few freckles on your nose bunch up in the most adorable way when you are annoyed with me."

She swallowed as he pressed a kiss to the tip of her nose, and his hand moved a little higher.

"Your eyes shine when you snap at me. Like you would love to fight with me forever." His hand traced along the curve of her waist, a heaviness settling in her center and a shudder of need coursing through her at the feather light touch.

"I would fight with you for eternity."

He smiled before he pressed a kiss to her temple. "You make me think about things differently." Another kiss to her other temple. "I need someone who challenges me. You do that."

His hand moved down between them, a small brush of his thumb against the sensitive space between her legs. She bucked against him, wanting more. Surprised that anything could feel this good when there was still so much space between them.

"It's not just that you're physically beautiful. It's that every action, every smile, everything about you makes me want more."

She wrapped her hand around him, letting instinct take over as she stroked him. "You've made your point, now please kiss me."

He obliged with a groan on his lips as he consumed her. There was no more thought. Only sensations—the heat of their skin. The feel of his touch as his fingers, deft and gentle, stroked languidly against that sensitive nub, making her movements more frenzied. The taste of each kiss. The scent of sweat and nature. Heat pooled, a new sensation deep within her that consumed every inch of her body. And as she came undone, he groaned against her throat and pressed another kiss to the curve of her neck, a small nip at her shoulder. Always more—this feeling would be something she could chase as long as it was with him.

But she wouldn't think about the future now, not when every second in this moment was perfect.

She caught her breath, then adjusted her position until he was lined up with her. He gave her a look that had her crumbling. Passion, desire—it was all there. Even something she couldn't quite name. He swallowed deeply, his throat bobbing, and she could tell he was nervous. Wanted to be careful with her.

"I trust you," she whispered.

"I..." He shook his head, a small grin peeking from the corner of his mouth. "You're certain?"

"Yes."

He kissed her. Long and deep. When they pulled away, he kissed the tip of her nose. "You're the only thing I've ever been certain about in my entire existence."

Every movement was slow. Gentle. Her body reacted to each touch, a shiver that moved down her spine. An electric current sparked between them as a lovely ache spread in her core. Sensitivity she chased. The moment he entered her, she tensed, the pain a small shock to her system. A stretch new and different. He was careful, didn't rush or push as she adjusted to the change. "Are you all right?"

She nodded then buried her face into his shoulder. With a flick of her tongue against his skin, she tasted the salt at the curve of his throat. He groaned as she relaxed under him. "Tell me to stop or slow down if you need me too."

He pushed gently further into her, and she arched against him. Her body adjusted, reacted. Everything felt as though she was on fire in the best way possible.

And as he undid her again, he kissed her hard, sharing in her absolute euphoria before he released his own groan and pulled out. She gasped at the sudden emptiness as he shifted aside, his body shuddering as he came.

Kora laid there, molded into the bed and wondered how she could ever consider leaving it again. Shade brought a rag over, cleaning her before everything else. Afterwards, he got back into the bed as she turned her back to him, his body curving around her. "How do you feel? Do you regret—"

She snuggled into him, cutting him off. "Never."

He kissed her temple, wrapping his arms around her. "I wish I could keep you, Wildflower."

"Let's not talk about that right now." She swallowed away her trepidation about tomorrow. "Right now, let's be together."

"The outside world doesn't exist," he agreed.

She threaded his hand with hers then kissed his knuckles. And bit back the tears that threatened to tear that moment apart.

Chapter 45
Kora

At some point, they had dressed only to curl back up together in the bed. She couldn't go back to the bonfire. Didn't want to leave him. Instead, she had fallen asleep in his arms.

"Kora?"

Kora woke at her twin's voice, and Shade groaned as she turned in his arms. He was awake, but from the look of his pinched eyes, he was annoyed at the interruption. When she met William's gaze, fury was written on his expression. She waited, expecting the blush to rise on her cheeks but it didn't. Instead, she sat up and met her brother's glare as her own frustration matched William's.

"What is this?"

Shade straightened beside her, running a hand through his disheveled hair, and she resisted the desire to grab his hand. "My choice, Will. This has nothing to do with you."

He laughed, but there wasn't humor in it. "What did you do?" William looked at the bed they sat at the edge of. "What in the hells are you thinking?"

She darted a glance at Shade, then back to her brother. "I don't have to answer to you."

"If your choice is *him*, then you need to reconsider your priorities." William's voice rose as he appraised Shade. "What do you think will happen? How do you think it will end?"

Shade sighed and took Kora's hand. "He's right." He turned to face her. "This was a mistake. You leave tomorrow."

There was sadness in his gaze, deep below the surface, that he attempted to hide by a mask of indifference. But she could see it. His words tore at her chest. He couldn't mean that. Nothing was a mistake. "I kissed you first. You can't tell me you regretted it."

The corner of his mouth rose into a half smile, and he brushed a wave of her curly hair behind her ear. "I would never regret anything with you. For the rest of eternity. But your brother is right, because there is nothing more that can come from it."

She blinked at the realization he'd laid at her feet. She pushed off the bed, putting the distance between them. No matter what she wanted, there was always something in the way of her achieving it. Her brother died, and she was told there was no bringing him back. Her parents' plans for her life interfered with her desire to go to university. Multiple experiments in her garden and nothing to show for it. And now this—the immortal that had made her heart soar would never be hers. "Do I not get to decide for myself? Maybe I don't want to go home tomorrow."

"Would you make that decision to stay for *him*?" William snapped.

Shade stepped between her and her twin. "First of all, don't speak to her that way. She's had to deal with a lot and has put you first in every way she could have these past seven days." He turned to face her. "And you aren't going to run away. Not for me. Not for him."

"I know," she breathed. The truth a balm and a sharp sting all at the same time. "But I want a say. I don't regret you."

Shade pulled her into his chest and pressed a kiss to her forehead. William stepped forward but stilled at the god's glare. Shade lifted her chin up to meet his gaze. "Thank you for showing me what it means to live and lose something."

She gripped his hand tighter, not wanting to let him go. Words caught in her throat. He squeezed her fingers and then slid free from her grasp.

William glared at the immortal as he passed then turned his attention to her. "Kora, seriously?"

"You don't get to say anything," she snapped back.

He snorted. "Oh yes, I do. I see you in bed with an immortal and you think I'm not going to comment?"

"No. Because my choice didn't get me killed." She snapped her mouth shut.

William's eyes widened.

"You stepped in front of me." The words came unbidden. "A mistake I have to *live* with." The memory of that day. The guilt she'd held within all this time. The words she hadn't been able to say came rushing out. "You didn't trust me enough to talk to me." Damn it to hells, the tears were starting again. "It was meant to be me that night, but you got in the way. Were torn away from us, from *me*." She wiped away the tears. "And I couldn't save you!" she screamed the last words, and her voice scratched from the pain of the truth.

"I tried to hold you together—your blood was on my hands." She held them up now, as if he could see the stain of his mortality. Kora choked on a sob. "You're my brother. My best friend. I'd have given everything for you—and you left me."

Her knees buckled, and she fell to the ground. William rushed to her side, wrapping arms around her. "I know—I wish it could be different. That I could have stayed, but I don't regret it. I'd always save you."

"I thought I had come here for a reason. There had to be a reason beyond gods playing games that Captain would bring me to the Isles of Nekrós." Her words fell silent. She couldn't say anymore. Didn't want to hear anymore. "I can't do this. Not now. Not like this, William."

His grip tightened around her. "I messed up. I shouldn't have gone that night."

Without thinking, the words flowed. "I was going to make things right. Captain said if I could force Shade back to the Isles of Nekrós, then you would be able to come home."

His hold loosened on her arm. His voice garbled. "What?"

"William." Her voice cracked. "I—"

"No!" William shook his head. "You need to hear this. Kora, I don't blame you for this, can't you understand that?"

"If I hadn't been there, then you wouldn't have died. You wouldn't have stepped in the path—"

"Then it would have been from something else. I understand how it might seem, but I know it wasn't a mistake. Never a mistake." He ran a hand through his hair. "Hells, Kora. Do you think I ever, even for a moment, regret being stabbed if it meant you got to live?" He stepped back. "You would do the same for me. Are trying to do the same for me. It was my time."

She'd known there was a reason she hadn't wanted to talk about that night. Why she lost him. "Even if it meant you left us?"

William looked at where he grasped hold of her arms. She couldn't even feel his touch. "It was my choice then and it's my choice now. You don't get to make it for me."

Kora paled, blood leeching from her face as realization dawned. "I'm just like them."

"Who?"

Kora met her brother's gaze. "The Immortals. Captain. Shade —" She cut herself off as she grappled with the truth. Captain hadn't let Shade decide the guidelines of his position. Had sequestered his brother on the isles with no one. And Shade, in his hurt and anger, had chosen those who stayed with him on the isles. He hadn't considered those in the mortal world because no one had ever considered him.

This whole time she had wanted to save William. Hadn't even wondered what he may have wanted. He'd gone along with the search knowing there was a chance, but he had already resigned himself to death. Had made his choice.

William gave her a sad smile. "You made your decisions

because you care, Kora. I don't doubt that. You shouldn't either. But maybe, next time, you should ask what others want too. And listen."

"I'm sorry." She wiped the tears from her eyes. "I don't like this, though. How do I say goodbye?"

"Why are we saying goodbye?" Michael appeared then, Branch at his side with a tight expression.

"Sorry," the soul said. "He didn't listen when I said we shouldn't interrupt."

Kora grabbed hold of Michael and pulled him into a hug. "Thank you, Branch. He should be here for this anyway."

Branch gave a firm nod and walked away, leaving them alone.

"Here for what?" Michael glanced between his two siblings.

"Tomorrow we are going home, and William can't come with us." Kora didn't know how to explain it in any other way.

"You said he would." Tears welled in his eyes and he glanced between his siblings. "We were meant to all go home."

Kora sighed. "I know. I tried—"

Michael wiped his cheeks. "We all tried. It wasn't just you."

She laughed, a real one. "True. You did help. So did everyone else. It's just going to be hard to say goodbye to him, and I don't know how."

"You don't." William gave her a half smile. "We say see you later. I'm always going to be with you. The memories. Our time together. All of it. The love we have for each other. Our friendship. That carries on with you."

"Not like you to wax poetic."

William chuckled. "And only you would find yourself in the middle of a dispute between immortals."

Kora couldn't help but smile.

Michael lunged for William and wrapped his arms around his waist, burying his face in his stomach. "I'm going to miss you so much."

Kora hugged them too, holding on tight to her family. Her siblings. "I love you."

"I love you too."

They sat on the logs for a bit, talking and crying. When it was getting darker, Michael reminded them that they were going to sleep under the stars together. "Please?"

William nodded. "Let's do that. But first, we should probably go spend a little more time with the others. They are going to miss you too."

Kora walked down to the edge of the beach, where the dirt turned to sand, then stopped. Shade was on the beach on the outskirts watching the festivities. They had remained close to the tree line this time, just in case. "I'm going to walk for just a little bit."

She saw the momentary concern in her twin's expression, but he just nodded. "Don't be long."

Kora walked to the dock where the souls waited. It was empty now. The sound of the boards clunked under her feet. She stopped at the end and gazed at the *Charon* in the distance.

Kora let the last of her frustration loose, calling out to the ship. "What was the meaning of this? Was it all for your selfish plans?" Kora fell to her knees and yelled into the expanse. "Well, it didn't work, did it? Now I'm meant to go home and neither of us get what we want. It's your fault."

A shadow silhouetted her, blocking the moonlight. Kora lifted her head as it settled. Her eyes widened at the figure, indescribable in the darkness. She opened her mouth to scream as they reached for her. But no one could hear her pleas.

Chapter 46
Shade

It was the first time Shade had wished he could have slept. To drift off into dreams of her. That it might allow him to feel her touch, the brush of her lips. The thought that it would never happen again caused an ache in his chest that only grew with each agonizing minute he stayed away from her. But she would leave soon, and it would get better. Hopefully.

Taea arrived, settling on the branch beside him, looking up at the star filled sky.

"Shade...?"

He rested on his back, his head laying on his clasped hands. To speak would betray every thought in his mind. The ones he knew best to pretend never existed.

"Astraea is waiting at the Fairy Circle. She offered time for the souls to say goodbye, and you could escort her to Camp."

He nodded, not caring if she saw it or not. The anguish. The pain. He didn't want to hide it.

"You seem upset." There wasn't a question in her voice.

Mistake. He'd told Kora it was a mistake when every moment with her had been a gift. It was only a mistake because he wanted her more now that he'd had a taste. Why did the Fates feel the need to mess with him? Had he pushed the bounds of his existence so much that they wanted to put him in his place. A living mortal. Beautiful, vivacious, brave...everything he never knew he wanted had just been pulled from his grasp. There wouldn't be another like her. "I'm fine."

They lay in silence as Taea hovered overhead, and somehow resisted peppering him with more questions. In the distance, the *Charon* bobbed on the Depth.

Taea fluttered upright and ran her fingers through her short hair. "It's time to meet with her and make plans."

Shade swallowed, wishing to make time stand still a little longer. Instead, he rose into the air. "Yes, it is." He drew his shoulders back, took a deep breath and held it for a moment before he let it out.

Taea started to follow him but stopped mid-flight. "Shade—"

He turned to face her, forcing his usual smile. He couldn't take it if she asked him what was wrong again. "What is it, Taea? Everything will be fine."

"No." She shook her head. "It's not that, it's just..." She trailed off, unable to look him in the eye.

An uneasiness settled in his gut. There it was in her body language, the way she curled a finger in her hair. Something wasn't right. "What did you do?"

A putrid green surrounded her. "It wasn't me. It was Captain," she spat.

Shade didn't wait for an explanation. He shot off towards Camp first, but no one was there. He flew over the remnants of the bonfire, not finding her there amongst the others who sat at the edge of the beach, talking and watching the fire die. He went to the treehouse, forcing the door open and breaking it off its hinges. He tore the blankets off the bed but didn't find her. He whirled around, searching the corners, hoping she was hidden. Nowhere, she wasn't here.

Taea's bell sounded at the door. He faced her, rage taking over, darkness spreading from his entire being. "Where. Is. She?"

"Captain. He had a plan, and you knew it involved her."

"You never said you knew. Not once." The darkness spread

out the door, calling for the tortured souls. If they came, he knew they would tear apart everything in their path. "If you don't explain now, I won't hold them back."

"She's a part of this, Shade." Taea straightened. "This is all to get you to come to the Isles of Nekrós."

His power dissipated. He knew this. Kora had told him. But why wasn't she here now?

William's silhouette entered the doorway. "What's happening?" Michael peered around the corner with the morning glow haloing him, fresh fear in his expression.

At the sight of the soul, the moment that Kora pulled him in for a kiss replayed in his mind. It couldn't have been an act. She wouldn't betray him. Through all of it, he didn't doubt that. He turned on the soul. "Do you know where Kora went?"

William's brow furrowed, and he peered over Shade's shoulder into the treehouse. "No, she didn't come back from her walk. I just came here to search for her." As though realizing what Shade insinuated, William forced past him. He tore apart the bedding and called her name. When he found it as empty as Shade had, he whirled around. "Where is she? What did you do?"

"I haven't seen her since we last parted. She didn't come down to the water."

"She needed a walk." William ran a hand over his face.

Taea raised her hands up. "When she left you, she went straight to Captain."

William scoffed, his hands fisted. "No, she wouldn't do that."

Taea laughed. "Maybe you don't know her anymore. What would she do if there was a chance to keep you alive? Captain is the only one who can help her now."

With those words, Shade stilled. Taea was fuming, but he noted the green envy twisted with the red that edged off her. All his brother wanted was for Shade to return to the Isles of Nekrós —and he'd use Kora however he wanted.

But Taea...

He snorted, a smile twisting his lips. "You spied on me, didn't you?"

"What?" Taea whirled around to face him.

He grabbed the tips of her wings, pinching them together. "You're twisting things now because you've known his plan all along. If anyone is in league with Captain, it's you." She kicked her legs out in an attempt to break free. "After everything we've been through together, it cannot just be jealousy. Why did you help him?" he bellowed.

Taea paled as she met his gaze. With a sniff, she turned a raging red. "It wasn't me. I told you that she was dangerous, and you didn't listen. He knew all along that she saw you that night. Used her because she prayed. If I didn't listen to Captain, he would have—" Her eyes widened in fear.

"He would have what?" A calm fell over Shade as he glared at the pixie. "It makes no sense—you've always been loyal. Been my friend. Or so you've claimed. What is it Captain holds over you that you don't want me to find out?"

"You can't go back there, Shade. If you do, you'll be trapped. Don't go for her. For anyone."

"What does he have against you?" Shade all but yelled the question, his composure cracking as power thrummed. All this time, it wasn't Kora who was stabbing him in the back, but his supposed best friend. "You might as well tell me now. There is no other reason for your actions. Liaison was one thing—spy is completely another. You've told me nothing but vague warnings."

The pixie reached into her pocket, removing a watch he'd seen her look at from time to time. Taea stopped fighting and tilted her head. The sneer that settled across her lips was one Shade had never seen before.

Shade's power thrummed through his arm towards the little pixie and wrapped around her body. She gasped for air.

Michael squealed in fear. Shade clenched his teeth and forced the darkness back. "I'm not going to ask again."

Taea glared at him, her wings still pinched between his fingers.

"I've worked too hard for so long to make sure you remained happy. Don't throw it all away for her and fall into Captain's trap."

"That's not the question I want answered, Taea. If you don't—"

The ground quaked, unbalancing the others. Screams echoed from the beach. Whatever caused it was strong judging by Taea's widening smile. "I killed Raz."

Shade choked on his shock, and Taea used that moment to tap the face of the clock. With a pop, she disappeared.

He fell to his knees as her words echoed in his ears as he searched the space for her. Where had the pixie gone? How?

"Taea?" Shade rushed to his feet, tearing through the furniture, barely cognizant of Michael's wails at the door.

"What was that?" The young boy clung to the wall, terrified.

"What was what?" Shade whirled at him, his eyes darting in the corners, searching for the pixie. Where had she gone?

"There was this thing. I felt frozen—couldn't move?"

Shade bent down in front of the youngest sibling as William curled an arm around his brother. "What thing? I didn't see—"

"It was too fast." Michael trembled. "It grabbed Taea and left."

"Can you describe it?" She wasn't there. Shade tried to relax his expression, knowing the darkness still shifted off him, and scared the boy.

"No. Everything was slow. There was a flash of something. That's it—that's all I saw." Michael curled into William.

The movement of her twin brought Shade's attention back to the true task at hand. Kora—he needed to concentrate on her.

"Shade, who is Raz?" William asked.

The mention of the pixie's name, the one he'd lost so long ago, sent an ache through his chest. Now he had the truth. It wasn't that the pixie had left him—but how and why would she do that? She claimed to be Raz's friend. Had offered to help find him. The first time he'd felt loss for another. That had been the moment he had begun to spiral and all this time, she had been sharpening the knife that would be used against him. She had been the one who stole a friend from him.

He sighed. "A friend. The pixie born of my first laugh. I thought he'd abandoned me." It was a wound that never fully healed, but now it was cut open anew. How had he not known his friend had died? This was his domain. Raz's loss had been the start of his desire to leave the Isles of Nekrós. The last stray after his mother had disappeared. His brothers had stopped visiting and forgotten him. When his obsession to understand life—and death—began. To grasp onto the concept of loss. Then Taea had arrived and filled a piece of that void by remaining by his side. Or so he thought.

"I'm sorry," William whispered.

Shade shook his head to dispel the memories. "I'll deal with her later. Captain's taken Kora to the Isles."

William covered his head with his hands. Michael rushed to his brother's side, surrounding Shade. "What does that mean?"

There was no time to waste, no questions to consider. He would get her and bring her back. "I have to go. She's leverage. I don't know what he would do when he's desperate enough to involve a mortal."

"Not without me." William rose, his sibling clambered for purchase.

Shade's jaw tensed. "If you come, you won't be able to return here. I should go alone."

"What if you fail to bring her back?" William countered.

"I need to be a few steps ahead, but there is nothing that would make me leave your sister in the Isles of Nekrós. She and your brother are returning to the mortal world today, William. Astraea is waiting at the Fairy Circle. Have Curly take you to there and bring her to the beach. Explain to her what happened, and I'll bring Kora back. I promise." He made sure all his conviction was visible in his face and audible in his tone.

William nodded. "Bring her back, Shade."

"Have the pixies take your brother home. It's the safest alternative for now." Shade turned to leave, hearing the wails of discontent from Michael. He hoped William would take it as more than a suggestion. The sooner the young boy was off the island, the safer he would be.

Shade wouldn't let anything happen to Kora. It was time she was allowed to make her own choices. She had woken something inside of him he thought never existed. He'd save her and make Captain pay for thinking he could use her.

He swam through the Depth until The Isles of Nekrós came into view and scanned the different portions of the realm he once called home. He couldn't touch the ground, otherwise it would hold him prisoner once again. If there was any chance he could free Kora without damning himself, he was going to take it.

Mizéria Isle's flaming volcanoes and fiery mountainside oozed lava that flowed around the realm of the torturous hell. The heat that surrounded Shade held a touch of adrenaline that both warned and strengthened him. The smell of burning flesh—all for show and to add to the levels of depravity for those who suffered —rose with their screams. Within the depths, the growls of the Giants could be heard, adding to the chorus of feverish complaints. He'd done his best to ignore their calls last time, but now it was more difficult.

A shudder slid down his back, chilling his bones. Once he passed the mountains, he flew over Lýpe. Here laments could be heard from the small orbs that floated about emitting heartbroken pleas. Their groaning was suddenly cut off when he reached the quiet Eiríni Isle.

Shade stayed on the outskirts, not passing over the center of the never-ending grassland. An occasional tree, a few flowers, dotted the space. Souls moved about in little orbs, no longer distinct and whole. Some congregated together, looking for companionship though they never spoke. Peace—this was what eternal peace was meant to be. Shade had always thought it interesting that they had searched for one another even with the base of their being gone. This was where many arrived and came to rest. It was where he expected to find Captain since Shade had spent most of his time here before, but neither the immortal nor Kora were present.

Finally, he went to the Iroes. The souls' silhouettes were floating about, a few clamoring together. Those who still spoke usually had an air of insolence and self-importance that only annoyed Shade. This was where the elite had come to rest, some awaiting their chance at reincarnation—and they never let anyone forget it. Even if the only ones who listened were just like them. That was why so many had become nothing more than silent souls, floating about like many of the orbs in the meadow.

The structures were small but not as dingy as what the Lost Souls had created in their Camp. There were buildings made similar to the Greek temples of old, others more modern. Whatever the builder needed would appear and form with a thought. That's when Shade realized where his brother had taken Kora. He veered towards the outskirts of the isle and one of the oldest buildings created. It had been Shade's home once. A place where, centuries ago, his brothers would come to visit. Before Shade was forced into isolation, and his power tied him to the Isles of Nekrós. He hadn't lived there for some time. Even before he had left his post. It held memories. Time with Raz. Visits from his brothers. He'd been left. Forgotten. Until he made them remember.

Chapter 47

Kora

Kora blinked and her eyes opened to a vibrant world. Surrounding her were tall Grecian pillars with thin gauze hanging stagnant between them from the lack of breeze. The air was stale, even with the cherry blossoms visible through a small opening that served as an entryway. Above, there was no ceiling, just a clear sky of blue. This wasn't home and it certainly wasn't Anamoní. Yet, it was familiar.

"It's good to see you again."

She stumbled to her feet at the sound of a familiar voice, turning to face the immortal. "Oh, so now you deign to visit."

He nodded as he stood from a marble bench. He bowed, whipping his hat around in a flourish before placing it back on his head. "I do hope Smith didn't frighten you too much. I cannot step foot on the Isle of Waiting, so I had to use alternative methods."

Kora sat upright, her attention lingering on the doorway. From the distance, she could now make out the etchings along the top—a helm. She'd seen this temple when she'd first woken to Captain.

"This was Shade's home." Captain brushed the tails of his long coat behind him.

"You lied to me." She met his gaze with a sharp one of her own.

"I did not. You have yet to bring him to the Isles." Captain's grin lengthened.

Her body shuddered at his words. "He did bring me here. You're the one who backed out on our deal." Even after the conversation with William, she couldn't let go of the chance to outsmart the King of the Gods.

If the words bothered Captain, he didn't show it. He took a seat again on the marble bench. "He didn't return as the God of the Dead, and you know it."

Fists formed at her side as her anger rose. Of course, another who thought she was nothing more than a pawn. Something to use and cast aside. She needed to think of a way to keep him busy and use him for what she needed. Turn the tables. "You've overestimated his attachment to me. He wouldn't fall for your schemes. Not when his freedom is on the line."

Captain laughed, the sound echoing despite the open building. "Then you shall remain. I have all the patience in the world. And with your brothers on the island, do you think they will let Shade forget what he's sequestered you to if he doesn't save you?"

She wasn't frightened. In fact, she was far from afraid. She'd survived her brother's death, almost drowned, and had to fight off the xéchase not once but thrice...what would a life on the Isles of Nekrós mean for her? She shrugged and ran a finger over the nearest pillar. It was cool to the touch, but no dust stuck to her skin. "It's clean, at least. I could make a home here, I suppose. Does that make me a goddess then?"

Captain scoffed, but she didn't turn to face him.

"I can't let that happen, Kora." Captain was suddenly in front of her, his mouth a thin line and no sign of laughter left in his expression. "If he doesn't come, then maybe your brother William will need to go to the Mizéria. Do you want to be plagued with his tortured screams?"

"You wouldn't," she snapped. "He doesn't deserve it."

"No, he doesn't. But the Judges and I have an understanding. They want Shade back as much as I do at this point. We will take any necessary steps to ensure it's done. If he doesn't come for you, we'll begin with your brothers, then the Lost Souls. Otherwise, I'll be forced to drag Shade to the depths of hell."

Kora gasped, covering her mouth with her hand. "How could you? He told me what his father had done to him and to you. You should be allies and that's all Shade has ever wanted. My brothers are not to blame, and neither are the others."

He lifted his chin. "If I must sacrifice a few to save many, I will."

"We didn't do anything to you." Tears threatened, stinging her eyes but she blinked them back. Not in front of him. She'd prove herself a worthy opponent. "If anything, you're the cause of the deprivation of the mortal world. You're the one who called back the gods and won't allow them to do their jobs."

Captain sighed. "He's twisted your thoughts, I see. I'm not surprised. It would have been near impossible to resist his charms." He rested one arm against a pillar, assessing her. "Do you have such little faith in him that you don't think he'll come for you? Taea seemed to believe otherwise."

"Taea? But she—"

"Will do exactly what I tell her," Captain finished.

She'd been stupid. Naive. Trusting. Kora shook her head. "After all you've done to him, you should be groveling at Shade's feet. Offering penance for leaving him here alone." If what Captain said of Taea was true, then Shade needed to know. Even if it meant that he would truly be alone, he deserved the truth. All those moments she'd observed him, she saw the reality in his eyes. What he craved. Freedom.

"You only believe that because you've fallen for him." He snorted. "Ridiculous, really. After I warned you. He's curious about mortals because he's been apart from them for so long. You should have continued to trust me."

"No. I never trusted you. I only learned to trust him because he let me see him—who he is." She straightened, her expression as cold and hard as stone. "It's because he craved companionship, friendship. Something the Isle of Waiting offered him—a sense of reprieve from the dead and sullen. You've been here how long now? Can't you see what you've done to him? How you attempted to imprison him? You think he's the villain, but in this story the villain is you." She pointed her finger into his chest, not realizing she'd closed the space between them. "I hope he doesn't come. That he never steps foot on the soil again. He doesn't deserve to be trapped here, but you do."

Kora's eyes widened as a smile cracked across Captain's face. "Oh, so you did find a little bit of information." He chuckled, swiping away the finger she left hanging between them. "Shade will come. He let you see him and there was a reason for it." The immortal leaned forward, the space between them thinning. "Or maybe you should stay with me? Now that I see more of that spark in your eye, I see the appeal."

She stepped back, her gaze thinning. "Never."

"She's going home, Captain."

Captain drew back and sniffed. "Took you long enough." He winked at Kora. "Told you he'd come."

Kora searched the skies above and settled on Shade who sat upon a pillar. One leg hung over the edge, while the other was bent, his foot settled on the flat top and his arm rested against his knee. Why did he come?

Shade leaned forward slightly. "I've had some time to consider why she saw me. For a moment, I thought it was because of something Astraea mentioned." Kora knew what he was referring to but didn't say. The immortal blood running through her veins. Shade continued, "Then I wondered if it might be all part of your plan—with a little help from Taea. But after some consideration, I realized that wasn't the case either. Taea's gone, so *your* pixie can't pull the strings from the shadows anymore."

Thank the *gods*, he knew.

Kora stepped aside as Captain locked a predator's gaze on his brother. Should she run? Before she could decide, something unseen dragged her to the pillar with her back and arms forced around it by invisible bonds. She struggled until Captain snapped his fingers, and her body went rigid. Trapped.

Captain strode forward, closing the distance between himself and Shade's pillar. His brother didn't turn his attention towards her. What was he playing at?

"My pixie?" Captain asked. "Taea isn't mine."

"Well, she sure isn't mine." Shade snorted. "If she was in anyone's pocket, it seemed to have been yours. But I don't think either of us knew to what extent she was playing her own game."

Captain raised his chin higher. "Did she tell you?"

Shade nodded, his face solemn. Kora wanted to go to him, but even if she wasn't trapped against the pillar, she didn't want to interrupt. Something felt important about this conversation.

"I cannot believe you never thought to come to me about Raz's death. You knew she killed him and befriended me but didn't say a word," Shade accused.

Kora's eyes widened.

Captain laughed. "I needed whatever leverage I could to force the pixie to assist me. You can't blame me for her actions. I didn't order her to kill Raz. We hadn't even met until I arrived here."

"Just used her and her circumstances against me instead of telling me the truth. I kept her by my side all this time."

"You wouldn't return to your post."

Shade's jaw ticked. "Let her go. She has nothing to do with this." His mischievous smile grew. "Are you sure you want to tempt fate, threatening the child of another immortal?" Shade stood upon the pillar now. "The trouble it could cause if her lineage was uncovered..." He tsked.

Kora tried to straighten, call on that power supposedly within her. But if it was there, it was dormant.

"What in the seven levels of hell are you going on about?" Captain bristled, his shoulders drawing back.

Shade shrugged. "Astraea's under the impression that Kora

may have some long distant immortal blood in her system. Maybe enough to use when one's defenses are low—and enough to make flowers sprout in desolate parts of the Isle of Waiting."

"She has a twin," Captain snapped, and her body went rigid. "And last I saw, he's dead. Those with even traces of our blood don't die easily."

"According to Astraea, it's not enough to grant them power or immortality in the mortal realm. When she and her brother came here, it was triggered. Awakened." Shade tilted his head, and Kora swore she saw the corner of his mouth lift further.

"You said so yourself—it's an indirect line, long forgotten. If they cared, they would be here now." Captain darted a glance in her direction. "Besides, many will agree with my tactics if it means bringing order to the Isles of Nekrós and allowing me to take my proper place again."

Captain held out his hand and a scythe appeared within his grasp. "It's been waiting for you—I know you've felt the call."

Shade turned his attention to the scythe. "We can do this if you want…" He pointed at Kora. "Let her return home now, and I promise we'll battle it out."

"Ha!" Captain snapped the end of the scythe against the ground. Clouds began to congregate above, encircling them.

A gasp sounded from outside the Grecian dwelling, and Kora saw, through a break in the stagnant drapes, silhouettes of figures floating away in small groups. It seemed they had attracted an audience who now thought it best to leave.

"Shade," Kora warned, her attention on the darkening skyline. His gaze met hers for the first time. That look alone held an unspoken promise that made her choke on any further words. He smiled and nodded before turning his attention back to his brother. There was no way he was leaving without her and that thought gave her a newfound confidence.

"I'm not playing the game any longer, boy. It's time. Take up your scythe, the title you deserve, and then this can all be over." The debonair Captain no longer remained. He tore the hat from his head, tossing it aside and his hair was brushed by a breeze brought on by the storm he gathered above. "After all, I just need one little tiptoe to touch the ground."

Shade's eyes narrowed.

Oh no. Kora took in a deep breath of air. "I'm sorry," she whispered. She instantly regretted divulging that information. Another pang of guilt.

"You assumed she was working for me, and you didn't think I'd find out your weakness?" Thunder clapped in the distance as Captain struck the scythe against the stone floor. "She let the truth just slip through her lips."

"I didn't mean to. I swear," Kora called, hoping he'd believe her.

Captain continued to click the tip of the scythe against the floor in a steady beat, the force rising with the storm. "See how it is, Shade? You would tempt fate for a mortal, and they draw you in with your curiosity."

Darkness inked out from Shade. Kora wished she could take her snappy comeback towards Captain back. She couldn't— wouldn't be the cause of him being stuck here. Somehow. "Shade, I'm so sorry. I didn't know. I care—"

Shade cast a glance in her direction, the sneer on his lips twisting into his mischievous grin. The armor of midnight began to spread over his body, appearing like a second skin. His features darkened once again as they had done above the Váthos Sea. Her mouth fell open in awe. Even with the power coursing through him, Kora couldn't turn away. Mesmerized by the immortal before her.

Shade chuckled and winked at her. "With all the possibilities, I think there is another reason I let her see me at her brother's deathbed. I didn't know it then." He pushed off from the pillar and met her gaze again. "It's because I saw the kind of love in her that I would always fight for. She emitted it—caught hold of me right here." He patted his chest, over his heart. "As much as I wanted to keep her at a distance, she was never a mistake," he said with his gaze pinned on her. "The only mistake was letting her get so close where it would be hard to let her go." He turned to his brother. "This is your last warning. Let her leave right now."

Those words weakened Kora's knees. It was the last thing she'd ever expected to hear from him. Not after what she'd just done. She was scared he'd thought they were a mistake.

If it wasn't for Captain's power holding her upright, she'd have fallen on the ground. She opened her mouth to respond when a crash of lightning sliced through the air, thunder reverberating around her.

"To think, my brother has learned what it means to care for others." Captain sounded bored. "Well, there is only one way to get her back. Land, Shade. Take your place."

"No, Cap. Because this is my domain. Even with the scythe in your grasp, I have more control than you." Darkness spread from him, and Kora inhaled deep as the cool shadows created a cocoon of air around her.

"You think I don't know what you're doing?" Captain bellowed as lightning tore through Shade's darkness, making the tortured souls momentarily visible. The immortal stood in front of her, his arms fisted and his shoulders rigid. "You can't have her!"

Lightning rained down, illuminating the xéchase around her but also tearing them apart. Kora screamed, pulling at the invisible bindings that held her in place and calling on the power she knew she could access if she only tried. For him, she'd find a way.

"Stay still." Captain whirled around on her as the thunder clapped, the sound and vibration almost rupturing her ears. He swiped his hand out and a bolt of lightning sprung from his palm, heading straight towards Shade. Kora tried to fling her body at him, but the pillar held her tight. "No!"

Shade dodged just as the bolt pierced the pillar he'd stood upon. Lightning pounded out of the sky, and Shade swerved and twisted through the air around them. But he wasn't completely on the defensive. As he flew, the creatures attacked Captain, coming in droves. They tore at his clothes, pulling him down. He flung them back with all his strength, but it wasn't enough. More came. He fought them back as her leg loosened. The creatures dove for her but hit an invisible wall. The xéchase clawed to break through.

She watched the battle, continuing to struggle as she trailed Shade's figure in the sky moving in and out of view. Somehow, she had to break out. *Think*. What else would force two immortals to come to an impasse?

Captain's concentration must have been waning because her left arm was now free. She fought harder, tugging her limbs in an attempt to free herself. Shade swooped down and grabbed her arm. He tugged but nothing happened. Another lightning bolt landed nearby, but Kora could see his brother was too busy to concentrate on Shade's location with the multitude of xéchase ambushing him.

"We'll get you out, Kora. Come on—fight it." He grabbed her shoulders, which hurt less than him pulling her arm, and dug his fingers in between her body and the pillar. "Grab your power. It's in your center—waiting."

He darted a glance over his shoulder, then met her gaze. "I'm sorry. You aren't and were never a mistake. I meant—"

"I know." She reached out a hand and squeezed his arm. "I know."

He kissed her forehead. "Fight it." She shimmied her torso, helping as best she could when Captain broke through the throng and charged them.

"Shade," she screamed.

He shot up in the air just as Captain reached them and the immortal bellowed, his arms outstretched and fists tightened. Lightning rained down and a bolt hit Shade in his shoulder. He roared in pain.

"No. Stop!" Kora pleaded as Shade rolled in the air, just grabbing hold of the top of a pillar. If he touched the ground, it would be all her fault. He couldn't be stuck in the Isles of Nekrós because of her. Not like this.

Shade pulled himself up, and his gaze thinned on his brother. "Do we really want to do this all day?"

Captain's jaw tensed, and his glare thinned. "No, I don't. Let's finish this."

He turned his attention on Shade just as the immortal sent a wave of xéchase. They stopped, frozen in mid-movement. Shade circled with confusion in his expression. He hadn't done that.

Kora concentrated on that power within. Just as she thought it wasn't there, she felt it—a strength in her center. She fell to the ground in a heap. She gasped, catching her breath for a moment, and then rushed to her feet. She looked towards Captain, the immortal standing between her and the God of the Dead.

Captain's smile spread. His eyes narrowed as the scythe settled in his grip. "I wondered if I could—I hadn't tried to control them against you."

Shade looked at the souls. At the control he'd lost on those he once beckoned. "You? You've been the one sending them to Anamoní?"

Captain laughed and with a wave of the scythe, the souls turned their gaze towards Shade. "It seems my time here has given me a little of what you threw away."

The creatures began to march towards Shade. Kora screamed as they climbed up on top of each other to reach him. Shade darted away when lightning cut off his path. Each twist and turn, he met a bolt and just missed getting hit. He was trapped between the pillar and the showers of bolts surrounding him.

Kora yelled as she ran, breaking through the darkness. The souls tore at her body, but she broke away from their grasps. Nothing would keep her from Shade—not even the power he wielded. Because she felt it too. The pull towards him. The need to be by his side. How he had made her feel so many things these past seven days. Not just the desire for him, but of the dreams she wished to discover. He'd brought her out of another type of darkness and made her see it. See life in a whole new way. The immortal that had done all he could to protect her—to save her brothers. A bolt crashed into the ground, and she jumped out of the way just in time. With a wave of her hand, vines sprung up, grabbing hold of the xéchase. Her eyes widened in surprise as instinct took over.

Captain growled. "No, you don't."

The souls seemed to multiply, tearing at her clothes, hissing if they touched flesh. Plants meant life—is that why they couldn't touch her? A consideration for later.

Just a little farther, the space around Captain was clear of the dead. Somehow, she'd reach him. Shade yelled, and Kora darted a glance towards him. The souls were pulling him to the ground. He continued to fight for control, his own power radiating off him. It wasn't enough. Another wave of her hand and another vine flew like a whip, tearing a few of the monsters down.

It didn't stop them, but it slowed them enough. With each of Kora's attempts to break through the souls, Shade was getting closer and closer to the ground.

She sent more vines, more plants, to pull and rip away their hold on Shade. They were hard to control, some hitting him, and she winced at the mistakes. With each swipe of her hand, she raced towards Captain. Lightning landed, her arm lifting to shield herself from the light. With another burst of speed, and a strength she didn't know she held, she tumbled straight into the King of the Immortals. He fell over with a grunt, and Kora's limbs caught in his.

With his attention diverted, the xéchase froze again. Shade was inches from the ground. Kora rushed to her feet and made her way to free Shade's clasped body. She knew she only had moments until Captain would begin his attack again.

Lightning flashed.

And this one didn't miss.

Chapter 48
Shade

Her scream tore Shade in two.

Another bolt hit his shoulder, and the souls fell into a tumbled mess on the ground below him as his back cracked into a pillar. He started to fall but caught his bearings enough to stop himself. With a quick turn, he looked for her.

"Where is she?" His yell reverberated, the earth rumbled and the pillars shook.

The creatures stilled, and Shade turned to lock eyes with Captain. "What did you do?" His tone held the steel of a thousand blades.

The storm clouds didn't dissipate but the lightning stopped. Captain looked to where Kora had been and when he'd broken the stare, Shade searched their surroundings.

Thump, thump...thump. Her heartbeat—he whirled around and roared as he flew to her side. "Kora!"

He found her crumpled under rubble and xéchases' broken bones. He turned her over, but her eyes didn't open. Although her heartbeat was there, it was faint. A blue line sparked from under her skin, starting at her shoulder and slid under the remains of her scorched clothes. "No," Shade mumbled. "No, no, no. Kora, wake up."

"I didn't mean for the lightning to hit her." Captain came to stand opposite her, his hands hanging at his side and mouth wide in disbelief. "Shade."

"No." He shook his head as her heart beat again. *Thump, thump.* "She's still alive. There is something we can do. There has to be."

Captain grabbed Shade's shoulders. For a moment, he thought Captain was going to force him down on the ground and take the glory he wanted, but he didn't. "She has immortal blood."

Shade swallowed and nodded.

"There is one possible way." He glanced towards the scythe on the ground. "The pomegranate."

Shade's brow furrowed in thought, tracing his brother's thoughts. It was a long shot, but it could work. "Then find it."

Captain's jaw feathered. "I can't. I never have been able to track it, Shade. The tree never appeared for me. Only for you. Why do you think I went through all this to get you to find it?"

"I haven't been able to track the tree since..."

Thump...thump.

Shade looked at Kora, his gaze raking over her pale face, searching for signs of life. He couldn't help the chuckle that broke free. "I never thought it would take a mortal to get you what you wanted."

He inhaled a deep breath as he closed his eyes. There was no need to second guess his decision. For her, he would go to the lowest levels of hell and back. He'd give up his immortality if it meant she'd live. That was nothing in the grand scheme of things.

Slowly, he lifted his hand in the air, his fingers sprawled wide. The scythe was suddenly in his grasp and with a swish of air, the power that longed to be his sizzled under his skin. He lowered until his feet touched down on the stone and as soon as he made contact, the bindings of the Isles of Nekrós tethered around him.

The armor stretched over his skin, a pointed helmet sliding up over his neck and resting on his brow. Power writhed over muscles, through veins and spread through his body. It surprised him how much he'd missed the touch of the darkness at the ready instead of held back and hidden.

But there were more important things to consider right now. *Thump...*

The scythe disappeared as he scooped Kora up in his arms. With just a thought, one of the gossamer drapes tore from its place and lay down on the bench. The warmth of her body was still present, the scent of spring filling his senses, and he committed it to memory.

As he carried her over to the bench, he regarded Captain. "You caused this so you're going to help. For this moment alone, you may step foot onto the Isle of Waiting to inform her brothers of what has happened. I told William to send Michael back with the pixies, but I doubt the soul listened. I'm going to find the fruit. Once your task is complete, return here." Shade peered at his brother from the corner of his eye. "If you cause any trouble, I swear you shall regret it."

Captain lifted his chin. "I didn't mean for this to be how it happened, Shade. You must know—"

"That in your own way, you cared about her...that this was all about the mortals." Shade pressed a kiss to her forehead, then laid her down on the bench. "If that's true, prove it now."

Captain's hand rose in the air and Shade grabbed his wrist, holding him in place for a moment. "If anything happens to her, Captain..." The edge in his tone held a warning his brother should never forget. "If this doesn't work—"

"Astraea might be difficult, but she is rarely wrong. If she has immortal blood, then this will work. It worked on you." Captain snapped his fingers, and he disappeared from Shade's hold.

He didn't want to leave her.

Thump.

But he no longer had the choice to stay. He leaned down and

wrapped the drape over her front, hoping the little bit of warmth it held would be enough. "I'll return. Hold on for me, Kora." He pressed one kiss to her cheek. The scythe reappeared as he straightened, and Shade rose into the now-clear sky. He hadn't noticed that Captain's storm had retreated. The tortured souls he'd called were frozen in place, waiting for his orders. Now that he was at his full power, they weren't as savage, uncontrolled, as they'd been previously. "Go back to where you came from."

They began to disperse, making their way towards Váthos. He closed his eyes as he lifted into the air. Concentrated.

If they were right, the tree they had been searching for should be all they needed to save Kora's life. Worst case, if it didn't work, then Kora would get what she wanted and could trade places with William. It wasn't ideal, and Shade cringed at the thought. He didn't want her dead, even if it meant she could stay with him.

If Kora had enough power within her veins, then her immortal life would be tied to the Isles of Nekrós. It would mean that a connection would be forged but not one that would force her to remain within the realm of the dead like he was. For the chance of seeing Kora's amber eyes again, to hear her laugh...it was a risk he was willing to take. There was no way she could die now that she'd chosen to live for herself. She'd given him so much. It was a choice that he hoped she would understand.

He opened his eyes and realized that he was floating above the Isles of Nekrós, the view of the realms spread out beneath him. It wasn't familiar to his eyes as it had been before, but his power—the darkness within him—came alive.

The pomegranate tree. He repeated the thought in his mind over and over until a bright light appeared in front of him. He lowered until the light floated away, towards the tip of the island. It led him along the outskirts at a slow and steady pace that he wished would quicken. There wasn't much time. Kora couldn't survive this forever. As if understanding his urgency, the light picked up speed towards the east.

When the light came to an abrupt stop, he looked down and

saw a grove of trees. He landed and began to search the branches for the red fruit. Of course, they would be found in Lýpe—the place for the broken-hearted. That's when he saw it on the second tree. One red fruit, circular in shape and as deep crimson as blood, hung from a branch that beckoned to be picked. He plucked it. The skin was smooth to the touch.

Without wasting any time, he pushed off the tree trunk to give himself speed and soared back towards Kora. Souls he'd ignored before waved figments of hands at him. A few others groaned with approval. He tried to return their welcome, but they could wait a little longer. Right now, his entire being was focused on getting back to her.

The thought of leaving Kora alone for too long was disconcerting. Even though Captain wasn't high on Shade's list of approved chaperones, he wasn't at the bottom either. The immortal had his reasons for what he had done. Shade had always known that. But Kora should never have been involved.

He reached the isle and landed hard on the marble floors of the Grecian temple. Captain stood there, another figure at his side kneeling over Kora. With a groan, Shade stopped across from his brother. "What in the hells made you think this was a good idea?" he snapped.

"It was mine." William straightened, piercing Shade with a look. "I know what my choice meant, but if anything happened, I had to be by her side."

Thump.

Shade's shoulders tightened.

"The Dikastés and I spoke, and they understand the situation. For now, William can be within the Isles of Nekrós and stay in this form." Captain clasped his hands behind his back. "Soon, though, he will be called to face judgment."

Shade ran a hand through her hair. "She's not going to be happy about this when she wakes."

"Are you certain this will work?" William darted a glance between the two immortals.

Removing the pomegranate from his pocket, Shade hit it against the side of the bench, cracking it open. "There are two options here." Shade ran a hand through his hair, not sure how the soul would take the news.

"Captain filled me in on what her immortal blood could mean, but what if you're wrong?" William held Kora's hand tight.

Shade breathed a heavy sigh and glanced at his brother before turning back to William. "Then she could switch places with you."

William whipped around. "No."

"Would she be all right knowing you wouldn't take the opportunity when it was offered to you?" Shade gripped the soul's shoulder. "If her heart starts to fail, then you should eat the seeds. For her. Don't make her sacrifice be in vain. Then she'd remain."

"What's the second option?" William looked over Kora, an indentation forming between his brows.

"If she does have an immortal line, then the pomegranate seeds will tie her blood to the islands. She will have to come back from time to time to...recharge." It was the easiest way to explain it and an assumption he was making. "It has never been done before. This is my best guess."

"Why can't she eat it once she dies and then return to the mortal world?"

Captain sighed. "Because she would die here. There is no going back from that. The Judges would feel that the quota was filled."

"But if she's tied to here..." William closed his eyes, running a hand over his face. "How is that any better than being dead?"

"You're right." He stared at her still body. *Thump.* "She deserves a choice."

Captain stepped in closer. "Are you sure?"

Shade's jaw flexed. "I need to consider what she wants first."

He crouched down beside Kora and pressed a hand to her forehead.

"What is he doing?" William whispered loudly.

"She's dying. He can speak to her soul."

Shade groaned. "Well, I could if you both would shut it. This takes concentration."

Silence echoed in his ears. He closed his eyes tight, pressed his hand towards her temple. When he opened his eyes, he was no longer on the isle, but in a bedroom. A young woman sat at a window seat, reading a book on the best crops to plant in spring. *Hells*, she was beautiful. After trying so hard to ignore that fact for so long, it was nice to take a moment to observe. Take her in.

Her entire body stilled, and she looked up, meeting his gaze. "Shade, why are you here?"

His expression softened. "Hello, Kora."

"Am I dead?" Her eyes widened, snapping the book closed.

"No." He wanted to eat up the space between them. To take away her fear or apprehension.

"Then how...?"

Thump. Her heartbeat was weakening. There wasn't much time. "I wish I could explain everything but..."

He told her all he could. The words rushed and sentences clipped. "You have a choice. I can feed you the fruit and your immortal blood will be tied to here, or I can let you go."

"And William is no longer an option?" She spoke quietly, as if she was embarrassed to ask.

Shade shook his head and gave her a soft smile. "He could, but William has made his choice. Now it's time to make yours. But you don't have much of it left."

"What would you have me do?" She folded her hands in her lap. Fidgeted.

He considered lying. "I could be selfish. Rush you to Anamoní and have you stay with me always. But it's not mine to make."

She stared for a moment at the space between them. *Thump.*

"Kora?"

She met his gaze. Smiled. "Someone once told me that to live is an adventure."

"If you're willing to fight for it." He rushed across the space and scooped her up in his arms. Held her close. Missed her scent that was absent now. The rush of her heart. "Thank you," he whispered into her ear.

She kissed him. The touch chaste. Delicate. "Thank you, too."

"For what?"

She cupped his cheek. "For showing me that there is more out there."

"It was you, Wildflower."

Kora scanned his face. "What was?"

"The first time that I didn't think my story was only meant to be a tragedy."

Just as quickly as he'd been in her arms, he was sprawled on the solid ground of stone, back at the temple.

He groaned as William assisted him to his feet. "What happened? What did she say?"

Shade didn't waste any time and grabbed hold of the fruit. He tore into the white flesh surrounding the bright crimson seeds. He pulled three seeds from within, slippery to the touch. When he spoke, it was to the soul. "She chose." He paused as he popped them into her mouth. As he grabbed three more with fingers stained red, he said, "I promise to do everything within my power to make it a life she won't regret."

Captain inhaled and his shoulders physically slumped as he turned to face Shade. "I..." His gaze fell to the young woman between them. "I never considered it that way, Shade. I was blinded by what I wanted and my own desires and didn't think about the consequences to others." Captain glanced at William. "For that I'm sorry. She didn't deserve this."

William nodded. He took up his sister's hand as Shade placed the last two seeds into her mouth. Her brother massaged her throat, forcing them down into her stomach. If this didn't work, he didn't know what he would do. To make Captain pay would be a good start though.

"And you didn't either," Captain said.

Shade stilled, his attention wholly on Kora as he listened.

Captain sighed. "I understand a bit more now. You've been here, alone, for much too long. It wasn't fair of us—of me—to do that to you."

"You have an eternity to spend figuring out how to make it up to me," Shade grumbled.

Thump...

"We can make something work. Maybe if I'd seen it sooner—and you hadn't been so stubborn we—"

"Brother." Shade cut off the immortal. "Later. If you'd shut up now, I'd appreciate it." He listened intently for the one sound that beat with passion, love—life.

Silence expanded around them and time stood still. None moved. None breathed, and thankfully it wasn't a requirement because as the moments ticked on, Shade was beginning to lose the last dredge of hope he still contained.

Captain reached for the pomegranate settled by her waist.

"No, not yet. There is still a chance." Shade picked up her other hand, squeezing it as he settled down on his knees beside her. Resting his head on her shoulder, he closed his eyes and whispered, "Don't leave yet, Wildflower. It isn't your time."

Thump, thump...Thump, thump.

"Kora?" William's voice cracked.

Shade lifted his head as Kora's grip tightened within his. He smiled through tears as she met his gaze. "Shade?"

He brushed the hair from her face and pressed a kiss on her forehead. "Hello, Kora."

Chapter 49

Kora

They filled Kora in on everything as she sat on that cold marble bench. She'd have to return to the Isles of Nekrós every few weeks. If not, her life span would be cut short. Well, if there was a worse fate, it wouldn't be this news. Even if she hadn't saved William. The promise of her return was imprinted in her skin now—the blue lines that veined through her arm and shoulder proof of the lightning that struck her.

William sat beside her with a protective arm around her shoulder. He'd barely spoken, only adding in bits and pieces as Shade and Captain informed her how they believed the fruit worked. Soon they would return her to the living world with Michael who, even with the order to return home, was in the Isle of Waiting with strict instructions to stay with Branch and Curly. As for William, he would never leave the Isles of Nekrós again.

Once complete with their hypothesis on how the fruit would affect her—a mortal with the blood of the gods wasn't commonly eating Nekrós pomegranates—Kora just nodded. As far as she was concerned, all of that could wait. She smiled at Shade and William, ignoring Captain altogether. Right now, she was tolerating his presence. The two immortals may have an unspoken truce, but she knew it would be short-lived if they stayed in each other's presence for long. "I need to speak to my brother. In private, please."

Captain opened his mouth, but Shade grabbed his brother's lapel and pulled him away. Kora smiled at the immortal. Shade looked different. That she couldn't deny. The power within him had darkened his features, and he looked taller, more forbidden. The rag-tag clothes he wore had been replaced by black trousers and a linen shirt with drawstrings hanging open at his chest. His armor was currently gone. Even with this new power radiating off him, the draw she felt was unmistakable.

"I still cannot believe you kissed him." William's arm fell from her shoulder.

Kora chuckled, nudging into him gently with her elbow. "William..."

She met his gaze, and her twin shrugged as if he knew what she meant to say. But he couldn't, because there was too much unsaid and not enough time for all the words she wanted to tell him. "I love you." It was the easiest thing to start with, and she bit back the tears that already threatened to pour down her face. "I'm also glad you're here, but why didn't you stay on Anamoní?"

William rested his hand on hers. The one that gripped the edge of the marble bench to ground her in place. "Because I had to be here. You never left my side—how could I leave yours?"

She bit her lip to drive back the tears. Gods, she never wanted to cry again after this. "But now you can't enjoy more adventures, and your soul will turn into one of those orbs and—"

William chuckled. "I wasn't meant to stay in the Isle of Waiting, Kora. Before you and Michael arrived, I had already considered coming here. My life may have been short, but do you know what?"

She waited. The damned idiot was going to make her say it. "What?"

"There's nothing worth doing in the Isle of Waiting without you there. You made the adventures worthwhile, and now that you'll be gone...I'm ready."

The tears came unbidden now. William wiped them away with a gentle thumb. "Well, it was Michael too. He helped."

His attempt at humor was lost on her as a new wave of tears broke free. "I'm sorry I couldn't save you." She leaned against him, no longer able to fight back the need to be close to him, to rely on him for just a little bit longer. "I'm sorry I kept so much from you—for everything." This was her last chance to say it all. And she was thankful for it.

William sighed and gave her a small smile. "You did save me, Kora. The one thing I thought I'd always regret was the pain I put you through. This time together was a gift I will always cherish. Don't ever tell Captain, but for that alone, I will be grateful he dragged you here."

He pulled her in close. "When you go back, hug Mother and Father for me. Consider the options they give you. Stand up to them if you think they are wrong. But don't miss out on adventures because of me. I feared their disappointment more than I should have, Kora. Don't live that way."

She wiped her face then wrapped her arms tight around him. He did the same, holding her close. Kora never wanted to let him go, but if she'd learned anything these past seven days, life didn't owe her anything. But it had given her these moments with him. "You're a hero, William. Maybe not in the conventional sense, but I'll always remember you that way."

He chuckled, the feeling reverberating against her body. She couldn't help the smile, even with all the pain. "I'm going to miss you."

When she still hadn't loosened her hold, William whispered, "Did a god admit that he loved you, or was that just a lie Captain told to get me to stay in the Isle of Waiting?"

"What?" Kora's eyes widened as she pulled away, biting her bottom lip.

William laughed and the sound echoed in her ears, one that she wanted to commit to memory. "So, it's true?"

Her cheeks flushed bright red. "Not exactly—but why would he tell you that?"

"Because he thought that it would be enough to let me know you weren't alone. Stupid twit. What did he think I'd do?" William continued, relaying his version of what happened from the time they discovered she was gone, to the deal with the Judges, and until she woke. They laughed, talking about the past few days and the events no one would ever believe had happened to her when she returned to the mortal world.

"So immortal blood, huh? Wish we had known about that before. You don't look different. How do you feel?" William scanned her from head to toe.

"Did you expect I would sprout a third eye or something? It seems that this immortal blood thing may have been a part of you too, you know." She chuckled as William searched her forehead for the accosting extra pupil and set of eyelids. "No, I don't feel different," she said between clenched teeth. "But I was able to make vines come out of the earth."

It was William's turn to be shocked. "Tell me everything."

She did her best to recount the entire story as best she could and even though there were moments when William looked concerned, he listened intently. Then he wrapped an arm around her and held her close. "Stop finding danger."

"It finds me."

"It's time."

Kora and William looked up to Captain standing over them. Although he still wore his impeccable crimson overcoat, there was something relaxed in his posture that hadn't been there before. Shade came up beside her as Kora and William stood.

The twins wrapped each other in a hug once more. Another set of tears. A few more mutters of "I love you." William held her at arm's length and squeezed each shoulder. "Forever. Remember that."

She nodded, unable to form words.

William smiled again, then turned his attention on the

immortal by her side. "I'll know if you ever hurt her. Somehow, I will find out. I promise that no matter what island you venture to, that I'll stick to you like a parasite and make you regret it."

Shade laughed, his head tilting back. "If any soul could find a way, it would be you, William. I don't doubt it for a second." The two clasped hands, giving a firm shake.

Captain turned on his heels but stopped to allow William to lead the way. Kora watched as her brother's shoulders drew back, and he gave her one last smile. "Live your life, Kora. With everything you have."

"I will."

Shade wrapped an arm around her shoulder. She rested her head against him as she watched William and Captain disappear. "Where do you think he will be placed?" She didn't know why she asked, but the words came unbidden from her lips.

"No less than Eiríni." Shade pulled her in closer to his side. "Don't worry. He was ready for this. The question is, are you?"

Kora blinked, letting the realization of everything she learned settle over her. A small smile grew. "Yes and no." She turned her face up to him. "I know it won't always be easy and that I'll miss him, but I'll be all right."

His own smile thinned, and his eyes grew distant. "I'm sorry for all of this. For dragging you into this battle. The curse you now have upon you. It's all my fault."

She reached a hand up and rested it on his cheek, pulling his attention back to her. "Did you mean what you said? The reason why you saw me was because you saw love?"

Shade straightened. "You love so strongly. I saw it in the fight for your brother's life. Everything is still new, but..." He shook his head. "It's ridiculous, I know that. I have nothing to offer you, Kora. If you don't want—I have no expectations."

"I do, though." She pressed a finger to his lips, and he fell silent. "What do you mean?" Stretching up on her tiptoes, she pressed her lips to his. A gentle kiss, with just a touch of the want, the feelings she had for him. She pulled back and searched his expression. "You've already given me so much. Because of you, I now have a chance to really live."

He wrapped his arms around her waist and pulled her close. She smiled, feeling the comfort and warmth within his hold. "As you said, life is an adventure. Let's see where it can take us."

The smile that extended on those perfect lips, the way his features brightened at her words had her kissing him again, capturing every memory she could of this moment.

CAPTAIN HAD BEEN GIVEN one last task by his brother. To return them to Astraea before he left for Synnefo.

"I thought you should know." Captain sighed as he landed them on the dock and gazed towards the rowboat. "The Judges believe your brother was meant for Iroes. He won't be exactly as you remember him, but he will be there to see you."

She'd never been so happy to hear such news. Even if it meant he wasn't home with her, there had been another gift that she couldn't despise Captain for. "Thank you."

He had nodded, then waved one final farewell before disappearing from the realm in a flash of light.

She'd returned to the Isle of Waiting to find her younger brother on the beach. Michael had cried when he realized William wasn't returning. She'd comforted him, no tears left to shed, while he recounted how William had said a proper goodbye—as if he knew this was it.

Astraea had brought them home with the promise to return, once they had reached the living world, Kora was suddenly sleepy, eyes refusing to stay open. She fought it, didn't doubt that this exhaustion was otherworldly. Yet—

Kora woke with a start. Her room. Her bed. The street lanterns below illuminated through the window. It worked. She was home.

Michael lay snoring beside her, a hint of dawn coming

through her window. For a moment, she wondered if it had been a dream. But the feeling of Shade's kiss was still warm against her lips. The words he spoke an echo in her mind. And in case that wasn't enough, the strange blue lines that inked out were visible under her skin, faint but still there under close scrutiny.

Everything was as if they'd never been gone. Even her clothes were mended. The dress that had been stained and torn nearly to shreds now whole and clean.

The one thing that had changed was the hollowness she had felt the last time she laid in bed. William's absence was still present. Kora had a feeling it always would be, but she didn't feel like all hope was lost.

A soft knock sounded, and Kora extracted herself from under Michael's heavy weight. She opened the door with a creak. Mother stood in the hall wearing a nightgown with a robe tied around her waist. It was rare she knocked. How funny to think it had only been one night for her mother while for Kora it had been days. It took some will not to wrap her mother in a hug and inhale the scent of lavender soap she always washed with before bed.

"I couldn't sleep most of the night. I didn't mean to wake you."

Kora shook her head. "You didn't."

"Can we talk for a moment, dear?"

Kora peered behind her as Michael rustled about in her sheets. She slid through the crack of the doorway so as not to cast any further light into her room and closed it with a click. Her mother walked down the hall towards a door and opened it. A doorway Kora had not entered in weeks.

She walked into William's room and a fresh wave of grief pressed against her, but with it came a comforting warmth. Mother took a seat and patted the bed beside her. "I come in here from time to time."

Kora inched slowly across the room and took the spot allocated for her. "You do?"

Tears tracked down Mother's cheeks. "He was my oldest boy, Kora. A piece of my heart is given to each of you once you're born. Or at least that's what I believe anyway." She sniffed, pulling a handkerchief from the pocket of her robe and dabbed at her face. "So now a piece is gone forever and—" She inhaled and met Kora's gaze. "No parent should have to bury a child."

"I know. I said some things I shouldn't have." Kora took her mother's hand in hers. "There is no doubt in my mind that you love Will. I'm sorry."

Mother nodded. "I know. We all said some things we shouldn't have." She squeezed Kora's hand. "And I owe you an apology too. This is selfish of me, but I forgot that I wasn't alone in my grief."

Kora rested her head on her mother's shoulder. "No, you aren't alone. We all feel how you do." She bit her lip, considering her words. "I'm always going to miss him."

Mother pressed a kiss to the top of Kora's head. "I know you are. So am I."

She stood up and headed towards the door, but Kora didn't move. "Mother, there is more." It was now or never. William had reminded her of how important her dreams were to her. If she let her mother walk out of this room without saying something, she knew she'd regret it, and it would only become harder.

"Yes." She sat back down.

"I don't want to go to England. But do you think we can discuss it together tomorrow?"

Mother opened her mouth, but Kora rushed forward. "I know we have discussed it before, but I really want to attend university. There are opportunities in England as well, and I'd love to visit. I just don't want us to leave for the wrong reasons. And this feels rushed."

Her mother blinked in surprise. Kora kept going. "I'm asking for a chance—even just one semester. Then, after it is over, we can discuss further. It's not that I never want to meet a man, fall in love and start a family. It's just that I don't want to do that yet.

Has there ever been a time that you had wanted to do something for yourself?"

Even if she'd already met someone, she didn't think it would get her anywhere to mention Shade—ever. That was something to be figured out later. A choice the two of them would make.

Kora grew silent, knowing she needed to allow her mother a chance to think. To respond. Maybe it would have been better if she waited until Father was present. Or—

Mother cleared her throat. "Do you know I wanted to study art?"

Kora shook her head, surprised at the admission. Just like William.

"I did. Painting to be exact. Before I met your father, I had an easel and as many paints as I could collect within a little corner of my childhood bedroom that overlooked the park. For hours, I would spend time recreating what I saw from that window onto that blank canvas. Not to brag, but I was quite good too."

Kora smiled. "I would love to see some of your art someday."

Mother chuckled. A quiet sound. "I haven't touched a brush in years. But you know what I found this evening as I was getting ready for bed?"

There wasn't time to answer the question. Mother pulled from her pocket a thin paintbrush with a wooden handle. "It made me think of the dreams I'd let slide because of what was more important. You—a family. Those dreams were on the forefront of my mind when I met your father. The desire to paint— the same that we admonished your brother for having—they were forgotten."

Kora held a bated breath as Mother slid the brush between her fingers, analyzing it. "I always wanted a house, a husband and children of my own. Those dreams were more vivid than my desire to study." She met Kora's gaze now. "That isn't the same for you, is it?"

All she could do was shake her head.

A corner of Mother's mouth lifted. "I'll have to speak to your father to see if he'll agree, but I'm willing to give you a chance, Kora. To see what else is out there in this world. Either here or in England."

"Really?" Kora's eyes widened in surprise. In her wildest dreams, she'd never imagined this. But, of course, the past few days have proven anything is possible.

"This might be difficult to believe, but your father hoped England might be a better fit for all of us right now. We need each other, and he wanted a chance to spend more time with our family." Mother's smile lengthened as she searched Kora's face. "I cannot make any promises. But tomorrow, after your father returns from work, you and I can sit with him together. How does that sound?"

Kora wrapped her arms tight around her and buried her face into Mother's neck. "Yes." She could dance with excitement. "Thank you."

"We want you to be happy, Kora. Don't ever forget that." Mother breathed into Kora's ear.

A shadow, a quick slip of darkness flashed out of view from the corner of her eye. Kora knew Shade wasn't here, but maybe another was. She lifted her head and smiled in the direction of whoever spied, hoping they would relay the message to the immortal.

William's words flashed through her mind. "I won't. I promised William I'd remember to live."

Epilogue
Kora

Three months had passed since she'd returned from Anamoní. One month since she had expected someone to arrive and take her to the Isles of Nekrós. There hadn't been a sighting or a peep from anyone, and Kora was attempting to deny the desperation that clawed at her. Had he changed his mind even if it meant she'd lose years of her life? Did something happen in the time they'd been apart?

Classes would begin in two months. Kora was excited, but the desire to speak to Shade was more torturous than she had imagined. The move to England had been postponed for one year, and her parents had agreed she could take a semester of courses before deciding if she wanted to move with them and have the opportunity to study at Oxford.

Bachelors still occasionally arrived for dinner, but the pressure was taken off of the visits. Instead, she'd had lovely conversations with a few of them and didn't sit in brooding silence as she waited for a chance to speak her mind. Without her mother's manipulations, Kora had learned a bit more about these young men and they her. One she now considered a friend—but nothing more. She told herself it wasn't because she was waiting for Shade, but the truth was that he remained in her thoughts each day and was a constant presence in her dreams.

The living world had changed as well. While things hadn't been fixed overnight, rain had returned, crops began to grow, which meant more medicines were becoming available again. The people praised the return of the immortals. Although no one claimed to see one, the people knew they must be the reason for the Earth's slow mend. So, Kora began to pray. To Shade, who she hoped heard her as she thanked him for the sacrifice he made.

Ariana had also begun to travel with her father again. She missed her friend but anticipated her letters that arrived every other week about her most recent adventures. With an upcoming trip to see the universities in England, Kora had hoped to visit her friend too.

And she still felt the weight of William's loss in her chest. That grief would probably never go away. Even with a goodbye that most could only dream of, she missed her brother. Her twin. But she could live with it and did her best to change her sadness into happiness by thinking of a happy memory with him and thankful she had those to hold on to.

Every night, she left her window unlocked, hoping it was enough of an invitation. Some evenings, she sat on her window seat watching the stars and counting their position to find the direction to the Isle of Waiting. Second star to the right...

Tonight was no different. She was wrapped in one of her thicker quilts, with a book in her lap, opened and ignored. She was unable to concentrate on the words. Instead, she stared at her garden below now flourishing with her constant care and the touch of power she still possessed. It would be time to make another delivery of produce to the grocer soon. She didn't control the plants like she had been able to do, but she was able to assist them to grow strong and healthy. Fresh fruit and vegetables thrived. Wilflowers grew along the edges as a reminder of where she had been. Who she was to someone.

Michael shifted from his spot beside her, wrapping his arms around her neck. "Good night, Kora."

He didn't spend every evening curled up in her bed. She still told him stories each night though. Now they were mostly about their adventures on the Isle of Waiting. And William.

"Love you." He squeezed her extra hard before trotting from the room in his bare feet and night clothes. Kora smiled at his retreating form. So far, there hadn't been anything more than a sighting of a few extra birds coming to her window when Michael was present, but if that was a signal of a power untapped, Kora didn't know. Astraea didn't seem to consider it anything to note.

The cool mid-winter air brushed her toes through the open window. This would be the last night, she'd promised herself. After this, she would let him go. Like he obviously had her. Maybe they had discovered she didn't need to return to the Isles of Nekrós. If he didn't want to see her, the least he could do was let her know and say goodbye.

"Deep in thought?"

Kora jumped, the book tipping off her lap and landing with a plop on the floor. She looked up with wide eyes.

Shade stood in the center of her room, dressed in all black with the darkness hugging his silhouette. The smile on his face warmed her inside and out.

But she was still annoyed with him. "Where have you been? I thought someone would be here a month ago?"

His jaw dropped. "Really? You think I wouldn't have come for you sooner. I didn't trust anyone else to retrieve you."

"Seriously?" She glared, her mouth forming into a pout until she remembered his newly reinstated responsibilities. "Wait, how are you here?"

The immortal chuckled and rested his hands on his hips. "I can't come for long, but I found balance. Can even visit Anamoní for a few days now and then."

Her mouth fell open in awe, a sense of pride washing over her. "I'm happy for you."

Shade crossed the room in two quick strides, and she stood so he could wrap his arms around her, drawing her close. "I apologize for the delay. I didn't think you'd want to come back so soon."

She pushed up to her tiptoes and kissed him. He relaxed into her until she pulled back gently. "Silly immortal, don't you know much I missed you?"

He grinned. "I've missed you too. Besides figuring out how to come here, there was a bit of a mess to clean up. Even with Captain overseeing things, he didn't have everything organized."

Kora wrapped her arms around his shoulders. "Look at you acting all grown up."

A small blush colored his cheeks as he shrugged. It was the most attractive thing she'd ever seen. He kissed her again, and she wished for it to never end. "After this, how often shall you come for me?"

"Every month you will join me for seven days in Nekrós. Does that work for you?"

"Does that mean you owe me three weeks now since you're late?"

Shade grinned. "I wish. We can't have your family worrying for you, Wildflower."

For a week every month, this was what she would become accustomed to. The idea was both exciting and sent a dozen butterflies loose in her stomach. He rested his hand on her neck, brushing his thumb along her jaw. "What this also means is that in between trips, I can come visit from time to time. If you want, that is?"

Kora inhaled deep, searching his expression for any jest, but he only smiled back. "Yes, Shade. I would like that."

He stepped back, slow and timid. "Are you ready to go now?" He peered out the window, then pulled a small satchel from his pocket. "While the lights are low?"

"What's that?"

He opened it to a familiar shimmering powder that brightened the space between them. "Pixie dust—are you ready to fly?"

"Yes!" She almost squealed the word. He laughed, sprinkling it over her head and the shimmering particles stuck to her body.

"Think happy thoughts."

A few weeks ago, that may have seemed impossible. Now, with a future before her, her brother's memory in her heart, and this immortal by her side, any and everything was possible. "Let's go on to our next adventure."

He kissed her as her body began to rise in the air. "Lead the way."

Somewhere Else - Taea

THEY SAY pixies are born from laughter. What they don't say is what kind. Some laugh through tears. While others laugh at the expense of others. Taea was created by a laugh so vindictive, she sprung out with vengeance coursing through her veins.

She settled against the crook of the dark slate, leaning her head upon the cool stone. "I gave you as long as I could."

"Yes, you did." The voice was deep and gravelly. She couldn't see the speaker but didn't need to. Taea knew exactly with whom she spoke with. The voice sighed, "It is patience that I have trouble with. I need you to do something for me."

"More? Don't you think I've done enough?"

"You're mine, Taea. My pixie. You don't belong solely to yourself."

She glanced out at the Váthos Sea. "What is it you want from me?" Taea swallowed, glancing over the weakening prison.

"It's time to leave Nekrós and return to the mortal world."

"I hate it there." All those humans. They believed themselves necessary when they piddled about in their meager existence.

"I know you do. But I have need of you." The tick-tock of the clock in her pocket sounded louder. The sound that followed was between a sigh and purr. "I see you, Taea. I know you question if you should have done what you did to Shade. But remember our cause."

The pixie smiled, her dust changing to a shimmery pink. "Yes, I'll remember." She zoomed out of the cavern towards her destination, a faint laugh following her out.

And they all *hoped* to live
Happily Ever After

ACKNOWLEDGMENTS

This book started out as a small idea about mixing fairytale with mythology. From there it grew and expanded into a story of grief and loss. It was a long one that took years to cumulate over time. And with insight and readers that really helped it grow and develop. Thank you so much to some of the very first readers and members of the Query Wenches: Johanna Randle, Lily Mehallick, L.J. Thomas, Michelle Tang, Olivia Woods, and Ruby Martinez. To Tania Joy who took the time to try to bring order to my chaos. Another very important shout out to Lindsay Fortin who was a wealth of information and resources on all things Greek mythology. To the Secret Writers Guild who were there with support during sprints and bouncing off ideas when this story was nothing more than a blob of words on the page.

It also wouldn't be what it is now if it wasn't for my fantastic and wonderful CP, Ashley Wilson, who read this book more than once and was up to chat and bounce off ideas! Thankful we were put into each other's lives by Writing With the Soul. Another thank you to the ever-impressive editing by Megan Amato who has worked long and hard on this book. I think we are finally figuring this whole thing out (maybe I shouldn't write this down here because now I'm worried I jinxed us).

To the readers—the one's that found *A Nameless Curse*, were patient as I learned things about writing a sequel, and stuck around (im)patiently checking in and snuck into my DM's to ask about what I was working on next. You don't know how much that kept me going sometimes!

And of course a thank you to my kids who pretended to be

excited when I got character art, tried to understand when I said I was almost done with a chapter, and usually went to dad when I was deep in the writing zone. To my husband who doesn't understand me all the time but supports me anyway, and to my parents, sister, and in-laws who ask, "How's the writing going?" which always seems to make my mouth go dry and my mind to forget how to form words, but is appreciated nonetheless. Thank you and love you all!

ABOUT THE AUTHOR

GW Prouse has a heart for travel and a love of the outdoors that inspires her settings and worlds. While she lives near the beach, she prefers redwood trees, fog covered lakes and mountain peaks. If she's not writing, reading, or rushing her family around to the countless activities her children can accumulate, she can be found crafting, camping, or cuddling up with her family for a movie.

Thank you so much for reading and please take a moment to leave a review. To follow GW Prouse or more details about her other books, please **Follow Along Here** or Scan the QR code:

www.ingramcontent.com/pod-product-compliance
Lightning Source LLC
Chambersburg PA
CBHW022300310726
48973CB00001B/144